An Unknown World:
Two Years on the Moon

An Unknown World:
Two Years on the Moon

by
Pierre de Sélènes

translated, annotated and introduced by
Brian Stableford

A Black Coat Press Book

Visit our website at www.blackcoatpress.com

ISBN 978-1-61227-302-0. First Printing. July 2014. Published by Black Coat Press, an imprint of Hollywood Comics.com, LLC, P.O. Box 17270, Encino, CA 91416. All rights reserved. Except for review purposes, no part of this book may be reproduced or transmitted in any form or by any means, electronic or mechanical, including photocopying, recording, or by any information storage and retrieval system, without permission in writing from the publisher. The stories and characters depicted in this novel are entirely fictional. Printed in the United States of America.

Introduction

Un Monde inconnu, deux ans sur la Lune by "Pierre de Sélènes," here translated as *An Unknown World: Two Years on the Moon*, was originally published by Ernest Flammarion in an undated edition attributed to 1896 by the Bibliothèque Nationale catalogue. That publication date is undoubtedly correct, as numerous reviews of the book appeared in periodicals in the last few months of 1896, but the internal evidence of the text, which places the action in the 1880s, suggests that most of it, at least had been written more than a decade earlier. The book was dedicated to Jules Verne, and is, in effect, a sequel to Verne's two-part novel *De le Terre à la Lune* (1865) and *Autour de la Lune* (1870), initially translated into English in a single volume as *From the Earth to the Moon direct in 97 hours 20 minutes, and a Trip Around It* (1873).

The catalogue of the Bibliothèque Nationale records that the pseudonym attached to the book was that of "A. Betolaud de La Drable." Some other sources give the author's birth-date as 1863, although it is not clear what evidence there is for that attribution; it appears to derive from a catalogue annotation of the 1898 Spanish translation of the book, and may well be an invention or an error. If it is correct, then the author was presumably the grandson of Armand-Ludovic-Eugène Betolaud de La Drable (1808-1888) and his wife Louise, née Tillette de Mautort (1820-1895). The name A. Betolaud de La Drable appears in a number of directories published after 1896, including a membership list of the Parisian Astronomical Society, but as some of the directories in question also list a Madame Betolaud de La Drable, née Tillette de Mautort, resident at the same address, one might be inclined to wonder whether the references are to a living individual. It is not inconceivable that the Armand Betolaud who died in 1888 is the person belatedly indicated in the directories, and the author of the book,

5

although it might also be the case that his similarly-named son or grandson had simply married a cousin (as one of the heroes of the novel does).

Wherever the author actually figures in the Betolaud family tree, there is no doubt that he belonged to the old French aristocracy, to a family that, as the popular expression puts it, went back to the Crusades, and had long been in the habit of marrying the members of other families of similar aristocratic descent. That is of some significance because *Un Monde inconnu* is a curious hybrid story, which deliberately fuses the Vernian romance from which it takes it immediate inspiration with an older tradition of utopian romance—older being the operative word, in this case, because it differs from almost all the other utopian romances written in France since the mid-18th century in taking a rather reactionary view of the ideas that prompted and succeeded the 1789 Revolution, embedding its supposed commitment to liberty, equality and fraternity within a stratified, hierarchical society equipped with a "natural" aristocracy and a similarly "natural" religious culture.

The eccentricity of the utopian model featured in *Un Monde inconnu* does not stop there; again, it is by no means the only French utopian novel to propose that Earthly humankind is ill-fitted for a utopian existence for physiological reasons, but the modifications it proposes are a peculiar mixture of the radical and the conservative. The author follows a proposal advanced by Camille Flammarion in several of his otherworldly visions, that it would be more convenient for a species with ambitions toward perfection if it could do away with the messy business of nutrition, defecation and urination and obtain its nutrition by way of respiration, excreting wastes by exhalation. Flammarion was, however, fully aware of the fact that such a variation would require adaptation to an atmosphere radically different from that of Earth, and considerable physiological and anatomical adaptations of the species enjoying that exotic ecology. The author of *Un Monde inconnu*, wanting his utopians to live up to standards of human beauty in no uncertain terms, and to allow human visitors to their world to breathe the same air, fudges those issues in a decidedly unconvincing fashion, although such imaginative audacity is perhaps not out of keeping with the initial hypothesis that the Moon might be inhabited by human beings, internally if not externally.

Some license, of course, must be granted to utopian writers, on the grounds that the strategies they employ for locating their hypothetical societies are convenient literary devices rather than rational hypotheses, and it is a matter of opinion whether any such device can really be said to be exceeding legitimacy. If any can, however, the one employed in *Un Monde inconnu* must be a strong candidate, perhaps all the more so because of its attempt to plunder the apparent plausibility of Jules Verne's novel, which did try hard to pretend to rational plausibility, even though few people have ever been convinced that one really could travel safely to the Moon and back by means of a projectile fired by a gigantic cannon.

The novel's faults do not stop there; it was the author's only book, and that shows. The text is prolix and repetitive, and frustratingly inclined to devote detailed consideration to trivia, while sidestepping more pertinent matters, in both the dialogue and the narrative commentary. Such faults are not unusual in speculative fiction, and are illustrative of the enormous difficulty of writing such fiction, and, as in many other cases, that kind of *gaucherie* is compensated here by the ardent desire on the author's part to imagine and describe things that no one had ever imagined or described before, in the quest to widen the horizons of the imagination. Many other writers made a better fist of it than he did, but there is a sense in which every book of this kind has some value and interest by virtue of its obligatory uniqueness. Nobody else had ever written a book like *Un Monde inconnu* before, and nobody has done so since; if it is a monster, in more ways than one, it is nevertheless an intriguing monster.

The novel has inevitably received something of a bad press from lovers of Jules Verne, who consider its very exist-

7

ence to be a crime of lèse-majesté. The fact that the novel's basic narrative device is borrowed, is, however a subsidiary issue; if authors of speculative fiction were deemed to have intellectual property rights in the novelties that they invent, entitled to maintain them free of infringement, the genre would be infinitely poorer than it is, whole subgenres having been condemned. *Un Monde inconnu* is unusually detailed and specific in its borrowing, perhaps to the point of breach of copyright, although not of plagiarism, but there is a sense in which, in science fiction as in science, ideas have to be treatable as common property if progress is to be conceivable, let alone feasible. There does not seem to be any record of Ernest Flammarion consulting Verne before publishing the book, but it is not improbable that he did, and not improbable, either, that Verne told him that he had no objection. Whether the novel has any right to exist or not, it does, and is therefore available for consideration.

French interplanetary fiction was, in general, an extremely hesitant subgenre in the 19th century—considerably more so than in Britain, where several authors took a much more robust attitude to the possibility of interplanetary flight, if only as a matter of arming a narrative device with a gloss of plausibility. Verne's work, classic as it is, stops short of allowing his tourists actually to land on the Moon, and when he attempted a much bolder interplanetary fantasy in *Hector Servadac* (1877; tr. as *Off on a Comet*) his publisher, Pierre-Jules Hetzel, who was always striving mulishly to keep Verne on a tight imaginative rein, insisted that he changed the ending in order to conform with his own idiotic notion of plausibility, although the alteration only succeeded in reducing the text to incoherence. Either the author of *Un Monde inconnu* suffered a remarkable failure of nerve at the end of his own novel, or Ernest Flammarion followed Hetzel's example, fortunately with less ruinous consequences (although the reader will probably find it advantageous to ignore the last few paragraphs of the text). That endemic tentativeness did not last long after the publication of the present text, although it required crucial examples from abroad, in translations of H. G. Wells, to blow it away completely, but *Un Monde inconnu* came closer than any other domestic product, including Verne's, to breaking the mold, and deserves some credit for that.

All things considered, *Un Monde inconnu* is primarily interesting as an exotic historical specimen rather than a viable work of art, but it holds a significant place in the history of French interplanetary fiction, and interplanetary fiction in general. Of all the fictional developments of Charles Cros' suggested program for interplanetary communication, first outlined at Camille Flammarion's salon in 1869 and subsequently reprinted as a pamphlet and in the periodical *Cosmos*, it is the most detailed and the most enthusiastic. It is perhaps also the one that has the most accurate appreciation of the difficulties that such communication would entail, even if it fares no better the any other in suggesting ways of overcoming such difficulties. The problem was to be explored in earnest a century later by the scientists who took up the notion in connection with the SETI (Search for Extra-Terrestrial Intelligence) program, but they had better technology on which to base their ingenuity; the strongest reason for believing that *Un Monde incomnu* was written in the 1880s rather than the 1890s is that it has no inkling of the possibility of wireless telegraphy. Of all the proto-SETI fantasies written in the absence of that narrative convenience, it is perhaps the most thought-provoking, precisely because of the conscientiousness of its hopeless struggle.

The following translation was made from the version of the Flammarion edition reproduced on the Bibliothèque Nationale's *gallica* website.

Brian Stableford

PART ONE

I. The Announcement in the New York Herald

"Yes, my dear Marcel," said Jacques, placing his elbows on the table and putting his head in his hands, "You see in me the most unfortunate of men, and I really don't know whether it wouldn't be wiser for me to go dive head first into the Seine than continue to drag out a miserable and henceforth aimless existence. That's what I was thinking, seriously, when you ran into me just now and brought me in here."

"What! You're reduced to that, my old Jacques? Two years ago, when I left for the Rocky Mountains, I left you so valiant and confident in the future, and now I find you as desperate as this! After brilliant medical studies crowned with countless successes in your examinations, along with a personal fortune—which doesn't hurt—that gave you time to build up a clientele, you were able to envisage life without anxiety, and now you're defeated in advance without having battled!"

"Oh, you don't know how I've suffered. Listen, and see whether I've got reason to be absolutely discouraged. You know that, having been an orphan since I was fourteen, I was brought up by my guardian, my mother's brother, the French scientist François Mathieu-Rollère, known throughout Europe for his astronomical work and his famous paper on the satellites of Uranus. But what you don't know is that I was brought up in his house with his daughter Hélène, my cousin; that we lived together in close proximity, and that from that pleasant communal life a sentiment was born that gradually became an ardent and profound love. We swore ourselves to one another. It's in that hope that I've lived, and it's to assure Hélène of a future worthy of her, in order that she could be proud of her husband, that I've devoted myself to dogged labor, and that I

11

wanted to become one of the foremost physicians of the new school."

"But it seems to me," Marcel put in, "that you've succeeded rather well."

"Yes, perhaps—but what good has it done me? When I made my request of Hélène's father, he looked at me with a surprised expression. 'My dear boy,' he said, 'I've devoted my life to science; my daughter will only ever marry a man who has as a dowry some striking discovery of an astronomical order.' I was amazed by that declaration; nothing had led me to anticipate such an obstacle. Utterly preoccupied by my love and my future, I hadn't realized that my uncle's passion for science was gradually turning to obsession and mania. Now it was all-consuming; the disease was incurable.

"In vain, the woman I loved and I tried to change his mind; his resolution was as immutable as the course of the stars he observes. Weary of my persistence, he banned me from his house and told me not to appear before him again until I've fulfilled the condition that his scientific egotism had imposed on me. Too meek to resist paternal authority, Hélène could only weep before the obstinate refusal that broke her heart. I left her desperate, not knowing whether she'd ever be allowed to see me again."

"And you haven't made any attempt to satisfy the intractable scientist?" asked Marcel, with an expression that seemed to be pierced by a slight irony.

"What could I have done? Devoted to the study of a science to which I've devoted myself entirely and to the extreme limits of which I've advanced, how could I have started a life of study over again, with a different goal? To reach the point where a mind can extend the boundaries of a science and realize some great conquest of the unknown, it's first necessary to have absorbed all the knowledge that humankind has stored up in that order of ideas. That required ten years of ardent study, with no guarantee of success. No, the struggle is impossible; I renounce it, and abandon myself to my unfortunate destiny."

"Man of little faith," said Marcel, smiling, "I thought you were braver and more resolute. How love can weaken a soul and soften courage! Well, I can bring you salvation."

"You?" exclaimed Jacques.

"Yes, me. Look."

And he unfolded before his eyes the fourth page of an American newspaper dared 1 June 188*, which he took from his pocket, and on which the following announcement was made with a headline in gigantic letters:

NATIONAL SOCIETY
OF INTERSTELLAR COMMUNICATIONS
SALE BY PUBLIC AUCTION FOLLOWING BANKRUPTCY

Sir Francis Dayton, receiver in the bankruptcy of the National Society of Interstellar Communications, incorporated in Baltimore (Maryland), has the honor of informing the public that he will proceed, on 10 February next, in the main hall of the Baltimore Auction Rooms, with the sale by auction of:

1. The gigantic cannon known as the Columbiad, founded and established by order of the Gun Club of the said city of Baltimore, which served to send to the Moon the projectile in which the celebrated voyagers Barbicane, Nicholl and Michel Ardan took their places on 4 December 186*;

2. The aluminum projectile, cylindro-conic in form, equipped with portholes, protective plates and bolts, and interior padding, which enabled the aforementioned voyagers to effect the said voyage;

3. The hangars and various constructions erected in the vicinity of the Columbiad, having served as storage facilities and workshops during the first experiment;

4. The lifting-apparatus—blocks, pulleys, cranes and chains—having served for the loading of the said shell, still in a perfect state of conservation, as well as the electric batteries, piles, coils, conductive wires, etc., employed for the deflagration of the Columbiad's charge.

The aforesaid sale will be made in a single lot, with a reserve price of two hundred thousand dollars.

The sale will take place under the surveillance of the honorable Harry Troloppe, legal commissioner.

Jacques returned the newspaper to Marcel.

"What's the meaning of this joke?"

"It's not a joke," Marcel relied, "and if you care to listen, I'll explain it briefly.

"I left, as you'll recall, at the beginning of 187- for the Rocky Mountains. I thought I had recognized significant deposits of copper on a previous voyage to the northern territory of Missouri. I had resolved to verify those initial observations and, if my anticipations were not mistaken, to attempt a large-scale exploitation.

"To that end, equipped with adequate authorizations, I organized a small expedition to complete the work. I spent two years of the harshest existence in that arid and mountainous country, in the middle of a desert, incessantly obliged to fight for my life against the Indians in the midst of whom I was camped, who accused me of violating the sacred lands of the ancestors with my endeavors. At every moment, in fact, my drilling operations were sabotaged and my assaying workshops destroyed; I had to start over continually.

"I would have died of boredom if the mountain of Long's Peak hadn't risen up some twenty miles from the deposits I was exploring—twenty miles is nearby in that scarcely-inhabited area.

"You doubtless haven't forgotten that during the famous attempt made in 186* to reach the Moon, the Baltimore Gun Club had constructed on that summit, one of the highest in the mountains, a giant telescope designed to follow the audacious explorers in their flight.[1] A friendship was established between the astronomers at the observatory and me. In that remote sta-

---

[1] The mountain of Long's Peak is real, but the observatory constructed there in *De la Terre à la Lune* is fictitious.

tion, 4,350 meters above sea level, they didn't often encounter anyone to talk to, and gave me the most gracious and attentive welcome. All the free time that the explorations I had undertaken left me, I spent with them. I usually stayed there for several days in succession, during which I considered myself not as a guest but as one of the observers attracted to the astronomical post.

"I had felt a very pronounced liking for the science of the heavens awakening within me, and soon, the manipulation of meridian circles, reflecting and refracting telescopes had become familiar. My imagination was excited by memories of 186-, and I couldn't tear my eyes away from the ocular of the big telescope. That admirable instrument brought the Moon to a closer distance than the most powerful optical instruments previously constructed.

"I observed our satellite for a long time, and was able to rectify several areas of the map made by Beer and Mädler, which was then reputed to be the most complete and the most exact. I was able to make new observations that seem to me to present all the characteristics of an exact certainty. Thus, I was able to establish that the recent astronomers who have written about the Moon were mistaken when they observed on its surface the presence of a certain quantity of water. It's now established, so far as I'm concerned, that it isn't water but air that they've seen; that's what can be induced from the appearance presented by certain slightly blurred contours and ridges at the edges of the lunar crescent.

"For me, the large depressions that exist on the surface of our satellite, such as the one called the Sea of Cold,[2] enclose in their lowest parts a layer of air whose thickness is doubtless exceedingly slight, but sufficient in my opinion to maintain, at least in those regions, the life of animate beings. And then, who knows? In the rapid enlightenment that permitted them to

_____

[2] I have translated the author's French names for lunar features into English, although scientific parlance usually retains the Latin names, in this case Mare Frigoris.

glimpse the portion of the Lunar disk that is always invisible to us, didn't the Gun Club voyagers think that they perceived water, wooded mountains and profound forests? Weren't the fulgurant gleams of the bolide that almost pulverized them reflected from the surface of vast oceans? That would be in accordance with the hypothesis of those astronomers who maintain that what remains of the lunar atmosphere might have condensed on the invisible part of its disk. That would be, in any case, a matter for verification.

"In brief, I sensed growing within me the desire to accomplish what the Americans had attempted, with the hope, this time, that no unwelcome bolide would arrive to throw me off course and prevent me from attaining the goal.

"An unexpected event hastened my resolution.

"I had for an assistant in my endeavors an Englishman named John Parker, in whom I had every confidence. Ingenious and adroit, fertile in resources, he had been a great help to me in carrying out my operations and directing the workmen I employed for drilling and assaying. It was to him that I left the supervision of the workshops and to whom I confided my plans and notes when I went away on my explorations.

"I had always found him so faithful and reliable that I had got into the habit of prolonging my absences.

"One day, 27 July of last year, on returning to my station after spending a month at the Lon's Peak Observatory, I was surprised to find workers that I didn't know installed there, and an administration functioning under the name of the Great Western Copper Mining Company. When I demanded explanations, they replied by showing me a legal document, duly drawn up, granting the exploitation of mines throughout the region I had explored to the new company. I tried to protest, but they laughed in my face; I got carried away and cried theft, but the barrel of a revolver aimed at my chest told me that I could expect nothing from the new occupants.

"I soon had an explanation of the mystery. The day after my departure, John Parker had run off, taking all my plans and sketches, my notes, my assay reports and my specimens—

everything, in short, that established the reality of my discovery. He had gone to New York and sold it all to the Great Western Copper Mining Company, whose director, with links to influential members of Congress that he had liberally bribed, had stolen the concession in a matter of days. My workers had been dismissed, with a severance payment, and new workers brought in—and as the results I'd obtained were conclusive, the preparatory work of exploitation had begun immediately.

"I had been vilely robbed, but what could I do? To what jurisdiction could I address myself? How, above all, could I establish the priority of my claim now that I'd been completely stripped?

"I might perhaps have attempted to obtain justice; I might at least have searched for that wretch John Parker in order to blow his brains out, if I hadn't been tormented by the thought that I mentioned just now. I had soon made my decision, therefore, and having gone to some trouble to recover from my thieves certain objects that were of no value to them, and which I'll show you shortly, I resolved to devote myself entirely to the realization of the project by which I was haunted. A few days later I was in Chicago, where the announcement I've just shown you fell before my eyes, and my project began to take on substance."

"That's all very well," Jacques put in, with a smile, "But thus far I can't see anything that permits you to affirm that our satellite is inhabited, and given that, I can't see that, even if you succeed in reaching it..."

"Listen," said Marcel, lowering his voice. "In a little while you're going to come home with me to the Rue Taitbout, and I'll give you undeniable proof not only that the Moon is inhabited but that its inhabitants have attempted to enter into communication with us. You can adopt an expression of incredulity if you like, but you'll be forced to yield to the evidence."

"Well, so be it," said Jacques. "Let's see now how you count on realizing this enterprise, which, until there's proof of the contrary, appears to me to be utterly extravagant."

"My plan is quite simple," said Marcel, "and I've been in France for a week precisely to realize it. I'm going to found a company, under the name of the Anonymous Society for Astronomical Exploration, with a capital of five million francs, divided into a thousand shares of five thousand francs each, for our enterprise mustn't have anything commercial about it, and the people who associate with me must only be motivated by a disinterested love of science. I have no doubt that I'll succeed promptly in France, where every generous and noble enterprise finds numerous adherents, in obtaining the modest capital necessary to us. There's even a well-known financier in Paris who has a passion for science, who has already given striking proof of his interest in astronomy, and to whom that science already owes important foundations. I'm sure that when he knows the details of my project, he'll judge it practicable, and won't refuse considerable cooperation. As soon as the funds are subscribed, I'll leave for Baltimore, buy the Columbiad, its shell and all its accessories, which certainly won't be disputed by many enthusiasts; I'll repair it all, complete my preparations and, on 15 December next year, we'll repeat, but this time with complete success, the attempt made by Barbicane, Ardan and Nicholl."

"Damn!" exclaimed Jacques, laughing in spite of his friend's enthusiastic assurance. "You're going a bit quickly—I haven't decided yet."

"Doubter!" said Marcel. "Come home with me, and you'll be convinced. Waiter—the bill!"

The conversation we have just reported took place in Paris, in the Café Anglais, on a fine morning in August 188*. The two young men who were talking with open hearts were almost the same age, between twenty-eight and thirty, but they were different in stature and appearance.

Marcel de Pouzé, tall and broad-shouldered, with supple and robust limbs and a head covered with a dense forest of reddish blond hair, had a highly-colored face divided by a long moustache. His big blue eyes, wide open, radiated frankness and cheerfulness. His slightly think red lips expressed a slightly disdainful bounty. One might have thought that he was just a good and joyful fellow, always disposed to look at life on the bright side, if the glint that sometimes animated his gaze and the crease that hollowed out his forehead had not denoted an energetic determination at the service of a keen intelligence capable of the highest conceptions.

Jacques Deligny offered a striking contrast with his companion. Not as tall in stature, but elegant and well-built, he seemed to realize a type of rare distinction. His delicate and intelligent face, framed by jet-black hair and a beard, offered the mat pallor of those whom patient and difficult studies have kept enclosed in a study or a laboratory for long periods of time. His slightly tight-lipped mouth seemed to have forgotten how to smile. His high forehead was that of a thinker, and his rather deep-set eyes were ordinarily veiled by a hint of melancholy.

They had known one another since childhood, when they had sat next to one another at the Lycée Louis-le-Grand.

Later, when Marcel had gone on to the École Polytechnique while Jacques had followed the course at the École de Médecine, they had never lost contact with one another, and the bonds that united them, formed by an element of protection on the part of Marcel and a great confidence on Jacques' part, had only become tighter. Then life had separated them. Jacques had remained in Paris, pursuing his laborious studies for his examinations and his internship, while Marcel had gone to another continent in search of a vaster field in which to exercise his exuberant activity.

Marcel was an orphan, and his personal fortune permitted him to travel and await without too much impatience the success of one of the great enterprises that his ardent imagination was always caressing.

When they parted, they had promised to write, and had indeed corresponded for some time. The letters had soon become rarer, however, and then had ceased entirely. The two friends had often thought about one another, however; the separation had not weakened their affection, and when chance had brought them together again, it was with a veritable joy that they had fallen into one another's arms. As they had many confidences to exchange, they had gone into the first place they had come upon and had chatted while savoring the delicious lunch that they had just finished.

II. The Document

As the two guests, shaking the ash from their cigars, were about to leave, a waiter came up to Marcel and presented a vellum card to him on a silver tray, saying: "the person whose name is here solicits the honor of being introduced to you."

"To me?" said Marcel.

"Yes." And with a sideways glance, the waiter indicated a neighboring table, at which Marcel directed a rapid glance.

The man sitting at the table appeared to be between forty and forty-five years of age, and was recognizable at first glance as a native of Great Britain. His symmetrical and energetic face was imprinted with considerable nobility. His full beard was blond, striped with a few silver threads. His eyes, of a changing blue, seemed to reveal a rare firmness of mind, and yet one seemed to distinguish therein an expression of lassitude and ennui. All his features, in fact, seemed slightly fatigued and gave the same impression; spleen had passed that way.

He was dressed very fashionably, and once sensed that he belonged to the highest society. Although he was sitting down, it was obvious that he was tall and that his limbs ere well-proportioned. His long, slender hand, which was toying with a horn-rimmed monocle, was entirely aristocratic. There was nothing common or vulgar about him; he was certainly not just anyone.

Marcel looked down at the card that had been handed to him and red: *Lord Douglas Rodilan.*

"What can that islander want with me?" he murmured.

With the natural courtesy of a man of the world, he turned to the stranger with a smile on his lips. The latter stood up and approached the two friends.

"Forgive me, Monsieur," he said, bowing to Marcel and also nodding his head to Jacques, "for the irregularity of my action, and since there is no one here who can serve as an intermediary, allow me to introduce myself. "He adopted a slightly solemn tone to say: "Lord Douglas Rodilan, afflicted with an annual income of fifty thousand pounds sterling."

As Marcel made a haughty gesture at that brutal declaration, the Englishman added: "Excuse me, Monsieur, but that detail, to which I attach no more importance than you, will soon reveal its relevance when I've told you the motive that made me desire to converse with you."

"Speak, Milord," said Marcel, "but first permit me to introduce my intimate friend, Dr. Jacques Deligny."

The two men bowed to one another.

Marcel invited the Englishman to sit down.

The latter continued: "First, I must beg your pardon for an involuntary indiscretion. A few words of your conversation reached me; my curiosity was provoked by the boldness of your conjectures and the audacity of the enterprise that you're planning, and, without further deliberation, I took the resolution to enable you to realize without waiting for the establishment of a company, which might be slow in formation, and whose interested shareholders could create difficulties for you in future."

"What!" cried Marcel. "You want..."

"Simply to put at your disposal the funds necessary to purchase the famous Gun Club cannon and underwrite all the expenses of the expedition."

"But Milord..."

"I put only one condition on the offer—that you accept me as a traveling companion and that I go with you."

The two young men stared at their interlocutor in bewilderment. He perceived that, and smiled as he continued: "I can see that it's necessary for me to explain the reasons for that proposition, which might appear singular, to say the least. My father, Lord Glennemare, died shortly after my sixteenth birthday. Left in possession of an immense fortune at a young age, I've traveled the world with no other care than satisfying all my whims, seeking new enjoyments—soon exhausted—

from the most various countries and the most refined civilizations. I've drunk my fill of every kind of savant and delicate luxury that the great capitals of Europe—Paris, London, Vienna and St. Petersburg—could furnish; I've tasted all the pleasures invented by the over-excited Far East: India China and Japan have nothing left with which to tempt me.

"I've traveled the primitive countries of Africa, where I've hunted ostrich and slept in a tent. I've even led the rude existence of gauchos and trappers in the pampas and savannahs of the New World. The diplomatic functions with which I've been charged on various occasions while undertaking those voyages have given me access to all courts. From those observation posts I've been able to study all societies, to familiarize myself with humans of all climates and all degrees of civilization. I've experienced the emotions of war, braved tropical cyclones and typhoons, requested from science the enjoyments that it reserves for its adepts. Nothing has been able to dissipate the immeasurable ennui with which the incomplete satisfaction of ever-renascent and always unsatisfied desires has left me.

"Firmly decided not to prolong any further a search for happiness that I deem to be utterly unrealizable, I've resolved to quit this world, so poorly equipped for those tormented by a desire for infinity, and the tour of which is so rapidly completed. Only one point still made me hesitate; I sought a new and original means by which to leave this narrow valley. I wanted my death to bring me some new enjoyment, something that no man before me had been able to experience. What I overheard of your conversation appeared to respond to that secret desire of my soul.

"I won't hide it from you that I'm perfectly convinced that the enterprise in which you're about to engage will end in a frightful catastrophe. If you succeed in getting out of the Earth's zone of attraction once again, you'll infallibly fall on to our satellite, and if the laws of gravity are accurate, you'll be shattered into a thousand pieces on its rocky crust. Well, that's what tempts me. That vertiginous plunge, sufficiently prolonged for one to feel oneself falling, to analyze one's multiple sensations from second to second, attracts me invincibly. Do you want me, in the conditions that I've just indicated to you?"

"He's a madman," Jacques murmured, leaning toward Marcel.

The Englishman heard, or at least divined, what he had said. "No," he continued, with the utmost calm, "I'm not mad, and I give you my word that if you refuse to accept me for your traveling companion, I shall blow out my brains this very evening. Judge now whether, in the interests of the science you love so passionately, you ought not to accept my proposal. By ensuring the realization of your project, it would save you all the difficulty that might delay its execution or render it impossible."

"Well, so be it, Milord," said Marcel. "I accept, but while imposing one condition on you in my turn. You must swear to me that if, as I'm convinced, we reach the Moon safe and sound, you'll renounce your suicidal plans."

"Oh, wholeheartedly," said Lord Rodilan, "for then I'll have found a powerful interest in life, and will no longer have any reason to renounce an existence that will bring me so many new emotions inaccessible to the vulgar. But you'll permit me, until further notice, only to see this second voyage as a pure and simple folly, with which I'm associating myself because I shall find my reckoning therein."

"Well, Messieurs," said Marcel, rising to his feet, "would you care to follow me to my home? If what I have to show you can't triumph over your incredulity, it will be to the despair of human logic."

In a matter of minutes they arrived at the house in the Rue Taitbout in which Marcel occupied a small entresol apartment furnished with elegant simplicity. He left them alone in the drawing room for a moment, went into the adjoining bedroom and came back, carrying, with considerable effort, a kind of chest with solid iron reinforcements, which he deposited carefully on the table.

His two companions got to their feet and looked at it; their faces displayed expressions of keen curiosity.

Marcel opened the mysterious box and took out a round object about twenty centimeters in diameter, reddish brown in color, seemingly very heavy, which he placed respectfully on the table.

"But that's a vulgar cannonball," said Jacques, laughing. "It dates from the taking of Quebec by the English."

"Wait, skeptic—you'll see," said Marcel.

Picking up a screwdriver, which he had brought out along with the singular object that he was showing to his companions, he pointed out a number of small, almost imperceptible grooves; then, introducing his screwdriver successively into each of them, he drew out two tiny narrowly-threaded screws and removed a thick plate embedded in the metallic mass. That plate sealed the orifice of a rectangular hole that extended along the radius of the sphere, and with the aid of forceps he withdrew a tablet made of a bizarre violet-tinted white metal with changing reflections, about twelve centimeters long, half as wide and two centimeters thick.

A number of characters were engraved on its two faces, the first depicting two human beings standing to either side of a circle clearly marked with the outline of the African continent and part of South America, with a crescent beside it, and a second circle to the right of the ensemble, with a shaded circle contained concentrically within it, and another crescent with a horizontal projection terminating an a conical bulge extended toward one of the human figures.

The other face depicted two circles, one marked with the outline of the Americas and the other with East Asia and Australia. There were no human figures this time, but there were horizontal projections to the left of each circle, one of them attached to a crescent with an intermediate circular bulge and the other with a terminal conical bulge. To the right of the circle connected to the crescent there was a smaller, shaded circle, connected to it by two horizontal lines, one interrupted by a circular bulge and the other a conical one.[3]

Jacques and Lord Rodilan leaned over and looked at this singular document curiously.

"Good God, what's that?" exclaimed Jacques.

"Do you believe," Marcel said to him, "that The English would have been able, in 1761, to inscribe at length on a metal plaque the authentic history of the Gun Club experiment, in order to send it graciously to the French besieged in Quebec?" He became more animated. "No, my friend, what you have before your eyes is a message sent to Earth from our satellite—the response to the audacious voyage of the immortals Barbicane, Arden and Nicholl."

"What madness!" murmured the young physician.

Lord Rodilan was looking on indifferently, and a smile that was almost pitying was playing upon his lips.

The word *madness* had exasperated Marcel. "Madness!" he said. "Well, know how this strange object came into my possession, and if you're in doubt after that, it's because you're determined to deny the evidence.

"One day, in the Rocky Mountains, a few weeks before the catastrophe that caused me to lose the fruits of my long labor, I had my workers start digging a shaft that was to serve to increase the ventilation of tunnels that were already well-advanced. They had reached a depth of about fifteen meters when the pick of one of the workmen broke on an object of exceptional hardness. I thought at first that it was a boulder, or an errant block deposited there in the wake of a volcanic eruption, but the workers, having soon disengaged the obstacle, set before my astonished eyes a metallic fragment of singular form. The external surface offered the appearance of a section of a regular sphere, which corresponded on the other face to another, no less regular, concave section. The edges of that fragment, which was about thirty centimeters thick, presented

---

[3] In the original text these images are represented graphically, and these verbal descriptions are improvised.

the appearance of a fracture similar to that of a projectile broken in the aftermath of an explosion. I obviously had before me a fragment of an enormous hollow ball whose radius measured about forty-seven centimeters—which is to say, of a diameter of about ninety-four centimeters. Now, as far as I know, there is mo machine on Earth, except for the Columbiad, capable of launching such a projectile."

"There is none, in fact," said Lord Rodilan.

"Very intrigued, I ordered my men to continue digging with the greatest care, taking every possible precaution in order for me to be able to take account of the relative positions of all the fragments, for I had no doubt that others would be found.

"After some time, in fact, I had collected a dozen fragments of unequal size, all of which presented the characteristics I have just described, confirming my initial hypothesis. Soon, my astonishment reached a peak when one of my workmen brought me a spherical object, which was none other than the ball you've just seen. Increasingly intrigued, I stopped the work; I ordered that the location of the hole should be surrounded by a fence, in order that nothing could be disturbed, and I took my strange find away.

"After having got rid of the clayey soil covering it in part, I examined the ball minutely and did not take long to discover two tiny rectilinear grooves that appeared to form the diameter of little circles traced in the metal; they were obviously the heads of two screws. After much effort, I succeeded in unscrewing them, and took out the tablet that you've just seen, carefully fitted inside, as you'll be able to ascertain for yourselves.

"It took me a long time to understand those mysterious signs. One day, however, light dawned in my mind and it became evident to me that I was looking at a message sent to the Earth by the inhabitants of the Moon, in response to the Gun Club's abortive attempt.

"It was immediately beyond doubt that, if our neighbors had thought of entering into communication with us, they could not, in our reciprocal ignorance of one another's idioms, have recourse to phonetic characters; they were obliged, in consequence, to use a kind of ideographic writing and to refer to some event which, while interesting them, was well-known to us.

"You can see in fact, that everything is there.

"The first symbols evidently represent the Earth and the moon—which is to say, the two heavenly bodies between which it's a matter of establishing communication. You can have no doubt about that, since the old terrestrial continent is drawn on the first figure, and the form of a crescent given to the moon gives a perfect account of the aspect it presents to our planet at the beginning of its cycle. Thus, there are astronomers among them, and their instruments of observation have attained a high degree of perfection, since they can distinguish the exact form of our continents, As for the human figures standing beside the two bodies, they demonstrate that the inhabitants of the Moon, being constituted, to judge by appearance, almost identically to us, have assumed that the Earth is inhabited by beings analogous to themselves, with whom it is not impossible to communicate."

"If this is all the proof you have," Jacques out in, "it's rather meager."

"Don't be in too much haste to judge," Marcel replied. "Just listen." He continued: "Next you see a symbol clearly representing a shell—the Gun Club's—heading for the Moon. The following symbol shows us the same shell, which hasn't reached its goal, describing a curve around our satellite, and finally heading back to Earth, on to which it did, in fact, fall."

"All that doesn't prove very much," Jacques repeated, incorrigible in his skepticism. "What do you think, Milord?"

"Oh, said the Englishman, "all this leaves me indifferent. As you know, I'm only making the journey in order to crash appropriately on the surface of the Moon."

That observation cast a chill.

Marcel went on: "Now here's a shell departing from the Moon and heading toward the Earth; it's obviously the response to the Gun Club's shell. And as we can assume that the Moon's astronomers haven't limited themselves to a single dispatch, not knowing where their projectile would fall, the large sphere whose debris I found is certainly only one of the messages by means of which they've tried to enter into communication with us.

"The following signs confirm that demonstration: look at the projectile going from the Moon to the Earth and the one that is following a similar but parallel trajectory; isn't that a manifest indication of permanent and sequential communications between the two worlds by means of message-bearing projectiles circulating in a regular and normal fashion? Isn't it the realization of the ideal of which the most eminent astronomers have dreamed, and which the Gun Club attempted to bring into the practical domain?"

"But it's a joke, my dear Marcel!" Jacques exclaimed. "You have in your hands some commemorative inscription devised by a member of the Gun Club or some other witness of the experiment of 186*, and there's nothing but lunacy in your hypotheses."

"Mock and jest as much as you like, but explain to me all the circumstances in which I made this singular find. As I said just now, I had the hole at the bottom of which my workman's pick collided with the object we have before us surrounded by a fence. I went back to examine that hole, and observed that the projectile had traversed the upper layer of soil formed by humus mixed with sand, as well as a layer of reddish clay constituting the subsoil, and had finally run into the granitic rock whose upthrust forms, a few kilometers away, the foothills of the Rocky Mountains. There, the surrounding sphere, of which I've retained this fragment, shattered, and its debris was buried in the earth in all directions.

"What corroborates my observations and the consequences I've drawn from them, is that the ball was resting on a layer of exceedingly fine white sand, of which no vestige is seen in the layers traversed. It's therefore certain, so far as I'm concerned, that the people who fabricated the ball took every possible precaution to ensure that it arrived intact at its destination. They enclosed it in a hollow sphere, filling the space enclosing the interior ball entirely with compressed sand, in such a fashion that, no matter how violent the impact might be, the sand would deaden it and preserve their message.

"Can you imagine that anyone, wanting to preserve the memory of Barbicane's voyage, would amuse himself by taking such a luxury of precautions to protect a document that it would have been sufficient to deposit in any museum, and burying it at a depths of fifteen meters in a deserted region where no one would ever have gone to look for it? For you've admitted yourselves that no terrestrial cannon could have fired that colossal projectile."

"Yes, murmured Jacques, visibly shaken. "That's something I can't explain."

"Ah! You're coming round," said Marcel. "Look at this now. You're a chemist—tell me what this metal is." And he presented to his eyes the plaque on which the signs for which he had just furnished an explanation were engraved.

"In truth, I have no idea. It would be necessary to assay it."

"I've assayed it; I detached a minuscule fragment from that corner. I heated it to incandescence and analyzed it with a spectroscope. Well, I can assure you that this metal has no parallel on our planet."

"You're telling me that..." As if talking to himself, Jacques continued: "What a magnificent dream that would be! To establish the presence on our satellite of a human race with which we can enter into fruitful communication! What new horizons opened to science! What inappreciable discoveries the future would reserve for us! Where would human genius stop then, and what glory would not be reserved for those who took the first step into the abyss of space!"

"It seems to me, Doctor," said Lord Rodilan, "that you catch fire very easily. So reserved a little whole ago, you're now as enthusiastic as your friend."

"In truth, I can't deny it; that strange message, the circumstances in which it was discovered and this unknown metal have all stirred me strangely. And you, in spite of your British phlegm, don't you feel a trifle shaken?"

"Oh, personally," said the Englishman, "I have no interest in the question and, as one of your writers said, my seat is taken. I only want an original means of dying and I don't think I'm paying too dearly for it be lending you my collaboration—for if there's one thing of which I'm perfectly convinced, it's that if we escape the initial shock at the moment of our departure, we'll inevitably shatter into a thousand pieces on the rocks of out inhospitable satellite."

"Ah! Permit me...," said Marcel.

The Englishman interrupted him. "No, my friend—I'll ask you, in fact, for permission name you thus, since our destinies will be so narrowly linked—we'll come back to the subject later, since it appears to interest you."

"And I hope to convince you," Marcel concluded, extending his hand.

The Englishman shook it vigorously, as well as Jacques' hand, murmuring: "Oh, that I doubt!"

III. The Auction

On 10 February 188*, as midday drew near, the large hall of the Baltimore Auction Rooms exhibited an unaccustomed animation. The sale by auction of the Gun Club's famous Columbiad cannon and its accessories was about to begin.

According to all indications, the number of potential buyers ought not to have been very large, and it is quite probable that the sale would have passed unnoticed and that the monstrous engine that had excited so much public curiosity twenty years before would have been sold for scrap, if something entirely unexpected had not occurred. The curiosity-seekers assemble in the hall, well before the time fixed for the sale, told one another urgently, with abundant commentary, that serious buyers were going to appear. People who seemed well-informed said that a month before, two Frenchmen and an Englishman had disembarked in Florida.

In spite of the mystery with which they surrounded themselves, their actions had been noticed; they had been seen talking to the men posted to guard the cannon; they had examined all the apparatus carefully, visited the aluminum shell and had even made a descent into the depths of the Columbiad, whose side walls they had carefully inspected.

While these items of information circulated in the crowd, the honorable John Elkiston, the auctioneer, had installed himself behind the table on which the precious objects for sale were usually exhibited. For lack of the Gun Club cannon, which would have been difficult to transport, the crier displayed to the gaze of the curious massed on the other side of the table plans, drawings, blueprints and photographs representing all aspects of the object of the unusual sale.

"Gentlemen," Elkiston said, "You must have heard mention of the unforgettable voyage effected eighteen years ago[4] into the lunar regions by the illustrious members of the Gun Club, Impey Barbicane and Captain Nicholl, accompanied by the bold Frenchman Michel Ardan. You all know that a company was formed in order, by means of the results obtained, to establish regular communications between the Earth and its satellite. In the beginning, the capital flooded in, but the zeal of the backers soon relented; the instigators of the enterprise abandoned it and the company went bankrupt.

"The time is approaching, however, when, according to the most irrefutable astronomical calculations, he experiment that had been on the point of achieving complete success can be renewed. So the honorable receiver of the company has judged the moment favorable to proceed with the sale of the Columbiad, and thus provide the organizers of scientific expeditions with the means to effect a new departure.

"We have no doubt that a number of courageous and devoted men will be found on the soil of the Union who will want to retain for our fatherland the monopoly on all audacities and the glory of a success that will make all the universities and scientists of the old world pale with jealousy. Hurrah for the Union! Pay attention—the sale is about to begin."

In spite of this expenditure of eloquence, the audience seemed rather cold. There was no agitation or hubbub, none of the urgent interjections of a crowd impassioned by a great idea or excited by a glorious enterprise. People looked sideways and sniggered, ironic smiles creased lips. People seemed to be wondering whether anyone could be found who was mad enough to launch forth on such an adventure. There were muted whispers to the effect that the reserve would not be reached

---

[4] Given that the text explicitly dates the Columbiad's first voyage to the 1860s, the figure of 18 years establishes that the date of the present events cannot be later than 1887. Eighteen years from the 1865 publication date of Verne's novel would be 1883.

and that the debris of the colossal monster that lay buried in the soil of Florida would doubtless be condemned to stay there indefinitely, corroded by rust, destroyed by time—a lamentable monument to human folly, a sad witness to overweening ambition and immeasurable disappointment.

Now one, however, had noticed the entry into the hall of three foreigners who had slipped in quietly; they were Marcel de Rouzé, Jacques Deligny and Lord Rodilan.

The auctioneer resumed: "The Columbiad, with all its accessories, projectile, electrical apparatus, cranes and lifting-tackle, plus the hangars in which these objects are conserved, are offered for sale with a reserve of two hundred thousand dollars, and will be sold to the highest bidder, even if there is only one bid. The bids are open."

The auctioneer repeated: "The Columbiad, at two hundred thousand dollars."

Silence.

"Come on, gentlemen, make up your minds. No more magnificent opportunity has ever presented itself to lovers of science to repeat the famous attempt that impassioned the two worlds."

No one breathed a word.

John Elkiston became agitated behind his table.

"Come on," he said, "it's not possible that the gigantic effort made to sound the abysms of space should be lost forever. Is there no one in the United States to pick up and bring to a successful conclusion the greatest idea of the century? Have the children of free America lost all courage, all spirit of initiative? Has the appetite for heroic adventures disappeared with the illustrious Barbicane and Nicholl?"

The auctioneer's eloquence remained ineffective, and he was doubtless about to postpone the sale until another day when Lord Rodilan suddenly said, coolly: "Two hundred thousand dollars."

All gazes turned toward him. The auctioneer's voice was exultant. "Bravo, gentlemen! There is a bid of two hundred thousand dollars. I knew that an endeavor so glorious could not go to waste. But you Americans wouldn't want to leave to a foreigner the honor of succeeding where our fellow citizens have failed."

The members of the audience, however, continued looking at him with mocking expressions, and, on seeing the way in which they were staring at the singular bidder, it was evident that they were not far from considering his to be an eccentric, if not a madman.

As for the person who was the object of that curiosity, he remained impassive, scanning the crowd with an indifferent gaze.

The voice of the auctioneer made itself heard again: "There is a bid of two hundred thousand dollars. Any advance on two hundred thousand dollars?"

No voice went up to raise the bid.

The auctioneer's hammer was raised. "Going once," he said, "at two hundred thousand dollars. No one? Going twice..."

Silence still reigned over the assembly.

"Two hundred thousand dollars," he repeated. "All finished...? No regrets...? Sold!" And the hammer came down on the table.

The Englishman was the owner of the Columbiad. A few minutes later, the saleroom was deserted.

IV. Mathieu-Rollère

While Marcel, accompanied by Lord Rodilan, who seemed to be lending the enterprise in which he was engaged more interest than he wanted to admit, went to Florida to direct the preparations for the projected voyage, Jacques Deligny, with the consent of his two friends, set off for Europe in order to accomplish what he considered to be a sacred duty.

The old astronomer François Mathieu-Rollère had been living for nearly thirty years in the Rue Cassini in Paris, near the Observatoire. It was there, in a pleasant small house surrounded by a large garden that he had come to take up residence with his wife when he had been appointed to the post of astronomer at the Observatoire de Paris. The young scientist would have been completely happy with a spouse he loved and the science to which he had devoted his life if Heaven had blessed their union. For many years he despaired of being a father, and seemed resigned to that suffering when a daughter was born, to whom he gave the name Hélène. But he paid dearly for that happiness; the birth of the child cost the life of her mother.

That unexpected death threw the scientist into great despair. To divert himself from his grief, he plunged even more resolutely into science, which was the only thing that could make him forget the person he had lost. Hélène thus grew up with a father who, entirely given over to his scientific work, scarcely gave her a thought and seemed no longer to remember how ardently he had desired to have a child. Although his aged housekeeper, the worthy Catherine, had transferred to her all the affection she had had for the deceased, the life of the child, deprived of maternal tenderness, who spent her days between a scientist lost in his books and an old maidservant, was rather sad. She rarely went out and never joined in with the games of children of her own age.

She was eight years old when the arrival of a young companion profoundly modified her life.

The astronomer had a sister married to a naval officer whom she loved profoundly. A brilliant future had opened up before ship's lieutenant Deligny when, in the course of a campaign in the Far East, death had suddenly snatched him from the tenderness of his wife. The latter had followed him to the grave not long after, and Jacques, their only son, then aged fourteen, had been left an orphan. His uncle, whom the law appointed as his guardian, had taken the boy, who was then finishing his studies at the Lycée Louis-le-Grand, into his home.

From then on life had changed for young Hélène; a close affection had not taken long to unite the two children. That sentiment, growing with age, had become a serious love that nothing seemed likely to disrupt. The old scientist seemed only to be interested in matters of the skies; it did not seem likely that he would ever oppose the union of the two young people, and Jacques worked with confidence to build a secure and honorable situation for the person he adored. So, his surprise and despair were great when, on asking for Hélène's hand, his uncle had replied with a categorical refusal. He knew that nothing would make the astronomer go back on his decision, and he had gone away heartbroken, and said to Hélène while stifling his sobs: "I'll go in search of a means of being worthy of you."

From that moment on, life had been very sad for the young woman; she was consumed by a wait that every day rendered more desperate. Since his departure, Jacques had given no sign of life, and she sometimes wondered whether the man she loved might have forgotten her, or whether he had died in some perilous adventure. Her complexion had paled, her eyes had lost their gleam, and her health seemed to deteriorate.

The old scientist, however, completely absorbed by his work, did not notice anything. He scarcely darted an occasional distracted glance at his daughter, whom he only saw at meal times; he did not notice the changes that had taken place in her.

Eight months had gone by like that since Jacques' departure; Hélène was no longer hopeful.

One morning, in the latter days of February, the bell at the garden door rang noisily, as if shaken by a vigorous hand, and Hélène, who was sitting in her room, felt a shock in her heart without knowing why. The old maidservant went to open up.

The visitor was Jacques.

He erupted joyfully into the little room where he had so often sat between his uncle and his beloved. The old scientist, who was getting ready to go to the Observatory, had just come into it.

"Oh, Uncle!" cried Jacques, throwing his arms around his neck. "How glad I am to see you! You're going to be pleased with me. But where's my cousin? I want to hug her too."

"Gently, gently," said the astronomer, who had nearly been knocked over by the young man's greeting. "You leave like a madman, you go away for eight months without sending any news, and you come back like an aerolith. What does it all mean?"

Meanwhile, Hélène, overcoming her emotion, had run downstairs and come into the drawing room. Her cheeks were now covered with a vivid blush; her eyes had recovered a gleam that had not been seen there for a long time. She offered her forehead to Jacques, and while he deposited a burning kiss thereon, she murmured: "Wretch, how you've made me suffer."

When lunch was over and he was savoring his coffee, Jacques told his uncle and his cousin everything that he had done since he had left them.

The young woman listened avidly to the story, in which she sensed all the love palpitating with which Jacques heart was filled. The old man only lent a distracted ear to it—but when the narrative reached his encounter with Marcel de

Rouzé, and the most recent events that had filled his life, concluding with the audacious voyage that he had decided to undertake, the astronomer's eye became animated, his attention became sustained, and an old residue of blood flowed to his cheeks; he was gained by his nephew's enthusiasm, and in the end, his joy overflowed.

"Bravo, my dear boy!" he exclaimed. "That is indeed a great and noble enterprise, which will make all the astronomers in Europe dry up with jealousy, and furnish science with an inexhaustible mine of rich documents and discoveries, whose range can't yet be anticipated."

"But Father," put in Hélène, whose joy seemed suddenly to have faded away, and who felt gripped by an inexpressible anguish, "you can't think that! To consent to Jacques engaging in this insensate adventure is to send him to certain death and to condemn me too—for I certainly won't survive him."

"Ta ta ta!" said the old scientist. "That's little girls all over—ignorant and timid. If one listened to them, one would never attempt anything and science would remain immobile. But, ignoramus that you are, this voyage that causes you so much dread has already been made once, and they came back. It's a matter today of beginning again in conditions of absolute security. You've been told that up there, on our satellite, there are people waiting for us, who are eager to enter into communication with us. Nothing will be easier for those who will have reached the Moon than to come back again."

Hélène did not share her father's enthusiastic conviction, and during the days that followed, she used all her influence on Jacques to make him take back his terrible resolution—but her efforts were futile; Jacques had gradually become intoxicated by the thought of that voyage into the immensity. Marcel's ardent faith in the ultimate success had won him over. In any case, he could not see any other means of obtaining the hand of the woman he loved.

His love rendered him eloquent and persuasive, and although he did not succeed in making the young woman share his confidence, he eventually contrived to stop her opposing his plan. She wanted at least to remain close to the man she loved until the last possible moment, however, and to follow him in his perilous enterprise with her eyes.

"I can see," she said to her father one day, "that everything I might try to persuade you, Jacques to abandon this enterprise, and you, Father, from approving of it, would be pointless. It's necessary, therefore, for me to resign myself to it. But why shouldn't we accompany you to America? And since there's a telescope in the Rocky Mountains that permits the projectile to be followed in its flight, why not go there in order to remain, for as long as possible, in communication with the person who is so dear to us?"

"You're right!" exclaimed the astronomer. "That's an excellent idea. Nothing will be easier than obtaining a special mission from the Observatoire."

It was therefore agreed that they would leave together for New York, and that while Jacques went to Florida, the old scientist and his daughter would go to the Rocky Mountains, there to await the departure of the Columbiad's projectile.

V. Preparations for Departure

For several months, an extraordinary activity reigned in the Florida peninsula. Several crews of European workmen had disembarked there. New workshops had been constructed, replacing those that had been built eighteen years before and which, greatly neglected since that era, had fallen into ruins and become useless for the new enterprise. There was, in fact, no more need for the innumerable furnaces that had served to found the Columbiad; the number of workmen required for what needed to be done now was much less considerable.

A few temporary houses sufficed to lodge them, but it was necessary to retire to working order the railway liking Tampa to Stone's Hill, by which all the machinery and necessary provisions would reach the construction yards, for that track, which had been so busy for a few months and had transported so many materials and passengers had become singularly dilapidated in the interim.

It was no longer a case, as before, of digging the vast hole in which the gigantic cannon would be encased, or of pouring in the enormous quantity of cast iron that was to form its walls. All that colossal, frightful labor, which had surpassed all known proportions, had been carried out magisterially and brought to a successful conclusion by the forerunners of our explorers. Even the aluminum shell that had served them as a habitat was there, under the sealed hangar, with its internal furnishings.

It was, however, necessary to review the cannon and the projectile very carefully. How would both of them stand up at the moment of departure? Had they not suffered in some measure from the long abandonment in which they had been left? Undoubtedly, the public advertisement that had appeared in the American press had affirmed that they were in good condition, but our men were too shrewd to trust in such an assertion.

The National Society for Interstellar Communications had taken care to have a kind of roof erected above the orifice of the Columbiad in order to protect it from bad weather, but such precautions could not be taken for granted; it was necessary to carry out a serious and profound examination.

Marcel and Lord Rodilan directed the work. The presence of Jacques, who would not have brought any special competence to those circumstances, had not been judged to be indispensable. He had, moreover, informed his two comrades of the result of his conversations with his uncle, and they had obligingly let him know that he could make preparations for the departure of the astronomer and his daughter for the Rocky Mountains completely at his ease. They both took responsibility for making sure that everything was for the best, given the epoch in which the journey had to be undertaken.

The orifice of the Columbiad was cleared of its protective roof, and lifting-tackle was installed in its place that would permit penetration into the depths of the gigantic tube, to check its condition. Marcel did not want to entrust the responsibility for that examination to anyone else. Equipped with a powerful electric reflector lamp, he descended slowly along the walls, and recognized with satisfaction that the barrel of the cannon had been coated internally along its entire length with a thick layer of tar in order to protect it from damp. He was able to ascertain by scrupulous inspection that the layer had not cracked anywhere, which was sufficient proof that the cast iron cylinder, sustained by the solid mass of masonry in which it was encased, had resisted the formidable gas pressure admirably.

It was now a matter of proceeding with a new boring process to remove the tar and returning the polish it had lost to the inside of the barrel. To do that they had only to follow the example of the constructors of the Columbiad, and the work, directed and supervised at close range by Marcel—who was everywhere at once and communicated to the souls of the workmen the ardor by which he was animated—got the job done in as little time as possible.

Lord Rodilan, to whom it made no difference to parade his ennui in one part of the globe rather than another, did not take a very active part in those preparations. He followed them with a slightly mocking expression; Marcel's robust confidence had not shaken his incredulity, and he did not spare his friend his unkind reflections and sinister predictions.

"For me, my dear fellow," he told him, "you're the object of a sufficiently interesting curiosity, and I really would admire you if I were capable of experiencing such a sentiment. To see the seriousness that you bring to all these preparatory operations, one might that you were sure of arriving safe and sound at the end of your voyage."

"Am I sure of that? But my dear Lord, so far as I'm concerned, that is mathematically demonstrated, and it's necessary for you to shut your eyes to the evidence in order not to be convinced by the calculations I've so often submitted to you."

"La la—don't get annoyed, incorrigible engineer that you are. Since I'm leaving with you, what more do you want? I certainly hope that we'll have a memorable fall up there—can you have a *fall up there?* That's what's original—that and the fact that we'll be smashed to smithereens before even being able to recognize the color of that satanic satellite that's attracting you like a veritable magnet."

"But we won't fall, as you know very well. Perhaps we'll come down a little quickly..."

"Yes, yes, I know, the famous rockets, which won't allow the shell to fall on to the Moon."

"Agreed—but this time, I hope, we won't encounter an inconvenient bolide that will throw us off course, and my new system of rockets will prevail against any event."

Marcel was, in fact, preoccupied with that question; he had remade the calculations of Barbicane and Nicholl, and remained convinced that the means they had devised for slowing down the rapidity of the descent to the lunar surface was absolutely insufficient, especially given the absence of an atmosphere, the resistance of which the shell would not have to overcome. But the idea of rockets whose ignition would oppose the shell's fall and deaden its impact was ingenious. Marcel was determined to stick to it; he merely thought it useful to increase their number and to organize three series, which would be brought into play at calculated intervals in inverse proportion to the distance to be traveled. He would thus obtain three successive resistances, which, if his calculations were accurate—and he did not doubt their exactitude—ought to allow the travelers to arrive at their destination without an excessively violent impact.

The shell that the first expedition had used was also subjected to an attentive examination. It had successfully resisted the pressure of the gas whose explosion had projected it into space and its formidable plunge into the depths of the Pacific. The thick walls had been made of pure aluminum and, having the resistance of a single block, had not been subjected to any considerable deformation. Only the interior fittings had suffered much from the insults of time.

The padding of the walls and the circular divan had been completely replaced, and Marcel took advantage of that circumstance to have the fine but resistant steel springs replaced, which had rusted over time and lost their elasticity. The lenticular panes of the portholes and the metallic frames in which they were held were similarly renewed. It was also necessary to reestablish the metal plates designed to protect them against the shock of the departure, which the original voyagers had simply thrown outside. Finally, all the containers were replaced: the boxes of water and food, the gas reservoirs, and the Regnault-Reiset apparatus designed to maintain the respirability of the air throughout the journey.[5]

---

[5] Henri-Victor Regnault and Jules de Reiset worked in collaboration during the 1850s on respiration processes, conducting many experiments on animals; among other devices they developed a system for removing exhaled carbon dioxide from air and replenishing the oxygen consumed, which maintained its respirability in a closed environment for some time. The

With the certainty that he had of encountering living beings on our satellite with whom it would be possible to enter into intellectual communication, Marcel had wanted, if to instruct them or cause them to marvel, at least to acquaint them with the degree of civilization and moral development that their terrestrial neighbors has reached. With that in mind he had take care to equip the projectile-vehicle in which he was about to visit them with everything that he thought likely to inform them of that. To the most improved and carefully-wrapped optical and mathematical instruments—telescope microscope, compass, chronometer, theodolite, sextant, etc.—he had added a small printing press, a phonograph with several cylinders, capable of reproducing the most beautiful of our operatic arias, a telephone, an instantaneous camera fitted with the latest improvements, specimens of our various metals, seeds of the most useful and precious vegetables, including a dozen saplings of the fruit-bearing tree species that were most productive and easiest to acclimatize.

He had taken care, above all, to establish a rich collection of albums containing photographs of terrestrial landscapes and seascapes, and our most famous monuments; works of art, including paintings and statues by the greatest masters, were abundantly represented therein, as well as our principal industrial, agricultural, navigational and locomotive apparatus.

An atlas of the terrestrial globe completed that collection, in which all the effort of centuries and all the conquests of modern civilization were summarized. Everything concerning everyday life among the various peoples covering the surface of the world—habitations, furniture, costumes, weapons, utensils and objects of every sort—were encountered there in sufficient quantity.

They took with them a few advanced weapons: repeating rifles and revolvers, with ammunition. "Because," Marcel said, "We don't know much about what we'll be dealing with,

---

idea was still new when Jules Verne adopted it in *De la Terre à la Lune*.

and in spite of the hospitable inclinations of which they seem to be giving evidence, we might also encounter people of a difficult humor, with whom it will be necessary to reckon."

Everything had been carefully calculated with regard to volume and weight, in order not to clutter the projectile or make it unreasonably heavy. As they were not taking dogs with them, as had been done on the previous voyage, they had more space at their disposal and their cargo was both more complete and less cumbersome than that of the first explorers.

The shell itself, which was to serve as a receptacle for such numerous and various objects, and in which the three travelers were going to live for an indeterminate time, had to undergo a few indispensable adjustments. Although, as has already been said, it had not suffered any external deformation, it was necessary to polish its surface again, but that was a trivial matter. It was necessary to reestablish the broken partitions that had succeeded so well in deadening the initial shock during the first departure. On that point there was nothing to change, so wisely and skillfully had the precautions taken eighteen years before been executed; it was sufficient to repeat what had already been done.

But one important point remained to be set right; Marcel, it will not have been forgotten, had calculated that the rockets with which Barbicane had equipped the shell would be insufficient to deaden its fall, not being sufficiently powerful, In addition, since 186-, the science had made progress; the ingenious chemist Cailletet had discovered a means of liquefying some of the gases that had thus far resisted all other attempts.[6] Evidently, that liquefaction could only be obtained under enormous pressure, but once the gas had been reduced to liquid form and enclosed in receptacles of proven resistance, one had a considerable expansive force in a very small volume, easier to manipulate than that of the numerous and varied explosives that modern scientists have recently discovered. Mar-

---

[6] Louis-Paul Cailletet first succeeded in producing droplets of liquid oxygen in 1877.

cel therefore decided to substitute liquid oxygen for the powder previously employed, and to dispose around the hull of the projectile the three new series of rockets on whose action he was relying absolutely.

While these preparations were being made in Florida, the old astronomer François Mathieu-Rollère, entirely given over to the new idea that now impassioned him, had done everything he could to facilitate the execution of the project suggested to him by his daughter. Without revealing exactly what he had in mind, he let it be known that he was interested in checking and completing, with the aid of the giant telescope in the Rocky Mountains, the observations commenced by the Observatoire de Paris of the constitution and the motion of recently discovered nebulae. And as he had a great skill in astronomical research, Admiral Mouchez, the illustrious director of the Observatory, who valued him highly, had obtained a special mission for him from the Ministry of Public Education.[7]

Neither Marcel nor Lord Rodilan attempted to generate any publicity regarding the projected enterprise; they both judged that the blizzard of advertising that had accompanied the first voyage—the loud announcements thrown to all the echoes of publicity, the entire populations invited to witness a scientific experiment as if it were a fairground spectacle—were unworthy of true scientists. It was, in fact, a matter of a serious attempt to resolve an interesting problem of cosmography, and not a pretentious and almost charlatanesque exhibition in which the pride of an ignorant crowd could find its pleasure.

---

[7] Amédée Mouchez (1821-1892) was appointed director of the Observatoire in 1878. His naval career had mostly been spent in hydrographic studies and attempts to perfect the measurement of longitude with the aid of scientific instruments; he had also made important observations of the 1873 transit of Venus from the Indian Ocean.

In any case, the conditions were no longer the same. The Gun Club, which had initiated the first enterprise, had been far from capable of raising the considerable sum that it had cost; it had been necessary to appeal to the public of the Old and New worlds, to bring national pride into play, and to provoke, especially among Americans, the surge of patriotic enthusiasm that had caused capital to flow into the explorers' coffers.

Today was not at all similar. The complete failure of the Society for Interstellar Communications and the sale of all its assets, including the Columbiad, at a derisory price, had reduced the expenses of the initial establishment in considerable proportions; in addition, the generosity of Lord Rodilan dispensed with the necessity for any appeal to the public, and, in consequence, of any publicity. The entirely relative success obtained by Barbicane, Nicholl and Michel Ardan had been somewhat forgotten; a profound silence had fallen over that grandiose exploit. Other events had occurred that had deflected attention and impassioned public opinion.

Before going to the observatory in the Rocky Mountains, from which he would be able to follow the shell in its flight, François Mathieu-Rollère, perhaps also pushed by his daughter, who wanted to postpone the moment of supreme separation until the last minute, had decided to spend a few days in Florida to take account personally of the preparations for the enterprise in which he was taking such a keen interest. So, on 10 November, Marcel and Lord Rodilan, alerted by telegram, went to Tampa to meet the steamer carrying Jacques and his two companions.

"I hope, my dear Lord," Marcel had said, while they were waiting to meet the arrivals, "that you aren't going to alarm the funereal prophecies of our friend's fiancée. The poor child, if I can believe Jacques' letters, has only a very mediocre confidence in our ultimate success; she seeks to reassure herself, but can't always succeed. Don't increase her anxieties; at least let her hope."

"Oh, my dear chap," replied Lord Rodilan, phlegmatically, "I'm a gentleman; I know the regard one owes to a young woman, and although my opinion has not varied, I shall not allow it to appear—you can be sure of that."

The meeting was cordial and touching. Hélène, whose smile did not hide her anxiety, felt slightly reassured by Marcel's masculine confidence and robust gaiety. Lord Rodilan's phlegm also contributed to her reassurance; she could not imagine that such a correct gentleman envisaged the prospect of a frightful death with such tranquil indifference.

As for her father, he was entirely given over to his scientific preoccupations and did not perceive anything. The fortnight he spent with the three bold companions was employed in examining everything; he remade all the calculations on which Marcel's confidence was founded, and confirmed their accuracy. He wanted to go down into the Columbiad to verify its definitive condition, and carefully checked the projectile, whose new fitments he praised highly.

"My dear friends," he said, when he had inspected everything, "I'm now absolutely certain that you'll succeed." And he rubbed his hands together with evident satisfaction.

On 23 November he left with his daughter for the Rocky Mountains.

On the previous day, Jacques had had one last conversation with Hélène.

"So," said the young woman, "it's completely settled, and nothing can change your mind. You're going to leave on this frightful adventure, the mere thought of which chills my heart with fear."

"Don't worry," Jacques relied. "Your father has verified our calculations himself and declared that the journey is possible and devoid of peril. What we have done in order to reach the goal that we're pursuing, nothing will prevent us from doing the same to return. Look at Marcel; he doesn't have an instant's hesitation or doubt. Look at Lord Rodilan; isn't his superb calm the guarantee of a sure success?"

"Oh," said Hélène, "those men aren't in love, and aren't leaving behind someone who loves them."

"But dear heart, it's precisely because I love you and want to win you that I've resigned myself to causing you such anguish. You know very well that I have no other means of bending your father's will. When I come back, he'll grant me your hand. If I refused to leave with my friends now, I'd be dishonored; your father would banish me from his presence forever; all hope of being your husband would be lost, and I'd have nothing left to do but die, sad and desperate."

"Die, Jacques, you! You know very well that I wouldn't survive you."

"But I'll come back; I have an unshakable conviction as to that. Don't take away, at this cruel moment of separation, the courage that I need to distance myself from you."

"Go, then," she murmured, stifling her sobs ineptly. "And may God protect us all."

VI. The Observers at Long's Peak

The day of departure was drawing near; it was 1 December. The operations necessary for the loading of the Columbiad had begun. After numerous reflections, after having passed in review and submitted to the regulation of rigorous calculation all the recently-discovered explosive substances, the three voyagers had come back to the fulmicotton employed by their predecessors.

It will be remembered that, in spite of the error made by the Cambridge Observatory regarding the initial velocity that the shell would require to cross the zone of neutral attraction, the charge of four hundred thousand pounds of fulmicotton had been adequate to obtain that result. They had, therefore, maintained that figure, and on 10 December the charge was complete.

Although the planned attempt had not been announced far and wide, like the preceding one, only the scientific societies of the two worlds having been notified, and although the political preoccupations then agitating the United States had deflected public attention elsewhere, a fairly large number of people, mostly attracted by a love of science, had gathered in Tampa and were following the progress of the gigantic project with interest.

It was, therefore, in the midst of a numerous crowd that the three companions embarked. Marcel had brought a young engineer from France, named Georges Dumesnil, previously attached to a factory at Creusot, of proven experience, who had helped him in the technical part of all the preliminary operations. It was to him that he confided the delicate mission of supervising the descent of the shell into the barrel of the Columbiad and launching the electric spark that would set fire to the fulmicotton charge and hurl the projectile into space.

The departure took place as he had foreseen on 15 December at ten forty-six and forty seconds in the evening. The shell, launched with prodigious force, escaped the blazing flanks of the Columbiad in the midst of the cheers of an enthusiastic crowd.

The experience of the first departure had not been useless, and the disasters that the previous explosion had occasioned were mostly avoided. It is true that the witnesses felt a violent commotion, and a considerable number, in spite of being warned, fell to the ground, but no trains were derailed, no ship broke its anchor-chain and the vessels crossing the Atlantic were not disturbed in their progress. The sky was not even obscured by unusual vapors, and the observers whose eyes was fixed to the ocular of telescopes like that in the Rocky Mountains saw the passage through our atmosphere of a sort of incandescent asteroid, which they would have taken in any other circumstance for a vulgar bolide. Alerted as they were, they recognized it as the Columbiad's projectile.

The scientist Mathieu-Rollère stamped his feet. "Ah!" he cried, rubbing his hands together vigorously. "There they go, those brave young men. They're exactly on time. Now the vehicle transporting them, leaving our atmosphere, has disappeared into the depths of space. But in three days we'll see them again; we'll follow their fall step by step, and witness their triumphant arrival on our satellite."

Hélène wept silently.

During the three nights that followed the departure, the astronomer was at his post, trying to sound the darkness that filled space and follow the shell carrying the three audacious individuals in its flight—but the darkness was impenetrable and, although he knew scientifically the route that the projectile would follow, the giant eye of the telescope could not perceive anything; the jealous night kept its secret. Exhausted by fatigue, he had fallen asleep on the afternoon of the fourth day when suddenly—it was about five o'clock in the evening, but night falls quickly at that time of year in those northern regions—one of the young astronomers taking shifts at the telescope uttered a cry: "There they are! There they are!"

Mathieu-Rollère, immediately alerted, leapt to his feet.

On the broadly-illuminated disk of the Moon an almost imperceptible black dot stood out, which, as they were able to ascertain with the aid of the micrometer, was definitely moving.

"It's them, no doubt about it," murmured the scientist.

In fact, the moving dot in which the astronomer recognized the projectile was at that moment over the western part of the Sea of Rains, where the craters of Aristillus and Autolycus rise up.[8] It seemed to be advancing in the narrow valley limited by the extreme tip of the Caucasus chain and the two craters.

Although the movement of the projectile was almost insensible at such a distance, it was evident that the fall was taking place with frightful rapidity.

All the astronomers usually present at the observatory, and a considerable number of other scientists attracted by the desire to follow the strange experiment, had come successively to fix their eyes to the ocular of the telescope, and all of them had observed the displacement of the dot observed by Mathieu-Rollère. They all shared his opinion.

He took his place at the ocular again. The other astronomers, their gazes attached to the hands of a sidereal clock, calculated the moment at which the travelers would arrive at their goal. It was at eleven fifty-nine and sixty seconds that they ought to reach the surface of the satellite.

"They're getting close," murmured Mathieu-Rollère, "but there's something I can't explain. They ought to be able, with the aid of the rockets at their disposal, to slow their ve-

---

[8] The "Sea of Rains" is the Mare Imbrium. The reason why the craters are said to "rise up" is that the author is taking it for granted—as many astronomers then did—that the lunar craters are volcanic, and must be situated on top of mountains. That mistaken assumption plays an important role in determining the notion of the Moon's surface and history developed and depicted in the novel.

locity—but doubtless, at such a distance, such an observation is impossible."

Suddenly, he uttered an exclamation. They hurried around him. "I can no longer see them!" he stammered.

They all approached and looked in their turn.

"Of course!" cried the honorable W. Burnett, the director of the observatory. "They've fallen into a fissure." He added: "Look, in fact, at that crack in the lunar surface snaking from the foot of the Caucasus chain; it only appears to us as a thin line traced in ink, but in reality it's several kilometers wide—sufficient space to give passage to thousands of projectiles of that caliber."

He turned to Mathieu-Rollère. "And it's doubtless because they perceived the direction in which the shell was headed that they left until the last moment the rockets designed to deaden their fall."

"But what will become of them in the depths of that abyss?" said Mathieu-Rollère, his voice trembling with emotion.

"My God," said the American, "That's a question I can't answer. The fissure into which they've fallen, originating from a fracture of the lunar crust, will, in all probability, have sheer vertical sides, and getting out of it will be difficult. On the other hand, if, as recent observations permit the supposition, low-lying lunar areas still enclose air, they have a greater chance of encountering a breathable atmosphere when they emerge from the shell.

"On my soul," muttered one of the young staff-members of the observatory, "I wouldn't give ten cents for their hides."

Hélène had fainted, and the old scientist was trying to bring her round.

For all the observers in the Rocky Mountains, the three voyagers were irredeemably lost.

VII. The Fall

"Hurrah!" cried Marcel. "We're falling!"

"Are you are of that?" said Jacques.

"Perfectly sure. We've just crossed the neutral zone in which, the shell being subject to the double attraction of the Earth and the Moon, weight was annihilated, and you must have felt, as I did, that we were to longer weighed down to the floor of the projectile."[9]

"Oh yes!" said Lord Rodilan. "And I must say that I've never experienced anything similar to that strange sensation. It seemed to me that I no longer had a body, and that I'd become a pure spirit. That alone was worth the trouble of making the voyage. But there's nothing durable in this world, and now we've become heavy and material again, as before. Fortunately, it will soon be finished and in a little while we'll..."

"That's understood, my dear friend," said Jacques, "but keep it to yourself. We have the means to deaden our fall and we'll disembark as tranquilly on to the soil of the Moon as passengers descending to the platform of Charing Cross station."

---

[9] The mistaken assumption that travelers from the Earth to the Moon would only experience weightlessness briefly, while crossing a "neutral zone" in which the attractions of terrestrial and lunar gravity are equal, is an error of which dramatic use is made in *De la Terre à la Lune*. As well as being reproduced here in passing, the idea was afforded much greater melodramatic importance in Georges Le Faure and Henri de Graffigny's *Aventures extraordinaires d'un savant russe* (tr. as *The Extraordinary Adventures of a Russian Scientist*, Black Coat Press, 2 volumes, ISBN 978-1-934543-81-8 and 978-1-934543-82-5), whose first three volumes appeared in 1888-1890 and a fourth in 1896, although *Un Monde inconnu* was probably written before its publication.

"A thousand guineas," said Lord Rodilan, "that we'll be reduced to pulp."

"Done," retorted Marcel, laughing. "I'm sure that, if you win, you won't be claiming the price of the wager from me."

"For myself," said Jacques, "I'm fully confident. I sense that I shall see Hélène again.

"Bravo, my son," said Marcel solemnly. "It's necessary to have faith in science. And now, pay attention! Gunners to your cannon!"

Beneath the gaze of the voyagers, the dry bed of an immense sea extended, oval in form, from which a few isolated craters emerged with steep and tormented slopes. Toward the west, three of those craters, arranged in a triangle, were near the mountains that formed the boundary of the plain in that direction. In the midst of those mountains a large strait opened that connected with another sea, smaller in its dimensions.

The Sun's rays, the force of which was not attenuated by any vapor, poured a dazzling light over that desolate landscape. The soil, absolutely arid, where no trace of vegetation could be seen, seemed only to present to the gaze the rocky foundations of an extinct world; its surface, irregularly hollowed out by profound depressions, was bristling with peaks that jutted up abruptly; even the flat regions seemed swollen by an infinite number of blisters that might have been mistaken for tightly-packed granulations at a distance.

The whole of that strange panorama offered a spectacle of incontestable grandeur to the eyes of the marveling voyagers.

"How beautiful it is!" murmured Jacques, as if overwhelmed by admiration.

Even the Englishman, in spite of his phlegm and detachment from everything, was unable to conserve his indifference. "In truth," he exclaimed, "I've never seen anything as splendid."

As for Marcel, he was triumphant. "Look," he said to his companions. "We're about to arrive in what is perhaps the most interesting region of our satellite. That great depression extending beneath us is obviously the bed of an ancient ocean, which astronomers have baptized with the name of the Sea of Rains. The three craters you see a little to the left also have names. The largest is Archimedes; beside it is Aristillus, and a little further to the north Autolycus. The strait that separates those two mountain chains you can see—the denser one extended to the south is known as the Apennines, the lesser one heading northwards the Caucasus—leads to another plain that is none other than the Sea of Serenity. To judge by the direction of our fall, I imagine that we're going to make a soft landing in the Marsh of Mists, which extends from the foot of Autolycus in a north-easterly direction.[10]

"Soft, eh?" said the Englishman, sniggering.

"Well, you'll see," Marcel replied.

His hand was on the lever designed to displace the gaskets on the tubes forming the first series of liquid-oxygen rockets, and he pulled it down abruptly.

Suddenly, the voyagers felt a shock so violent that they were thrown to the floor. The movement of recoil imparted to the projectile had been such that, gripped as it was by its vertiginous fall, it would inevitably have been shattered into tiny pieces by the two contrary forces if it had not had the solidity of a single block.

The velocity of the descent was completely annihilated for a few seconds, and the projectile began to fall again as it that momentary arrest marked the initial point of its fall.

"Well, Milord, what do you say to that?" said Marcel.

---

[10] The Sea of Serenity is the Mare Serenitatis. The "Marsh of Mists" (*Marais des Brouillards* in French), first identified in the rather quaint map drawn up by Montanari in the seventeenth century, was more usually known as the Palus Nebularum before the feature was banished from lunar maps entirely, although it was still included in the maps reproduced in *The Moon* (1876) by Edmund Neison, which the author of the present work might have used for reference.

"That, I agree, is a nice trick, but you've worked it in vain, and I can already make up the points of rocks beneath us that will tear up apart before long. For my part, I couldn't console myself if it were otherwise."

"Well, it will be otherwise, I can assure you. Prepare yourself to make an entrance worthy of a gentleman in the middle of the lunar plain."

Jacques was entirely absorbed in the contemplation of the marvelous scene that was unfurling before his eyes. From one second to the next the summits of craters toward which the shell seemed to be heading were growing and appearing more distinctly; their sharp ridges stood out with a clarity that rendered the absence of atmosphere even more precise; dark precipices were hollowed out on their profoundly uneven flanks, filled with a shadow whose blackness was undiminished by the diffuse light. All around, the ground was streaked by crevasses and abrupt crags; one might have thought that the waves of an ocean had been suddenly taken by surprise and frozen in the midst of a raging tempest. Nowhere, however, could anything be perceived that might indicate the presence of animate beings.

Marcel pressed the lever again. For the second time the oxygen fused. That shock was less violent than the first and the pause less noticeable. The young engineer was able to take exact account of the progress of the projectile.

"We're going to pass over the group of craters!" he cried. "We're going to fall in the Marsh of Mists."

"Where are we going to land, then?" asked Jacques.

"On the banks of the Acheron," murmured Lord Rodilan.

No one bothered to reply to that quip.

Marcel's face expressed a certain anxiety; Jacques was grave.

As they were about to reach their goal, those exceedingly well-tempered men, whose audacity had not recoiled before the perils of such a voyage, were gripped by a secret anxiety. What would become of them? How would they arrive on the soil of our satellite? Would they arrive there alive?

"Ah!" exclaimed Marcel, suddenly. "We're going to pass between the craters of Autolycus and Aristillus, and will surely fall in the valley that extends from the foot of the craters to the last peaks of the Caucasus chain."

Lord Rodilan, sitting on the circular divan, did not seem to be listening to that feverish conversation; he was lost in a profound reverie, as if everything that surrounded him was completely foreign to him.

"But what's that?" asked Jacques, suddenly. And his finger designated a large fissure in the lunar ground, the sinuosities of which snaked through the middle of the valley. It broadened as the projectile got closer, and between its edges a somber abyss opened up, the sides of which were bristling with rocky asperities, and whose mysterious depths the eye could not fathom.

Marcel had seen it too. His forehead creased, his eyes fixed and his face pale, he gazed at the gulf silently, which was growing from one instant to the next. Its edges seemed to be opening up as if to swallow them.

"I've foreseen everything, except that," he murmured. "It's a fissure, and we're falling directly into it."

The grandiose horror of their situation had even snatched Lord Rodilan from his imperturbable phlegm. All three of them were now on their feet, as if ready for the final sacrifice.

Marcel had made his decision. He kept his final rockets as an ultimate resource. At the precise moment when the shell arrived with frightful rapidity at the level of the crevasse, he pressed the lever for the last time. The projectile seemed to leap backwards. At the moment of pause, the three men gripped one another forcefully, and, their eyes tranquil and their faces calm, without a single muscle quivering, they plunged proudly and resolutely into the entrails of the world they had come to conquer.

VIII. At the Bottom of the Pit

The most profound darkness and the most complete silence reigned in the projectile. Were the three men dead? Had Lord Rodilan's somber presentiments been realized? Was an obscure and inglorious, but certainly original death the denouement of so much effort and courage?

Marcel was the first to recover consciousness. He got up painfully and, unable to see anything or hear any sound, felt his heart gripped by a mortal anxiety.

"Where are we?" he said. "What's happened?" And he called out: "Jacques! Milord!"

There was no reply.

A cold sweat trickled over his limbs; he shivered in horror. He searched his surroundings, groping, and his hand soon encountered a copper button, which he pressed abruptly. A jet of electric light illuminated the interior of the shell. Jacques and Lord Rodilan were lying on the floor, motionless. First, Marcel leaned over his childhood friend; the young physician was as pale as a corpse; his heart was only beating feebly.

"My God!" Marcel murmured. Lifting his up cautiously, he lay him down on the divan, his head supported by cushions. He loosened his clothes precipitately, baring his chest. But it was in vain that he made him breathe smelling salts, in vain that he rubbed his temples and forehead with vinegar, and in vain that he poured a few drops of a powerful cordial between his clenched teeth. Jacques remained unconscious.

Marcel felt gripped by despair. Discouraged, he no longer knew what means to employ, when a feeble sigh escaped the invalid's lips. Leaning over him, the shivering Marcel then started massaging him vigorously in the region of the heart.

Soon, his respiration became stronger and the colors of life began to reappear in his cheeks.

"Oh, my dear Jacques, you gave me a scare!" he murmured.

"Oh well," said Jacques, in a voice that was still weak and hesitant "What happened?"

"Ah! As to that, I know absolutely nothing—but before we try to find out, it's necessary to see what state our traveling companion is in."

"Is he injured, then?" asked Jacques.

"I don't know. I only thought about you to begin with. I'll see to him now."

"And I'll help you, my dear Marcel, for I've almost got my strength back."

They lifted the Englishman's body carefully.

As if he had only been awaiting that contact to return to life, Lord Rodilan opened his eyes abruptly and uttered a formidable oath.

"God damn it!" he groaned, in an irritated voice. "What do they want with me now? I'm dead—leave me in peace."

"No, Milord," said Jacques, laughing in spite of the fearful situation, "you're not dead and you've lost your bet."

The Englishman pulled a face. "Well," he said, "I have no luck at all. But wait a minute—if we're not dead, we're not much better off."

"That's what we need to find out," Marcel put in. "But since we're alive, well and truly, we need to think about getting out of here."

They remained immobile for a moment.

"Hold on," said Marcel. "One might think that our shell is moving. Is our voyage not over? Is it continuing in the bowels of our satellite?"

The projectile did indeed seem to be animated by slow and feeble oscillations, as if it were not resting on a solid base.

Abruptly, Jacques, who could not resist his anxiety, removed the bolts retaining the aluminum plate of one of the portholes pierced through the wall of the shell; then, seizing the electric lamp, he approached it to the widow.

He uttered an exclamation: "But we're in water!"

His two companions came running. Lord Rodilan seemed to have forgotten his bad mood; keen curiosity was painted on his features.

The electric beam, forcefully projected by the reflector with which the lamp was fitted, fell upon a tremulous surface from which it was reflected and scattered.

There was no doubt about it; they were floating.

The profound darkness that reigned in the place they had reached did not permit them to distinguish anything more.

"Let's see," said Marcel. "For the moment, we're afloat; that's certain. On what, I don't know yet, but we have time to think about it. Before anything else, we need to know whether the space in which our projectile has emerged is filled with breathable air."

"But we can't open one of the portholes," said Jacques. "All the air enclosed in the projectile would escape in the blink of an eye, and it's a precious reserve that we might need to eke out carefully."

"I've thought of that," said Marcel, "and I have a means to collect a sample of the gaseous environment in which we're immersed, and to see whether it includes the elements necessary to the conservation of life."

So saying, he had picked up a wrench, and, gripping the end of a powerful bolt that traversed the entire thickness of the wall of the shell, he started unscrewing it.

As the steel stem emerged from the hole that it was filing, without losing a second, he screwed in a platinum tube fitted with a tap. The operation was carried out so quickly that there was no loss of the air contained in the projectile.

Jacques had understood. "You're a careful man," he said, "and I can see that you've thought of everything. I understand what you're going to do, and I'll help."

Lord Rodilan, completely recovered from his bewilderment, was looking at them attentively, seeming very interested.

From one of the crates in which the scientific instruments were contained. Marcel carefully removed a simple apparatus familiar in laboratories. It consisted of a glass tube mounted vertically, maintained on a copper rod along which it was able to move, plunging into a crystal bowl. Then he picked up a long stick of phosphorus. In the meantime, Jacques has placed a shelf underneath the tap on which the apparatus was placed. The tube and the bowl were filled with water, and a rubber tube, fitted to the tap and immersed in the water, was adapted to the lower extremity of the tube, into which the stick of phosphorus had been introduced. Then the tap was opened, and the three voyagers saw the gas forming the exterior atmosphere penetrating the tube in bubbles, and gradually taking the place of the expelled water there. After a few seconds the tube was full and the tap was closed.

"Now," said Marcel, "while we wait for our experiment to be concluded, we have some time in hand, so we'll have lunch."

"Is it lunch or dinner?" asked Jacques.

"It would be more logical to call it supper," said Lord Rodilan, "as we're in pitch darkness."

"As you please," Marcel replied. "For myself, I have a furious appetite. "All this excitement has made me terribly hungry."

"In truth," said the Englishman, "since we're not dead yet, I could gladly eat something."

"There," said Marcel. "A tin of Crosse & Blackwell turkey, of which you can give me your opinion."

And all three of them, sitting on the circular divan, started to tuck into the wings and thighs of the turkey preserved in a savory jelly and strongly perfumed with truffles. First-rate biscuits served as bread. The Englishman tucked in more conscientiously than anyone else.

"I can see, my dear lord," said Jacques, laughing, "that for a man disgusted with life, you're not so disdainful of the means of sustaining and prolonging it."

"By Jove!" Lord Rodilan replied, his mouth full. "I don't mind being crushed, but it's not in my program to let myself die stupidly of starvation. But when one eats, one ought to drink. What do you have to give us, Marcel, to wash down this succulent nourishment?"

"In truth," said Marcel, "on that point I have to ask for your indulgence. I've only brought a few bottles of a light wine, sufficiently digestive, which, I hope, won't go to your head—because, you understand, I was obliged to anticipate and fear the malevolence of the juice of the grape."

The two friends grimaced significantly. Marcel smiled beneath his moustache. He took a tightly-sealed bottle out of a case, where it had been carefully enveloped in a straw sheath.

"Damn!" said Jacques. "A lot of precautions for cheap wine!"

Having carefully uncorked the bottle, Marcel poured into the glasses that his companions were holding out a liquid whose amber color and penetrating perfume caused the Englishman's nostrils to dilate.

"My dear Marcel," he said, "I believe you're making fun of us." Savoring the precious liquid respectfully, he beamed and exclaimed: "It's the 1865 Clos de Vougeot. Damn it, comrade, if you've got many like that, I'm ready to follow you to all the planets to which you might care to take us."

Jacques laughed quietly; he had not believed Marcel's joke, knowing his friends practical sense too well to think that he had would have neglected such an important matter.

The generous burgundy had restored all the strength and confidence of the three voyagers.

"Now let's see how our experiment is going," said Marcel.

They approached the apparatus. The tube that had previously been completely full of the exterior gas now appeared to be empty to the extent of about a third of its length. Marcel looked at the graduation marked on the glass; the water had risen to twenty-six degrees.

"Oho!" he said. "We are indeed in the presence of breathable air, but rather heady air. The proportion of oxygen indicated by the tube is 26% instead of the 21% contained in the terrestrial atmosphere."

"Bah!" said Jacques. "All three of us have solid lungs, and we'll make use of it."

"Well," said Marcel, "it's necessary now to think about getting out of here and finding out a little more about where we are."

"Yes," said Jacques, "but it might not be prudent to expose ourselves abruptly to air supercharged with oxygen. Don't you think we ought to take a few precautions?"

"You're right," Marcel replied. "I'll unscrew my rubber tube. The exterior air will penetrate gradually into the shell through the hole sealed by the bolt, and the substitution will be complete in a matter of minutes. Nothing prevents us, in the meantime, from trying to figure out where we are with the aid of the electric lamp."

The luminous beam was, indeed, shone through the portholes in various directions. In the direction is which they had first detected the liquid surface on which the projectile was floating they could make out nothing further; the luminous beam was lost in the distance in unfathomable darkness. On the opposite side, however, the light projected by the reflector encountered a wall, black in color, of rocky appearance, the height of which could not be estimated, which seemed to be to more than five cables away. Its base emerged from a strand on which the waves of the subterranean lake or sea died away.

In the meantime, the exterior air gradually penetrated into the shell, and the three voyagers felt vivified by the oxygen-rich atmosphere, which they breathed delightedly. Jacques had feared momentarily, when Marcel had revealed the result of his analysis, that the air rich in the element of combustion might overstimulate the activity of vital phenomena, and that their organisms might have difficulty adapting to it. The precaution they had taken of measuring out the entry of the external air soon reassured him. A little cerebral excitation, a slightly more active and rapid respiration were the only physiological phenomena that he observed in himself and his two companions, whose pulse his experienced finger had interrogated.

"We can be reassured," he said. "The stimulation we're experiencing at present, which comes from a slightly rapid transition from our ordinary atmosphere to more oxygen-rich air shouldn't alarm us, and won't last long. We're all healthy and vigorous; our organs are well able to adapt to the ambient environment. We'll even find, I'm sure, a surplus of vitality that will augment our strength, and our brains will draw an unsuspected intellectual force from it."

Jacques' anticipations seemed to have been realized already. Since they had recovered the use of their senses, the three friends had found themselves in a singular state; they felt animated by an unusual vigor; their bodies seemed to have lost weight; all their movements were carried out with an ease and facility to which they were not accustomed. They were astonished to be moving without effort, able to toy with objects that would previously have seemed heavy; their feet no longer weighed upon the floor, and Lord Rodilan, having tried to reach up to take an object from a high shelf, found himself carried by his movement all the way to the top of the projectile, where he bumped his head on the superior padding.

"Where are you going, my dear lord?" exclaimed Jacques, laughing. "Are you taking flight in order to leave us?"

"My God!" said the Englishman, falling back gently on to the floor. "That's bizarre! Damned if I understand it."

"It's quite simple, though," Marcel interjected. "And it's sufficient proof, if any doubt remained, that we really have arrived on—or in—the Moon."

"Bah!" said Lord Rodilan, intrigued.

"Yes, my dear friend. You know that on the Moon, weight is six times less than on Earth. Thus, your honorable person, which would weigh 148 pounds on the Yacht Club scales, only weighs about 21. That's why all the objects you touch seem so light, and the slight effort you made just now was sufficient to lift you up so high."

"That's all very well," said Lord Rodilan, "but if I have to continue living, I'd rather not remain too long in this darkness; it's not worth the trouble of being alive to be buried like this."

"Oh," said Marcel, "We're not so badly off. I can't yet estimate the distance that separates us from the lunar surface, but it must be considerable. First, we need to get out of here and reconnoiter the place where we we've ended up."

The exterior air had finished filling the shell; they could now open the portholes. When that was done, Marcel hastened to consult the instruments of observation with which the projectile was equipped. The centigrade thermometer marked 18.5; the barometer indicated a pressure of 641 millimeters, corresponding to an Earthly altitude of 1,480 meters. The needle of the Saussure hygrometer had stopped at ninety—which, according to the table constructed by Gay-Lussac, corresponded to a saturation of 0.791; it was an atmosphere heavily charged with humidity.

"All that's very reassuring," said Marcel. "Now it's necessary to know the nature of the liquid on which we're floating."

Immediately, Jacques dipped a pewter goblet into the exterior liquid, and brought it back full of a colorless transparent liquid. Marcel examined it attentively, poured a few drops into the palm of his hand, and moistened his lips with it.

"It's water," he said, "but with a slightly saline taste. At least we can be sure that we won't die of thirst."

It was now a matter of reaching the strand, which seemed all the more urgent because Marcel thought he had noticed that for some time the shell had seemed to be moving away from it gradually. He made that observation to his companions.

"It's probable," he told them, "that this lake overflows into some inferior basin, and the current is tending to draw us God knows where. It's therefore important to land without wasting any time."

As they had been expecting to fall on to the surface of the Moon and to have to walk over very uneven ground, they had prudently equipped themselves with long and sturdy iron-tipped walking sticks. Two of these sticks were bound end to end and firmly fixed.

"To you, my dear lord," said Marcel then, "one of the most glorious champions of Oxford, goes the honor of steering over this lunar lake the first terrestrial vessel ever to venture thereon."

"All right!" replied the Englishman. "And it's a great pity that some Cambridge champion isn't here to witness that navigation and shrivel up with jealousy."

"One can't have everything," murmured Jacques, philosophically.

Taking of his jacket and rolling up his shirt-sleeves, Lord Rodilan bared his muscular arms; then, seized the pole formed by the two iron-tipped canes, he passed it through the porthole opposite the shore, which was about two feet above the surface of the water. It reached the bottom. Bracing himself vigorously on the end of the pole, he gave it an energetic impulsion, and the heavy machine began to move, drawing nearer to the shore in a sensible fashion.

It was evident that the subterranean lake into which they had fallen filled a depression of considerable depth, similar to the crater of a volcano. The shell must have fallen near the center; then, having come back up to the surface, it had been gripped by the current, which, by reason of the sinuosities of the shore, sometimes seemed to be drawing it toward it, and sometimes away from it.

Marcel and Jacques stood at the other porthole, illuminating the direction to be followed by means of their electric lamps. As the shell, cylindrical in form, could not advance in a rigorously straight line, they indicated to Lord Rodilan the direction in which he ought to steer the inconvenient skiff.

The Englishman toiled ardently. His robust limbs had lost nothing of their flexibility and skill, and his strength was multiplied tenfold in an environment where weight was diminished in such a remarkable fashion. So, in spite of the difficulty of the task, scarcely an hour had gone by when the shell ran aground on the gradually raised bed and stopped about fifty meters from the strand.

"Ah!" said Lord Rodilan, flexing his arms. "That bit of exercise has done me good." Approaching the porthole facing the shore, he laughed and added: "Good! Now we'll have to take a bath. After violent exercise, that's very hygienic."

The shell was, in fact, some four feet deep in the water, and it was necessary to wade across the distance that separated the voyagers from solid ground.

Detaching the mobile iron ladder that they used to reach the baggage stored in the upper section of the projectile, they passed it through the porthole and plunged it into the water, where its weight maintained it immobile. The three friends had rapidly put on impermeable rubber garments over their clothing, which enveloped them from head to toe. Thus equipped, they crossed the distance separating them from the shore in a few strides.

As they set foot on the fine sand that formed the floor of the cavern, which had never been trodden before by any terrestrial creature, Marcel experienced a surge of triumphant excitement.

"Victory, friends!" he cried. "Here were are in the bosom of the mysterious world of which our audacity has dreamed of penetrating the secrets. The calculations of science are confirmed. Let's give thanks to God, who has brought us here safe and sound, and *vive la France!*"

Jacques shook his hand with an emotion that he did not try to hide.

"Pardon me, my dear Marcel," said the Englishman. "Since I'm not dead, allow me to participate in your joy and also to associate England with it. Don't you think it's only just to shout with me: *Hurrah for England?*"

"With all my heart, my dear Rodilan, and whatever the future has in reserve for us, there's life and death between us now."

And the three friends embraced delightedly.

The shell was then moored to an overhanging rocky out-crop, not far from the place where they had landed, with the aid of a cable that Marcel had fixed solidly to the interior and unrolled as he advanced toward the shore.

IX. Exploration in the Unknown

"By the way," said Jacques, "what day is it, and what time might it be?"

"I haven't thought about that," said Marcel, "but it's easy enough to verify." He took out his chronometer; it indicated seven forty-five.

"Good," said Lord Rodilan. "That's the hour, but what day is it?"

"Let's see—we left on Saturday 15 December[11] at ten forty-six and forty seconds in the evening. Our journey to reach the lunar surface lasted ninety-seven hours thirteen minutes and twenty seconds. I'm leaving out the time that it took us to traverse the lunar crust. We fell into the sea on Wednesday the nineteenth at eleven fifty-nine and sixty seconds—which is to say, at midnight. So it's now Thursday 20 December, at seven forty-five in the morning.

"And then again," said Jacques, "how is it, since our projectile was able to get this far without breaking, that we can't see any opening, any trace of light indicating a communication with the exterior?"

"In truth, my dear chap, you're asking too much for the moment. It's probable that the fissure which gave us access narrowed; its doubtless several kilometers deep, in which case the solar light wouldn't penetrate this far. In all probability, we've fallen into a part of the cavern where the water is very deep, and thanks to the invisible current whose action we've already observed, we've been drawn toward the shore."

---

[11] December 15 fell on a Saturday in 1883, supporting the notion that that is the year in which the present action is taking place, although the author's arithmetic then goes awry, as the original incorrectly records the 19th as Tuesday and the 20th as Wednesday; I have corrected the days to make them consistent with the first date.

"All that's very interesting," said Lord Rodilan. "We haven't come here simply to devote ourselves to scientific dissertations, though, but to explore. I suggest, therefore, that we explore, and I won't hide it from you that I'm in haste to see the sun again."

"Well then, let's explore," said Jacques. "I'm beginning to get tired of this darkness myself."

All three of them picked their electric lamps and directed them at the wall at the foot of which they were standing, which rose up for some twenty meters above the lake. It was formed of solid and compact granite. Projecting the beams of light as high as they could, they could not perceive the summit on which the vault of the cavern must be braced.

"In my opinion," said Marcel, "there's only one thing we can do: follow the shore until we find some tunnel or fault that permits us to get back to the surface.

"Since we're justified in believing that the Moon is inhabited on the side that's invisible from the Earth," Jacques said, "our efforts ought to be directed toward reaching that region."

"That doesn't seem to me to be very difficult," said Marcel. "It's obvious that in the epoch when there were many active volcanoes, each one had its chimney, and furthermore, that the continual disturbance of the satellite's crust must have led to the extension of fissures and crevasses of various sorts around each nucleus. We'll doubtless have plenty of choice."

"Let's get a move on, then," said Lord Rodilan. "I've had enough of this inaction, and I wouldn't be sorry to make the acquaintance of our new compatriots."

Having made that resolution, the three friends commenced their exploration. At the place where the shell had run aground the shore was only a short distance from the wall, but the space son expanded, the interior lake became more distant. As they were searching for a way out through the mountain, they continued to follow the wall, studying it intently. They had been walking for about an hour over fine sand when Lord

Rodilan, who was in the lead, exclaimed: "Here we are at the end of the cavern, I think."

Projecting the beam of his lamp, he pointed at a mass of rocks that abruptly interrupted the strand.

"It's an obstacle to go around," said Marcel, after having looked at it carefully. As far as I can tell, the rocks diminish rapidly in the direction of the lake."

After a few minutes, in fact, they found themselves back at the edge of the water, into which the granite wall plunged to form a kind of cape. The chaotic disorder of the profoundly uneven rock, with sharp ridges, neat fractures and polished faces, which the combined light of their lamps allowed them to distinguish clearly, dispelled any idea of climbing over.

"What shall we do?" asked Jacques.

"Well have to go into the water and try to swim around it, of course," said Lord Rodilan. He was already advancing into the water.

"Be careful," said Marcel. "Use your iron-tipped stick to sound the bottom."

All three of them advanced, while their guide carefully tested the terrain. They soon reach the extremity of the cape; they were waist-deep in the water. Although their rubber garments, hermetically sealed, prevented them from getting wet, the coldness of the subterranean water ended up chilling their limbs. An immense liquid sheet extended in front of them, which bathed the granite wall on the other side of the cape.

They hesitated momentarily.

The absence of the strand at that place suggested that the depth of the lake might increase abruptly there, and that it was necessary to abandon any further research in that direction, but to return to their point of departure in order to go the other way was just as risky and would waste a lot of time.

As he was advising his companions to keep going forward, Lord Rodilan, who was holding his lamp above his head and illuminating the inferior extremity of the rocks exclaimed: "I'm not mistaken! Look, Marcel—isn't that, about a hundred meters away, the entrance to one of those fissures or tunnels you were talking about a while back?"

In the direction he was indicating, there was indeed an obscure opening.

"You're right," said Marcel. "We need to go that way."

They resumed walking and doubled the cape. They advanced slowly, weighed down and hampered by the rubber garments, and sometimes having water up to their knees and sometimes up to their shoulders, in accordance with the unevenness of the ground. After half an hour of that difficult march, they felt the ground on which they were walking rising along a gentle slope. The excavation they had noticed formed the arched entrance to a rather spacious grotto, into which they penetrated by ducking down slightly When they raised their heads again their gazes were dazzled and they uttered cries of admiration. The walls of the grotto were entirely coved with a shiny and polished substance that reflected the beam of the three electric lamps with an incomparable brightness.

It was a radiation of light in which the prismatic faces of crystals were sown in profusion, like rubies, sapphires, topazes and emeralds. One might have thought it an enchanted palace. Marcel approached one of the walls and detached a few fragments of the crystalline substance with the aid of his iron-tipped cane. He examined them attentively and uttered an exclamation of surprise.

"What is it?" Jacques asked.

"Half the treasures buried here would suffice to pay for the national debts of all the states of Europe and enrich the whole of terrestrial humanity."

"What have you found that's so marvelous?" asked Lord Rodilan.

"They're diamonds, Milord—genuine diamonds." He projected the beam of his lamp over the brilliant surface, and added: "And look: some are as large as a fist. All the dealers in London and Amsterdam would pale with envy before such riches. But these precious pebbles are no use to us at present; we have to think about continuing our journey." Darting a circular glance around, he exclaimed: "There are two openings that ought, in all probability, be the entrances to the tunnels we're looking for."

A short distance away, there were indeed two openings, whose depth it was impossible to estimate at first glance.

The first one into which they ventured followed a horizontal path initially, but seen sloped downwards steeply toward the core of the satellite.

"Damn!" said Lord Rodilan, turning back.

Marcel and Jacques remained silent, but their frowns testified to their disappointment and betrayed a commencement of anxiety.

They returned to the diamond cave and took the other tunnel without hesitation. They had only taken a few paces when Marcel's face cleared. "This time, I think, we're on the right path," he said.

The floor of the tunnel was, indeed, sloping upwards significantly. The vault was reasonably high and the breadth sufficient for the three travelers to walk abreast.

After having determined the direction of the tunnel Marcel stopped. "We can't go any further," he said, "without being equipped with food supplies and everything necessary for an exploration that might be long and difficult."

"Will we have to contend with this obscurity much longer?" asked Lord Rodilan.

"In truth, my dear friend, it's impossible to estimate our present depth, but it's certainly several kilometers. There's no proof, anyway, that this tunnel maintains the same slope, and God knows what other obstacles we might have to face. We need, therefore, to make provision for several days, perhaps more, of tortuous and difficult travel."

"Let's get on with it," said Jacques. "We'll see what the future has in store for us."

They went back to the shell, but the emotions through which the three companions had passed since they had come round from their profound unconsciousness, and the fatigues of their exploration, had exhausted their strength. While they had been animated by the sentiment of a strange situation, and the fear of being buried forever in that somber abyss, a nervous excitement had sustained them, but now that a ray of hope was shining in their eyes and Marcel had put into the souls of his friends the ardent conviction that filled him, nature imperiously reclaimed its rights.

Jacques, in his capacity as a physician, observed it first. "Friends," he said, "before departing for the unknown, we need to get our strength back; my opinion is, therefore, that we should obtain from reparative sleep all the energy that we'll need."

"You speak like a sage," Marcel replied. "Anyway, now that I think about it, I'm worn out."

"Perfect," said Lord Rodilan. "Let's sleep. We have nothing to fear from unwelcome visitors, and when we wake up, we'll prepare ourselves with a solid meal to present to the inhabitants of the Moon three correct gentlemen, very much alive!"

The three friends lay down on the circular divan, therefore, and the calmness of their respiration soon indicated that they were sleeping as peacefully as if they were in the best room at the Grand Hotel in Paris.

Ten hours later they woke up, and after a substantial lunch, in which the old burgundy was not spared, they each equipped themselves as if for a difficult climb. They packed enough food for three weeks.

Before setting out they carefully checked the mooring-rope securing the shell to the rock, and made sure that no oscillation could detach it; it was their unique and supreme resource in the fantastic world in which they were lost.

Returning to the cave of diamonds, they set off resolutely into the tunnel they had chosen.

During the first day, the journey was effected without overmuch difficulty. They were evidently following the chimney of an ancient volcano; the layers of rocks they traversed presented in their successive stratifications dispositions very similar to those forming the terrestrial crust. First they encountered primitive rocks, gneiss and mica-schist; then came the primary terrains. They had crossed the Silurian and Devonian layers and were on the third day of their march when the first traces of carboniferous terrain appeared.

"We're evidently getting close to the surface," said Jacques. "If we were on Earth, we could hope to see the light of the Sun within two or three days."

"Yes," said Marcel, "but how can we determine here the thickness of the lunar layers that still separate us from the surface? Who can tell, in any case, whether the volcanic eruptions of which the Moon has been the theater might have accumulated molten materials drawn from the depths of its entrails in the original layers? Who can tell whether we might not run into impenetrable walls of cooled lava?"

"We might have to fear an even greater peril," said Jacques. "For several hours it's seemed to me that respiration is more difficult and that more rarefied air is arriving in my lungs."

"That's true," said Lord Rodilan. "I attributed the difficulty in breathing from which I was suffering to fatigue, but Jacques is evidently right: the air's become thinner."

"That's what I feared," said Marcel. "I hesitated to make you party to my apprehensions, hoping to be mistaken, but there's no longer any doubt about it; we're experiencing what mountain-climbers on Earth call mountain sickness. But where has Lord Rodilan gone?"

"He must have gone on ahead," said Jacques.

Suddenly, from some distance away, they heard an exclamation. "Hurrah!" the Englishman cried. "Here are traces of living beings."

He emerged from a cleft in the wall of the tunnel brandishing an object that his two companions could not make out. They ran to him, and with a triumphant gesture, Lord Rodilan showed them a fragment of a tool similar to the picks that miners use to detach blocks of coal. Although it was corroded by rust, its original form could still be made out, and they could see the hole in the center into which the wooden handle had been fitted.

"There," he said, "is irrefutable proof that the Moon is inhabited."

All three of them went into the narrow passage in which this important discovery had been made. It was evidently the extremity of a mine-shaft that had once been exploited. They could still see traces of the workmen's picks on the walls; but no matter how hard the three friends searched, they could not find and exit from the short tunnel, which some roof-fall had separated from the rest of the mine in an indeterminate epoch.

"And to think," said Lord Rodilan, tapping the wall with his iron-tipped stick, "that behind this obstacle there might be beings like us."

"It proves, at least," said Jacques, "that the inhabitants of the Moon got down this far—so one can live in the surface."

Marcel seemed to be plunged into a profound meditation.

"You're not saying anything, friend," said Jacques, clapping him on the shoulder.

Marcel shivered. "There's something inexplicable here," he said. "If the air continues getting thinner as we go further, how is life possible? In particular, how will it be possible for us to survive on the lunar surface?"

"Forward ho!" sad the Englishman. "Anything rather than retrace our steps."

They resumed their march. The slope of the tunnel they were following becoming increasingly step, and the rarefaction of the atmosphere became rapidly worse. Only a few hours had gone by when their avid lungs lacked air; the blood was ringing in their ears, their temples were beating forcefully, a veil was descending over their eyes and droplets of blood were pearling at the surface of their skin. They were forced to stop.

"It's impossible to go on, my dear friends," said Marcel.

"What are we going to do, then?" asked Jacques.

"For the moment, there's only one thing we can do. We have to go back to the cave where we ran aground, and where we left all our provisions and resources in the shell. Evidently, the Moon is inhabited, we were certain of that when we attempted the voyage; the document you've had before your eyes is categorical proof of it, and the discovery that our friend has just made confirms it. Where can we find the human race of which we're in search? What are the conditions of its existence? Nothing thus far has been able to inform us. Are we going to lose courage, then, because we haven't succeeded at the first attempt? Lunar humankind exists; we have to find it, and we shall. Let's go back to our point of departure. We'll decide what to do there."

"Ah!" said Lord Rodilan. "I thought I was on the point of exchanging a vigorous handshake with a Selenite! I had a very poor inspiration in coming with you."

"No, my dear lord," said Marcel, smiling in spite of the gravity of the situation. "All your friends think you're dead. In their minds, you've exceeded Empedocles by a hundred cubits. Your goal is attained."

"Well, so be it," said the Englishman. "If we can't live here, we can always die here."

Sadly, the voyagers retraced the route that they had followed. The descent was effected without difficulty; they traversed the cave of diamonds again, without paying it any heed, and went back in haste to the place where they had landed.

But the shore was empty. A cry of amazement and despair escaped their lips. The shell had disappeared!

X. A Humankind That Does Not Want to Perish

Ever since human intelligence, too cramped in the narrow sphere in which it is confined, began to sound the profundities of space in order to study the laws governing the worlds gravitating in infinity, the satellite that has faithfully accompanied the Earth on its journey, and whose glow illuminates its nights at irregular intervals has been the object of its most constant preoccupation. While the poetic imagination of the Greeks divined the blonde Phoebe and made her descend from Heaven on a silvery ray to the shepherd Endymion, asleep on the bank of the Cephise, the Chaldean priests were calculating the orbit of our satellite, describing its phases and predicting eclipses.

In the Middle Ages, astrology attributed a harmful influence to the Moon. She it was who presided over nocturnal incantations; it was her indecisive and tremulous light by which witches unearthed cadavers, sought the redoubtable mandrake at the foot of gibbets, and made up powerful philters that distributed hatred, pleasure or death at their whim. It was on one of pale Hecate's rays that they rode to the Sabbat on Walpurgis Night, and by means of which they returned to their lairs when nascent dawn dissipated the phantoms, sent the souls of the dead back to their sepulchers, and made the infernal deities return to their somber domains.

With the progress of science, the Moon, observed with the aid of improved instruments, has gradually and successively delivered the secrets of her strange existence to us. Today, when telescopes, masterpieces of modern industry, have permitted her to approach to a distance of eighteen leagues, she is known in an almost complete fashion; she can be photographed, the height of her mountains has been measured, and the depth of her craters. Maps of the visible surface have been drawn, far more exact than those of the terrestrial surface, where many regions, such as the poles, the heart of Africa and the Australian continent, are still unexplored.

To judge by the appearance that the lunar disk presents, bristling with mountains, pockmarked by a multitude of craters of all sizes—all extinct, for the eye can perceive the depths of their blocked chimneys—it seems that the Moon is a chilled world from which all life is completely absent.

That is not so, however. Already, with the telescopes of Lord Rosse and Foucault,[12] astronomers believe that they have distinguished signs indicating the presence of an atmosphere in the lowest regions of the lunar soil; the contours of ridges that normally appear very clearly have been seen to soften and blur, as if veiled by mist. Phenomena of the refraction of light have been observed, and it has been logically concluded that, in these regions at least, there is air and water—which is to say that life is not impossible there.

Reasoning has confirmed the data of observation. In the unfathomable times when our planetary system was formed, when the sun projected from its blazing center the fulgurant drops that have become worlds, the eruption that gave birth to the Earth formed the Moon at the same time, which, detached from our globe, was retained in its orbit. The two worlds, at first in a gaseous state, began to condense, and passed successively through the liquid state and then to the solid state. The volume of the Moon being much less than that of the Earth, however, its transformation was much more rapid. In an epoch when the Earth was still a molten mass, the Moon had already formed a solid crust on which life was manifest with an exuberant abundance.

Then the centuries succeeded one another, and when the Earth arrived, with difficulty, at the point of giving birth on its surface to the first seeds of life and the primitive forms ap-

---

[12] William Parsons, third Earl of Rosse and Léon Foucault were important pioneers in the development of reflecting telescopes, the latter improving considerably on the latter's 1848 model in the apparatus he constructed a decade later.

peared, still crude and barely sketched, of gigantic vegetables and monstrous animals, the Moon saw a normal and progressive life established on its surface.

In that epoch, vast oceans filled the cavities of which our gaze now plumbs the dry depths; dense forests stood on the flanks of her mountains; a humankind superior to ours, because the conditions of life were more favorable there, was born and grew, and, under fortunate influences, attained an intellectual development and moral heights that we have not yet reached.

Lunar humankind had thus arrived at a surprising degree of civilization, science and morality when the first human beings—the prognathous individuals contemporary with cave-bears—had scarcely begun to appear on Earth. But the vital evolution of the Moon was to be much shorter than that of its neighboring planet. If it had arrived in its highest period sooner, its decadence also had to commence sooner. From age to age, the cooling of the lunar globe progressed; the heat retreated from the periphery toward the center, whose incandescent nucleus, the source of life, diminished slowly but ineluctably.

As on the Earth, for as long as the central heat had been considerable, the waters that filtered into the profound layers through the numerous fissures furrowing the Moon had been vaporized and thus returned to the general circulation of the surface, but in consequence of the gradual cooling, the water had ended up being completely absorbed. Thanks to that slow absorption, the still-fluid rocks enclosing the molten core had solidified and the chemical elements, still unstable, had combined.

At the same time, the oxygen in the air was fixed in the solid parts, and thus the atmosphere had gradually disappeared, along with the lunar seas. As the elements essential for the maintenance of organized beings such as we understand them diminished, like had gradually retreated.

But lunar humankind did not want to die.

When one studies a map of the Moon attentively, one notices fissures in a considerable number of its valleys, at the feet of its high mountain chains. At the distance from which we observe them, they resemble thin black lines, as if traced by a sharp point, but in reality, they are wide crevasses whose edges are several kilometers apart, and which often penetrate profoundly into the entrails of the soil.

The scientific explorations to which the inhabitants of the Moon had devoted themselves had enabled them to understand the intimate structure of the globe on which they lived, which had no more secrets from them. They knew that beneath the solid crust, where life had been manifest for centuries, a whole subterranean region existed where a still-primitive life was maintained far from the sun's rays.

At variable depths, estimated at between twelve and fifteen terrestrial leagues, in immense excavations, there were seas, continents, rivers and an abundant vegetation. There, in the caves closer to the center, where a mild and even temperature still reigned, the vaults of which rose to prodigious heights, where the air was denser and where, for lack of daylight, an electrically-sourced light maintained by cosmic phenomena reigned, there was room for an entire human race. It was there that the last inhabitants of our satellite had retired, with their sciences, their industries, their institutions and their laws, resolved to defend their lives until the last moment.

While terrestrial humankind was awakening painfully to intellectual and moral life, and rising, through long secular periods, from the Stone Age to the Bronze Age and the Iron Age; while the first human tribes, dispersed and wandering through the gigantic primitive forests, passed from the condition of hunters to that of pastors, and then agriculturalists, and finally industrialists, the inhabitants of the Moon continued their existence of uninterrupted progress in the subterranean world where life was maintained.

In those calm and tranquil regions, where the temperature was almost invariable, where the influence of seasons was not manifest, where humankind did not have to defend itself against the blind forces of a hostile nature, in which the struggle for existence did not have the bitterness that it presents among us, those beings, adapted to life in an environment supercharged with oxygen, and where vitality was, in consequence, more energetic and more resistant, had far surpassed the level of knowledge at which we had lingered for such a long time.

Afflicted with fewer needs than us, they were exempt from the majority of our vices and our avidities. Less preoccupied with the satisfaction of base or egotistical passions, they had devoted themselves more to the cultivation of their souls and their morality was as advanced as their science. After having experimented in previous ages with the various political forms between which we hesitate down here, they had arrived at a simple and rational social organization in which everyone occupied the exact place assured by their degree of intelligence and moral worth.

For long centuries, already, even before the cooling of the surface had constrained them to take refuge in their new abode, they had been preoccupied with the neighboring star whose enormous disk shone above their heads, in the orbit in which they moved, of which they knew that their own world was only the modest satellite. They had measured the distance that separated them and, thanks to powerful optical instruments that they had constructed long before us, they had observed it attentively and studied it carefully. No part of its surface had escaped their investigations, and its constitution was well known to them.

They knew, and were in no doubt, that the Earth was inhabited; they had even been able, in a certain measure, to track the development of its life. What had happened on the globe they inhabited had informed them regarding the history of the terrestrial globe. Their eyes had followed the transformations of its surface; they had seen continents emerge and disappear, and the vast forests of prehistoric ages diminish with the centuries. The great rivers that furrowed the terrestrial continents were apparent to them. In the principal valleys or mouths of the most important watercourses, they had seen patches appear of different color and appearance from neighboring regions, and in which the increasing perfection of their optical instruments had eventually enabled them to recognize the agglomerations of human habitations.

With the progress that they had accomplished in the astronomical sciences and natural sciences, having considerable forces of nature at their disposal, they had soon conceived the desire to enter into communication with the inhabitants of that neighboring world, and they had often tried to attracted their attention. In that epoch, however, the peoples that were beginning to cover the surface of the Earth were still too crude and barbaric to think of gazing at, let alone studying, the worlds orbiting over their heads. If, sometimes, their gazes has risen into the depths of night as far as those brilliant dots, their blind superstition had seen divinities therein, whose favor it was necessary to conquer, or whose harmful influence it was necessary to ward off, by means of prayers and sacrifices.

None of the efforts made by the inhabitants of the Moon had been crowned with success; all their interrogations had remained without response. So, discouraged, they had ended up thinking that, either their observations were inexact, and the Earth was uninhabited, or that the beings that populated it, deprived of intelligence, did not rise much above the animal level. And the attempts, commenced with a certain ardor, had remained unrepeated for long centuries.

Later, after their conditions of existence had changed so completely, when they were able to measure with an almost infallible certainty the duration of time that they still had to live, they had resumed directing their gaze toward the world that was still continuing its majestic course so close at hand.

Further improvements in the art of constructing optical instruments had made new and more precise observations possible. Signs appeared to them: traces similar to canals, geometrical figures that might be the walls of cities, whose regular forms seemed to reveal the presence of active and intelligent beings; monuments of which they were able, by measuring their shadows, to calculate the height, had told them that the inhabitants of the Earth were in possession of fairly powerful mechanical means, and they had concluded that they were somewhat advanced in the knowledge of sciences. Their desire to establish regular and sustained communication with them was augmented.

As the signs by means of which, in previous ages, they had tried to attract the attention of the inhabitants of the Earth with powerful luminous sources, had not succeeded, they had thought of other methods. Since they had not replied to appeals, it was necessary to compel their attention by sending them messages directly, brusquely if necessary, the origin and significance of which could not be mistaken. As the laws of ballistics had been familiar to them for a long time, it had been child's play for them to send projectiles beyond the two world's zone of neutral attraction, whose weight would then ensure that they fell on Earth.

But as seven-tenths of the surface of the terrestrial globe is occupied by oceans, the majority of the lunar messages were inevitably lost in the bosom of the seas. In addition, vast spaces on the various continents are either completely deserted or inhabited by savage, ignorant populations absolutely incapable of understanding such invitations and of responding to them. Finally, those lunar projectiles which the hazard of their fall had enabled to fall in civilized regions plunged, for the most part, deeply into the soil, which closed up after their passage and concealed them from the knowledge of the inhabitants of those countries.

It had required a prodigious combination of fortuitous circumstances for one of those messages to be conserved intact, discovered and understood.

That was the one that Marcel had shown to his two friends. Although he had not been able to suspect the conditions in which lunar humankind lived, the audacious engineer had not been mistaken in affirming its existence, and it was in the midst of that humankind that he was about to find himself thrown, with his two companions in adventure.

XI. The Arrival

"May the graces of the Sovereign Spirit descend upon your heads and put joy and serenity into your hearts," said the sage Rugel, as he penetrated on to the terrace where Marcel and his two friends were standing, contemplating a marvelous spectacle.

Extended before their eyes was a strange city, the like of which the imagination of Oriental story tellers had never dreamed. Its white habitations, elegant and capricious in form, whose bright and polished walls were heightened by the most vivid colors, artistically disposed, and enriched by mosaics of precious metals, descended in a gently slope to the sea shore.

The sea too offered an appearance of which earthly seas can give no idea. Its waves, rippled at that moment by a slight breeze, had neither the deep blue of the Mediterranean not the changing green of the Atlantic; as if light were dissolved within in, the water was iridescent, spangled with all the colors of the rainbow. Every movement that the light breath of the wind imparted to the mobile waves caused a thousand subtle rays to pass through them, which melted into a delightful mixture.

The individual who had just appeared on the terrace offered all the external appearances of a member of the terrestrial human race and seemed to be between forty and forty-five Earthly years old. His tall stature was well-built; all his well-proportioned limbs were supple and vigorous; his free and easy gait revealed the harmony of a well-equilibrated nature. His face, which was framed by long black hair glossy and curly, was imprinted with mildness and gravity. His developed forehead and his keen, penetrating eyes denoted a broad and prompt intelligence. He had a straight nose and a small mouth, habitually formed in a benevolent smile.

He was dressed in a kind of tunic that hung down to his feet, made of a glossy silken fabric whose azure color was very easy on the eye. It was retained at the waist by a belt, darker in hue, enriched with ornaments reminiscent of the finest embroidery. His feet were shod in sandals made of some kind of woven liana, which were attached to the base of the leg by intersecting ribbons. Over that simultaneously rich and simple costume, a vast dazzlingly white mantle was negligently thrown, fixed at the summit of the chest by a large fastener formed by a substance as brilliant as diamond.

The three friends stood up. Marcel took a few steps toward the newcomer and bowed gravely.

"Be welcome," he said, "you who have initiated us into so many marvels since we have been in this new world."

"Jacques and Lord Rodilan had drawn nearer and added their marks of respect and gratitude to Marcel's.

"Friends," said Rugel, "the moment that I announced to you has arrived. You now have a sufficient knowledge of our language to appear before the prudent Aldeovaze, our supreme and venerated leader, and the sages who assist him in the direction of our public affairs. The news of your extraordinary arrival reached him some time ago; our scientists have been occupied with it; he was the one who assigned me to you, with the mission of educating you, in order that you might enter into communication with us."

"And you have acquitted that mission with a zeal, a good grace and a kindness that has touched our hearts," Jacques put in.

"That's true," added Lord Rodilan. "I've never encountered in the world where we've lived thus far a finer and more intelligent mind, a gentler and more even-tempered character, and a more amiable benevolence than the one you've testified to us."

Rugel smiled. "I have only fulfilled the task confided to me by the Supreme Council," he replied, "And you will allow me to tell you, in my turn, that the task has been as pleasant as it as easy. When our Diemides—that, you will remember, is the name we give to the inferior ranks of our humankind—found your vehicle in the cavern where they had gone in search of the shiny stones that serve to ornament our edifices and our vestments, and where the hand of the Sovereign Being had directed your fall, they brought it, via the channel that serves the cavern's lake as an overflow, to the capital of the neighboring province.

"Our scientists had already witnessed the attempt made by the inhabitants of the Earth to enter into communication with us, so the magistrate governing the province had no difficulty understanding that the floating house must have served to shelter human beings, who had doubtless come from the Earth. On seeing the traces of impacts and the scratches on the walls, he was alarmed by the thought of the terrible hazards of that fall. It was evident that you had fallen into one of the broad and profound fissures that furrow the surface of our globe. You must have collided with the numerous asperities with which the walls bristle, bouncing and rolling through all its sinuosities until one last leap precipitated you into the lake, which deadened your fall.

"The cavern of which it forms the bottom is, in fact, situated at a much greater depth than you were able to suspect. The distance that separates it from the surface can be estimated at about a sixtieth of the Moon's radius."

"Which is to say," Marcel put in, "about sixty of our kilometers."

"The magistrate whom chance put in the presence of that strange discovery," Rugel continued, "expected only to find cadavers in the singular vehicle; finding that it was empty, he understood that the care with which everything had been disposed inside it had protected the voyagers, and judged that, if they had abandoned it temporarily, it was to explore the region to which hazard had brought them and put them in communication with us as quickly as possible. It was therefore necessary to go in search of them, all the more urgently because the voyagers, lost in the darkness, might find themselves in great difficulties, and perhaps exposed to peril.

"Emissaries were sent in all directions, and ended up discovering you on the shore of the lake where your projectile had been found."

"And you came to our aid just in time," said Jacques, with an explosion of gratitude. "Without you, we would have died."

"And the most ridiculous and humiliating death for gentlemen," said Lord Rodilan. "Death by starvation."

"Yes," Rugel went on, mildly. "For on your Earth you are submissive to the necessity of maintaining life within you by the absorption of foreign elements—a necessity from which we are fortunately liberated."

"We were, indeed, at the limit of our strength," said Marcel. "Our despair had been immense when we discovered the disappearance of our shell. That very disappearance proved that the Moon was inhabited, as we had thought, and that it was at the very moment of reaching our goal that we were about to expire. We did not want to leave that location, on the assumption that those who had already been there would come back, but need had exhausted us, and we were going to sleep for the last time when we were snatched from certain death."

The conversation continued for a little while longer in that tone of cordiality and amiable confidence; then Rugel took his leave of his guests, after informing them that their reception by the supreme magistrate of the lunar society had been fixed for the time when the Earth would be in its first quarter.

Since our three voyagers, having been miraculously saved, had been living in the bosom of lunar humankind, they had been continually and completely delighted. The people who had taken them in had found them unconscious on the shore of the lake in the dark cavern, and when their eyes had opened again, when they had been recalled to life by intelligent care, they thought they had been transported into a supernatural world.

They were lying on rich cushions in a vast hall, the large bay windows of which were open to a warm and seemingly-embalmed air. Pressing around them were beings whose beardless faces, long hair, mild features and long loose robes had betrayed their sex. Their voices were soft and they were conversing with one another in a sonorous and harmonious language whose rhythmically-cadenced accents caressed the ears.

Soon reanimated, Marcel and his two companions felt the tortures of hunger reawakening within them. They had despaired of making those surrounding them understand when Lord Rodilan, looking around, had recognized, piled up in the room where they were, various objects that had garnished the shell in which they had accomplished their astonishing voyage. He had pointed to a square box that they had hastened to bring him, and which he had opened with considerable effort. He and his two friends had started devouring the biscuits that they took out of it with a gluttonous avidity that Jacques, in his capacity as a physician, was not long delayed in moderating. The women surrounding them had given signs of the most complete amazement at that spectacle, evidently new to them.

"Why are they looking at us like that?" Lord Rodilan grumbled. "One would think that they'd never seen an honest Englishman satisfying his appetite."

And, as the little nourishment he had taken had restored his strength, he got up and went to fetch a bottle of old burgundy, of which he poured generous draughts for himself and his two companions.

On seeing them absorb that liquid, unknown to them, the inhabitants of the moon had passed from amazement to the most complete bewilderment.

"Singular individuals!" Marcel murmured.

Such had been the entrance of our three voyagers to the unknown world they had come so far to visit.

XII. The Lunar World

Their ignorance of the indigenes' language had at first been a source of embarrassment and difficulties, but all three of them had minds too agile for such an obstacle to be able to stop them for long.

Their arrival had caused a great sensation. People came from all over to see the representatives of such a similar humankind; they wanted to know what they were like, whether they were intelligent, good and gentle; they wanted to know how they had come, and never stopped asking questions about the circumstances in which they had been discovered.

The entire lunar world was in turmoil, and, without the precautions with which the governor of the province had surrounded them, the newcomers would probably have suffered a curiosity that was sometimes inconvenient. The news had been quickly transmitted to the capital of the Lunar State, where the Head of State and the Supreme Council were resident.

The sages making up the Council had decided that before presenting the three strangers to the depository of sovereign authority, it would be appropriate to teach them the country's language, in order that they could be questioned and furnish useful explanations of the world whose messengers they were.

It was thus that the wise and knowledgeable Rugel, one of the members of the Council, had been placed with them in order to prepare them for the solemn reception that was reserved for them.

Intelligent as they were, they had not taken long to familiarize themselves with the language spoken by the inhabitants of the Moon. That language, with soft and musical inflections, was logical in its extreme simplicity. The grammar and syntax, founded on clear rules in conformity with the very laws of thought, stripped of any unnecessary complication and all the exceptions that embarrass our European languages, were clear and straightforward. That sobriety of essential forms did not exclude richness however; the vocabulary was abundant and each of the most delicate nuances of thought had a precise term to express it, easy to remember, which, as often as not, formed an image, the melodious sound of which charmed the ear.

The same spirit of methodical exactitude presided over the script that served to represent the words of the language.

In fact, lunar humanity presented a single race, always subject to the same influences of temperature and environment. Its members had, therefore, only ever spoken a single language, which had been improved over time as civilization progressed and the conquest of science had brought new elements of thought. In that language one did not encounter the variety of radicals originating from different sources and the complexities of orthography that so many dead languages have left us. The words were depicted phonetically by a small number of characters, easy to grasp and trace. Everyone spoke well and everyone wrote well.

In any case, the curiosity of the explorers was overexcited by everything they saw, and the desire to learn, already natural to those elite minds, was singularly increased. All the forces of their intelligence were extended to understand and admire the world, in which everything seemed superior to the one with which they were familiar.

They went from one astonishment to another.

That humankind, which seemed to have won the right to live in a strange environment by force of science and determination; those beings of a more subtle nature, freed from the material care of maintaining their life on a daily basis by crude nourishment; those arts and industries, far more advanced than our own, which had already stolen from nature secrets that we scarcely suspect, and disciplined forces of which we are far from extracting all that is possible; that civilization, so advanced that it had succeeded in simplifying the conditions of existence, and achieving the disappearance of the rivalries and dissents that divide Earthly humans; their high moral culture, their enlightened love of good, their practical wisdom exempt from grim austerity and narrow rigor; and finally, those gentle mores in which affability and benevolence rendered all relationships amiable and facile, all enchanted and delighted them.

Marcel was in a perpetual state of excitement and enthusiasm. Jacques had not forgotten his love for Hélène, but in the midst of that milieu full of serenity, he thought about it without bitterness and with pleasurable hope. Even Lord Rodilan, reattached to life, had been cured of his spleen and did not regret having avoided death.

To complete their instruction in haste, Rugel had taken them traveling through the various regions in which lunar humankind lived, the number of whose inhabitants was no greater than twelve million.

The rest of the country was occupied by a sea of dimensions almost equal to our Mediterranean. The surface of that interior sea was strewn with numerous islands, some of very restricted dimensions and grouped into pleasant archipelagos, others larger and isolated, attaining the proportions of small continents. States such as Greece, Belgium or Portugal could have been accommodated there without difficulty.

Around those shores, which were hollowed out by numerous gulfs or extended by picturesque peninsulas, extended vast regions furrowed by numerous watercourses, along which flourishing cities were scattered, where populations much less dense than those crowded into our stifling cities lived at their ease.

The ground rose up at a gradual slope to a region of inaccessible mountains, overhanging rocks and unfathomable precipices, whose inhospitable flanks no one had ever climbed. It was beyond that impenetrable circle that the granite foundations rose up, simultaneously forming the wall and the vault of the colossal cavern that enclosed a world.

That environment, where the sun's rays never penetrated, was illuminated by a even and constant light produced by the diffusion in the atmosphere of an electric glow, the unexpected sight of which had surprised the three voyagers so strangely. That continuity of illumination, unvaried by any

94

alternation of day and night, gave the inhabitants of the lunar world an existence very different from ours. Life there was not divided into two parts of unequal length, one of which is filled with fever, agitations and fervent contests, while the other is plunged in darkness, in which nature and humanity seem entombed.

The surface of the ground was always full of life, as if smiling. Everyone devoted the necessary time to their occupations, without worrying about temporal divisions, since light never ceased to fill space, and they went to sleep when they felt the need to restore their exhausted strength.

Nature, ever logical in its foresight, had disposed animal life in view of the environment in which it had to develop. Like humans, the inferior creatures were organized in such a fashion as to maintain life by respiration alone. The struggle for existence did not arm against one another either the individuals of one species or those of different species. Thus, the gaze was not afflicted by the spectacle of those incessant combats in which the weak, always sacrificed, serve to nourish the stronger. There was no danger that that absence of relentless enemies would allow the various animal species to develop excessively; their limited fecundity was sufficient to fill the gaps left in their ranks by natural death without any of them being able to become invasive.

Animals, not having to defend themselves against incessantly renascent enemies, nor having to attack others in order to live, had no need of the arsenal of various weapons with which nature has gratified them on our world: no sharp claws, menacing teeth or venomous stings. Malevolent species were unknown there.

Mild and inoffensive creatures, never being forced to suffer the unjust attacks of humans, and, in consequence, to fear or mistrust them, and also being closer to them in their intelligence and instincts of an almost sociable kind, lived with them in a state intermediate between independence and domestication.

The species that seemed to hold the primary rank in that life of an inferior order offered striking analogies with our canine species. Simultaneously more delicate and stronger, slimmer and more elegant in form, its members lived in proximity with humans as affectionate and submissive companions.

In a narrower intimacy with the inhabitants of the Moon lived another animal, smaller in size, lest lively in its behavior, charming, supple and caressant in form, which was like an assiduous house-guest. Its coat, with long and silky fur, offered the most varied and sparkling colors. Like the plumage of our tropical birds, it was sometimes uniform and bright, sometimes variously hued, but always easy on the eye and pleasant to behold. Familiar and placid in their habits, the animals in question had none of the ferocious egotism and hypocrisy of our feline species. They seemed to have made humans the sacrifice of their liberty, and their eyes, soft and expressive, showed that they were sensible to the affection of which they were the object.

Other animals, whose stature and form were reminiscent of those of our hinds, stags and gazelles, the variegated coats of which were sometimes striped or capriciously spotted, like those of our tigers and leopards—of which they had neither the ferocity nor the bloodthirsty instincts—populated the rural areas.

The families of birds, which were much less numerous than on Earth, were, in compensation, remarkable for their beauty, the glossiness of their plumage and the harmony of their songs. As they had no more reason than any of the other creatures to fear the approach of humans, they came familiarity when called, populating the arbors that surrounded the habitations, and penetrating into the dwellings, which they enlivened with their chirping and their presence.

In the sea, the rivers and the lakes lived a few species of fish, whose tranquil existence was never troubled, and only seemed to be there, as the ancient poet put it, in order that none of the elements of nature should remain deprived of inhabitants.

In that almost completely closed environment, the light and temperature were only subject to slight variations. The illumination was analogous that that spread over the Earth when the sun rises on summer days veiled by the mists that form at the surface of ground chilled during the night. The light was soft, iridescent with all the shades of the prism, singularly tender and delicately nuanced, which seemed to succeed one another in harmonious undulations; it was only darkened when vapors rising from the sea condensed in the upper regions of the atmosphere in light and shifting clouds that sometimes resolved into a fine rain, the vivifying fall of which made the flowers bloom and augmented their perfumes. The temperature dropped a few degrees then, but never enough for any sensation of cold to afflict the inhabitants or diminish their activity.

That constant mildness of temperature and beneficent rainfall gave the soil a marvelous fertility. The rural areas were not cultivated, since the inhabitants of those fortunate regions were not constrained by the necessity of extracting from the soil, with difficulty, the aliments indispensable to an inferior and material life. Thus, the plants blossomed in complete liberty. Nevertheless, deprived of the light of the sun, the vegetation there offered a strange appearance, to which European eyes had some difficulty in becoming accustomed. The ground was generously covered by a thick, fine grass, pale green in color, which sometimes attained a color that was only slightly tinted white.

Against that pastel background rose up woody clumps of somewhat darker verdure. The elevated trunks, covered in bark that was sometimes pale and marbled, sometimes smooth and green, and sometimes striated by longitudinal bands of varying darkness, extended their leafy branches in bizarrely-shaped crowns. The leaves were not uniform in color. Some, light and feathery, were almost transparent, and the light that traversed them gave them a brightness similar to that of flow-

97

ers; others, formed of a delicate cottony tissue cut out like fine lace, seemed light and vaporous.

Sometimes, in the middle of grasslands, gigantic vegetables rose up, with colossal trunks, extending vigorous branches in all directions, charged with long broad leaves that undulated like veils of bronze-tinted gauze in the slightest breeze, and radiated light of various colors. Others, of lesser height, with smooth trunks of a more vivid green, raised thick-veined lanceolate leaves with pointed tips into the air, as if preparing for a duel.

All the trees, of various species unknown to the voyagers, bore flowers of strange and capricious forms, but the flowers in question, like those that decorated the countryside, were all in pastel shades, as if toned down. One did not see there, as on Earth, bright reds and bloody crimsons, rutilant yellows reminiscent of molten gold, or vigorous and profound blues and violets, but pale pinks, yellows that seemed attenuated by time, tender blues, and faded reds with hints of violet. Only whites caressed by the slightly blue-tinted glow of the atmosphere, obtained a bright glare from that contact.

In that fortunate climate, in which there was no winter, the forests never lost their adornment and the lawns were never devoid of flowers; they succeeded one another incessantly, and the gaze was always charmed by them.

For eyes habituated to the violent and sometimes clashing colors that the richest flowers affect on Earth, the general aspect of that nature could appear a trifle insipid and monotonous, but sight soon became accustomed to those infinitely soft tones, the thousand nuances and delicate diversity of which were delightful and restful at the same time.

The cities were numerous, constructed like the one in which our voyagers resided, and which was, properly speaking, the capital of the subterranean world, because it was there that the Head of State and the Supreme Council were based. The capital was not otherwise distinguished from other cities, however. As the land was in common ownership and no one had any interest in disputing the common property with anyone else, everyone had been able to give their dwelling the proportions required by the number of family members, or their own whim.

Unlike the Earth, there were none of the hives deprived of light and air formed by superimposed floors, in which numerous families were accumulated who were strangers to one another. Every family had a dwelling of its own, and everyone delighted in decorating it an ornamenting it with exquisite taste and variety.

The streets were broad and spacious, paved with a substance similar to glass, the various colors of which, artfully disposed, formed a kind of mosaic. The vegetables that bordered them, the gardens surrounding the houses, and the large spaces planted with trees and shrubs, always covered with foliage and flowers, gave all the cities a pleasant and placid appearance. Numerous electric vehicles, light, rapid and graceful in form, moving silently, went back and forth along them. The roads that linked the cities were merely the continuation of the streets that traversed them; they were paved and planted in the same fashion.

In the rural areas, some distance from cities, stood solitary habitations, the preferred abodes of a few sages anxious not to be troubled in their meditations by the activity of cities.

Thanks to a system of electric locomotion, which permitted the acquisition of a very considerable propulsive force with a very small volume, communication between the various cities was rapid and frequent. The people had, in fact, discovered a metal of which the geological constitution of the terrestrial globe has no analogue. Bluish in color, with a density inferior to that of aluminum, with a higher melting-point than platinum and more magnetic than iron, it had the property of drawing electricity from the air and storing it, thus forming veritable accumulators of great power and almost indefinite durability.

The principal cities were linked by a network of railways, the strangeness of which caused the three inhabitants of

Earth a profound surprise when they saw them for the first time. Everything about them was, in fact, new.

Picture light vehicles elegant in form, hollowed out at the top and inflated at the base, resting both sides on the extremities of an axle-tree serving as the axis of a kind of sphere formed of four large metallic circles intersecting at right angles, one of which, perpendicular to the vehicle and equipped with a groove, ran along a single rail.

How could such an apparatus be maintained in equilibrium? That was the question that the engineer Marcel asked himself initially, the solution to which, as simple as it was original, amazed him.

The scientists of the Moon had only had to apply the principle of the gyroscope to locomotion. [13]

It is well-known that a solid body, like a metallic disk, for example, submitted to a rapid movement of axial rotation, invariably maintains its plane of rotation, and in consequence its axis, so long as the initial velocity is not modified. It was on this principle that the physicist Foucault based the construction of the instrument that served to demonstrate the rotation of planets. His gyroscope, in fact, maintained itself in equilibrium, suspended in a frame, so long as it conserves the same speed of rotation.

In the apparatus that surprised Marcel, the same physical principle had been applied. At the center of the sphere on the axis of which the vehicle reposed, a disk was disposed—or, rather, a kind of heavy metallic flywheel, animated by a electric motor with an extremely rapid rotational movement in the same plane as the grooved wheel that rested on the rail. The diameter and weight of that flywheel, as well as the speed imparted to it, were calculated with a view to the load that the

---

[13] Intensive investigation of the properties of gyroscopes was conducted in France by Léon Foucault in the 1850s, and the development of electric motors in the 1860s created the possibility of causing them to spin indefinitely, thus opening up the possibility of this kind of application to speculation.

axis of the sphere was required to support. As long as it conserved its speed, the entire apparatus maintained a fixed and
invariable equilibrium, sufficiently stable not to be disrupted
by the comings and goings of passengers. The train thus
formed was set in motion by an independent electric motor
disposed in the first vehicle, which thus constituted a sort of
electric locomotive, whose sharply streamlined form diminished the atmospheric resistance considerably.

Since the ensemble ran along a single rail, the system reduced friction of a minimum, and increased the speed obtained
proportionately. Precious facilities also resulted for the establishment of tracks.

In fact, the rail rested on metal pillars placed at intervals,
the height of which, varying according to the inequalities in
the ground, maintained the track in an invariably horizontal
plane. That avoided the building of embankments and cut-
tings, which render the construction-work of terrestrial railways so difficult and tedious; there were no other works of art
than a few bold bridges, similarly metallic, extended over a
deep gorge or a watercourse.

Always careful to avoid possible accidents, the lunar engineers had anticipated the possibility that the electric motor
might fail for some reason, threatening the train with a loss of
equilibrium. They had provided it with an ingenious system of
brakes. The rail, of dimensions and a strength far superior to
those in usage on Earth, also had the cross-sectional form of a
mushroom, with the difference that it was hollowed out more
profoundly and more acutely in such a fashion as to offer on
either side a groove to which a steel plate could be exactly
fitted; that plate terminated, to the right and left of the rail, a
very powerful lever disposed beneath the vehicles and thus
forming an isosceles triangle of which the rail was the summit.

When the train was moving the two steel plates were
maintained far enough apart for no friction to be produced. As
soon as the current activating the gyroscopes ceased, or even
diminished, and the stability of the vehicles was compromised,

the two plates came closer to the rail, adhering to it forcefully, thus forming an unshakable base for the train.

To determine that approach, an automatic mechanism was disposed on the locomotive vehicle. Before the eyes of the train driver there were recording devices whose needles indicated precisely the number of rotations accomplished by the gyroscopes in a particular unit of time, along with the force and intensity of the electric current. As soon as the needle reached the permitted minimum, a trigger activated the plates of all the brakes simultaneously, gripping the mushroom of the rail, maintaining the train in equilibrium. It was, therefore, sufficient to interrupt the current activating the locomotive apparatus for the train to come to a stop, without a jolt, in a matter of seconds.

All of that was light, aerial and silent, and the three friends never wearied of admiring the fertile genius that had imagined the bold trains that they saw cleaving through the air so rapidly, their passage only signaled by a faint noise.

That transport system served for general and industrial needs, but for particular communications and individual displacements, other comfortable means existed that were easy to employ.

In the electricity-saturated atmosphere, in which ozone—which is to say, electrified oxygen—was dominant, there was an inexhaustible reservoir of natural forces, which the highly advanced science of the Moon's inhabitants had put to every use.[14] It was child's play for them, with the light and powerful motors at their disposal, to construct kinds of apparatus that, heavier an air and obtaining their points of support in the am-

---

[14] Ozone, whose chemical formula was determined in 1865 By Jacques-Louis Sorel, was considered for the remainder of the 19th century and beyond to be a healthy component of the atmosphere, to be eagerly sought out by those is search of a tonic; its toxicity, determined by its powerful oxidant effect, was only gradually realized in the 20th century, so the author of the present work was completely unaware of it.

bient milieu, could navigate safely in the atmosphere and travel considerable distances rapidly and without encumbrance.

An ingenious system of parachutes, which offered a broad resistant surface in a small volume and was deployed automatically, prevented the accidents always to be feared, even with the most improved engines, and ensured that mode of transport a complete security. After long research, the lunar physicists had recognized that the simplest and most practical mode of propulsion was that of the helix, which had only recently arrived on Earth.

The birds became fatigued in their flight in following light vehicles that a single person was sufficient to steer and maintain in the required direction.

It was also the electric fluid that powered the vessels of every sort that floated on the surface of the interior sea, went up the rivers, or even, diving beneath the waters, went to explore the deeper layers of those unknown seas.

Everything in that world, so different from the Earth, respired calm and peace of mind; everyone, liberated from material needs, seemed to have no other care but the development of intelligence, or abandoning themselves to the most tender and noble sentiments of the heart. The serenity of their features, the frankness of their gaze and the benevolence of their smiles demonstrated that their souls were free of all the paltry ambitions and egotistical passions that render the condition of terrestrial humankind so wretched.

No other sadnesses were known there than those that might result from the loss of cherished individuals—of some child taken away at the dawn of life from the affection of its parents, of a beloved companion, a friend or a venerated master—or from the anxieties and torments against which the souls of sages cannot defend themselves when, entirely devoted to the research of some important problem, they see the solution that they have been pursuing for so long slipping away.

Our voyagers wondered where, how and by whom the monuments that excited their admiration were constructed, as well as the machines and various kinds of apparatus that responded in such a complete and convenient manner to all the demands of life. Nowhere, in fact, in the cities or the rural areas that surrounded them, had they perceived any traces of industrial labor. They were to learn, as their sojourn in the lunar world was extended, that beyond the limits of the regions they had visited were other agglomerations of habitations different from those with which they were already familiar.

It was in the vicinity of the mountains that we have already mentioned that these truly industrial cities were located. There, useful or precious metals were extracted from the ground; there, they were put to work; from there emerged all the manufactured utensils necessary to the various usages of life and all the items of apparatus making up a very advanced state of civilization.

It was the class of Diemides that was employed in these multiple operations.

XIII. Diemides and Meolicenes

As in all gatherings of human, intelligent and moral beings submissive to the great law of progress, which rise incessantly along the path of an increasingly complete well-being,
an increasingly broad knowledge and an increasingly elevated
morality, lunar humanity had, from the beginning, presented
various aptitudes and different capabilities.

There, as everywhere we can conceive of living and perfectible beings, the struggle for existence, each forward step of
which is a victory over nature, the influences of environment,
selection and heredity had done their work. While the best
endowed and the best armed had been able to cultivate their
faculties in more favorable conditions and become superior by
virtue of knowledge and the practice of virtue, others had only
followed the route of indefinite progress at a slower pace.

Nevertheless, as the inhabitants of the Moon had not
been subject to the same necessities as those of the Earth, as
they were essentially less coarse by nature and less subservient
to the exigencies of matter, their point of departure had been
more elevated than that of our primitive races, and the development of that privileged humanity more rapid and more
complete. The distance that separated the extreme strata of
that moral hierarchy was much less considerable that that
which exists on Earth between the refined products of European civilization and the primitive barbarians wandering the wilderness of central Africa or the deserts of Australia.

Gentle and placid by nature, penetrated in large measure
by a love of goodness, respect for science and the legitimate
ambition to rise ever higher, the Diemides—which is to say, in
the lunar language, "those who aspire to a better condition"—
accepted joyfully the labor that served the common utility of
the great family of which they were a part. Furthermore, the
incessant discoveries of the scientists, whose stole some new
secret from nature every day, which was employed for their

usage, disciplining forces that are as yet unknown to us, rendered that labor ever easier and less repugnant.

Ingenious methods, machines whose functioning was as simple as it was sure, permitted the extraction almost without effort of the raw materials that the soil furnished in abundance, and the fabrication without difficulty of all useful objects, reducing human labor to a minimum and limiting its role to the guidance and supervision of the operation of advanced machinery.

In any case, the great sentiment of justice and love that reigned in that purified society made the condition of the Diemides comfortable and reserved for each of them the prospect of more precious recompenses. Everyone there had the exact rank assigned by merit and moral worth. Anyone who, by virtue of intelligence, services rendered or the provision of a good example, distinguished himself from those of the rank in which birth had placed him, was raised to the appropriate degree in the social scale.

From the ensemble of mores and institutions that was freely and spontaneously established between races naturally inclined to virtue, a fixed hierarchy had resulted with regard to the demarcations separating the various classes, but an essential mobility for individuals, who could always rise by means of the continuity of their efforts into the superior classes. That produced a social order from which all envy and base jealousy was excluded, in which a sentiment of duty accomplished reigned in all ranks, and was accompanied by peace.

At the lowest degree of the scale were those Diemides who were employed in the extractive industries; above them were the constructors, those who built houses or manufactured machines, movable objects and various engines; higher still were those who, under the direction of artists, painters, sculptors, architects and engineers, decorated buildings, sculpted or carved wood, stone or metal.

There the roles of the Diemides concluded. The hierarchy continued in the superior class known as the Meolicenes—which is to say, "people of intelligence."

To tell the truth, there were no other distinctions between the two branches of that great people than the nature of the work they did. So long as the work was entirely or primarily material, they remained in the class of Diemides. When the work to which they were devoted demanded the exclusive employment of the faculties of intelligence, they entered the superior class of Meolicenes, and there a progression continued rising to the most elevated rank, occupied by the sages whose vast intellect embrace the principles of all the sciences, the general laws of the universe and the great moral truths that served the humankind in question, already so far advanced on the path of perfection, as a guide.

As the worship and practice of goodness was, in those elite natures, in harmony with the extent of knowledge, the foremost among the Meolicenes combined the most complete sagacity with the most unalterable virtue. Detached from all the moral flaws and imperfections that might remain in the inferior ranks of human fallibility, they seemed to live in an ethereal atmosphere in which nothing base or impure survived. They were dominant by virtue of the power of the mind, and the almost complete possession of the secrets of nature, which put into their hands forces capable, if necessary, of destroying the world they inhabited, and, above all, by virtue of the serenity of their life and the authority given to them by the constant realization of everything good, honest and just.

They formed the Supreme Council of magistrates, which ruled that republic of sorts. The Head of State, whose powers were lifelong, was elected by the members of the Council and was always chosen from among them. In that assembly of sages there could be no question of intrigue or vulgar competition; it was always the most worthy who obtained the suffrage of his colleagues. His functions consisted of directing the deliberations of the assembly over which he presided, and of taking, on his own initiative, all the measures that he judged useful to the material and moral development of the entire society. He figured in the first rank of all public ceremonies; he was both the head of the religion and of the city. That double character, august and sacred, and the conviction of everyone that he was the foremost in science, wisdom and virtue, assured him of an authority before which everyone inclined respectfully.

In that milieu, where social situation was marked by personal value alone, no privilege was reserved for birth; all were born equal, and all were subject to the same proofs. Every child, whether issued from a Diemide or a Meolicene family, was raised until puberty in the boom of that family. Without distinction of sex, they received from the mouths of ages the elements of all the useful or agreeable knowledge that would permit them subsequently to fulfill the roles that nature destined for them. Young men drew therefrom the principles of the sciences that they would have to apply in the various functions that the social hierarchy retained for them. Young women, in whose souls the sentiment of beauty was especially cultivated, formed the culture of the arts there without those aspirations to the ideal ever being able to alter the natural modesty of their sex, which is the charm of life.

Those who were responsible for distributing information in that fashion, and who had the delicate mission of discerning each pupil's dominant aptitudes and favoring their development for the greater good of the common interest, were the most honored among the Meolicenes.

The most important task of all was considered to be that of forming the worship of the good, the beautiful and the true in the souls of future generations.

For the young women, their lives continued in the domestic hearth until the choice of a spouse removed them from the parental house.

As no one could think of enriching themselves or raising themselves above others by evil means, and as there was no individual property, everyone received their legitimate share of common funds, and in consequences, there were no transactions, no salaries, and no money of any sort. There could be no question, therefore, of fortune or dowry. Whereas, on Earth, people hurl themselves recklessly in pursuit of rich inheritances, and, without paying any heed to qualities of the mind or heart, only aim for opulent rewards or base expectations, happy and envied when their calculations have succeeded, love alone, confident and disinterested, presided there over unions whose happiness and dignity were simultaneously assured.

When a reciprocal sympathy brought two people together, when the sincerity of their sentiments, which they could not think of concealing, had consecrated the first movements of the heart, no one bothered to enquire as to the rank of the social scale on which those who wanted to unite and found a new family were placed. On that terrain there was no distinction between Diemides and Meolicenes.

Furthermore, the functioning of the institutions that regulated lunar humankind rendered the formation of an aristocracy of race impossible; people only inclined before the intellectual and moral superiority acquired by incessant labor and established by numerous and decisive proofs.

To take account of that, it is necessary to return to the education given to young people. When they entered into adolescence, all of them, without distinction, whether they were the issue of the most elevated of Meolicenes or the humblest of Diemides, to their places in the latter class, and a career of self-improvement and progress opened up before them.

They all began by being employed in purely manual labor, which only required the use of physical strength. Those kinds of work, however, which were, for the most part, carried out by the machines of which electricity was the inexhaustible motor, also gave them the opportunity to exercise their intelligence and artistic sentiment. Once raw materials had been extracted and put to work, there was no more to do than fashion them, give them definitive form and, whatever the purpose was for which they were intended—from the powerful supports on which railways tracks rested and the blocks that served as foundations for monuments to the most delicate components of complex apparatus and the furniture the equipped sand ornamented dwellings—everything among those eminently well-endowed people took on the forms of an elegant and harmonious variety. Those occupations, moreover, left them abundant leisure time, and while they were working for the common utility, they continued the cultivation of their mind and strove to render themselves worthy of a superior condition.

The scholars who directed their work and distributed tasks to each of them were also those who guided them in the development of their scientific sand moral education. There was thus a vast family, in which authority was loved and respected because it was always benevolent and just, where obedience was easy and meek, for it did not rest on the fear of a tyrannical or jealous power, but on a reciprocal affection and a constant desire to do well.

Those scholars, who were also sages, followed everyone's work with an attentive eye; they judged merit, efforts accomplished and results obtained, and as soon as one of those submissive to their direction had, by means of personal endeavor, augmented the sum of their own knowledge and rendered themselves capable of rendering services of a more elevated kind to society, they designated them to take their place in a superior class.

And those decisions, solely dictated by the spirit of justice and the sentiment of the common good, were accepted without protest, jealousy or envy. An individual raised in the social scale saw nothing around them but smiling faces and hands extended to congratulate them on their success; so much did conviction reign from the top to the bottom of the society that everything was supposed to tend, and did in fact tend, to the prosperity and happiness of all.

It was not, however, given to all those who formed the class of Diemides to march at an equal pace along the path of progress that was open to them. Those who, as is natural in any aggregation of humans, were less well-endowed from the viewpoint of intelligence never passed through the inferior steps and never emerged from the ranks of Diemides; but morality, the spirit of order and submission were the same for all of them. And thus was accomplished, in a regular and constant fashion, without opposition, regret or bitterness, the rational selection that ensured everyone the place that best suited them.

The condition of women was what one would suppose in a world exempt from passions, paltry ambitions and puerile vanities. Whether the spouse of their choice was a Diemide or a Meolicene, all were equally considered. Furthermore, if distinctions of class and hierarchical degrees existed for men, nothing similar was encountered for women, and the reason for that was simple. There were neither rich people nor poor people; material life, brought back to its simplest expression, reduced to mere child's pay the domestic concerns that are often so fastidious and repugnant among us. No one was reduced to the servile condition of rendering humiliating services to others. Everyone's dignity, no matter to what class they belonged, was thus respected, and no one had to suffer the degrading vices that domestic service engenders on Earth: the jealousy, hatred, deception and fraud that are so often hidden beneath complaisance and obsequiousness.

While men fulfilled their social functions—none was idle or unemployed—women reserved the care of ornamenting and embellishing their dwellings, bringing up children and cultivating in themselves the exquisite sentiment of the arts: drawing and painting, music and the delicate and charming works that heighten the glamour of garments, and adding to their beauty the attractions of adornment.

The taste that presided over their adaptations was always ruled by an exceedingly accurate sentiment of measure and decency; no one there was given to vanity, ostentation and the need for appearance that so often spoils the most precious qualities of the women of Earth. Their features, regular and pure, did not offer those specimens of painful ugliness that sometimes generate smiles and alienate all sympathy among us. Their faces were imprinted with an attractive gentleness and agreeable good humor. False and unhealthy artistry could not have added anything to it; nature was sufficient for them, and it would never have occurred to them to resort to vain artifice to exaggerate the opulence of their hair, the freshness of heir complexion or the brightness of their gaze.

They were equally ignorant of the desperate coquetry of women who do not want to grow old, whose frivolous spirit and light heart take fright at the first wrinkle or white hair. The thought of struggling against the laws that preside over the transformation of all beings could not arise in them; they passed without anxiety from youth to maturity and then to old age, always loved, respected and honored. In any case, their faces always retained, even at an advanced age, an evident air of nobility and bounty.

The frankness and absolute sincerity that were a law of their nature and the condition of their moral superiority rendered impossible in them those perfidious dissimulations, machinations and treasons that have so often caused despair and ruin on Earth. The lies, calumnies, insipid gossip and evil insinuations in which the idle or empty minds of the mundane societies of our inferior world ordinarily take pleasure were completely unknown there.

The bonds created by nature, consecrated by affection and heightened by great moral dignity were sacred and respected. Every family offered a complete picture of concord and love, in which was reflected the order and harmony that reigned throughout the society.

Religious beliefs were those that best suited that purified world. From the outset, its inhabitants had been sheltered by the power of their reason from the crude superstitions that have marked among us the slow development of our civilizations. The idea of an infinite Sovereign Intelligence, the source of all things, the center of all being and all beauty, had not need to be incarnated for them initially in the forms of barbaric materialism, gradually to become more abstract and more perfect. It had presented itself to them from the beginning in all its simplicity and unalterable splendor.

Never had they judged it appropriate to enclose the divinity in temples, nor submit the worship they rendered thereto to manifestations that were often cruel and bloody and sometimes puerile or ridiculous. Everyone, in their interior consciousness, rendered the divinity a free and pure honor, attributing to the Author of all things their joy or sadness, and abandoned themselves, outside of any narrow ritual or liturgy, in all the spontaneity of a conscience that no authority could constrain, to sentiments of gratitude and adoration.

At certain epochs the Head of State invited all the inhabitants of the lunar world to public ceremonies of a character both patriotic and religious, and it was to that entirely paternal appeal that the exercise of his religious authority was limited. For those ceremonies, which maintained the chain of tradition through successive generations, poets composed songs, inspired hymns, and musicians made the most delightful melodies heard. The memory of those whose genius had endowed humankind with some great and fecund discovery, and sages who had formulated the precepts of a sublime morality, was celebrated there, and the voice of an entire people rose up to the heavens in accents of joy and gratitude.

Nothing in that worship resembled the theological controversies in which blind fanaticism unleashes its intolerant furies, causing torrents of blood and tears to flow. Nothing, either, paralleled the vain and sterile philosophical disputes in which minds infatuated with their own power lose themselves in the fog of an incomprehensible metaphysics.

Everything was simple, noble and grand.

XIV. The Reception

The day fixed for the reception of the strangers had arrived. It was in the palace where the Head of State resided and the Supreme Council met that the ceremony was to take place, which would consecrate in an imperishable fashion the success of the most audacious enterprise ever undertaken by human creatures. The news of that solemnity had spread throughout the lunar world; everyone was avid to witness it and they were all in accordance in wanting to surround it with an exceptional magnificence.

The palace stood some distance from the shore where the tranquil waves of the sea came to break, in the center of a vast square bordered with marble porticos, the various colors of which recalled porphyry, portor and Paros marbles, bloodstone and jasper. Around the columns and pillars hung garlands of flowers and foliage in precious metals, marvelously wrought, whose glitter, alternately amber and azure, blended with the colors of the marble they were decorating. Along the entablements and the friezes ran arabesques of the most delicate workmanship.

Against that background of warm hues the palace stood out vigorously, its white hues attenuated by the multitude of ornaments covering its walls. Generations of artists had succeeded one another in embellishing that sumptuous monument, in which a kind of history of the lunar world was summarized.

In the center of the edifice a boldly elegant dome rose up, surmounted by a light and slender campanile, delicately perforated. The dome was covered with a lacework of metallic ornaments, whose sculpture allowed the perception through the capricious mesh of the dazzling whiteness they overlaid. It reposed on a series of colonnettes with richly-worked capitals, linked to one another by sculpted arches whose ribs, tormented and interwoven by a sure hand, formed a veritable lace.

The palace crowned by that dome affected, in its general disposition, the form of a cross with four equal branches. Above the one that was elongated along the axis of the square, a vast terrace extended surrounded by a light balustrade in gold and silver, and also the metal with violet reflections with which our voyagers were already familiar. It was, it will be recalled, on a plate of the metal in question that the mysterious signs were engraved that had given Marcel the idea of launching his superhuman enterprise. Everything was massive, and there again was found the inexhaustible whimsy that curved the metal, like a flexible branch, around the dome and in the gaps between the colonnettes. Above the other three branches of the cross, supported by light arches, stood bold campaniles, less elevated than the one on the central dome, and covered with sculptures.

All around the edifice extended a portico forming a covered gallery. On the tops of the high columns supporting it, the garlands of flowers and foliage reappeared, where precious enamels, skillfully inserted, imitated nature in their bright and varied colors.

Everywhere that the exigencies of construction had left flat surfaces—the faces of walls, the sides of pilasters, friezes or entablements—the chisels of skillful sculptors had burrowed into the marble to firm polychromatic bas-reliefs, whose characters were depicted with such a realism of attitude and such an intensity of expression that they offered all the appearances of life. Each of those pictures, whose tones were as rich and varied as those of a painting, represented some scene in the history of lunar humankind. But they were not, as among us, scenes of murder and carnage. The fortunate inhabitants of that superior world had been ignorant of war and its horrors for a long time. If, in the early ages of the planet, the avidities inherent in any newborn humankind had armed living beings against one another, the progress of science and mores had caused such fratricidal struggles to be forgotten many centuries ago, and their memory was only conserved in order to avow universal execration thereto.

Each of the bas-reliefs recalled some great or useful discovery, or some feature of devotion, still alive in the memory and gratitude of humans, the establishment of some sage law, or the memory of individuals illustrious for their services or their virtues. It was like a perpetual education placed before the eyes of the crowd, which maintained a generous competition in all hearts.

In spite of the profusion of ornaments that covered the palace, it offered in its harmoniously combined general lines an appearance of incredible lightness. Under the porticos, between the columns, air and light had free play, and the edifice rose up like the fantastic palaces glimpsed in dreams, the capricious and changing contours of which the eye can sometimes follow in clouds.

At the appointed moment, a delegation of the Supreme Council, at the head of which was Rugel, came to fetch the three strangers from their residence and take them to the great and venerable Aldeovaze.

The road that led to the palace, which they traveled on foot, surrounded by the sages who formed their escort, was lined by the crowds of inhabitants attracted by a legitimate curiosity. In the ranks of that multitude, however, there was no shouting, no tumult, no hasty and indiscreet fervor; they all kept to their places calmly and with dignity, and there, where all the members of the crowd had respect for themselves and their neighbors, there was no need for regulations or for police to avoid ill-timed or turbulent manifestations.

As the cortege went by, everyone bowed to salute the newcomers, with a smile of benevolent welcome, and only a slight murmur marked the surprise caused to those who were not yet familiar with them by the sight of the intrepid voyagers who had come in such a strange fashion from a neighboring world.

The weather was calm and mild; a slight breeze was causing light vapors to move through the air, which were floating like veils of fine airborne gauze. The little bay in the depths of which the old capital stood was covered with vessels

116

of various sizes filled with curiosity-seekers who had come from all points of the shore, avid to enjoy the spectacle that was in preparation.

At the very moment when the Head of State came to occupy the throne that had been reserved for him, around which was grouped the imposing assembly of the members of the Council, who were joined, for that exceptional circumstance by all the high dignitaries of the State and the provincial governors, the three strangers appeared on the terrace.

A long shiver of curiosity ran through the crowd, all the way to the most distant ranks of the audience. The strangeness of their costumes—they had conserved their European garments—identified them to the attention of the spectators.

They were momentarily dazzled by the magnificent scene they had before their eyes.

The face of the prudent Aldeovaze was imprinted with a majestic gravity tempered by an expression of benevolence and mildness. He had stood up to honor his guests, and his tall stature, uncurbed by the weight of years, his head, crowned with long white hair, and his beard, whose silvery waves descended over his chest, gave him an appearance of indescribable grandeur. The vivacity of his gaze, and the energy detectable in his regular features, which age had not withered, denoted a soul in which generosity had not been weakened in any way by the pressure of the will.

All those surrounding him had stood up with him. Guided by Rugel, their introducer, Marcel, Jacques and Lord Rodilan advanced, bowed profoundly, and waited.

"Inhabitants of Earth," said Aldeovaze, in a grave and sonorous voice, "be welcome among us. Since the day when your courage permitted you to cross the distance separating us, when you came as the messengers of a world imperfectly known thus far, we have conceived the hope, caressed for a long time, of finally entering into a sustained relationship with the globe around which we are gravitating.

"We wanted to give your reception an exceptional glamour, in order that everyone here would know that a new age is about to begin. Two humankinds, which seemed to be separated forever by the inexorable laws of nature, will be able, thanks to you, to enter into regular communication. We have no doubt that these communications will be fruitful.

"For a long time we have been thinking about it; our scientists have tried to attract the attention of their terrestrial brothers. Those attempts have been futile thus far; your audacity has resolved the problem. The genius of science, which is only one of the manifestations of the Supreme Power that rules the universe, has brought you to us, in the midst of perils over which your great courage was able to triumph.

"We hope that this is only a beginning, and it is perhaps permissible for us to anticipate a time when, thanks to the incessant progress of the human mind, the worlds that gravitate around a common center, linked to one another, will form a single vast family. That would be an immortal glory for us.

"Go and enter into communication with our scientists; study with them the geological constitution of our world, our sciences, our arts and our industries. Take account of the state of our mores, our customs and our institutions; and when you have acquired a complete knowledge of our civilization, instruct us in your turn and enable us to know the world of which you are the representatives."

Aldeovaze had finished speaking.

His words, collected by a vibratory apparatus and amplified, thanks to an ingenious application of electricity, arrived clearly and precisely all the way to the last ranks of spectators, who were watching the moving ceremony from the middle of the bay. Others apparatus transmitted the speeches exchanged in the capital as far as the most distant provinces, whose inhabitants, gathered in the public squares, were, in a way, attending the solemnities.

"Glorious and venerated leader of the world where we have received such a cordial welcome," replied Marcel, in an emotional voice, "The children of Earth salute you. The noble and generous words that we have just heard have filled our hearts with a profound joy and an eternal gratitude.

"The high hopes that you have conceived have animated us with a new ardor. We shall be proud to serve as intermediaries between the two humankinds, who are as yet unacquainted, and in order to arrive at that admirable result, we are ready, supported by your august benevolence, to make every effort, and to brave any perils."

A murmur of approval, which was the highest expression of enthusiasm in that calm and ponderous race, ran through the crowd.

Aldeovaze had descended from his throne and was conversing in a familiar fashion with Marcel. All the members of the Supreme Council surrounded Jacques and Lord Rodilan, charmed by the facility with which the newcomers spoke their language. They were interrogated regarding the tribulations of their journey; people wanted to hear from their own mouths the story of the impressions they had experienced during that formidable journey. They were asked what they thought about the world they had come to visit in such extraordinary conditions. Their courage was admired; their eulogy and their names were on all lips.

Jacques and Lord Rodilan lent themselves with a good grace to that insistent but always discreet curiosity. Everything that they had seen in the last four months—that humankind, so different from their own; that environment, relatively restricted, in which a precious specimen of an eminently perfectible race was conserved, as if in a hothouse; those people among whom nature alone maintained life without them being constrained to labor to that end themselves; those arts, so delicate, those sciences, so complete, those institutions, so simple and fecund—had maintained their souls in a perpetual state of admiration and wonder.

Jacques' preoccupations had dissipated, his melancholy had vanished, and, returned to his natural ardor and generosity, he delivered himself entirely to these new friends, whose sympathetic welcome had gone to his heart.

If some member of London's Pall Mall Club had been able to see Lord Rodilan at that moment, he would not have recognized the phlegmatic and cold gentleman who had paraded his inexorable ennui through the gilded drawing rooms of Waterloo Place. The atmosphere of spleen in which he had enveloped himself had definitively melted on contact with those sincere and disinterested affections. Everything he saw and heard excited his curiosity and his interest; he now found that it was well worth the trouble of being alive.

Thus, our two friends responded with a cordial enthusiasm and communicative cheerfulness to the questions that were addressed to them from all directions. Sometimes, the comments that brought out Jacques' expansive character, and Lord Rodilan's incisive and lively turn of mind even brought smiles to the lips of their serious listeners.

When the reception was concluded, Aldeovaze, accompanied by the three strangers and followed by the members of the Council and the dignitaries who had taken part in the ceremony, went into one of the rooms of the palace where all the objects removed from the shell, which were to be the objects of comparison and study for the scientists of the lunar world, had been set out in methodical order. It will be remembered that Marcel, convinced that he would encounter a new humankind on the Earth's satellite, had equipped himself with numerous items comprising specimens of our arts and industries, which could give an idea of the level of advancement of our sciences.

All of that was the object of attentive examination on the part of the learned assembly. Those serious and reflective minds rapidly took account of the progress that terrestrial humankind had accomplished, the various phases through which it had passed , and were sometimes astonished that a world so contemporary with their own was, in certain respects, lagging so far behind. Some of the theories exposed by Marcel and Jacques left them rather cold; they seemed to be saying: "It's a long time since we surpassed those phases of science."

Nevertheless, the photograph albums, of which the shell contained and abundant collection, excited their admiration.

At first, they had mistaken the pictures for drawings of an extreme finesse; their astonishment was great when they learned that it was solar light alone, captured and fixed on glass plates coated with a sensitive substance, which had designed those images. They were very familiar with the laws of optics, the refraction of luminous rays passing through lenses and their projection on a screen, but the idea had never occurred to them of trying to capture those fugitive images and rendering them durable.

Marcel enjoyed their astonishment. He showed them the photographic apparatus that he had brought and explained its functioning to them. When one of those gathered around him exclaimed: "It's very unfortunate that we're deprived of the light of the Sun," he reassured him, and promised to produce, with the aid of the light illuminating the lunar world, pictures similar to those that they had before their eyes.

Among the objects exhibited were the weapons with which the three explorers had equipped themselves: revolvers and repeating rifles of the latest model. The albums also contained images of powerful engines of destruction created by the genius of war, the irrefutable proof of the inferiority of our race. The scientists who considered those instruments of death or turned the pages of the albums had a profound knowledge of ballistics, but the men in question, who had always lived in an atmosphere of concord and peace could not imagine that human creatures reaching that point of sanguinary madness and killing one another to dispute the miserable shreds of the planet they occupied. At first, therefore, they only saw them as items of scientific apparatus.

Marcel was careful not to disabuse them. He decided that he would inform a few chosen scientists later, in confidential conversations, about the lamentable history of our humankind: its beginnings, when it was scarcely distinguishable from animality, and its slow progress, in which each step had been marked by bloody conflicts and every conquest had had its price in grief and tears.

He hoped that those minds, endowed with noble philosophical conceptions, would understand that human genius had required perseverance and faith in the future to triumph over so many difficulties and perils. He already sensed that that was the only means of elevating slightly the sad condition of the inhabitants of Earth in the eyes of those superior beings.

Some of the scientists making up the assembly had paused to examine a magnificent atlas of anatomy, and Jacques—who, they were not unaware, had studied the medical sciences and physiology deeply in his capacity as a doctor—was explaining the mechanism of the organs of nutrition. It was with the ever-alert curiosity of minds avid for knowledge that they considered the human structure, which only differed from theirs on that one point.

That point was, however, of great importance, and one of those surrounding Jacques could not resist saying to him: "Friend, I won't hide it from you that at first, when we saw that nature, less generous to you than to us, had not liberated you from the painful obligation of renewing the elements necessary to your life every day, we thought that your race must have very little leisure time left to cultivate its thinking faculties, so we were agreeably surprised to learn that you have advanced so far in the study of the sciences. What we see of your progress in all orders of knowledge amazes us and charms us at the same time."

"It's because the need to nourish ourselves," Jacques replied, smiling, "has done for the inhabitants of the Earth—to a lesser degree, I hasten to admit—what the love of truth alone has done for you. It's because they were constrained to those material necessities, and had to satisfy them at any cost, that humans became ingenious in seeking and finding. Each of their conquests, while satisfying their minds, also increased their well-being, and they found the compensation for their efforts therein."

In the meantime, Lord Rodilan, deploying a terrestrial planisphere before the eyes of another group, explained to them in broad terms how civilization, born between two rivers whose courses he designated on the Asian continent, had gradually developed, following the march of the Sun, and had initially passed to an almost imperceptible country with profoundly fragmented coasts named Greece, to establish itself thereafter in the neighboring Italian peninsula and eventually to advance to the shore of the great Atlantic Ocean.

Then, placing his finger on two small islands that formed the most advanced point of the occidental continent, he exclaimed: "Now, there is the center of modern civilization! From those islands, so tiny in surface area but so great in the genius of their inhabitants, thousands of vessels incessantly set forth to all parts of the globe in search of the most useful products and the most precious merchandise, in order to distribute them thereafter over the surface of the Earth. There isn't a single country in which its language isn't spoken. England is the name of that nation, the foremost in the world, and there isn't a point on the globe that doesn't recognize its supremacy. Vast and rich regions are submissive to it."

And his finger ran proudly over the Indian peninsula, the Australian continent, southern Africa and the entire country north of the St. Lawrence. He drew himself up to his full height; all his British pride revived. One might have thought that he believed himself to be in the midst of one of those conferences in which intractable Albion defends its most unjustifiable pretentions so arrogantly.

"Now, now," said Marcel, suddenly, having overheard his companion's last words. "It seems to me, Milord, that you're selling France short." Then, turning to his listeners, who seemed surprised by the vivacity of the argument, because they never departed from their calm and gravity in their own discussion, he said: "Far be it from me to have any thought of diminishing the illustrious nation to which our friend belongs, for you've already suspected, given the warmth of his pleading, that he's talking about his own country, but it's permissible for me to claim on behalf of my own country, France"—he indicated with his finger the part of Europe of what all peoples have successively pronounced the name with envy or love—"the share of glory that is her due.

"If England is great in terms of commerce and industry, France is no less so in terms of heart and thought. Always in the human avant-garde, it has always held the torch of progress high, lighting the way that other nations have followed. There is not a great and generous idea that she has not propagated and for which she has not shed blood. Her disinterested devotion has always been at the service of justice and right; she has fought for all just causes; an enemy of all oppressors and a friend of all the oppressed, she has seen her name blessed by all those she has freed; her triumphs have made all other peoples pale with jealousy, and although she had sometimes been defeated, she has only been crushed by weight of numbers or surprised by treason."

While Marcel was allowing himself to get carried away by his patriotism Jacques had drawn closer to him and shook his hand forcefully.

"Bravo, friend!" he said.

A little blood had risen to Lord Rodilan's ordinarily pale cheeks, and he was doubtless getting ready to reply with some acerbity when the prudent Aldeovaze, who had been listening attentively to the debate, stepped forward, smiling.

"I see," he said, "that you belong to two great nations of the Earth, and the audacity of your enterprise proves to us that you must count among the most eminent of your compatriots. But at the distance you find yourselves from your fatherlands, is it really fitting to reawaken rivalries that we cannot appreciate here? The work to which you have committed yourselves is only just beginning; you ought to devote yourselves entirely to bringing it to a successful conclusion."

"Wisdom is speaking through your mouth," Marcel replied.

And the three friends shook hands.

XV. The First Signals

Seven months had gone by since the departure of the shell launched by the Columbiad toward the lunar regions when, all of a sudden, improbably, unprecedented and amazing news spread through the scientific world.

The Scientific American, in its 29 July 188- issue,[15] published the following telegram, immediately reproduced by the press of the old and new words:

> *Long's Peak Observatory, Rocky Mountains, 28 July, 8 a.m.*
>
> *Alphabetical luminous signals appeared distinctly last night at irregular intervals on dark part of lunar disk, near Hansteen crater, southern part of Ocean of Storms.*
>
> *W. Burnett*

At first it was thought to be one of those colossal hoaxes familiar in American puffery, but the universally-recognized serious character of the director of the Long's Peak Observatory did not permit long hesitation over that point.

From then on, from St. Petersburg to the Cape of Good Hope, and from New York to Melbourne, a thousand telescopes were feverishly aimed at the Moon.

All the scientific journals and reviews were resounding with passionate debates. Each of the observers, in accordance with the power of the optical instrument at his disposal, interpreted in his own way the supposed luminous signals that the astronomers in the Rocky Mountains thought they had seen. The majority had widened their eyes in vain, without anything appearing in the field of their telescopes or binoculars, so they

---

[15] Although *Scientific American* did not publish a issue on 29 July 1884, it did publish one on 19 July of that year.

flatly denied the phenomenon and treated the honorable W. Burnett as a visionary, with insistent mockery.

A few had indeed perceived, beyond a doubt, luminous points in the indicated region, the existence of which had never been observed before, but they recalled, triumphantly, with supportive evidence, that analogous phenomena had been reported in other areas of the satellite in various epochs, which had then ceased to appear, never to be repeated. They did not hesitate to affirm that this time, as on previous occasions, the more or less authentic signs would quickly disappear without leaving any trace.

There was, however, one person that the important communication emanating from Long's Peak had thrown into a veritable stupor, and that was the astronomer F. Mathieu-Rollère.

On reading the telegram addressed personally to him by his American colleague, which had been handed to him in his study at about ten o'clock in the evening, when he was still at work, he had been struck dumb, his limbs agitated by a nervous tremor. He had read the text of the dispatch several times, as if, at first, he had not fully grasped its meaning. He could have been heard to say, as if talking to himself: "Is it really them?"

Then he had hastened to the Observatory and, bustling everything out of his way, had glued his eye to the ocular of the large Foucault telescope.

But the night was foggy, as it often is in Paris, and veils of vapor were passing before the disk of the Moon, which was then approaching its first quarter. He searched the region of the satellite indicated by the telegram, which was then in shadow, but he could not discover anything definite. It sometimes seemed to him that he glimpsed a few fugitive gleams, but was it an illusion? Might his ardent desire to discover something be deceiving him? He could not affirm anything.

Daylight surprised him in his hesitation. He went home, where a further surprise awaited him. On his work-table there was a new telegram that had just arrived. It was conceived as follows:

Long's Peak Observatory, Rocky Mountains.
Confirming yesterday's dispatch. Reliably observed at one hour intervals recurrence of luminous letters MJR. Height of letters measured by micrometer 300 feet. Friends found. Please come for observation next lunation. Cordial felicitations.

W. Burnett

And the old astronomer, exultant and triumphant, launched himself toward his daughter's room.

"Hélène, my child," he stammered, "they're alive—they've sent us news. Your presentiments were right. Get ready—we're leaving."

A cry escaped the young woman's throat. She went pale and almost fainted into her father's arms.

When the astronomers in the Rocky Mountains, following the flight of the projectile though space with the giant eye of the telescope, had seen it suddenly disappear into the fissure that opened almost at the foot of the crater Aristillus, they had thought that it was all over for the bold explorers and that three more names had just been added to the martyrology of science.

However, even though they were convinced of their loss, they had not wanted to abandon all hope. They knew their friends' strength of character, and they knew that men of that exceptional stripe would attempt anything to escape the threat of death. They told themselves that, after all, if they had not perished in the fall, they might be able to get back up to the surface of the satellite and give some sign of life.

Thus, they had resolved not to quit the field of observation until they had acquired a definitive certainty. In any case, the French astronomer was urged by his daughter not to give up. Having recovered from the emotion that had overwhelmed her at the moment when it was believed that the projectile had been lost, Hélène had felt reanimating in her soul a robust faith that had never abandoned her; she wanted to hope against all probability.

François Mathieu-Rollère had, therefore, remained in the Rocky Mountains, and the observations had continued with an untiring zeal and perseverance. Every time the Earth's satellite had shown some part of its illuminate disk above the horizon, the astronomers' indefatigable eyes had scrutinized the luminous field. But nothing had appeared, and every time the ardently-observed star had disappeared, in order to return later, it was with a profound sigh of regret that the scientists had said: "Nothing yet; let's wait for the next phase."

But weeks, and then months, had gone by; six times already the Moon had shown her face illuminated by the sun, and six times she had plunged into celestial darkness again. No sign had been glimpsed that might offer hope that the travelers had reached the goal of their enterprise safe and sound. Discouragement had overtaken all hearts, and when the old astronomer had resigned himself to returning to the Observatoire de Paris, even Hélène no longer felt in her heart, where doubt was beginning to take root, the courage to stay on.

Since she had moved back into the little house in the Rue Cassini, she had worn the costume of a widow. If the man to whom she had pledged herself was no more, she would spend the time that remained for her to live in mourning; she would not belong to anyone.

Scarcely recovered from the surprise caused by the unexpected news from America, the young woman read the telegram addressed to her father over and over again, avidly.

"God be praised!" she said. "M, J, R—Marcel, Jacques, Rodilan: they're all alive. They've reached their goal; they'll be able to come back."

The preparations for departure did not take long. Soon, an express train was carrying the astronomer and his daughter to Le Havre. They disembarked from the Transatlantic Company's *Labrador* a week later in New York, and on 17 August

188- they arrived at the astronomical station of Long's Peak, where the greatest animation reigned.

Mathieu-Rollère obtained a long explanation of the conditions in which the observation of 28 July, which had caused such a stir in the scientific world, had been obtained.

"I was at my observation post," Burnett told him. "The big telescope was aimed at the Moon, and I was observing the part in shadow when an unusual gleam attracted my attention. I couldn't make out its nature and disposition very clearly at first, and in order to be able to define it more clearly I adapted a lens of greater magnification to the ocular. Then I seemed to make out a kind of irregular streak, whose contours were vague and sometimes seemed to be interrupted. I didn't hesitate to employ the greatest magnification at my disposal. This time the image appeared clear and precise; they were neatly-drawn straight lines, forming angles of which, at first glance, I couldn't take account. It vaguely resembled a geometric figure; one might have thought it two parallel lines cut by secants.

"I sought in vain for a explanation of the phenomenon, when an idea suddenly crossed my mind 'It's an M!' I exclaimed. 'It's the engineer Marcel who's signaling his presence.' My emotion was so intense that my vision was disturbed, and for a few seconds it was impossible for me to make out anything.

"At that moment I was alone. Beside myself, I quit the ocular of the telescope and went down into the observatory. My face was so distraught that my colleagues hastened around me, asking me anxiously what had happened. It was a few moments before I could reply; then I said: 'If my eyes aren't deceiving me, I've just had proof that the Columbiad's voyagers are alive on the Moon. Come on, see for yourselves whether or not I'm mistaken.'

"Everyone ran, climbing the ladder that led to the telescope with the same urgency. The first to arrive had scarcely fixed his eye to the ocular than he cried: 'I can distinctly see an M!' Everyone made the same observation in his turn. So, I hadn't been the victim of an illusion; my eyes had really seen it; it really was our friends giving us news. Another surprise awaited us. While the last one was looking in his turn we heard him exclaim: 'I can no longer see anything—it's disappeared.'

"For an hour nothing appeared on the dark part of the Moon, and we were about to go back downstairs to discuss the miraculous event when I took one last look n the ocular. Imagine my astonishment on perceiving a new letter: the letter J. This time, it was the first letter of the name Jacques. If any doubt had remained about the identity of those who were corresponding with us in that manner, that second apparition would have dispelled it completely. We resolved to remain at our post all night.

"We saw the letter R succeed the first two; then the others reappeared in their turn, and we established that each of them remained visible for an hour, and an hour separated it from the next one. Everything was calculated with mathematical precision to produce certain impressions and avoid any confusion.

"We continued the observations for the ten nights that followed, and always, in that region of the Moon, which remained plunged in shadow, we saw the same signs with the same intensity of light."

Mathieu-Rollère had listened to that story with visible satisfaction. He rubbed his hands together vigorously and murmured in a low voice: "Oh, the brave fellows! What a triumph for science and for France!"

When Burnett had finished speaking, the old astronomer stood up and, striding back and forth resolutely, said: "What a pity that I wasn't here to receive the first message from our friends personally. Now we'll have to wait for another two weeks before we can recommence our observations." Then, shaking the hand of the director of Long's Peak Observatory energetically, he said to him effusively: "It's to you, my dear colleague, to your perseverance, that we owe this important observation, whose consequences, I can already foresee, will be incalculable."

"It's also, and primarily," said Burnett modestly, "to the admirable instrument at our disposal that we owe this magnificent result."

It will be remembered, in fact, that the Rocky Mountain telescope had been specially constructed in order to be able to distinguish objects having a dimension of nine feet—which is to say, equal to that of the shell—on the lunar surface. There was, therefore, nothing astonishing about the fact that the luminous lines, measured by the American astronomer's micrometer as 300 feet long, should appear distinctly in the instrument's field.

Mathieu-Rollère's daughter had listened to the conversation, and her heart had blossomed tenderly at the good news. When the sign representing her fiancé's name had been mentioned her face had been tinted vividly red, and a serene confidence had animated her gaze. The future now appeared to her illuminated by a ray of hope; she had been right not to doubt.

The days that separated the astronomers from the next observation were fruitfully employed. As they were already sure of not being mistaken, they devoted themselves to thinking of means by which they could let the three voyagers know that their signals had been perceived and understood. It was necessary, in fact, not to leave them in uncertainty for a long time; it was not known how they had succeeded in producing the signals, or whether the resources at their disposal permitted them to renew them frequently.

In order to have a specialist on hand, they had hastily summoned the engineer Georges Dumesnil, the friend of Marcel's who, after having triggered the electric spark in the depths of the Columbiad, had remained on the site to guard the installation and see to the maintenance of all the machinery. The telegram sent from the Long's Peak Observatory had not surprised him overmuch; Marcel had infected him with his masculine confidence. Without knowing anything about the conditions of lunar humankind, he was firmly convinced that

131

the Earth's satellite was inhabited, and expected every day to learn that the audacious explorers had succeeded in their enterprise.

A kind of council was held to discuss the surest and quickest means of responding to the signals whose return was impatiently awaited. Dumesnil put forward a plan whose ingenious simplicity rallied all support. It was a matter of choosing, in the desert region of southern Algeria, an open plain in which a kind of network could be laid out, a hundred meters square, divided like the canvas of a tapestry into one meter squares. At the center of each square a powerful electric light would be placed, each one connected by wires to a commutator permitting it to be switched on and off instantaneously. On a network thus disposed, it would be easy, with the aid of the lights, to spell out the various letters of the alphabet.

"I've drawn up a plan of a kind of keyboard," the engineer continued," each of whose twenty-five keys marks one letter, and which will permit the lights depicting the letter one wants to produce to be switched on at will. One can form words and phrases in that fashion quite easily.

"It's evident that in making the signals that you've perceived, our friends, who know the power of your telescope, have calculated the luminous intensity of the signals in such a way as to be clearly perceived by the instrument. We have to assume that they too have optical instruments at their disposal sufficiently powerful to be able to distinguish on the Earth signals of the same intensity as those they've sent to us. In any case, we ought, for the sake of prudence, to exaggerate the dimensions of our luminous letters and establish our signals in a country where the limpidity of the atmosphere is as complete as possible."

"It's doubtless for that reason," said Mathieu-Rollère, "that you've chosen Algeria to set up your electrical network."

"Precisely," the engineer replied. "It's the purity and transparency of the air in that region that initially attracted my attention to it. Then again, I won't hide the fact that it seemed just to me, since the idea came from a Frenchman, that the experiment should remain completely French." He nodded to the American astronomers. "I hope that your honorable collaborators won't think that pretention excessive. The glory will always remain to them of having been the first to perceive the signals sent from the Moon. Without the Long's Peak telescope, nothing would have been possible."

"Oh, our part is very slight," replied Burnett. "The principal glory reverts, in reality, to the great Barbicane, who was the first to think of the possibility of a voyage to the Moon, constructed the Columbiad and audaciously launched into space with unprecedented confidence, and would have succeeded in his enterprise if forces impossible to avoid hadn't deflected him from his route."

At these words, pronounced with a legitimate pride, everyone nodded their heads in assent.

"But I've thought of something else," Dumesnil went on. "Before we can establish our alphabetical network a certain amount of time will necessarily go by. First, we need to obtain the authorization of the French government."

"Oh, that won't take long," Mathieu-Rollère put in. "I have influential friends at the Ministry, and anyway, the question that might have held us back—that of the expense—won't be an obstacle, because we have disposable funds at the Observatory."

"Good," said the engineer. "But to install our network in the middle of the desert, forty kilometers south of Biskra, we'll need to transport everything on the backs of humans or camels, unless we can set up a Decauville railway—which would be infinitely more practical."

"We'll set one up," affirmed Mathieu-Rollère, who now had no more doubt about anything.

"Perfect—but we'll need steam engines, and thus considerable provisions of fuel, numerous powerful dynamo-electric machines, ten thousand large arc-lamps, each one equipped with a parabolic reflector, and kilometers of wire. That's not all; it will be necessary to shelter all that; it will be necessary to lodge, feed and supply all the personnel necessary for the permanent functioning of the signaling system, because you can assume that once regular communications are established, they won't stop."

"Undoubtedly. All that can be done."

"Yes, but it will take time. I'll get back to my idea. Don't you think it would be useful to let our friends know as soon as possible that their signals have been seen? If we have to take several months—and I don't see any alternative—before giving them and sign of life, isn't there a danger that they'll become discouraged and renounce their attempts?"

"Perhaps you're right—but what can we do?"

"Well, this: we can install a powerful system here—1,500 lamps, for example—that we can switch on at an opportune moment and then switch off, in order to light it up again at regular intervals. Obviously, they'll have aimed the instruments available to them at North America, where they know that the only telescope capable of distinguishing their signals is located. They'll see the luminous point; they'll understand that we've seen them, and they'll wait patiently for us to organize a means of correspondence analogous to theirs."

"Bravo!" exclaimed Burnett. "I'll take charge of all that."

That same day, they telegraphed New York, and a fortnight later, fifteen hundred electric lamps combined in an immense array were ready to function. Everything had been foreseen and arranged, and they waited impatiently for the next lunar phase.

On 26 August the Moon was approaching its first quarter, and the concordance of lunar and terrestrial nights rendered observations easy.

The telescope was aimed at the night star, and each of the observers took turns anxiously interrogating the mirror in which the satellite was reflected. They succeeded one another at the ocular in vain, but nothing appeared on the dark surface.

During the days that followed, the ardent observation continued, passionately. At first, they were not overly surprised not to see anything. Mathieu-Rollère had, in fact, explained that the moment when the illuminated lunar crescent appears is also the one when the Earth, being full in relation to its satellite, sends it the greatest quantity of reflected light. In consequence, on the dark portion of the Moon, there is a reflection that astronomers call "ashen light." It is not until the approach of the first quarter that that reflection disappears, the Earth, then in its final quarter, no longer sending half as much light.

As soon as the part of the Moon where the first signals had appeared was plunged into veritable shadow, the powerful light-source prepared by Dumesnil was illuminated like a star twinkling in the depth of the darkness. The luminous jets, cleaving the night with their dazzling light, lit up the entire region, and within a radius of fifty leagues the surprised inhabitants thought it was some astonishing aurora borealis. There was no doubt that the gigantic beam, traversing the terrestrial atmosphere, would carry all the way to the satellite the signal that the observers of Long's Peak assumed to be anxiously awaited.

For an hour the torrent of light traversed space, and when it was extinguished, Mathieu-Rollère already had his eye glued to the ocular, interrogating the dark part of the lunar surface.

He remained there, attentive and breathless, for an hour, but he did not see anything.

"Let's start again," he said.

And all night long, at hourly intervals, the 1,500 lamps were switched on again, transmitting their futile appeal through the atmosphere. There was no response.

"Could you have been mistaken?" murmured Mathieu-Rollère, addressing Burnett.

"No, no—a thousand times no," the astronomer replied, with a vehemence that contrasted with his habitual phlegm. "I'm as sure of my eyes as my instrument—and all my collaborators saw what I saw."

"Well," said Mathieu-Rollère, "we'll try again tomorrow and the following nights. We don't know what's happening up there, but we must suppose that our friends are awaiting our signal with an impatience equal to ours, and that they'll respond to it as soon as they can."

But the nights went by, and nothing appeared on the surface of the satellite. The Moon became full again without any manifestation confirming the hopes of the observers. When that negative result was known in Europe, all those who had greeted the American astronomer's telegram with incredulity were noisily triumphant.

For some, Burnett had been the victim of an optical illusion; for others, the famous dispatch had been nothing but a gigantic hoax designed to trick the old world. Only the director of the Observatoire de Nice, the eminent Perrotin,[16] did not share in his colleague's jubilation. Without having been able to define the luminous signals that had been produced distinctly, he had been able to determine their regular intermittence, and had seen enough to convince him that they were indeed the effect of an intelligent and reflective will. He too had observed the Moon attentively during its recent phases, expecting the reappearance of the phenomena, and could not understand why they had not been manifest again.

For him, as for the American astronomers, it was a troubling and redoubtable mystery.

---

[16] The Observatoire de Nice, founded by the banker Raphael Bischoffheim (the philanthropist whom Marcel mentioned, without naming him, when first explaining his plan to Jacques) began operations in 1880, when Henri Perrotin was appointed as its director.

XVI. Study and Research

Since the day when they had been solemnly received by the supreme magistrate of lunar humankind, a new existence had commenced for Marcel, Jacques and Lord Rodilan. Having become, in a sense, citizens of that new fatherland, they had undertaken, under the direction of their friend Rugel, a profound study of the mores and institutions regulating the society that as so different from ours.

In perfect possession of the language, of which they now had a thorough knowledge, they were able to converse with everyone they met, and to see and judge things for themselves. In addition, their renown had penetrated all the inhabited regions of the Moon; thanks to the rapid means of communication, the ceremony of their reception, the speeches that had been exchanged, and the hopes to which their fortunate arrival had given birth, were known everywhere. So, wherever they went they were welcomed with a benevolent enthusiasm; everyone was delighted to receive them and to contribute to their education.

For them, everything was new and everything was to be studied.

They shared out the task in accordance with their aptitudes.

Marcel had the right to the extensive domain of the sciences and their applications; that of physiology, medicine and the natural sciences belonged to Jacques, which offered him an infinite field of observations. Lord Rodilan had reserved for himself the study of the political institutions and history of the unexplored world.

Profoundly versed in the study of the sciences to which he had devoted his life, and endowed with a rare faculty of understanding, Marcel had soon run the gamut of the new and bold applications ventured by the genius of the scientists of the lunar world. Rugel and a few other elite minds, who had quickly placed themselves at his disposal, were amazed by the facility with which he got to grips with the most arduous problems and, in a sense, divined their solutions as soon as he was provided with a demonstration. He often paused before one of the simple but powerful machines that carried out operations of force or speed, thought about it for a moment or two, and soon discovered the principle of the mechanism, and gave the relevant formula; those who had taken responsibility for his initiation looked at him with approving smiles.

The optical instruments applied to astronomy attracted his particular attention; astronomy was his passion. In libraries and museums, which he had visited carefully, he had seen models of telescopes whose proportions seemed to him to be colossal. He had often wondered how the inhabitants of the Moon, enclosed by a granite vault, were able to observe celestial space, and one day he interrogated Rugel on that subject.

The latter replied, smiling: "Patience, friend; we'll show you our observatory, which will astonish you, I'm sure; leave me the pleasure of reserving that surprise for you."

Among the numerous inventions that entered into everyday life, one of those that charmed Marcel the most was undoubtedly the transmission over distance of sensible speaking images. The physicists of the Moon had solved the problem of simultaneously transmitting the image of a living person, the movements that he carried out and the words and the words that he pronounced. The same electric wire served as a vehicle for luminous waves and sonic waves.

One could thus witness the strange spectacle of a person sitting before a screen on which the person with which he was in communication suddenly appeared; he could see him, hear him and converse with him just as in a face-to-face conversation, and each of the interlocutors thus had the person with whom he was conversing in front of him.

For that superior humankind, subject to fewer needs than terrestrial humankind, the range of industrial applications that we demand from science seemed rather restricted. Their intellectual activity and ardor for speculative research had not been diminished. All the problems that our scientists have glimpsed and which, at the limits of modern science, excite the spirit of investigation or exalt the imagination of a few precursors, had been tackled and solved by them. A long time ago they had found the electric motor for which our physicists are still searching, and which, developing a great deal of force within a small volume, obtained an applicable power that our rudimentary trials are far from attaining.

After having passed, like us, in aeronautical matters, via the theory of balloons founded on the lighter than air doctrine, they had not taken long to recognize its radical impotence. The observation of the flight of birds had rapidly led them to the adoption of the opposite principle, that of heavier than air flight, and with the motor at their disposal, they had soon been able to construct the light and resistant aerial craft that we have already mentioned, which had attracted the admiration of the representatives of a less advanced world.

In a purely scientific interest, without even thinking about practical applications of which they had no need, they had extracted the most mysterious secrets of nature.

The liquefaction and solidification of gases had been familiar to them for a long time, and Marcel was able to contemplate in their laboratories, maintained under formidable pressures, the various gases contained in their atmosphere.

They had discovered a long time ago—and it was not the least of Marcel's astonishments—the transformation of luminous waves into sonic waves for which our scientists are still searching, their attempts so far having been fruitless. They were thus able to collect the music of the spheres rotating in space and hear the mysterious concert of infinity that Pythagoras had defined and whose melodious effects Cicero, by a kind of prophetic intuition, had described.[17]

---

[17] Author's note: "Scipio Emilian recounts that he was, in a dream, lifted into the heavens by the soul of his friend Scipio Africanus: 'What is that sound,' I said to him, 'so powerful and harmonious, that fills my ears.'

Delicate and special electrical apparatus disposed on the surface of the Moon received in various notes the sonorous impression produced by each of the heavenly bodies of our planetary system, and those amplified sounds combined in an inexpressible harmony.

In the domain of all the sciences that proceed from reasoning and observation and in which calculation plays a role, Marcel observed the same progress, the same bold and profound insights. There was enough therein to save all the institutes of terrestrial humanity several centuries.

'It is the sound that results from the course and movement of the stars themselves," he told me, "which rotate in unequal times but whose variety is fixed by an immutable law, and which, mingling their low and high notes, form in their ensemble a melodious concert. For not only is it impossible that such vast movement should continue in silence, but, by a natural law, the outermost elements produce a low note on one side and a high note on the other. Whereas the highest of all, the celestial zone of stars whose revolution is more rapid, moves with a high, sharp note, this one of the moon, because it is the lowest, produces the deepest tone of all, for the earth, remaining motionless, is firmly located at the center of the universe. The revolutions of those eight spheres, two of which have the same force, produce seven sounds with distinct intervals, and that is the mystic bond of all things in the universe. By imitating this with stringed instruments and melodies, learned men have opened the way back to this place for themselves, like other men of noble nature who have followed god-like aims in their human life. But human ears overpowered by the sound have become deaf, and you have no duller sense than hearing.... The sound of the whole universe revolving at the highest speed is so awful that the ears of men cannot bear it, just as you are unable to look directly at the sun, being overpowered by the force of its rays.' Cicero *Republic*, Book VI: Scipio's Dream."

Similar surprises were reserved for Jacques in the fields of study attributed to him. He was unable, from the outset, to avoid being struck by the physiological conditions of those beings, so similar to us in many respects, but so different with respect to one capital point. The inhabitants of the Moon were not constrained by the most imperious of our needs, that of nourishment. Among them, in consequence, there was no digestive tract—no esophagus, no stomach and no intestines.

It was in the gaseous state that elements indispensable to life—oxygen, carbon, nitrogen and hydrogen—penetrated into their organism and, drawn into general circulation, went to renew the tissues.

Oxygen they took directly from the air by respiration; their lungs, much more developed than ours, presented a larger surface area capable of absorbing a greater quantity of the vivifying gas. Carbon and nitrogen were assimilated by a veritable chemical decomposition of the carbonic acid and ammoniac gases in suspension in the atmosphere. To that effect, the digestive tract and its annexes had been replaced in them by an ensemble of special mucus-lined organs of extreme delicacy, which, under the influence of the nervous system, separated the elements of those gases almost as the green parts of plants do under the influence of solar light, decomposing the carbonic acid and retaining the carbon.

The large quantity of ammoniac gas existing in the air came from the decomposition of animal bodies. In that world, in fact, where no life was nourished on any other life, maintained as it is by gaseous elements, the existence of the bodies of animate beings was not abridged by the necessity of furnishing other living beings with solid aliments. They all went to the term of their vital evolution; nature operated its work of dissolution and these that death had struck rapidly returned to the living the elements that the latter assimilated in their turn in a perpetual exchange.

How, finally, was hydrogen found in a free state in the air? It was because the of immense caves was eminently hydrated, and the powerful electric currents that traversed it incessantly, by decomposing the water vapor therein, enriched the air with that gas, so light that it penetrated all partitions. Thus was explained the constant absorption and assimilation of hydrogen by the tissues of the human body in the lunar world.[18]

In that physiological life of a superior order, no impure and unassimilable element, like those that nutrition brings to our organs, entered into their economy to be expelled subsequently. It was not necessary for their blood, like ours, to dispose of coarse elements by means of a special path. A particular organ, a kind of gland situated above the respiratory apparatus, filtered the blood, as it were, eliminating the unnecessary molecules that had become harmful. It filled a role analogous to that of the kidney, with the essential difference that the residues of that elimination were expelled in a gaseous state, as much by expiration as by evaporation through the epidermis.

As their mode of nutrition did not imply any work of mastication, their teeth might have appeared unnecessary. They had them nevertheless, but the ones furnishing their mouths did not play the same role as ours. Smaller and not as dense, they merely served to regulate the passage of air during speech and to produce in association with the movement of the tongue and lips the articulations of pronunciation. Ivory white, they were never deteriorated by any the causes that degrade and destroy them on Earth, their brightness contrasting with the bright red of the gums, where they were set like pearls in a jewel-case.

---

[18] It is not obvious why the author thinks that hydrogen needs to be absorbed by his modified organisms in the pure state rather than in combination in water vapor, while nitrogen needs to be combined with hydrogen in ammonia. His seeming unawareness of the toxicity of ammonia (at least to visitors from Earth) and the necessity of small quantities of many other elements in composing living flesh is also odd.

In that less complex organism, the function of the liver, instead of being double, as in us, was simple. There was, in fact, no need for any secretion of bile where there was no alimentation or digestion, but the liver conserved its activity of producing the glycogen that gives birth to glucose, the role of which is so important in respiration and the renovation of tissues. The vital mechanism, in that hyperoxygenated environment, was much more energetic, so physical development was more rapid than on Earth and ten of our years sufficed for human beings to reach adulthood. Those physiological conditions maintained a constant vigor, a youth that was prolonged until a very advanced age and a permanent equilibrium of all the concurrent elements of life.

One did not encounter among them temperaments disequilibrated by the predominance either of the nervous system, the lymph or the blood. One did not find any neuropathic individuals, anemic individuals with pale and wan complexions who only give the appearances of life, or sanguinary and plethoric natures irremediably doomed to congestion or apoplexy. The field of disease was, in consequence, restricted, and only presented rare complications: a few irritations of the respiratory tracts, which were easily remedies by ingenious doses of respirable air; occasional engorgements or inflammations of the abdominal organs; and cephalgias caused by an excessive expenditure of muscular force or cerebral tension composed their entire pathology.

In those superior beings, therapeutic treatments were very simple. As respiration was for them the unique mode of maintaining life, it was by respiration that all curative agents were transmitted to the organism. Their profound knowledge of chemistry and the means they possessed of acting on various substances permitted them to render such agents into the gaseous state easily and administer them to patients by way of inhalation.

For a long time, too, they had been in possession of methods of hypodermic injection, to which they had recourse in particularly serious cases, or when it was a matter of rapidly putting certain energetic substances into circulation, prompt and decisive in their action.

As for the traumatic effects that might result from the accidents inherent in an active and laborious life, especially in the class of Diemides, the science of surgery usually reckoned with them easily. The list of anesthetics and antiseptics, much more complete than ours, furnished them with the means of carrying out the most delicate operations in the greatest security, without having to fear the deadly consequences that often render them so redoubtable among us.

Everything, in any case, was favorable to them: the air they breathed, supercharged with ozone; a milieu essentially hostile to morbid germs; and, most of all, the simplicity of their organism, which rendered the diffusion of medicament substances easy and devoid of peril.

One day, when Jacques was telling his friends about the singularities that his observations had revealed to him concerning the physiological constitution of the inhabitants of the Moon, Lord Rodilan interrupted him by exclaiming: "Ah, this is a land where the damned sons of Aesculapius are sure of never making a fortune!"

"Do you have something against those unfortunate physicians, then, my dear friend, who so often risk their lives to snatch their fellows from the jaws of death?" asked Jacques.

"Yes, I know, there are some, like you, who are worthy fellows, always ready to soothe the poor world—but I'm talking about those charlatans who brag about being princes of science and have no aim but to sell at fantastic process the slightest words disdainfully emitted by their sibylline lips."

"You've been skinned, then, by some of my savant colleagues?"

"Oh yes, and I still remember it. For some time I was racked by stomach pains, with regard to which I consulted a number of physicians, each one with more diplomas than the rest. They competed in drugging me and sending me to the most fantastic bathing stations—and of course, all those peregrinations only profited those who had advised me to go, for everyone knows that the gentlemen in question don't disdain to accept a more or less reasonable commission of each patient they send to fashionable establishments.

"In brief, they ended up sending me to a celebrated specialist who was said to work miracles in such cases. He lived in London; I was then in Calcutta. I made the voyage especially, so keen was I to digest my food like anyone else. Scarcely had I arrived than I went to see him. I went into a splendid house that bore more resemblance to a palace than the abode of a scientist..."

"Pardon me," said Jacques, smiling, "but it was a matter of a prince of science."

"Indeed—but the cage was worth more than the bird. After having waited for a long time—a very long time—in a sumptuously decorated drawing room heaped with artistic masterpieces and already full of a crowd of devotees awaiting the oracle of their destiny, I was introduced into the sanctuary in my turn. I found myself in the presence of a grand old man with a receding hairline and a red face framed by long white side-whiskers. His cold eyes seemed to be looking into your soul, and perhaps into the depths of your purse; his thin lips could never have opened in a benevolent smile; the first impression he made was antipathetic. With a grave gesture he indicated a chair placed opposite the raised armchair into which he fell himself, looking down at me from a great height.

"I studied him curiously, for I've never let myself be taken in by the solemn expressions of those clowns who always seem to be pontificating and treating as mere livestock the unfortunates whose imprudence puts them within range of their claws. Leaning back in his chair and crossing his legs while he gazed with profound attention at the fingernails of his left hand, he uttered the words: "I'm listening, Milord.'

"I explained my case, and enumerated the various tortures to which those of his colleagues I'd consulted had submitted me. He listened to me, sometimes nodding his head, and limited himself, when I was about to pause, to saying: 'Go on.'

"I arrived at the nomenclature of the thermal baths I'd tried and told him, without attaching any particular importance to it, that the use of Vichy water seemed to have procured me some relief. That was a revelation. 'Ah!' he cried. 'Vichy did you good. Well, Milord, go back to Vichy!' He stood up. Amazed, I did likewise. The consultation was over. He added, obligingly: 'That's three pounds.'"

Marcel laughed frankly.

"You've had the bad luck," said Jacques, "to happen upon one of those fakers who exploit public credulity in the name of medicine. But all that results in useful information. If your stomach was tormenting you, it was because it had excellent reasons to do so. One knows that dinners as delicate as they're lavish are routine in diplomatic society, and, without wishing to offend you, you'd abused them somewhat. Since you've been reduced to a regime that has the precious advantage of rendering any excess impossible, your stomach has left you perfectly tranquil."

"That's possible," Lord Rodilan replied, "but at the risk of a few cramps, I wouldn't be sorry to find myself sitting at a table in the Yacht Club."

By means of attentive study of the physiological structure of the members of the lunar human race, Jacques eventually observed a particularity that had escaped his notice at first, and which explained, to some degree, their moral superiority.

Freed from the cares of nourishment, they had no need of a sense of taste, and nature, which does nothing unnecessary, had not endowed them with one. Among them, the papillae of the tongue and palate did not receive any impression of various savors, but fulfilled another function. Endowed with a sensibility whose delicacy we can hardly imagine, they formed a kind of electric emission apparatus, and the movements elaborated in the brain that their will imposed on that organ produced waves, which, although very weak, were transmitted to other individuals by means of a receptive organ of equal sensitivity.[19] That organ was located in the ear, where a second membrane, analogous to the tympanum but infinitely more delicate, vibrated in its turn and conveyed the impression to the brain.

Thanks to that sense, with the aid of were translated ungraspable states of mind that escape our observation, thoughts, in being transmitted from one person to another, expressed idea, sentiments and determinations sincerely, and without it being possible to dissimulate them. That sense functioned at the same time as speech.

In the same way that, among us, several senses exercised simultaneously collaborate in the complete expression of thought or sentiment—the voice in translating ideas; the eyes, the movements of the face and sometimes even gestures completing the manifestation—in the individuals that Jacques was studying, that unknown sense made sincerity the very law of nature.

Beings who could not dissimulate any of their thoughts or sentiments had never been able to conceive of the idea of lying. There was, in consequence, no scope among them for hypocrisy of fraud. In consequence, there was no deceit, no secret machinations and no intrigues to the profit of unavowed ambitions. Being unable to hide anything, they never thought of hatching plots, planning maneuvers or setting traps. It was impossible to have one thing on the lips and another in the heart. In sum, among the fortunate inhabitants of the Moon, diplomatic science, which is more often than not a science of artifice and lies, was absolutely unknown.

Jacques had also wondered how, during the many centuries that lunar humankind had been living in those new conditions, the increase of population, if it was subject to the same

---

[19] As the author has no knowledge of Hertzian waves, this hypothetical speculation is more enterprising that it would have seemed by the time the novel was published, and it is a pity that he did not see fit to imagine any technological extrapolations of the hypothesis.

principles as ours, had not already filled the limited space it inhabited to excess. He had soon realized, however, that births, submissive to the same physiological conditions as on Earth, escaped the law of progression. Nature, in its foresight, had sagely enclosed the development of life, for the human race as for animal species, within inviolable limits. It was content to replace losses; unions were far from being as fecund as among us, and the number of births never exceeded that of deaths.

Thanks to the vigor of their constitution, the inhabitants of the Moon lived for a long time, beyond the limits we know. They frequently attained a hundred and twenty-five or a hundred and thirty of our years. And in those robust natures, of which no morbid cause damaged the functioning, bodily strength and the faculties of intelligence were conserved without noticeable deterioration into the most advanced age.

The period of weakening that preceded death was relatively short. Organic activity decreased first, leaving almost intact what physiologists call the "life relationship." An old man, whose physical strength gradually abandoned him and in whom the nutritive function—which is to say, respiration—diminished, retained his clarity of mind and the vivacity of his sentiments until the end. Resigned, thanks to a sophisticated philosophy to which he owed the incontestable demonstration of a future life, he was slowly extinguished in the midst of his family, addressing his final advice to them, and the last words he pronounced embodied not a desperate adieu but an *au revoir* full of promise and hope.

In that sage conclusion, similar to the slumber of someone going to sleep on a completed task, there was nothing lugubrious and sinister, as among us. One never saw the repulsive spectacle of those decompositions that seem to anticipate the tomb, those deplorable collapses of an intelligence that appears to be extinguishing in fragments and leaving nothing in the hands of those surrounding an old man but a miserable rag retaining nothing human but the form.

XVII. Letters and Arts

A society whose intellectual and moral culture was so highly developed could not remain inferior in the domain of the arts. All of them, those manifest in time as well as in space, had been assiduously cultivated there for many centuries, and served to maintain the love of the beautiful and the sentiment of virtue.

In the first rank was literature.

All genres were represented there, from lyric poetry, whose generous flights rose up toward God in sublime verses, to amiable and charming tales, in which fantasy mingled the gracious creations of a disciplined imagination—which never departed from respect for oneself or others—with the gravest conceptions of reason. The poets celebrated in their hymns the grandeur of the Sovereign Spirit, the marvelous spectacles of nature, the revolutions of the worlds in space, and the leaps of the soul toward infinity—everything that might draw humans out of their inferior condition and reveal within them the sensation of their immortal destiny.

Admirable epic poems, more beautiful than our *Iliad*s and *Odyssey*s, inspired by an ardent love of humankind, retraced the exploits of ancient times for the education of new ages. There was nothing therein of the cold and incoherent mythology in which the inhabitants of Earth, adoring themselves, divine their worst passions and their most reprehensible actions. Heroes with pure souls passed through them, tall and strong, having in view not the satisfaction of gross desires of culpable ambitions, but the welfare of their fellows. They struggled against natural forces in order to liberate other humans from that servitude and joyfully giving their lives, if that was the result, for those for whom they were making the sacrifice, in order to accomplish progress and increase the sum of happiness. It was in past ages, in the times when lunar humankind had lived on the surface of the satellite, when it too had been obliged, by dint of courage and perseverance, to win its independence and advanced civilization from a hostile nature, that the divine singers found those noble figures for whom respect imposed universal admiration.

One did not encounter, in that purified literature, anything similar to our dramatic poetry. Among us, in fact, tragedy only puts to work the most disorderly passions. If a flash of grandeur and heroic devotion occasionally traverses that dark night, one only perceives by its light a confused swarm of ardent hatreds, frantic jealousies and unrestrained ambitions; our tragic stage is always streaming with blood and tears.

Comedy, such as we can conceive it, does not show our sad humankind in a more favorable light. That, it must be said, is because it is merely the excessively faithful reproduction of what we really are. If the catastrophes with which the characters are mixed up are less cruel and less frightening, they are nevertheless more refined and more subtle in their perfidy. One finds nothing there but knavery and duplicity, unhealthy intrigues in which appeal is made to the vilest passions, and the basest kinds of avarice are displayed. Libidinous old men who are the victims of tricksters, adulterous and coquettish women, young women whose false innocence hides a precocious depravity, thieving valets, procurers of every sort—those are the characters usually agitating in a plot whose complexity and confusion are often the sole merit. And the public guffaws and admirers, as if delighted by the spectacle of its own turpitudes.

Authors doubtless flatter themselves that they are correcting mores by means of laughter, but that laughter only underlines the immorality of their conceptions, familiarizing the spectators with their miseries and rendering them less odious and more acceptable by familiarization.

Although, among those beings of a higher moral level, inaccessible to our weaknesses, once could not imagine analogues of our tragic or comic poems, they had not renounced seductive charms and scenic representations in consequence. At the most solemn festivals, the assembled crowds were given spectacle of nature to elevate souls and maintain a cult of gratitude to those who had been the benefactors of humankind. As there was in those ceremonies a character simultaneously religious and patriotic, it was an honor to figure in them and play a role therein, so the actors, if one can give that name to those who were invested with that highly prized mission, were recruited from among the noblest and most intelligent, those who possessed to a high degree the rarest qualities of intellect and imagination.

It was not a matter, in fact, of reciting, with a more or less perfect memory and a mime more or less adapted to the character of a fictitious individual, the work of a poet traced in advance and invariable in its expression. A theme was given— some great act of devotion, one of those glorious enterprises that had contributed to the emancipation of humankind, to augment the sum of its happiness and prosperity—only the broad outlines being traced. Each of those who were to figure in the drama chose his role, the best adapted to his own nature and sentiments. He then identified with the character he was to represent, penetrating profoundly into his intimate personality, in such a way as to think, feel and act like him. When he had mastered the part, he abandoned himself on the stage to his own inspiration. As the incidents of the action unfolded, he experienced all the sensations involved in those various situations; he spoke in accordance with sentiments truly felt. It was his own personality that was in play, and the spectators had before their eyes not a vain and cold illusion but life in all its reality, in everything that it possesses of the most noble and the most generous.

The manifestations of the musical art were also concurrent, among the inhabitants of the Moon, with the imposing grandeur of those solemnities. But there, as for the scenic art, works of absolute sincerity were required for people who could only be moved by the truth.

Thanks to the progress that had been made in the science of acoustics, they could obtain a contribution from all of nature, and give it a role of sorts in their artistic conceptions.

They had already taken note of the mysterious sound of the spheres that gravitate in the immensity. Similarly, they perceived and fixed the most fugitive of harmonies, the sound of waves that sometimes break softly on the shore and sometimes, under the action of the wind, crash with a deafening din, the murmur of streams running over plains, birdsong and the delicate rustle of the breeze in foliage.

On those themes, furnished to them by the environment in which they lived, inspired artists embroidered the most various creations of their fantasy. According to whether they were penetrated by joy or sadness, enthusiasm or melancholy, they adapted those rich and various motifs to their sentiments. They added the expression of their own passions, and they made a whole of it, in which it was impossible to distinguish what they owed to nature from what their creative genius had added.

Melodies resulted of an inexpressible charm, harmonious concerts whose softness cradled souls tenderly, revealed the noblest sentiments in hearts, and formed a marvelous accompaniment to the great dramatic scenes that unfurled before the eyes of the emotional spectators.

It was in the capital of the lunar world that these festivals were celebrated, which owed their magnificence not to the puerile or pretentious accumulation of vain ostentations, but to the delicate choice and grandeur of artistic conceptions of which they were the pretext and the occasion. Its inhabitants were not, moreover, the only ones to enjoy these magnificent spectacles. With the means that science had already vulgarized in that privileged world a long time ago, everything that was done and everything that was said on those grandiose stages was immediately transmitted to all the cities and the most remote villages. Those who were unable to go to the place where the government was seated had those imposing before their eyes, with the most scrupulous fidelity. They saw the actors, and they heard and perceived the sound of the instruments. Nothing was lost for them, and, on the days when the cult of the fatherland and virtue was exalted, the entire population of the Moon was united in a common surge of fervor and love.

Vast halls, expertly designed for viewing and acoustics, received the numerous spectators that the festivals attracted. On widely-spaced tiers, everyone was comfortably seated, and no one was inconvenienced, as in our narrow theaters where people are crammed into the point of asphyxiation, either by neighbors or by the comings and goings of egotistical or distracted individuals who have no scruple about disturbing twenty people to return to their seat. There was no lack of air or space, and furthermore, all the audience members, penetrated by the gravity of the performances, enjoyed the great scenes that unfurled before them with a meditative mind and an emotional heart.

As those who went to the solemnities in question did not do so to show themselves or to make an ostentatious display of jewels or garish costumes, but in order to abandon themselves to the noblest enjoyments of artistry, the architects who had constructed those vast edifices had taken care to leave the audiences in the shadows and project all the light on to the stage where the actors in the heroic or lyric dramas were moving. What was set before the eyes was life in all its reality and all its intensity.

Faithful to the traditions of the beautiful, which were transmitted without alteration from generation to generation, painters and sculptors inspired the noblest and purest sentiments. Nothing falsified their superior judgment, the worship of purified form and the sentiment of the ever-renewed beauties of nature. There was never anything therein of the paltry or the contorted, nothing pretentious or artificial, and above all nothing that might degrade souls and, under a false exterior of plastic beauty, give birth to the appetite of vile instincts and degrading acts.

The gymnasia in which, under the direction of respected masters, the disciples of the great art were formed, did not resound, as among us, with the noise of the quarrels of rival schools; there were no disputes there over form or color; no

153

one there bandied around such labels as "impressionist" or "symbolist." Only one form of art was known there: the one that combined in a sovereign expression the splendor of form and the nobility of idea.

Thanks to the greatly perfected means at their disposal, writers and composers were not enslaved by the necessity of noting down their thoughts painfully with the aid of slowly-drawn signs in which the movement and warmth of inspiration is often lot. Special kinds of apparatus seized, at the very moment of production, the words emerging from the poet's lips and the sounds that the musician drew from the instrument that gave his emotions a sensible form. And the work, forever fixed, thus appeared still utterly vibrant with the impulsions of the soul that had given them birth, in the splendor or grace of spontaneity.

Rich libraries filled with all the remarkable works left by previous ages, and the periodicals that recorded on a daily basis the incessant conquests of a science ever on the alert, furnished inexhaustible treasures to all. Everything that the progress of the art of typography, illustration and engraving had been able to realize was combined to place before the eyes of those who turned the pages of the vast collections the conquests that the genius of the ages had realized by dint of toil and perseverance.

The simplicity of methods, the clarity of demonstrations, the abundance of observed facts and the rigor of critical intelligence that presided over their classification rendered accessible to all minds the knowledge of problems that, among us, are the privilege of a few elite intelligences. And thanks to that scientific diffusion, those beings, so well endowed with regard to comprehension and reasoning, maintained an intellectual level that we can hardly imagine.

In that world, where everything was harmonious and simple, social organization was fixed and sheltered from all the revolutions that are excited on Earth by the ambition or fury of parties. Nor was what we call "current affairs" known there, so they enjoyed the inappreciable advantage of having no newspapers. In consequence, the ardent polemics in which unleashed private interests make a *tabula rasa* of public interests were unknown, as well as the injurious diatribes in which, to satisfy savage hatreds or base grudges, the most reputable men are vilified, vice and perfidy exalted, and honesty and virtue dragged through the mud.

Nor was there anything similar to the scandalous enterprises in which, under the pretext of serving general utility, a multitude whose avidity matches their stupidity is deceived, the worst passions are subject to speculation, individuals enrich themselves at the expense of others, and the sickening spectacle is provided of colossal fortunes founded on gambling and double-dealing, on the ruination of a host of victims.

While Marcel and Jacques studied the lunar world from different points of view, moving from one surprise to another, Lord Rodilan was not inactive. His philosophical mind had been forcefully struck by the simplicity of the mores and institutions that regulated that society of a superior order. His skepticism, maintained by the contradictions and incoherence that were encountered in the bosom of terrestrial humankind, had not held up before the harmonious reality of a numerous gathering of human beings living in perfect concord, with a minimum of laws and government that utopian dreamers had scarcely dared to glimpse.

He had given himself the task of studying in depth everything that concerned religion, mores, and political and civil institutions, and he intended to summarize the results of his research in a monograph, which, combined with the summaries made by Marcel and Jacques, would certainly constitute the most unexpected, most unusual and most interesting of treatises. What a marvel it would be for the scientific world of the Earth to receive that strange book one day, printed on the Moon, full of photographs, drawings and paintings—the masterpieces of lunar artists—representing human beings, animals, monuments and unknown landscapes!

How could such a work reach the cognizance of those for whom it was intended? The English diplomat did not worry about that, for the moment, but worked on it ardently.

His task, in any case, was easy.

The political institutions that he had undertaken to study were uncomplicated; there was no meddlesome authority jealous of its prerogatives, ever ready to measure its importance by the annoyances and difficulties caused to those it administrates. Bureaucratic tyranny was unknown, as were the vexations of paperwork and the odious inquisitions to which the poor humans of Earth are subjected, cleverly composed and disguised under the soft euphemisms of liberties and administrative guarantees.

There, one did not have before one's eyes the afflicting spectacle presented, among the Earthly peoples who claim to be the most civilized, by the organization of repressive justice. Disputes between individuals were rare and easy to settle, the equity and good faith of the contracting parties was amply sufficient to regulate them. As for crimes against persons or the public good, most often products of the bitter struggle for existence, they were completely unknown. Hence, there were no courts, no police, no jails and no executioners. No one had to fear perfidious denunciations, interested accusations, to tremble for himself or his loved ones, to dread the surprises of the law or the traps of chicanery.

Everyone lived openly, without having anything to hide, and hence nothing to fear.

XVIII. A Gigantic Ascent

While occupying themselves with their important research, however, the three voyagers had been obliged to worry
about a problem that was of the greatest importance for them:
that of ensuring their survival in an environment so different
from the one in which they had lived thus far. Undoubtedly,
the provisions with which they had taken care to equip themselves when they left the Earth—tinned food of every sort,
biscuits and various beverages—would be sufficient for quite
a long time, but in the six months that they had been living in
the lunar world they had already made large inroads, and
could see the time approaching, not without anxiety, when
their stock would be exhausted.

On the other hand, the phenomenon of living beings being nourished other than by the simple absorption of air, with
the aid of material elements, had intrigued the inhabitants of
the Moon. The three strangers had been the object of a study
that, without their profound sentiment of propriety, might have
become indiscreet. It will be remembered, however, that
among the documents contained in the shell was a recent and
complete atlas of anatomy. It had therefore been easy for the
scientists to take an exact account of the physiology of terrestrial humankind, and they too had thought about finding the
simplest and most effective means of supplying their guests
with the means of survival.

Marcel, who had examined the important question with
them, had manifested the desire to use for that purpose the
various seeds of cereals and legumes that he had brought from
Earth, and also to attempt the cultivation of fruit-producing
species, with which he was also provided. A fairly large area
had been set aside for that purpose. On Marcel's instructions,
the Diemides put at his disposal had manufactured agricultural
implements, and the three exiles from Earth were soon able to

contemplate a cultivated field reminiscent of their native planet.

There was one of them, however, who only raised a mediocre smile at the prospect of that vegetarian nourishment, and that was Lord Rodilan.

"Tins of corned beef, ham and game are all right," he said, in a pitiful tone, "although they can't compare to a large slice of bloody roast beef, but your cabbages and carrots—pooh! Sad fare. I'm not a rabbit, to live in that fashion, and I can't do it."

He often darted covetous glances at the lovely and graceful animals bounding in the plains, or the fish with glittering scales that moved like silver streaks through the clear water of the sea and the streams. He said that with a good hunting rifle or one of the improved fishing lines that were presently on display in the palace museum, he would soon be able to procure a tasty meal.

He had not been able to resist the temptation to mention it to Rugel, but the latter had responded, smiling, as if he understood the exigencies of that British stomach: "It's necessary, alas, for you to renounce that hope. Murder is unknown here; all beings live in complete security; life, the emanation of the omnipotence of the Sovereign Being, is sacred. The fact that in your own world, where sad necessity obliges you to feed on animate beings, you're led to imitate the example that nature itself provides, is understandable and excusable, but nothing can render such a crime against the order and harmony of our world admissible. Don't worry, though; our scientists have been thinking about you; they now know the elements indispensable to your existence; they have anticipated the possibility that the experiments attempted by our friend Marcel might not furnish you with everything you need, and they're studying the composition of an aliment that can replace the animal nourishment to which you're accustomed, in a much reduced volume."

The Englishman pulled a face and murmured to himself: "That's all well and good, but reeks damnably of pharmacy. We shall see."

It was not long, in fact, before he did see. A few days after that conversation, Jacques, who was spending almost all of his time with the lunar scientists in their laboratories, came back triumphantly and presented his two friends with a flask filed with a clear liquid, as transparent as pure water.

"Good God, what's that?" asked Marcel. "And why are you so cheerful?"

"My friend," said Jacques, "we're now assured of never having to regret the succulent meals whose memory still haunts our dear Rodilan."

"What!" said the Englishmen. "Are you claiming that your mixture can efficaciously replace Durham beef, Yorkshire mutton and Westphalian ham—the mere mention of which makes my mouth water?"

"Exactly, my dear chap. To begin with, what you call, profanely, a *mixture*, is the result of a marvelous combination in which are united, in scientifically determined proportions, the nitrogenous elements with which animal flesh furnishes us on Earth. There's enough in this little flask to nourish all three of us for several weeks, but if we were to make exclusive use of this aliment, we'd soon be victims of a superabundance of life and harmful congestions. Fortunately, the fields sown by Marcel will furnish us with a sufficient quantity of fresh nourishment. The elixir that I have the honor of presenting to you will be our meat."

"Pooh!" said the Englishmen. "I knew that it would all finish with drugs."

"Just taste it," said Jacques, laughing. "Pass judgment afterwards." And he poured a few drops of the precious nectar into a glass.

Lord Rodilan peered at the unknown liquid, sniffed it, and then, closing his eyes and pulling a face, like a child about to swallow medicine, he swiftly absorbed the contents of the glass. Collecting himself, he said: "One can't say that it's excellent, but, all things considered, it's not bad. I very much doubt, however, that it has what it takes to replace a steak!"

"Wait a few minutes," said Jacques, "And tell me what you think. Look at our friend Marcel—he's not making as much fuss."

In fact, scarcely half an hour had gone by when Lord Rodilan, completely sated, felt full of a new vigor, as if he had sat down at an abundantly served table.

The experiment was decisive; the new aliment was adopted with no further difficulty, and the three friends felt reassured against the fear of dying of hunger. It even seemed to them that the almost immaterial nourishment in question brought them a little closer, in their own eyes, to the superior condition of the inhabitants of the Moon. More than once, in fact, they had felt humiliated by the sad necessities imposed on them by terrestrial nature, and they thought that they had glimpsed expressions of surprise and pity in the gazes of the witnesses to their meals, so they frequently made provision to take their nourishment in private.

Since they had been living in the lunar world, Marcel, Jacques and Lord Rodilan had observed a great deal and learned a great deal. Nevertheless, Marcel had not forgotten the mysterious remarks that Rugel had made on the subject of the observatories from which the scientists of the Moon were able to follow the courses of the stars. He wondered how they were able to sound the depths of space from the depths of the gigantic cavern were they lived.

The granitic vault that imprisoned the humankind in question did not present any breach in its continuity; furthermore, even if some communication with the exterior had existed, he knew from his own experience that the atmospheric column did not extend as far as the surface of the satellite, and that the rarefied air soon became unbreathable. Several times he had reminded Rugel of his promise; the time was near when he was to be completely informed on the subject.

The profound studies to which he had devoted himself had not distracted Jacques from thinking about the woman he had left behind on Earth. He was in haste to let her know that he had emerged from the redoubtable enterprise alive. He often talked about that to Marcel, and his preoccupation had not escaped the sage Rugel, who, interrogating him affectionately, had had no difficulty discovering the cause of his sadness. The love, so noble and so pure, for which Jacques had not hesitated to risk his life, was one of the sentiments that the elevated soul of their new friend understood; he had encouraged Jacques benevolently not to despair. From a few remarks that he had allowed to escape, Jacques thought he had understood that people were investigating means of informing the inhabitants of the Earth of the safe arrival of the bold voyagers. It seemed to him to be taking a long time, though, and he was becoming impatient.

One day, Rugel appeared smiling. "I'm bringing you good news," he told them. "In a few minutes, if you wish, we can go to visit the observatory that I've already mentioned to you. The moment is propitious; the part of the Moon facing the Earth is now in shadow, and you'll see your homeland brightly lit.

"Finally!" said Marcel, with a surge of joy, shaking the hand that Rugel held out to him energetically.

"Thank you, friend," said Jacques, his face radiant with pleasure.

"All right!" said Lord Rodilan. "I'm going to see joyous England again. What a pity, friend Rugel, that we can't empty together, in her honor, the last bottle of champagne we have left."

"Empty it," said Rugel. "I'll be with you in heart, not only for England, but also for France—for the entire world that you have left behind."

The wine was soon sparkling in the glasses; cried of "Vive la France!" and "Hurrah for England!" were heard, and Rugel contemplated with a tender gaze the joy that he seemed to feel himself, and which, in spite of his impassive serenity, touched his heart.

In the meantime, an aeroscaph had come forward; it was an elegant and solid vehicle.

Marcel, who had familiarized himself with the mechanism of such craft some time before, took the tiller, and set a course for the point on the horizon that Rugel indicated. The apparatus rose upwards, cleaving through the air rapidly.

After a few hours, the interior sea that extended across the center of the immense cavern had been crossed, and they arrived at the foot of a colossal mountain of granite: a kind of sheer wall that seemed absolutely insurmountable. Between the foot of the mountain and the strand where the waves broke there was a small town, severe and tranquil in appearance. The people who lived there, in order to be close to the place where they usually worked, were members of the class of Meolicenes with a particular responsibility for astronomical observation. Their functions were highly prized in lunar society; they were the ones whose mission was to maintain a kind of communication between that subterranean humankind and the exterior universe. Without them, and their constant endeavors, the inhabitants of the Moon would have been completely estranged from what was happening in the sidereal world, as if enclosed in the darkness of an eternal prison.

Bulletins emerged from that scientific research center incessantly, identifying all manner of celestial phenomena as they were produced, thus maintaining among the highly intelligent people—who knew that the end of the world they inhabited was already marked within a space of time that could already be calculated—the desire to enter into communication with the neighboring humankind.

Rugel and his three companions were welcomed on arrival with the most benevolent cordiality. Although they had never been to that distant region, Marcel, Jacques and Lord Rodilan were sufficiently well-known. They renewed their acquaintance with some of the eminent people with whom they had already conversed in the capital, and all the rest were informed as to their endeavors. The room in which they were received was vast, and almost entirely decorated with sidereal maps, in great detail and the most perfect accuracy.

Marcel noticed, however, that there were no instruments of astronomical observation.

"Where is your observatory, then?" he said to Rugel. "It's not from here that you can study the sky!"

"Patience, friend," Rugel replied. "We'll get there."

One of the scientists surrounding them made a sign. A large door opened at the back of the room, giving access to an electrically-lighted corridor.

"Follow me," said Rugel.

The corridor led to a small room, circular in form, furnished with seats and divans. An electric lamp in the ceiling illuminated it with a soft and even light; save for the door by which they had entered there did not seem to be any trace of an opening.

"Sit down for a moment," said their guide, "and you'll be satisfied before long."

The three friends, surprised and passably intrigued, obeyed without further response.

"Our observatories," said Rugel, "will not offer you any surprises from the viewpoint of the instruments you're doubtless expecting to see. Given the drawings that you've shown us and the explanations you've provided, we've been able to ascertain that the theory on which your astronomical instruments are based consists of the laws of reflection and reflection of luminous rays. Those laws are general; only their applications can vary in accordance with different environments. Our eyes are like yours, the phenomenon of vision occurs in the same way among us as among you; all the optical apparatus that has the objective of extending the field of observation into the infinitely large and the infinitely small are merely eyes magnified or refined. If other means exist—and we have no evidence that they do—of sounding the depths of space or scrutinizing the secrets of life in their most infimal manifestations, those means must only be accessible to beings whose conformation is different from ours. Already, before our humankind was reduced to taking refuge inside our world, important research had been carried out and serious results obtained. I shall soon show you the entire series of preliminary endeavors through which we passed."

For a few moments Marcel had seemed preoccupied; slight tremors seemed to be agitating the chair on which he was seated, in an almost imperceptible fashion, and the floor on which his feet were set. At the same time, he could hear a faint, almost ungraspable noise. One might have thought that he was searching for the cause of that movement and sound.

Rugel, who had noticed that, went on more urgently, as if to distract him from his reflections: "You'll see that, like you, we've been using reflecting and refracting telescopes for a long time; but you know that reflecting telescopes are always difficult to handle and don't support magnifications as considerable as those founded on the principle of refraction. We've succeeded in manufacturing lenses of such perfection and have been able to construct refractors of such a diameter that we've renounced the use of reflecting telescopes."

Rugel obligingly explained, at length and in great detail, the ingenious and precise methods with whose aid they obtained marvelous and gigantic objective lenses, and the simple and powerful mechanisms that moved the apparatus without difficulty, the proportions of which surpassed anything that terrestrial science had so far been able to realize.

Marcel and his two friends, keenly interested by the descriptions that Rugel was giving, by the memories of distant ages that he was evoking, and by the successive phases of the scientific progress obtained over the centuries, that they did not notice the time passing, and that several hours had already gone by since they had entered the strange redoubt in which they were still present.

"All that is very curious and very instructive, friend Rugel," said Marcel, cheerfully, "But is it only to give us a lecture on the history of lunar astronomy that you've brought us here?"

164

"Always impatient," Rugel replied smiling. "Don't worry—we've arrived."

"Arrived?" exclaimed Marcel, Jacques and Lord Rodilan. "Where? How?"

"On the surface of the Moon," replied Rugel, simply.

XIX. The Observatory

The door was open; the three inhabitants of Earth, under the influence of a sharp emotion, followed Rugel into a broad tunnel, rather dimly lit, which opened before them. At the far end another door yielded to their guide's pressure; they took a few more steps and stopped, wonderstruck. They were on a vast terrace inundated with light, whose brightness, slightly veiled by a blue tint, was not reminiscent that of the Sun, but rather resembled that with which the Moon, when full, illuminates terrestrial nights, but with an infinitely superior intensity.

They looked around in surprise, and contemplated admiringly the strange landscape that extended before their eyes: an immense plain with a cracked and profoundly tormented surface, in the center of which rose up the gigantic edifice in which they were standing. On the distant horizon, there were formidable masses of mountains and capriciously-formed rocks: denuded peaks with sharp ridges, raising their summits toward the sky and projecting long, fantastic shadows.

They were still under the influence of that emotion when Rugel, raising his arm, pointed at the sky extended above their heads.

They raised their eyes. A sudden tremor agitated their limbs, and with an irresistible impulse, they hugged one another ardently, their eyes bathed with tears. As if under the impression of an unspeakable anguish, they were only able to stammer: "The Earth! The Earth!"

In the profoundly black sky, at an angle of 1°54, was an immense round globe, as bright as fourteen full moons, which was pouring over the lunar landscape waves of a intense but soft and tranquil light.

It was the world they had left six months before.

The Earth, full at that moment, was turning the hemisphere containing the old continent toward the Moon. The three friends could make out with the naked eye the brilliant contours of the land and the darker masses of the oceans, recognizing Europe, with its profoundly indented coasts, the vast surface of Asia, with the peninsulas that terminated it, and triangular Africa to the south. But it was specifically on France that Jacques and Marcel fixed their avid eyes, while Lord Rodilan repeated, in a voice that tension rendered hoarse: "England! England!"

Rugel watched them silently, seeming to share their emotion.

"Come on, friends," he said to them. "You're going to see the Earth at closer range."

They tore themselves away from their contemplation, as if with regret, and marched behind Rugel, not without turning their heads and raising their eyes toward the enormous disk shining above their heads.

The terrace on which they were walking was on top of an imposing construction that stood in the middle of a vast depression within the Ocean of Storms, in the vicinity of the crater Hansteen. It was a kind of palace of colossal proportions, square in form, composed of several stories. The lower part, surrounded by massive walls about fifteen meters high, was pierced by large bays fitted with thick crystal, extremely transparent, and separated by tall columns half-integrated into the wall. Large rooms had been accommodated there, which served as libraries, museums and work-rooms for the astronomers who spent their lives observing the sky.

A tapering construction rose up to the height of the frieze supported by the columns, around which was a terrace ten meters broad, hermetically sealed by huge glass panels, arched in the upper sections to form a dome, supported on the platform on top of the central block and serving itself as the base of a final story, where the instruments of observation were installed.

It was to that glazed terrace that the travelers had been brought initially, and from which they had contemplated the

167

Earth, the sudden sight of which had thrown them into such sharp emotion.

There were more surprises to come.

Soon, an electric elevator transported them, with Rugel, to the upper floor. They emerged in to the ultimate platform, and again, through the glass framework that formed a completely airtight cupola about twelve meters in diameter, they saw the world to which all their thoughts reported.

Their visit had undoubtedly been announced, for when they appeared they were surrounded by scientists attached to the observatory, who hastened to wish them welcome. People were looking at them with curiosity mingled with respect.

The man who appeared to be the foremost in that elite company stepped forward. "We are glad to salute your arrival among us," he said. "We know of your heroic adventures; we rejoice, along with the entire lunar population, in the coming of our terrestrial brothers. We share the hope that your presence has inspired in the eminent man who governs us, and we shall do everything in our power to assist its realization. For the moment, however, while awaiting something better, we're going to bring the sight of the globe that is so dear to you closer."

And he designated with his hand three chairs in which each of them found themselves in close proximity with an enormous cylinder projecting from the interior of the cupola and terminating in a lens set in a metal tube, similar to the oculars with which Earthly astronomical instruments are fitted.

"Look," he said to them.

Three exclamations sprang forth at the same time.

"France!"

"Paris!"

"London!"

Thanks to the power of the instruments put at their disposal, the Earth had drawn nearer in an incredible fashion; it was so close that one could distinguish all the geographical details, as if a vast map had been extended before their gaze: mountains, forests, rivers and cities.

A precise mechanism permitted the apparatus to be moved effortlessly, and paraded over the entire surface of the terrestrial globe—and their insatiable eyes could not detach themselves from the places where they had lived.

While Lord Rodilan searched the gigantic city of London, which appeared to him as a large gray patch striped with imperceptible lines that must have been streets, and divided by the black line of the Thames, Marcel and Jacques palpitating with emotion, kept their eyes obstinately fixed on Paris. Although the magnification furnished by the marvelous instruments, which Marcel estimated at about twenty thousand times, was such that it ought to have been possible to make out all the monuments, the thickness of the terrestrial atmosphere singularly diminished its clarity. A kind of veil was extended between the observers and the surface of the Earth, which blurred all the contours, caused lines to oscillate, and prevented the eye from bringing things into focus.

For the astronomers of the Moon, who had only been able to establish conjectures on the basis of those troubled and uncertain impressions, it was difficult to orientate themselves in that indecisive milieu, but Marcel and Jacques easily located the places where they had spent such a large part of their lives and which they knew so well. A few moments had sufficed for them to get their bearings. They could now distinguish, to the west of the great city, a starry point that was obviously the Place de l'Étoile, with its dozen broad radiating streets, and with that reference-point established, they had soon assigned to each monument, in that almost alarming map, the location that it ought to occupy.

Thus, one of them saw once again, or at least thought that he saw, the Observatoire quarter where he had tasted such sweet pleasures, experienced such cruel dolors and left behind all his hopes. The other, whose attention was not attracted to any particular point of the capital, scanned France affectionately in its entirety. He went from Dunkerque, bathing in the waves of the North Sea, to the cities of the Midi that were mirrored in the transparent waters of the Mediterranean; from the extreme tip of Brittany to the snowy mass of the Alps, whose summits, profiled in a less dense atmosphere and above the region of the clouds, stood out with a dazzling whiteness. He never wearied of following the course of rivers and recognizing in passing the cities they traversed: Rouen, Nantes, Bordeaux and Lyon attracted his gaze in their turn.

Then, while Lord Rodilan, after having cast a glance over London, delighted in passing in review all the points on the surface of the globe where the avid English nation had planted its flag, and felt his heart swelling with an insolent pride. Marcel, crossing the frontiers of France, paused—not without a melancholy regret—on the provinces violently separated from the fatherland.

Soon, however, wrenching himself from that contemplation, which revived such cruel memories, he crossed the Rhine, passed over Germany, at that moment covered in clouds but which, with the aid of his imagination, seemed to him to be bristling with weapons, to run along the banks of the Neva, where his patriotic soul seemed to divine future allies. Soon, descending again to southern Europe, he followed the picturesquely-indented coasts that the atmosphere, more transparent in that region, permitted him to distinguish with greater clarity.

There was Greece, displayed like a mulberry leaf, Italy reaching toward the Africa continent, Spain striped with chains of mountains, Algeria sandwiched between the Mediterranean and the Atlas, and the Sahara unfurling its long yellow plains all the way to central Africa, with its unfathomable mysteries.

But his gaze always returned to France, the beloved fatherland that one could quit but never forget.

As time marched on, however, the terrestrial globe rotated on its axis; Europe gradually disappeared, and already the coasts of the American continent seemed to be emerging from the Atlantic.

"Friends," said Rugel then, "forgive me for tearing you away from that spectacle, which, I understand, is charming your hearts, but you're at home here and you'll have time to contemplate the Earth in all its phases at your leisure—for your sojourn in our observatory can be extended for as long as you deem necessary. Let me show you the apartments reserved for you, and then I'll abandon you to the care of the savant Merovar, my colleague on the Supreme Council, who directs the astronomical observations here. He has already studied, as you will soon discover, a means of putting you in communication with those you left behind. As for me, the demands of my responsibilities oblige me to separate myself from you for some time."

He took them to the lower floor, where spacious rooms had been prepared for the voyagers, furnished with a severe and elegant luxury. Everything there had been arranged with an attentive care to satisfy all the needs of the strangers, so different from those of the inhabitants of the Moon.

The three friends bid farewell, not without a certain sentiment of sadness, to the man who had been their faithful and voted guide since their arrival, and had testified a veritable and sincere amity toward them. Then they took possession of the places where they were going to live for some time. It was with a real satisfaction that they found themselves alone, for, after the violent emotions through which they had just passed, they felt gripped by an invisible need for repose.

In the days that followed they were the object of the attention and thoughtfulness of all the astronomers of the marvelous observatory. Everyone was enthusiastic to initiate the visitors into the secrets of his work and have them admire the perfect instruments that they employed. Jacques, and even Lord Rodilan, ended up with a strong interest in the superior science of astronomy, the privilege of the boldest minds, in which the results furnished by observation aided by calculation put on all the colors and have all the charm of the most brilliant and fantastic fantasies of the imagination. How, in any case, could they have remained indifferent when it was to that very science that they owed the visual connection that they maintained to the world to which they were still linked by such powerful bonds?

XX. Mechanics and Optics

A problem of mechanics was troubling Marcel. He was wondering by what means it had been possible to transport him and his companions from the depths of the lunar world to its surface. As he already knew, the immense excavation that served as an abode for the refugees from a world that had become uninhabitable was situated at a depth of about fifteen terrestrial leagues. What powerful methods did the engineers of that strange humankind have at their disposal to raise such considerable weights vertically to such heights? It seemed to him that it required, in fact, that everything required in the construction and equipment of the observatory must have been transported to the periphery. That was enough to trouble the most audacious mind profoundly.

He had soon ascertained, and remained amazed, by the simplicity of the means employed to obtain such astonishing results. He remade with the savant Merovar the journey that he had already accomplished with Rugel, and with that enlightened guidance he examined everything and took account of everything.

It was the chimney of an ancient volcano that the inhabitants of the Moon had used to install the mechanical apparatus that permitted them to communicate with the exterior world. They had an inexhaustible motive force at their disposal in electricity; they had only to establish an elevator cage about five meters wide within the long, almost vertical corridor, whose walls they had evened out. The uprights and cross-pieces were formed of highly resistant steel plate; the various sections were linked together by solidly riveted bolts, which gave the ensemble the rigidity of a solid body. At intervals, sheet metal beams extended to the four corners of the cage, similarly bolted, necessarily of variable length, in accordance with the distance separating the uprights from the rocky wall, and profoundly embedded in that wall.

The elevator that traveled up and down that chimney was equipped, at each of its corners, with two toothed wheels, one at the top and one at the bottom, which engaged with four hooks disposed along the uprights. Movement was imparted to them, with a velocity of about twenty kilometers an hour, by a powerful electric motor with a relatively small volume, fitted to the bottom of the elevator. That motor, propulsive when it was a matter of taking the elevator up, served during the descent as a moderator and brake. Everything was calculated with such mathematical rigor, the materials employed were so homogeneous and so resistant, and the operation was so perfect, that it all functioned with the safety and softness of a precision apparatus, and the probability of any accident had been reduced to an infinitesimal proportion.

For greater security, and in order to leave nothing to the unexpected—always possible in human endeavors—the lunar engineers' foresight had disposed, beneath the elevator's point of departure, in the same axis as the cage, a profound cavity filled with water, the density of which was increased by the addition of a chemical mixture, and the elasticity of which would, in case of a fall, deaden the terminal shock.

Marcel was gripped by admiration for that colossal endeavor, which extended to a height of fifteen leagues, the mere conception of which seemed frightful.

How had human beings, limited in strength, been able to imagine and carry out such a project?

On reflection, he reminded himself that the prodigious quantity of material employed represented, on the Moon, a weight six times less than on Earth; he knew, from having seen remarkable applications, that the lunar engineers had succeeded in solving important problems of mechanics as if they were child's play, and that their scientific genius, triumphing over the resistance of matter, had invented the most powerful and varied machines, reducing the individual labor of humans to virtual negligibility.

Nevertheless, what he had before him was so extraordinary, and seemed to surpass all expectations to such an extent that he could not believe his eyes.

Merovar appeared to enjoy his astonishment.

"Fortunately," he said, "we have been favored by circumstances. When our humankind, constrained to quit the surface of our globe, retreated into the subterranean regions that it occupies today and which the Sovereign Spirit seemed to have prepared for us as a last refuge, our scientists did not resign themselves to being separated forever from the external world and the infinite space in which the stars pursue heir immutable courses. They directed their investigations everywhere; no accessible location remained unexplored. Thus, we were able to observe the existence of numerous chimneys of extinct volcanoes.

"Almost all of them were irregular in form and oblique in direction; their sinuous courses did not lend themselves to the establishment of apparatus permitting us to communicate with the surface—but we eventually found the one through which you have just traveled. Its vertical direction and narrow diameter made it marvelously appropriate to the usage we wanted to make of it. Unfortunately, it was, like all the other craters of the Moon, obstructed some distance from the surface by a thick layer of lava and accumulated volcanic ejections. It was necessary for us to bore a passage through those extremely hard materials, and we had to have recourse to explosives with a considerable expansive force to do that. To even out, as far as possible, the asperities with which the walls were bristling in many places, we employed powerful rams."

"I'm amazed," Marcel put in, "by the magnificent results obtained by your industry, but I wonder how you managed to create a respirable atmosphere in this chimney, of such prodigious height, and especially in the observatory, which is on the very surface of the Moon. I know from my own experience that it isn't necessary to rise very far above the level of the cavern into which we fell to arrive at levels where the air is rarefied and incapable of sustaining life."

"That's true, but you'll understand how the problem was solved, as easily as the others. At the bottom of the chimney in which our elevator moves, powerful pumping machines are established, alimented by the air that forms the atmosphere in which we live; that air, aspired by them, is incessantly pumped into the chimney with a pressure that raises it to the surface and accumulates it in the observatory. The force of the machines in calculated in such a fashion that the ascendant column and the atmosphere that fills the entire edifice, hermetically closed in all its parts, is maintained at a constant pressure virtually identical to the one we experience in our subterranean world. The action of the machines, functioning incessantly, furnishes the chimney and the edifice at the top with a current of air that is incessantly renewed and always respirable. The unnecessary elements are drawn away and rejected into general circulation, where it is purified and retransformed. You can see for yourselves that respiration is easy on all that all the floors of the observatory and that life at this height has lost none of its activity."

"All this is marvelous," Marcel murmured.

The optical instruments whose formidable power the three friends had observed became the object of an attentive examination on their part. The great difficulty that had presented itself initially to the lunar astronomers consisted of the impossibility of operating in the open on the surface of the Moon. On the other hand, observations were only possible with instruments articulated in such a fashion as to be moved in all directions and capable of searching all the regions of the celestial vault. It had therefore been necessary to find a combination such that the observer, remaining in a rigorously sealed environment filled with breathable air, could nevertheless maneuver his instrument in the external void without effort and without displacement.

The system of equatorial telescopes, which is the one most commonly used on Earth, could not meet that objective, the observer being obliged to move at the same time as the telescope. But they had found the means they sought in jointed telescopes, and it was not the least of Marcel's astonishments to observe that the kinds of optical apparatus to which terrestrial astronomers had been led by the sole desire to render their observations more comfortable, and hence more precise, were exactly those to which their colleague on the Moon had had recourse by reason of the very special conditions to which they were subjected.

The kind of telescope devised by Monsieur Loewy, one of the most ingenious and knowledgeable astronomers at the Observatoire de Paris, is well-known.[20] The body of the instrument is formed by two cylindrical sections mounted at a right angle; one, which bears the ocular, is parallel to the axis of the world; the other, the one equipped with the objective, is parallel to the equator. A kind of rectangular bolt is fitted to that objective, enclosing a silvered glass mirror inclined at 45°, able to rotate in such a fashion as to face all the points of the sky above the horizon.

The image of any star whatsoever, reflected by that mirror and refracted by the objective, encounters a second mirror similarly inclined at 45° and positioned at the point where the two parts of the instrument form a elbow. That mirror, in its turn, reflects the image thus received and transmits it to the ocular, which is nothing but a powerful microscope—and it is that image, thus amplified, which the observer's eye examines.

It was on that principle that the telescopes used by the lunar astronomers were founded, with the particularity that the tube bearing the ocular, which projected from the interior of the observation hall, penetrated it through a cylindrical opening that was hermetically sealed, while being able to pivot on its axis, along with the entire body of the instrument.

As for the telescope itself, which was almost entirely outside, it rested, at the extremity of its horary axis, on a solid

---

[20] The Austrian-born Maurice Loewy (1833-1907) began work at the Observatoire de Paris in 1860, and eventually became its director in 1896, after which he supervised work on a monumental atlas of the Moon, eventually published in 1910.

mass in which a system of gears, activated by an electric motor of extreme precision, permitted it to follow any star in its course, at the observer's whim.

Another mechanism permitted the astronomer to direct the objective mirror at the star he wished to study. One of the four faces of the observation hall, disposed in the meridian plane, had been adapted in such a way as to receive three of those items of apparatus of equal dimension and similar in all respects, with regard to disposition, to those in use on Earth, but differing on one essential point: their colossal proportions and their absolute perfection. The objectives, in fact, measured no less than 3.5 meters in diameter, and could support magnifications up to a factor of 25,000. That explained the prodigious effect produced on the three voyagers by the sight of Earth so close to them. Three other telescopes of similar construction but not equatorial were disposed symmetrically on the opposite face, permitting all points of the sky to be swept and astronomical research completed.

It was to render possible the simultaneous observations required to ensure effective checking that the lunar scientists, who counted neither time not effort, had multiplied the number of those gigantic telescopes. As for other astronomical instruments—divided circles, meridional circles, etc.—they offered considerable analogies with ours, and necessarily so, astronomy being an exact science founded on mathematical laws that are the same throughout the universe.

Such expert astronomers could not have neglected the fecund source of observations furnished by the spectral analysis of stars, and in that domain of physical astronomy, as in that of the pure science, the results they had obtained far surpassed those attained on Earth. That part of the science, very recent among us, had been familiar to them for a long time, and they had been able, thanks to the excellence of their methods and the superiority of their instruments, to analyze much more completely the physical constitution of the worlds comprising our planetary system.

It had also not escaped Marcel's attention that the lunar observers were working in unique conditions much more favorable than those on Earth. The long nights of three hundred and fifty-four hours that the rotation of the Moon provided for them every month, offered the marvelous facilities. They were, in fact, able to devote themselves to long and sustained observations, the course of which was untroubled and uninterrupted. In that immutably pure sky, never thickened by any vapors or veiled by any cloud, from which light always arrived clearly and frankly, the stars could be discerned with the most rigorous precision. In addition, in consequence of the slowness of rotation, the apparent motion of the stars was extremely slight, almost the same as that of our pole star. They were, therefore, able to follow with exactitude the movement of the star that the visual field of their telescope embraced, and none of its potential variations could escape them.

In such conditions, they had found the solutions to a considerable number of problems that terrestrial astronomers were still posing.

Thus, they had been able for a long time to draw complete maps of Mercury and Venus; they had discovered that the axial rotation of the former planet was effected in a time effectively equal to that of its rotation around the sun, and that strange astronomical phenomenon, which the scientists of Earth had not yet suspected, had caused Marcel profound surprise.[21]

Mars, with its continents, its gigantic canals and its polar ice caps, no longer had any mystery for them. The thick atmosphere that envelops Jupiter had veiled its surface from them, as from us, and their studies of that planet were little

---

[21] Author's note: "This discovery, since revealed by Schiaparelli, has been confirmed by Monsieur Perrotin." This note was obviously added some time after the text was written; the "discovery" in question was announced by Schiaparelli in 1889, and Perrotin supported the claim shortly thereafter; the error was not corrected until the 1960s.

more advanced than ours, but they had resolved the rings of Saturn, and Marcel was able to convince himself with the evidence of his own eyes that each one is composed of an infinite number of tiny bodies, tightly packed, rotating around a central nucleus with such rapidity that the light reflected appears continuous. As for Uranus and Neptune, lost in the profundities of the sky, they had been able to discern different hues on their disks that led them to believe in the presence of continents and oceans, but the extreme distance of those worlds had not permitted them to make any precise determination. Finally, at the extreme limits of our planetary system, they had discovered, initially by the power of calculation and then by direct observation, the hypothetical world whose existence our scientists can only suspect.

They had taken their sidereal astronomical research far in advance, and the results obtained had been no less fecund. Around a considerable number of the nearer stars they had been able, thanks to the powerful means of investigation at their disposal, to observe numerous satellites—or, rather, veritable planets—effecting their orbits around the central star, as in our solar system.

When Marcel, abandoning himself to his taste for astronomy, searched the celestial vault resplendent with stars with those gigantic telescopes, his wonderstruck gaze contemplated those myriads of suns strewn in the immensity, some white like ours, other blood red, emerald green, deep blue or golden yellow, he wondered with amazement what inconceivable power maintained those worlds suspended in infinite space, and regulated their various revolutions with an immutable harmony.

And his imagination, exalted by that dazzling spectacle, was launched beyond the planets that he had seen orbiting the nearest suns; he told himself that around all the others—those which astronomical instruments could distinguish clearly, those that can only be vaguely glimpsed in the confused mass, those even more distant, the faint light of which is revealed on sensitive plates, and those, finally, that the mind alone divines, succeeding one another endlessly in incommensurable spaces—other worlds are gravitating.

And there again, always and everywhere, he sensed that humankinds lived, how various and how different from ours and that of the Moon! His imagination exhausted itself relentlessly trying to picture them, and life in its multiple forms, from the most rudimentary and the most primitive types to superior conceptions drawing ever closer to perfection, circulating everywhere in the boundless universe, celebrating the glory and the grandeur of the unique and sovereign force from which everything emanates.

And his soul lost itself in an ineffable delight.

XXI. On the Lunar Surface

While Marcel plunged into the contemplation of so many scientific marvels and admired the genius with which so many great problems had been resolved, his two companions, who were not animated with an equal zeal by the passion of astronomy, began to feel more personal preoccupations. During the first phase of their sojourn in the observatory, they could not detach their gaze from the terrestrial globe, but at length, the constant uniformity of that spectacle and the impossibility of being able to see more, had begun to give birth to certain surges of impatience in their souls.

Jacques, in particular, who was attached to Earth by such strong bonds, suffered in seeing his friend forget what, in his eyes, ought to be the sole objective at which they were to aim—which is to say, the establishment of regular communications with the terrestrial world.

He broached the subject with Marcel one day.

"All these studies in which we're absorbing ourselves," he said, "are very interesting, and like you, I'm glad to have been able to get to know this superior world in which we've learned so much, and where there doubtless remains a lot more for us to learn. Don't you remember, though, that we've left friends behind us who have been keeping their eyes avidly attached to the lunar disk for months, believing us to be definitively lost and doubtless mourning us?"

"I beg your pardon, my friend," Marcel replied. "My passion for knowledge hasn't rendered me egotistical, and I have thought about the problem that's troubling you. But you know that outside of the enclosure in which, thanks to artificial means, we're able to live at present, like is impossible on the lunar surface. It seems to me to be very difficult, from this narrow enclave, to contrive signals that might be perceptible on Earth. Nevertheless, we ought to try everything, even the impossible, to reassure our friends, and I've decided to talk to

Merovar about it—for it's quite evident that, in order to construct this observatory and dispose their optical instruments outside, they must have found a means of moving and acting in the ambient void. Your anxiety, which I share, has served to prompt me to act. We'll go right away, with a clear conscience."

Lord Rodilan, when informed, shrugged his shoulders.

"You're wrong to worry about it," he said, smiling. "We've been assumed to be dead for a long time, and our names figure among those of all the lunatics who wanted to render their name immortal by some insane enterprise—Herostratus, Empedocles and many others. Take my word for it, don't be in such a rush; it's not as if you don't have anything else to worry about than reassuring people who are surely no longer sparing us a thought."

"I have more confidence in the hearts of those who live us," Jacques replied, hotly. Turning to Marcel, he added: "Let's go find the astronomer right away."

As soon as the two friends began to speak, Merovar, seemingly unsurprised, replied: "I've been expecting you. From the day when the prudent Aldeovaze, in welcoming you, expressed the hope of soon seeing, thanks to you, communications established between your world and ours, we've been preoccupied with practical means of achieving that result, and we'll be able to give you satisfaction very shortly."

He deployed before their eyes a highly detailed map of the region in which the observatory was located. The crater on which it was constructed, one of the smallest that the eyes of astronomers have distinguished on the surface of our satellite, which they have not seen fit to designate by a particular name and is not marked by an symbol on the most complete maps, was situated at 9°31′ south latitude and 49°16′ west longitude, and was isolated in the middle of an immense plain in the southern part of the Ocean of Storms. The vast depression to which astronomers have given that name, after being extended from the radiant crater Kepler to the large circus of Hevelius, plunges southwards in a sort of gulf in the depths of which rise the crater Hansteen and, even further away, that of Billy. It was a little to the north-west of the former crater, and on a line linking it to that of Flamsteed that the narrow chimney was hollowed out that the genius of the lunar scientists had adapted to facilitate their communications with the exterior.

Hazard had served them marvelously; nothing impeded their observations, and it was on a distant horizon that the jagged summits or tormented walls of mountains and craters appeared, which the absence of atmosphere permitted them to attain. Around it extended a large flat space on which none of the blisters was observable that ordinarily render the surface of the Moon so irregular. One might have thought it a vast liquid plain suddenly frozen during calm weather.

"It's there," Merovar said to them, "that we count on establishing the apparatus with the aid of which we'll send news of you to those who are doubtless awaiting for it anxiously."

"There, on the surface of the Moon, in the void!" Marcel exclaimed. "But no one can live there."

"Oh," said Merovar, "you haven't run out of surprises yet. A long time ago we found the means of traveling on the desolate surface of our world, and if you care to follow us there, you can make some curious observations."

"We're ready," said the three friends.

They went down to the lower floor of the observatory and went into a vast room, in which mannequins of a vaguely human form were arranged along the walls.

"That," Merovar said to them, "is the apparatus that permits us to live and move in the exterior void."

"But they're ordinary diving suits!" exclaimed Lord Rodilan, laughing.

"Yes," said Merovar, "but inverted diving suits. When it's a matter for human beings of living under water, the apparatus in which they enclose themselves has to be able to resist the pressure of the ambient environment, which increases as one descends through the liquid layers. Here the problem is the inverse; as it's impossible to live, as you now, without an exterior pressure establishing an equilibrium with the forces of expansion with which our organism is animated, it's necessary that we are, in a permanent manner, enveloped by an atmosphere carrying sufficient tension. It's for that reason that we're obliged to enclose our entire body in an apparatus of this sort. On the lunar surface, there's no pressure that can counterbalance the pressure of the air that fills them, so it's necessary to construct them with materials sufficiently resistant and flexible to permit the person who puts one on to move and act in complete freedom. In any case, you can judge for yourselves."[22]

And, setting them an example, he started putting on one of the suits disposed along the wall.

"Each of you chose one appropriate to his height," he said, "but be careful to close all the openings hermetically, for the slightest crack might expose you to serious danger, by letting the air the surrounds you escape."

Soon, the three travelers and their guide were clad in the costumes, whose strangeness provoked Lord Rodilan's laughter. Only their heads were still free,

"If my friends on Earth could see me in such an outfit, they'd certainly have difficulty recognizing me," he said.

"None of them, at any rate," Jacques retorted, "could boast of having attempted an expedition similar to the one we're about to undertake."

The apparatus in with they were tightly enclosed was made of a material that was both supple and tenacious, and coated with a substance that rendered it absolutely impermeable. The traveler's head was imprisoned in a sort of metal sphere equipped in the front and at the sides by crystal plates permitting the gaze to scan almost all of the horizon. In that sphere the orifice of a conduit opened, which brought the air

---

[22] Although this was not the earliest description of a fictitious "space suit" by the time the Flammarion edition was published in 1896 it was probably the earliest when this passage was written, and is more sophisticated than the descriptions of unpressurized suits contained in other 19th century novels.

necessary for respiration. The air came from a metallic reservoir placed on the back, in which it was compressed under considerable pressure; thanks to an automatic mechanism regulated with rigorous precision, it escaped in a continuous fashion at a constant tension. The quantity was calculated in such a way as to be able to maintain life for a duration of ten hours.

To furnish an exit for the air that escaped from the reservoir, whose accumulation would have ended up causing the apparatus to burst, and which, moreover, charged with the products of expiration—which is to say, carbonic acid and water vapor—would not have taken long to become unbreathable, a special valve had been fitted into the middle of the torso. When the interior pressure exceeded a certain level, the valve opened of its own accord, and then closed again thanks to a powerful spring, and the occlusion was complete.

After being diverted for a few moments by that new disguise, Marcel, Jacques and Lord Rodilan were astonished to retain, within that seemingly rigid envelope, the free use of their limbs and the facility of all their movements.

"Not only can we act and move," Merovar told them, "But we'll be able to communicate with one another." And he drew their attention to small microphone receivers at the level of the ears in the sphere, and a transmitter in front of the mouth; the whole was a marvel of delicacy and economy. A metal wire linked the receivers to a small electric accumulator fixed to the air reservoir.

Externally, a mobile wire about two meters long and furnished at its extremity with a ring, permitted each tourist, by fixing his ring to his neighbor's sphere with the aid of a hook provided for that purpose, to enter into continuous conversation with him, speaking to him and hearing his responses.

"All this is extremely ingenious," said Marcel, "And denotes the greatest practical sense on the part of your physicists. I'm in haste to experiment with these charming items of apparatus, which no one has yet thought of utilizing in this fashion on Earth."

"Let's go, then," said Merovar; and he took them into a small hermetically sealed room, whose door he was careful to close.

"Here," he told them, "we're in an air-lock, and only this wall separates us from the exterior void. It only remains for us to fit the spheres on our heads."

When they were ready, Merovar opened the door that led to the outside, and scarcely had the bolts securing it been loosened than it escaped of its own accord under the pressure of the interior air, in spite of the springs with which it was furnished. The four men, violently pushed forward, would have fallen if they had not braced themselves on the solid iron staffs with which their guide had taken care to equip them.

At first, they experienced a strange sensation; the apparatus in which they were clad, abruptly inflated by the dilatation of the air it contained, rounded out about their limbs in the form of puffed sleeves in which they seemed to be floating. After the first moment of surprise, however, they realized that, thanks to the elasticity of the fabric of which it was made, the liberty of their movements was not hampered; they scarcely perceived that their fingers were enclosed in gloves.

Marcel was then able to understand how the observatory had been built, the construction of which had previously seemed inexplicable. He realized that an army of Diemides, brought to the lunar surface, had been able, thanks to the apparatus that he was now wearing, to fashion the rocky blocks that the slopes of the crater furnished in abundance, and which it would have been impossible, because of their mass, to bring up by means of the elevator. He took account of the fact that, weight on the moon being six times less than of Earth, the bold constructors had been able to move the masses, whose proportions would have seemed enormous to us, without overmuch difficulty. On the other hand, he calculated that, in order to obtain a stability equal to that of terrestrial monuments, it had been necessary to give the base of the observatory and the thickness of its walls much greater dimensions—

with the result that, if the effort seemed less, the proportions given to the project almost restored parity.

The three voyagers then paraded their gazes around them. The Sun, its ardent light untempered by any atmosphere, was inundating the lunar surface with its rays. The spectacle was dazzling.

They found themselves on a kind of platform surrounding the edifice. The orifice of the crater, which measured no less than eight hundred meters in diameter, had been filled in, with the exception of the chimney that served both the cage of the elevators and as a conduit for the air that came from the depths to the observatory, and it was at the center of that artificial ground that the colossal monument rose up from which they had just emerged.

Under the guidance of Merovar, who preceded them, they went along a kind of pathway grossly carved into the rock. Never, since they had arrived in that world, where everything was strange, had they experienced in a more complete manner the singular effects of the law of gravity. Their specific weight was diminished in astonishing proportions; their feet scarcely posed on the ground; the slightest effort enabled them to cross considerable distances; they had descended the steep and tormented slope of the crater with marvelous facility, and when they looked back at the route they had followed, they wondered with a kind of horror how they had not broken a limb a thousand times over.

After an hour, they found themselves at the foot of the crater, in a plain limited in the distance by confused masses of rocks. On the surface of the extinct world, everything was dismally bleak, and the blinding sunlight, inundating the ground, increased that appearance of supreme desolation even further. Everything was dead and motionless, and in that universal silence, untroubled even by the sound of their footfalls, the three inhabitants of the Earth were almost surprised to find themselves alive.

Having recovered from that initial emotion, they paused, penetrated by a profound satisfaction. To tread the soil of that previously inaccessible world; to contemplate from their base those immense mountains and craters of which they had only had distant and fugitive images before their eyes; to fathom with the gaze those monstrous precipices that they had only been able to suspect; to have that unknown world beneath their feet—what a dream and what a triumph!

They felt the souls of conquerors quivering within them. The great Columbus must have experienced something similar on the day when he had planted the standard of Castille for the first time in the new world that his genius had, in a manner of speaking, caused to emerge from the ocean. But how much greater and more astonishing was the conquest due to their courage and perseverance!

For them, what the most audacious imaginations had barely dared to conceive had been realized. The fictions of poets and romancers had been overtaken; the dream was now an accomplished fact.

As if he had divined the thoughts that were agitating them, and understood the sentiments that were making their hearts beat, Merovar left them to their reflections for some time; then, resuming his march, he headed toward the enormous crater of Letronne, followed by his companions.

The ground on which they were advancing was bristling with asperities that often rendered walking slow and difficult, in spite of their agility; there was no trace of soil or sand, but bare rock everywhere, with sharp and trenchant ridges, reflecting the raw white light with an unsustainable intensity. Without the precaution that had been taken of adding a deep blue tint to the crystal plates that permitted them to look out, they would not have been able to tolerate the glare.

About four kilometers away, they found themselves in a completely bare region, the ground of which no longer presented any irregularity. One might have thought it the surface of a tranquil lake, suddenly frozen.

Merovar stopped and hooked his telephone wore to the sphere covering Marcel's head.

"This," he said, "is the location we have chosen to set up the luminous signals that will be perceptible from the Earth.

"It seems perfectly suitable to me," Marcel replied, "but I don't see any of the preparations you seemed to be announcing."

"Have no fear—you'll soon be edified in that regard." He explained that the astronomers of the observatory had thought of attracting the attention of their colleagues on Earth by means of powerful electric lamps, and that everything had already been done to the laboratory to realize the project. They were convinced that the signals would be seen this time, especially now that attention had been awakened by the fortunately-successful attempt made by the voyagers. It only remained to settle with them the form of signals capable of being understood and of reassuring their friends.

Jacques and Lord Rodilan, who had attached their wires to Marcel's sphere, listed to that communication and, to the extent that their strange costume permitted, manifested considerable excitement. Jacques especially, who thought that Mathieu-Rollère and his daughter would still be at Long's Peak, felt his heart beating faster at the thought that he was finally going to reassure the young woman who, he had no doubt, was waiting for news of him with cruel anxiety.

As for Lord Rodilan, in spite of his skepticism, which was more apparent than real, he was agitated by other sentiments; his pride was secretly flattered by the idea that his name would be flying from mouth to mouth with those of his two companions in both terrestrial hemispheres.

They all approved the choice of location enthusiastically, and Marcel, after consulting his companions rapidly, settled on the idea of depicting, with the aid of prepared lamps, the three initial letters of their names as the surest way of making their safe arrival in the lunar world known to their friends.

They returned in haste to the observatory, into which they went, employing the same precautions that they had taken when emerging from it.

They were approaching the period when that part of the Moon was about to enter into darkness. Merovar had calculated that they still had a duration of daylight before them of approximately seventy-two Earthly hours, and that time seemed to him to be sufficient to arrange everything. A hundred Diemides received the necessary instructions, and at the appointed time, they were ready to attempt the experiment. It had been agreed, after long and scrupulous calculations, that each of the letters to be traced would be three hundred feet high. To form them, six thousand enormous lamps had been disposed, linked together by wires that terminated inside the monument, in the observation hall. Powerful accumulators installed in the lower section of the edifice would furnish the current that was to animate the entire gigantic apparatus.

The observatory had been reached by the line of shadow about twenty-four hours before, and it was now plunged in thick darkness.

All the astronomers had gathered around Marcel and his companions; there was no one who was uninterested in the unprecedented experiment, which might, if it succeeded, have incalculable and decisive consequences. Until now they had acted at hazard; it was without any certainty of being understood or even perceived that they had attempted to attract the attention of the inhabitants of Earth. Now they were sure of being awaited. The telescope at Long's Peak could distinguish objects on the lunar surface nine feet in height; the luminous letters were three hundred; there was no doubt that the message would reach its addressee.

Evidently, it would be necessary to wait for some time before receiving a response from the friends with whom they had been put in communication, but doubt was no longer possible; success was assured—and after so many centuries of waiting, they could easily resign themselves to a few days of patience before obtaining absolute confirmation.

Marcel wanted the first letter to be the R—Lord Rodilan's initial.

"It's you, my dear friend," he said to him, "who furnished us with the means of getting here. You should have the honor of inaugurating the series of interplanetary communications."

"Oh, no!" said Lord Rodilan. "You have been the soul of the enterprise; that honor belongs to you."

"Well then, to settle the argument we'll start with our friend Jacques; there's someone down there who's suffering from his absence and in haste to be reassured."

"I oppose that formally," Jacques put in, forcefully. "But for you, we wouldn't have attempted anything; but for you, I'd still be plunged in despair. If the future has any happiness in store for me, it's to you that I owe it."

"Oh well, so be it, since that's what you want," said Marcel, cheerfully. And, seizing a crystal handle fitted into a metal plinth serving as a support, and at which all the wires coming from outside terminated, he pulled it down with an abrupt gesture.

Everything suddenly lit up: two thousand electric lamps of an incomparable power had just been switched on at the same time. A flood of beams of blinding light traversed space, bearing with them the exiles' wishes and hopes. A fiery M of colossal proportions stood out in the darkness, and to judge by the glare that spread around them, one might have thought that daylight had replaced the darkness, so clearly apparent were the craters, the mountain chains and distant peaks that limited the horizon.

For an hour, the two thousand lamps radiated into space, and the hearts of the three men quivered at the thought that at the same moment, those who loved them would, after long anguish, be reassured on their account. Then everything was extinguished, and the darkness that enveloped the entire landscape again seemed even darker after that dazzling illumination.

They let an hour go by before sending a new signal, and a J as colossal as the M initially traced was soon resplendent in its turn. It shone for an hour; another interval went by, and then it was the turn of the letter R. The three voyagers had signaled their presence.

And for the rest of the time when that part of the lunar disk remained in shadow, the signals were assiduously repeated, rigorously giving each one the same duration. That regularity ought to be certain proof for the terrestrial observers that nothing about the phenomena was random, and ought to dissipate all doubts.

The lunar astronomers, who never ceased to observe the star with which they were seeking thus to enter into communication, and were following its phases, were careful to interrupt the signals throughout the time when the Rocky Mountain region was in daylight. They applied themselves, moreover, to calculating the exact epoch when the Moon, during its period of shadow, ought to be above the horizon of observers at Long's Peak.

The first interplanetary message had been launched from the Moon to the Earth; it was now up to the Earth to respond.

XII. Catastrophe

Marcel resigned himself quite easily to waiting, but Jacques and Lord Rodilan were tormented by impatience and demanded incessantly why, throughout the time that their signals had lasted, which represented six terrestrial rotations, no response had been made to them.

Jacques, especially, was alarmed.

"Oh," he said, "in order for no one to have replied to our appeal, some frightful misfortune must have occurred. Who can tell whether some cataclysm might not have destroyed the observatory at Long's Peak, and whether Mathieu-Rollère might be dead, and Hélène..."

"Gently, my dear Jacques," Marcel put in. "At the pace you're going you might as well predict the end of the world. Believe me, your imagination's running away with you; you're seeing everything in black for no reason."

"But after all," exclaimed Lord Rodilan, "Why aren't they replying? What are they waiting for? Oh, if they were English, they wouldn't have left us in uncertainty for so long. But these Americans, these Yankees, are a bunch of loud-mouths who can't do anything right."

"Calm down, my dear friend, and think about it. It's seven months since we left. Evidently, in the first weeks, the big telescope at Long's Peak will have been aimed incessantly at the Moon throughout the time the world was observable. Then...well, the surveillance must have relaxed."

"Why?" said Jacque. "Personally, I'd have kept it up for ten years if necessary."

"Undoubtedly; but remember that our friends, who were easily able to follow us to the lunar disk, must have seen us fall into the fissure that swallowed us up. Do you think they were able to conserve any great hope that we had escaped death?"

194

"Personally, I would have conserved hope regardless," said Jacques.

"An Englishman never despairs," growled Lord Rodilan.

"I believe too," Marcel went on, "that our friends haven't despaired, and that's why I haven't hesitated to attempt to enter into communication with them. But it's necessary to take account of the manner in which things might have happened. We've sent signals for the space of eight terrestrial nights; it's quite possible that they weren't perceived immediately, for it would have been an extraordinary stroke of luck if there had been someone there to observe them, at the exact moment we began. Several nights might have ne by before they were seen."

"Well," said Lord Rodilan, "Why, if they ended up perceiving them, haven't they replied straight away?"

"Damn! How fast you go, my dear lord! Supposing that they only recognized the signals during the later nights of their appearance, it was first necessary for them to think about means of responding, to examine and discuss what it was appropriate to do, and, once the matter was settled, to execute he plan. In my opinion, they can scarcely have thought of anything but establishing some luminous signal. Now, the Rocky Mountains are poorly equipped for such an enterprise. It would be necessary to procure the necessary equipment at a distance, dispose them and get them into a functional state, and all that will obviously take a lot of time. Add that perhaps, when our signals arrived, there were only junior staff at the observatory; it's quite probable that Mathieu-Rollère, recalled to Paris by his important work there, left America some time ago."

"Oh," said Jacques, in a sad tone, "Hélène wouldn't have allowed him to leave."

"But my poor friend, you're not taking account of the situation: you know that you're alive, but your fiancée doesn't. She must, in fact, believe you to be irredeemably lost. After seven months, what arguments could she have opposed to her father, if he had judged it futile to wait any longer? I understand your fever and your fears; I also understand your impatience, Milord, but in truth, you're not being reasonable. The wisest thing is to wait. Besides which, what else can we do?"

"That's true," said Lord Rodilan. "But are we going to wait like this, arms folded?"

"Until the next period of shadow there's nothing else to do. But as soon as the region we're in is dark again, we'll direct our telescopes toward North America. If we don't perceive anything, we recommence our signals—and this time, I have a profound conviction, we'll get a response. I don't know what, but we'll get one."

"Well then, let's wait," said Jacques, with a sigh.

There resigned themselves to it, since there was no alternative—but the period of time that separated them from the moment so ardently desired was perhaps the cruelest they had spent since leaving the terrestrial world. They felt ready to resume contact with everything they had left behind them, and wondered anxiously whether their hopes were finally about to be realized. The fever of waiting had affected Marcel too, in spite of his self-control, and Lord Rodilan was more agitated than he had been for a long time, The most troubled of all was, however, Jacques, all of whose love seemed to have reawakened with a new ardor now that he felt that he was close to the goal he was pursuing.

The three friends went back and forth incessantly, incapable of staying in one place, their nerves always taut, their eyes shining, their minds haunted by obsession; they wandered at hazard, continually putting their eyes to the ocular of a telescope, as if they might catch sight of what was happening in the Rocky Mountains.

Their agitation had not escaped the attention of those surrounding them; everyone understood the impatience that was devouring them, and by common accord people pretended not to notice that their behavior was strange and unusual, especially in an environment as tranquil and so completely unaccustomed to mental disturbance and passionate disorder. On the contrary, they were surrounded with consideration; a discreet sympathy enveloped them. Merovar, in particular, made great efforts in their regard, trying to distract them and render the tortures of waiting less painful.

The moment was approaching, however, when they were able to recommence the interrupted attempt. Two days more and darkness would reach the region in which the observatory was situated. Marcel, Jacques and Lord Rodilan were counting the minutes.

As if they wanted to hasten the moment when his experiments could resume, the engineer was incessantly occupied in visiting his communication apparatus, making sure that they were in working order. He was checking them for perhaps the hundredth time when it seemed to him that he perceived, in the room where he was, a singular odor. It was very faint, but characteristic; it was a vague odor of sulfur.

At first, he did not attach any great importance to it, but as it persisted, he looked around, to see whether it was coming from the next laboratory. Not discovering anything, he went back into the interior of the edifice; the odor was also sensible there; it even seemed to him to be slightly stronger.

He was about to go down to the lower floor when he met Merovar, who seemed to be looking for him.

"What are these unusual emanations in the air we're breathing?" he asked. "Do you have chemists here who are carrying out some experiment with gases derived from sulfur?"

"No," said the astronomer. "We're only occupied with astronomy here, and I can't explain this phenomenon, which I've noticed too. Let's go see whether we can discover the cause."

Accompanied by Jacques, Lord Rodilan and a few other scientists who were working at the observatory, they visited the various parts of the vast monument. Everywhere they received the same impression, but it became stronger the further down they went, and as they got closer to the cage of the elevator.

Already, everyone was experiencing the disagreeable sensation, and without anyone showing anxiety as yet, they were beginning to worry about it. They examined everything with the greatest care but in vain; there was nothing abnormal that might explain the phenomenon.

Marcel, his mind still haunted by his obsession, did not take long to leave Merovar to continue his investigation and return to his apparatus. He was joined by Jacques and Lord Rodilan, more impatient than ever to see the problem that was impassioning them so much resolved.

"Let's leave our friends to find the cause of what's happening," said Jacques. "We have more important things to do. How long will it be, Marcel, before we can resume our signals?"

"Don't worry—it won't be long before we can get started. The penumbra's already approaching. In twenty-four hours the darkness will be deep enough for out illuminated lamps to be perceptible from Earth. But if our calculations are correct, it will be daybreak in the Rocky Mountains at that moment, and we'll have to wait to least another twelve hours before our friends can perceive our signals and respond."

"How long it all takes!" said Lord Rodilan. "In truth, it's necessary to be exiled on the Moon to learn patience."

"In truth, my dear lord," said Jacques, smiling, "it's certain that your friends in London would no longer recognize in you the gentleman—so cold, so correct and so impassive—that they were accustomed to seeing."

"That's because all this has finished up getting on my nerves. Since I left the Earth I've seen so many extraordinary things that nothing seems impossible any longer, and it irritates me to see that people as clever as you are can't find a quicker solution to a solution that seems to me to be so simple."

"That's phlegmatics all over," said Marcel, laughing wholeheartedly. "As long as they're in the midst of the ordinary course of life, nothing astonishes or excites them; they're disdainful and blasé. If something new and unanticipated comes, their imagination runs wild; from one day to the next they become the most impatient of men. You see, Milord, true wisdom consists of always maintaining, whatever the circumstances, dignity and calmness of mind, not disdaining anything or finding anything tragic, avoiding all discouragement as well as all extravagant hope—and, as ancient wisdom put it, taking things as they come and people as they are."

"Moralize away, my dear Marcel, since you have the time and liberty of mind to do it—but in truth, what's happening? That odor of sulfur is becoming unbearable."

In the meantime, in fact, the sulfurous emanations that had already been attracting the attention of the observatory's personnel for some time had become increasingly sensible, and breathing was beginning to become difficult.

"There's something inexplicable here," said Lord Rodilan. "It's absolutely necessary to discover what's going on."

Marcel and Jacques, poring over the apparatus, seemed oblivious to their surroundings.

As the Englishman got up to go in search of information, the door opened. Merovar appeared on the threshold.

"Friends," he said, "our investigations haven't discovered anything, but as the situation is becoming increasingly serious, I thought I ought to inform the Supreme Council of what's happening here without further delay. Doubtless we'll soon see the arrival of scientists familiar with questions of physics and geology. They'll certainly discover the cause of the abnormal phenomenon and take the necessary measures to counter it. So far as I can judge, it's probable that a crack has occurred in the elevator's chimney, letting out gases accumulated in a neighboring cavity. At any rate, we'll soon know."

Almost at the same moment the elevator arrived, containing three scientists delegated by the Supreme Council to discover what was happening and find a remedy.

News of the unexplained phenomenon produced at the observatory had spread promptly through the lunar world, exciting considerable emotion. Everyone knew that the three inhabitants of the Earth had been installed there for several weeks, with the intention of organizing, if possible, communications with the terrestrial world. As had already been seen, everything touching that important question interested the entire population keenly. A great hope had been born since the arrival of the voyagers of seeing the realization of a project long caressed, but which had only given rise to failed attempts thus far. Everyone was wondering anxiously whether hopes were to be dashed again.

The newcomers had soon recognized the nature of the gas whose presence was vitiating the atmosphere; it was hydrogen sulfide.

"Your conjectures," they said to Merovar, "are evidently well-founded. Although no shock was felt in the subterranean regions, which we would certainly have detected, revealed the event, it's certain that a crack has developed somewhere in the elevator's chimney, giving passage to the mephitic gas. It's therefore necessary to evacuate the observatory, because the air is becoming more unbreathable by the minute, and it won't be long before everyone is asphyxiated.

Merovar immediately gave the order for everyone to prepare to leave, and ran to warn the three friends.

Absorbed by the feverish wait for the signal that might confirm all their hopes, estranged from everything that was happening around them, they were all in the upper part of the observatory, which wires linked to the electrical apparatus outside.

The region had been plunged in darkness for several hours, but, as Marcel had calculated, when darkness had reached the observatory it had been daylight in the Rocky Mountains, and there were several hours more to wait.

With their eyes glued to the oculars of gigantic telescopes, they were following the rotation of the Earth anxiously, watching the light recede gradually toward the western coast of the Atlantic.

Merovar came in hurriedly. "Friends," he said, "the situation is becoming perilous. The envoys of the Supreme

200

Council have decided that the observatory has to be evacuated; there's no one left here but us. Let's make haste to go down while there's still time."

Marcel did not appear to have heard him.

Jacques and Lord Rodilan also seemed insensible to the imminence of the peril. Merovar renewed his insistence.

While he was speaking, a muffled noise was heard, like a distant explosion, but none of them paid any attention to it.

Meanwhile, the atmosphere became increasingly laden with emanations of the deleterious gas. Already, their faces were becoming congested, their eyes bloodshot and their respiration hoarse. In their state of overexcitement, however, they did not appear to notice it. Even Jacques, forgetting that he was a physician, had not noticed the redoubtable symptoms.

Merovar became more urgent.

"Go without me, then," exclaimed Marcel. "I won't abandon my post at such a moment for anything in the world."

With a gesture, without even taking their eyes away from the oculars, Jacques and Lord Rodilan made it understood that even the threat of death could not shake their resolve.

"The shadow's approaching," Jacques murmured.

"It's already reached the Rocky Mountains," said Lord Rodilan, in a voice trembling with emotion.

"Friends," said Marcel, in an indescribable state of excitement, "We're reaching our goal. In a few moments, we'll know whether our signals have been perceived and whether the great problem of interplanetary communication has been solved."

In the presence of that sublime abnegation, that sacrifice of life, accomplished with so much heroism and sacrifice, Merovar felt moved in spite of his self-mastery. The memory of great devotions to science, of which the history of the lunar world offered so many remarkable examples, came to mind and prompted admiration.

Mute and immobile, he folded his arms and waited.

Suddenly, three superhuman cries sprang forth at the same time:

"The signal!"

"The light!"

"Hurrah!"

In the center of the field of the three telescopes aimed at Long's Peak, a sudden light had just appeared, which, in spite of the frightful distance, stood out clearly and brightly, and was sustained.

Breathless and bewildered, three-quarters asphyxiated in the atmosphere that was becoming more intolerable to their exhausted lungs by the second, they could not tear themselves away from that contemplation, and did not perceive that death was approaching rapidly.

A few moments later, Marcel got up, with a painful effort, and looked at his companions. Asphyxia had already done its work. Slumped in their seats, heads tilted back and arms dangling, they were no longer giving any sign of life.

Merovar was lying on the floor.

"It's death," Marcel murmured, "but at least let our friends know that we've perceived them. Our last thought will have been for them." And he staggered toward the commutator that would illuminate and launch through space the luminous letters bearing their message.

Just as he was about to reach it, however, he collapsed and fell, like an inert mass.

PART TWO

I. Rugel's Villa

About twenty terrestrial leagues from the capital of the lunar world, in the direction opposite the shore of the interior sea, the first buttresses were encountered of the formidable granite wall on which the vault of the cavern was supported. There, in a delightful spot, a lake was alimented by streams descending from the nearby mountains.

That pure and transparent lake was surrounded by hills clad in rich vegetation, whose thick carpets of moss sloped down to its sinuous edge. Nothing was more charming than that enchanted solitude, enlivened by birdsong and gentle breezes playing in the foliage.

Almost in the center of the lake, there was an islet, small in size, where trees of the most precious species came together with the most perfumed specimens of the lunar flora. Everything there seemed prepared to please the eye.

In that exceedingly calm and peaceful world, the place seemed to be even calmer and more peaceful. One might have thought it an inviolable refuge reserved for study or meditation.

A short distance from the shore, a spacious habitation in a style that was both delicate and graceful was seemingly posed on a lawn that sloped gently down to the bank. Against the pale green background it stood out brightly, with its walkway sustained by slender colonnettes, its white walls decorated with paintings and mosaics, its terraces with elegant balustrades, its campaniles and perforated bell-rowers, whose apparent whimsicality nevertheless presented a savant harmony.

Floods of air and light entered through wide open bays. In that fortunate region, the atmosphere was exceedingly pleasant to breathe; one could not have asked for a more marvelous abode to render peace to troubled souls and health to enfeebled bodies.

It was to that retreat that the sage Rugel came to rest from the labors that his elevated functions imposed upon him. The wife who had been his companion in life had died some time ago, only leaving him as a pledge of her love a daughter on whom he lavished all his affections—but the memory of the one he had lost had never been effaced from his mind. He could not think without sadness about the happy times that he had spent with her—hence the hint of melancholy that always veiled his features, but which took nothing away from the nobility of his soul and the generosity of his heart.

When her education was complete, Orealis had returned to the paternal household; she had attempted to fill the void left by her mother, whom she had scarcely known; and sometimes, on seeing her always so loving and gentle, the father thought he had rediscovered the spouse that his heart regretted incessantly.

Orealis, Rugel's cherished daughter, was splendidly beautiful. She was at the age when a girl becomes a woman, and still unites all the graces of childhood with the penetrating charm of youth. Her symmetrical, expressive features were brightened by two large dark eyes, which, in her pale and slightly rosy complexion, shone like two somber diamonds. Their glare was tempered an infinite softness; they were the interpreters of a pure soul, accessible to the most elevated sentiments and the most generous passions. Thick ash-blonde hair framed that radiant visage and fell in silky waves over her shoulders. A narrow circlet of gold, embedded with sparkling stones, was posed on those adorable tresses, their thousand fires scintillating in the mist of its soft tints. She wore a dresses made of a light and vaporous fabric, dazzlingly white, whose floating sleeves left the forearms bare and which, raised at the sides, uncovered an azure tunic with silver embroidered. Her tall figure was slim and shapely, offering admirable proportions. Phidias could not have dreamed of a more perfect model when he extracted from marble those young immortals in which the most perfect forms of the feminine body seemed to be bathed in a divine atmosphere.

Her gait was harmonious and supple, her gestures noble and dignified, and, on seeing her advance at a rhythmic stride, one would not have been able to help murmuring the poet's line: *Et vera incessu patuit Dea.*[23]

Sometimes, when a joyful thought agitated her softly, as when she saw her father after a time of absence, her face, ordinary calm and tranquil in its lines, lit up with a celestial smile.

One could not see her without being influenced by the attraction that emanated from her; all those who approached her loved her and surrounded her with a religious respect.

Three of Rugel's female relatives helped her, in that peaceful dwelling, to surround with care and affection the man whose high intelligence was universally admired and whose generosity was universally cherished. Orealis surpassed them all in charm and beauty, however, and if absolute equality had not reigned in that superior world, one might have thought that she was a young queen in the midst of her court.

In that house of Rugel's, ordinarily so calm and almost silent, there had been an unaccustomed agitation for some time. It was there, after the catastrophe in which they had almost found a horrible death, that the three voyagers from Earth had been transported.

It was to Rugel that they owed their salvation.

At the first news of the accident that had occurred at the observatory, he had become alarmed and anxious regarding the fate of his friends. In the palace, where the prudent Aldeovaze was sitting surrounded by the Supreme Council, the result of the mission entrusted to the scientists charged with investigating the causes of the phenomenon had been awaited impatiently.

---

[23] "The true goddess was revealed in her step." The quotation is from Virgil's *Aeneid.*

Soon, they had learned that the order had been given to evacuate the observatory, which had become untenable, and that the entire personnel was coming down. Only the three inhabitants of Earth and Merovar had refused to leave.

Rugel understood. "Oh, the great hearts!" he cried. "They're going to perish, victims of their love of science—but I shall save them in spite of themselves, if necessary."

And he had left in all haste.

Having arrived at the foot of the elevator's chimney, he found it full of unbreathable mephitic vapors. While he was being given a brief explanation of what had happened, a sound like a thunderclap was suddenly heard, which, reverberated by the echoes of the rocky walls, descended with a dull rumble.

Almost immediately afterwards, a kind of hissing became audible, and the column of air, driven back and heavily charged with sulfurous emanations, caused everyone to recoil.

"They're doomed," murmured one of the scientists. "The fissure has widened under the pressure of the gas. The whole shaft is filled with poisonous gases; there's nothing more to be done."

Rugel made an energetic gesture.

"I'm going," he said, simply.

"You won't go alone, then," said the scientist who had spoken. "We'll go with you."

And, equipped with respirators of compressed air similar to those used to go out on to the surface of the satellite, Rugel and the three scientists had hastened into the elevator, which rose up again with vertiginous rapidity.

Having arrived at the observatory they headed without hesitation for the observation hall, where they were sure to find those they sought. Thanks to the apparatus they were wearing, they were able to traverse the deadly atmosphere with impunity.

The four bodies were lying on the floor, showing no sign of life. Without waiting to discover whether they were still breathing they picked them up and carried them to the elevator, which immediately went back down. During the journey the cares that their condition required were lavished on the four unfortunates: doses of ozone expertly graduated with the aid of improved inhalers; massages with energetic reagents; rhythmic pressures on the thoracic region—everything was put to work to bring back the life that appeared to be extinct.

Merovar, whose constitution was quite different from that of his three companions in terms of the development of his respiratory apparatus, which offered more resistance to intoxication via the airways, had already shown a few signs of life before the elevator reached the ground, but nothing could extract the three inhabitants of the Earth from their unconsciousness.

They were transported to a large room whose large windows permitted generous aeration, and the active and intelligent treatments that had proved futile thus far were continued there.

Rugel, in particular, was anxious and troubled.

"The unfortunates!" he said. "What terrible imprudence—or rather, what sublime obstinacy! Are they going to perish, then, without reaping the fruits of their efforts? Provided that Azali arrives in time..." Turning to one of the scientists who were attending to the three friends, he said: "I've summoned the skilful Azali; he'll be able to tell us whether any chance remains of reviving them—here he comes now..."

He went to meet the newcomer.

Azali was a man in his prime. His high forehead denoted a meditative turn of mind, and his eyes sparkled with the keenest intelligence; his features were grave and gentle. He had studied the sciences of life in depth and was justly reputed to be one of the most knowledgeable individuals with regard to all questions related o the organism.

When he arrived, Merovar had already recovered the use of his senses and was taking account of what was happening around him, but, still weakened by the shock to his entire system, he was unable to do anything but watch the efforts made to save his friends, an emotional but impotent spectator.

Azali approached the three bodies, which were lying on a broad couch, and ordered that their clothing should be removed. He examined them carefully, and then, straightening up again, said: "All hope isn't lost, but we need to hurry."

He made a sign to a young Diemide who had accompanied him. The latter went away, and came back with three special devices that Azali had taken care to equip himself in anticipation of their possible necessity. Each apparatus consisted of a king of cage formed by metallic wires closely fitted to the thorax, disposed in such a fashion as to allow free movement. The wires were arranged in such a way that their tips rested on the muscles whose contraction and extension determined the movements of aspiration and respiration in a living being. An electric current, of an intensity proportional to the result to be attained, acted with the aid of the wires on the muscles of the breast, thus determining an artificial respiration of perfect regularity.

The three inanimate bodies were fitted with these devices, which, under the influence of the electric fluid, immediately began to function. The physiologist followed the operation with an attentive gaze. At the same time, inhalers set in motion with minute care caused the breasts of the patients to be penetrated with beneficent waves of ozone, designed to replace the vitiated air in the lungs and purify the tainted organs.

That patient and assiduous work went on for several hours. Nothing changed in Marcel's cadaverous appearances, but Jacques and Lord Rodilan seemed to be slowly coming back to life. Their skin was more supple and less cold, their cheeks colored with an almost rosy tint, and their eyes, whose lids Azali lifted from time to time, became less vitreous. Their pulse, previously insensible, began to make itself felt.

"There's no longer any danger to their lives," said Azali, straightening up. Leaving the others to care for those two, he returned to Marcel.

The engineer was still in the same condition; all appearances of life seemed to have abandoned him, and in spite of the action of the electric currents, the artificial respiration was still ineffective.

He absorbed more poisonous gases than his companions," the physiologist murmured. "It's the toxic effects that we have to combat."

He had anticipated the possibility. Arming himself with a small metallic instrument analogous to the syringes used on Earth for hypodermic injections, he injected a colorless liquid deeply into the muscular tissue of Marcel's left side; it had a powerful antitoxic effect. The pain of the insertion had not caused the patient the slightest shudder, but soon, under the action of the injected agent, the heart, whose movements seemed to have ceased, resumed beating feebly. At the same time, the circulation of the blood resumed its activity, determining respiratory movements.

Azali's somber features cleared. "Courage!" he said. "We'll save him."

He gave the patient two further injections, and after each of them, the vital movements were seen to revive and accelerate.

After an hour, Marcel too was out of danger.

Rugel, who had followed that struggle of science against death with emotional attention, shook Azali's hand; his face was radiant with joy.

"Don't rejoice too soon, my friend," the other replied. "Their material life is assured, but the poison they've absorbed has acted profoundly on their organism, principally on the brain, the center of all thought and sensibility. They'll need time and a great deal of care before they recover the free exercise of their functions and the integrity of their intellectual faculties."

"I'll take responsibility for that," Rugel replied.

And it was thus that the three friends were transported to the tranquil refuge where their recovery was to be completed.

II. A Love without Issue

Azali's anticipations were realized.

Thanks to the devoted care of which they were the object, Marcel and his two friends recovered their physical health fairly promptly, but a strange phenomenon had been produced. Under the influence of the poison that had invaded their bodies, their intelligence remained torpid, as if their minds were plunged into profound darkness. Their memories had disappeared; they could only string ideas together in a confused fashion; even their sensory perceptions were incoherent, as if incomplete.

To put it briefly, it seemed that their brain had become a *tabula rasa* in which nothing remained of acquired notions and stored ideas. They were like children opening new and candid souls to the impressions of life; they had to relearn everything.

It was a spectacle that was both singular and sad to see those robust men, in the full maturity of life, become ignorant again, as timid and hesitant as little children on the threshold of existence.

During the days that followed the terrible shock, they had been the object of the most vigilant solicitude on the part of Rugel's daughter.

Like all the other inhabitants of the lunar world, she knew their story and had not been able to help feeling a sentiment of profound admiration for the men who had made such a heroic sacrifice of their lives. She wanted to supervise the care that was given to them personally. She followed the rapid progress of their resurrection with an emotional gaze, and when she saw that, in spite of the return of physical health, their minds were delayed in recovering all their power and lucidity, she was profoundly troubled, and admitted as much to Azali.

The young scientist had been the friend of her heart for some time. They had lived side by side and, in that world where sentiments developed in complete freedom, without any propriety ever constraining them, they had been attracted to one another and had abandoned themselves to the charms of a shared affection. As they had nothing to hide, and could not hide anything of what they were experiencing, Rugel was aware of that reciprocal penchant as soon as it was born. Everything about that love, which bore no resemblance to Earthly passions, was pure, simple and honest. That was how things happened in that privileged milieu; in all probability, they would soon be married and found a new family around Rugel.

The accident that had befallen the inhabitants of Earth had brought the young woman even closer to the man that everyone who knew her already considered to be her fiancé.

Retained by the cares of which the three patients were the object, Azali rarely went far from the house to which they had been transported. The time that he did not spend with them he devoted to the one that his heart had chosen.

When Rugel was recalled to the capital by his duties, they often went for walks along the shores of the enchanted island or through the flowery arbors with which it was covered, doing so with the innocence and liberty of mores in which nothing impure ever germinated. Their conversations, grave and lively by turns, revealed the serenity of their souls and their calm confidence in the future.

Orealis displayed none of the tricks of coquetry, the clever maneuvers and studied provocations with which feminine shrewdness is exercised down here, when it is a matter of making sure, in the quest for a husband, of the conquest of a fine name or a brilliant fortune. And on Azali's part, there was nothing resembling the protestations of love that sometimes ring so false, the conventional exaggerations, the insipid and vulgar compliments beneath which, on Earth, dryness of heart and baseness of desires are so often concealed.

One day, in the course of their customary stroll, Orealis interrogated the young scientist on the subject that had begun to preoccupy her some time before. "My friend," she said, "I'm wondering with some anxiety whether we ought to rejoice at having snatched from death those it had already seized. Their bodies appear to have recovered a condition of health, but the state of their minds troubles and torments me. They seem to have retreated to the first phase of life; they have no more strength or scope than a child. Are they, then, doomed remain forever immure in that intellectual limbo? If so, we've only saved them to condemn them an existence unworthy of them, and utterly miserable."

"I too am troubled by the condition I see them in," Azali replied, sadly. "I know that the shock they experienced was profound, but I didn't think they were so gravely affected. Their memory of the past seems to have been almost completely abolished; they're entirely restricted to fleeting momentary impressions. What it's necessary to do to return them to themselves is to reawaken, by every possible means, the effaced sentiment of their personality.

"It's up to you, Orealis, good and gentle as you are, already so maternal in their regard, to make the memories that have been temporarily suppressed revive, by reminding them of the events through which they've passed. By that means, their intelligence will develop more rapidly and they'll soon recover the sentiment of their great designs and the will to pursue them, thanks to your generous influence."

"May the Sovereign Spirit hear you," Orealis murmured, having become pensive.

From then on she devoted herself entirely to the curative process she had undertaken. It was a charming and melancholy thing to see that tall and beautiful young woman becoming the patient and devoted instructress of the three men, bronzed by such rude vicissitudes, reverted to infancy, who listened to her avidly as to an elder sister.

In the marvelous stories that she adapted to their minds with an ingenious skill, the young woman caused them to relive before her eyes the terrible ordeals through which they had passed, the works that they had accomplished, and the hopes they had conceived. Gradually, the consciousness of their identity reawakened. They remaining hanging on her lips; sometimes, their eyebrows as if, in some labor on interior reflection, a corner of the veil that still hid reality from them had torn, and the moment could already be foreseen when they would recover full possession of themselves.

But it was Marcel in particular, more than his two friends, who seemed to be subject to the young woman's magnetic influence. The sound of her voice threw him into a kind of ecstasy; the charm that emanated from her entire person acted upon him irresistibly; confused movements of which he could only take imperfect account agitated his heart. And when, having returned to himself, he asked himself what he had experienced, he wondered, not without a certain alarm, whether that delightful sentiment was only gratitude, or whether it merited a more tender name.

Soon, it was no longer possible for him to labor under any illusion. He was experiencing emotions hitherto unknown. His active and questing mind, which had never been impassioned by anything but the solution of scientific problems or the realization of some bold enterprise, seemed to have lost its initiative and its vigor. A kind of languorous lassitude had invaded him; he now delighted in allowing himself to be lulled by soft reveries. Birdsong and the harmony of the wind in the foliage delighted him, his overexcited imagination incessantly showed him the beautiful Orealis; he could not tear his thoughts away from her, and when he was apart from her he remained plunged in a melancholy whose sadness was not without charm.

There was no longer any doubt about it; he was in love with the young woman.

The moment when that truth appeared to him unclouded was cruel. He knew that Orealis was the fiancée of a man to whom he was indebted and, in the rectitude of his conscience, he shivered at the thought that he could not abandon himself to his love without showing an odious ingratitude. And then again, there were so many obstacles between himself and the one to whom his heart was drawn!

Even supposing that their souls were able to reach an understanding and that the sentiment he was experiencing could be shared, how could a union be possible between two beings so different in nature?

Marcel was too innately honest not to judge his new situation sanely. He tried bravely to combat the passion that was gradually overwhelming him. That struggle was the cause of painful torments for him.

He now avoided the presence that he had previously sought out, but he had forsaken, along with the ignorance of the state of his soul, the repose and tranquility of his mind.

The state of disturbance and uncertainty in which Marcel was struggling had not escaped the observation of his two friends. Jacques and Lord Rodilan, who had been afflicted in the same way as the young engineer, had passed through the same phases. Thanks to the attentive and devoted solicitude by which they had been surrounded, they too had gradually climbed back up the slope down which their reason had slid; they had recovered all the liberty of their intelligence. Jacques had recovered his generous ardors, Lord Rodilan his self-possession and the slightly disdainful calm from which he had only rarely departed since leaving the Earth.

They were troubled by Marcel's strange sadness.

Its cause did not escape them for long; Jacques remembered what it had felt like when his own heart had opened to the love that now filled his entire being. That made his sympathy for Marcel all the greater and more affectionate.

As for the Englishman, what preoccupied him most of all was the question of the ultimate outcome of their enterprise. What would become of them if the natural leader of their expedition lost his lucidity of mind, and the energy necessary to see it through to the end, in a mad and unrealizable amour?

In spite of the singular adventures into which they had been thrown by his desire for new emotions and his disgust with the world that he knew too well, Lord Rodilan had not entirely rid himself of the man he had been before. The vicissitudes of the strange voyage had undoubtedly made his soul vibrate with sensations he had thought himself incapable of experiencing, and which had delighted him. The spectacle of this world, so different from the one he had quit, had not been able to leave him insensible, and more than once, in spite of his British phlegm and his desire not to be astonished by anything, he had felt surprised or gripped by admiration. That was something entirely new for a blasé individual like him, and it had moved him delightfully.

He had even promised himself to astonish the inhabitants of Earth in his turn—for he was counting on returning someday—with the description of this superior humankind, and it was for that reason that he had attached himself, with an ardor that even astonished him, to the study of the mores, institutions and history of the lunar world. And it was no slender satisfaction for his pride to think that, thanks to him, England would have its share of glory, and not the least, in the marvelous epic that would reveal to the Earth an unknown world, and would be the point of departure for an era of progress of which no one had so far dared to dream.

But if all that satisfied Lord Rodilan's mind, there were other exigencies against which he struggled, sometimes not without suffering. Although he had previously affected to be indifferent to the pleasures of a well-supplied table, on the pretext that nothing could be new for his weary palate, he had not taken long to regret what he had once disdained. He had not adapted well to the chemical composition that sufficed for his friends, and to which he referred disdainfully as "scientific nourishment." The attempts at cultivation made by Marcel, only a few of which had succeeded, furnished the three exiles from Earth with the cereals and legumes to which they were accustomed, but without any seasoning; and as all animal nourishment was forbidden to him, the unfortunate son of Albion suffered more every day in thinking about large slices of bloody roast beef, turtle soup and various pickles, the mere idea of which made his mouth water.

He was, therefore, thinking seriously about the return journey.

He had not yet talked to Marcel about it; he sensed that the young engineer might not welcome the idea so long as he had not realized the immediate goal of his enterprise—which is to say, establishing regular communications between the two planets. But if Marcel, surrendering himself to the tender sentiments that now seemed to be dominating him, were to lose sight of the project he had formed, the hope of returning might be postponed indefinitely. Even worse, if the engineer thought of devoting his life definitively to the woman he loved, what would become of his two companions?

Such was the question that imposed itself on Lord Rodilan's mind, and caused him to envisage the future anxiously. He was definitely not made for this superior world.

Rugel's daughter had not failed to notice the change that had overtaken Marcel's humor and character. She could not read the depths of his heart, because the inhabitant of Earth was deprived of the subtle sense that established such a close connection between speech and thought in the lunar world that no one there could hide anything. By virtue of the expression of Marcel's gaze, however, the tender inflections of his voice and the disturbance that afflicted him when he was in her presence, she ended up comprehending the sentiment of which she was the object.

At first, she had not seen in Marcel's desire to seek out her society anything but the manifestations of gratitude, something akin to the unconscious gratitude that a child experiences for the woman who watches over his cradle, smiles at his joys and soothes his suffering. Gradually, however, as Marcel's affection became more pressing his moods more changeable, she had become anxious.

When she saw that he had lost sight of the objective of his voyage, no longer talking about his great endeavor, seemingly enclosing his life in the narrow circle of that new intimacy, she observed him more attentively, and did not take long to become certain of the nature of his feelings for her.

That was a painful discovery for the young woman.

Certainly, she felt a profound sympathy for the hero of such a marvelous adventure, especially for one whom her care brought back to intelligence and the life of the heart, but her soul was too noble and her nature too superior for her to be able to abandon herself, in the presence of the love she felt, to the puerile joy of satisfied vanity.

There was no place in her heart for pride, and it was with sadness that she saw Marcel suffering thus from a love without any possible issue.

From then on, she strove to heal that wounded soul.

Far from seeking to irritate Marcel's passion by avoiding him, she created opportunities to encounter him and to talk to him, to bring him back, by showing him the serenity of her heart, to a more accurate sense of reality, to dissipate the chimeras that might be cradling his mind, and to revive the lofty ambitions to which he had initially devoted his life.

Together they strolled in the delightful gardens that surrounded Rugel's house; they wandering along the edge of the lake, where they sometimes climbed into a small boat and allowed themselves to be gently rocked by the perfumed breeze that floated over the tranquil water.

"Friend," she said to him, "does it not seem to you that the time has come, now that you've completely recovered your health, to resume the attempts that were so abruptly interrupted? Your friends on Earth are anxiously waiting for the response to the signals they've addressed to you. Do you intend to leave them any longer in such cruel uncertainty?"

"Oh," replied Marcel, with a movement of impatience that he could not dissimulate, "why snatch me thus from my enchanted dream? Since I've been living in your presence, Orealis, I feel happier than I have ever hoped to be. Are you already so weary of my presence, then? What have I done that you should seek to get rid of me like this?"

"Dispel such thoughts, friend," the young woman replied, gently. "if you could read my heart, you would see a profound affection for you there, and it's precisely because you're dear to me that I'm anxious about this unworthy repose in which you're forgetting yourself. I love your great plans, and the audacity of your enterprise, but I also love the glory that awaits you, and which I don't want you to renounce."

"Yes," said Marcel, vehemently, "you love in me that which now has little value in my eyes. What I'd like to see you love is me, my heart, full of you—for I can't retain any longer the confession that's burning my lips. Orealis, I..."

"Stop, friend," the young woman interrupted, swiftly, emphasizing the word *friend*, which seemed to ring false in Marcel's ears. "I know what you're going to say. Your secret has been known to me for some time, and I've made every effort to ensure that the sentiment you possess remained restricted by the limits of a sincere and honest friendship. Nothing else, in fact, can exist between us. Even if we were not separated by insurmountable obstacles, you know that I cannot respond to your love. I do not belong to myself; my faith is pledged to a man that you ought to love and respect. My heart has confirmed the choice of my reason, and it is solely from the man who has judged me worthy of him that I must expect the share of happiness to which every human being has the right to aspire. I don't know how things happen in the world from which you come, but here, our souls cannot pass from one love to another, and once our hearts have spoken, it is forever."

"Oh, you're torturing me," Marcel murmured. "What you're saying I've repeated to myself a hundred times; and it's only in being vanquished by the excess of my loved for you that I've let the secret escape that I would have rather retained in the depths of my soul. What breaks my heart is the sovereign virtue, the serenity of soul that sets you so far above our terrestrial passions, and perhaps it's because I know that you're inaccessible to my desires that I feel myself more violently attracted to you."

"Child," said Orealis, smiling. "It's always the impossible that tempts you; it's that desire to attain the unrealizable that drove you this far, and it's the same hope that is leading you astray today. To the same extent that the first ambition was noble and generous, the passion you're suffering now is regrettable and deadly. It will become wretched if it distracts you any longer from your great endeavor."

"Eh? What do you want me to do now that you've dashed the only hope that attached me to life and could give me the strength to carry on until the end?"

"What I want you to do is to be a man: to rid yourself of the vain chimeras that are obscuring your mind and troubling your will; to march with a form stride, enslaved to the duty that you've imposed on yourself, without looking back at the path you've traced, to pursue without weakness the realization of your fecund endeavor."

She became more animated. "Oh, I'm dreaming of a great and noble destiny for you. After having explored our world, I want you to return to the people of Earth, to tell them that an entire humankind exists here, eager to enter into communication with them. I want you to be the first pioneer of that route, into which human genius will enter. And my heart will follow you; I shall be proud when I think about you, and it will be pleasant for me to believe that the desire to merit my esteem and admiration has not been unconnected with the efforts that you have made to being that glorious design to a conclusion."

While she was speaking, her face had been transfigured, becoming radiant with enthusiasm; her eyes seemed to be flashing, her bosom was swollen with pride; she seemed magnified. One might have thought that she could already see in her mind's eye that brilliant future in which the two worlds, united in fraternal thought, would go side by side at an equal pace toward enlightenment and progress.

Marcel looked at her in surprise. She had never appeared to him so radiant and so beautiful; he had not suspected such a nobility in her sentiments, such an elevation in her soul. But he also understood how far distant from him such a perfect nature was. He felt the abyss that separated him from her hollowing out, becoming deeper and more insurmountable. And confused sentiments agitated his heart.

To renounce the love that had been cradling his life so tenderly for dome time seemed impossible. On the other hand, how could he not strive to be worthy of the magnificent hopes that Orealis has conceived?

The conflict raging within him was visible in his face.

Finally, that which was good and noble in his heart got the upper hand. "Well, so be it," he said. "It shall be as you demand. I renounce the hope of being loved by you. I'll content myself with your friendship and your amity. But I want them entirely, and since it's necessary, in order to obtain and keep them, to devote myself unreservedly to the completion of the work I've begun, that's what I shall do."

III. Stupidity and Routine

"Nothing again," said the astronomer Mathieu-Rollère, regretfully tearing himself away from the ocular of the telescope. "Three months have already gone by since our friends revealed their presence; I'm beginning to fear that some misfortune has befallen them and that we'll be forced to renounce the hopes that seemed so magnificent."

"Bah!" replied the Burnett, with his American phlegm. "It's necessary not to despair until it's demonstrated absolutely that success is impossible."

"Undoubtedly, but if they were able to make the first signals that you perceived, why haven't they done it again?"

"Why? How do I know? A thousand accidents might have occurred of which it's impossible for us to have the slightest idea, any one of which might suffice to explain their silence. Remember that, from now on, the mere fact that they were able to reach the surface of the Moon, and from there to put themselves in communication with us, even if only once, has brought science the solution to important problems."

"Yes, but I wish..."

"You're too impatient, my venerable friend. Isn't it already a great deal to know that life is possible on the surface of the satellite? And on that point, no further doubt is permissible. There's air, if not all around the Moon, at least in certain parts of it, since our friends are alive there and have been able to send us their signals.

"As for the signals themselves, it's difficult to be precise about their nature. To judge by their form and deliberate intermittence, they seem to be electrical in nature. But how were our voyagers, with the limited resources at their disposal, able to produce them? The response to that question is rather embarrassing. How were they able to make contact with lunar humankind? Thus far, we don't know anything about that, and only further signals can inform us."

"That's true, but it's precisely that absence of new signals that desolates me. If they could make the first ones, nothing prevents them from doing it again. Even supposing that one of them had perished, the others could have repeated the experiment. For nothing to appear, I'm afraid that all three of them must have been killed. And, I'll confess to you frankly, my dear friend, that thought is tormenting me obsessively. It's me who pushed my nephew to associate himself with that reckless enterprise; I wanted to realize, for him, for myself and for my country, a sublime conquest; I've separated Jacques from the woman he loved.

"My daughter hasn't lost confidence, she still remains sure that she'll see her fiancé again—but if my fears are, alas, well-founded, as I anticipate, and Jacques doesn't come back, what will become of me in the presence of her despair? Oh, I sense today the terrible responsibility I've assumed; in my mad scientific pride I didn't think about that, but now it weighs upon me with all its weight, and I ask myself with terror whether I haven't committed sacrilege in tempting Heaven thus."

"Don't worry, my friend; what they've done for us is a guarantee of what they might yet do. For myself, I have a profound conviction that after a pause that we can't estimate at present, they'll give us more manifest evidence of their presence. Isn't everything about this incredible odyssey marvelous? Have you ever wondered how our voyagers, whom we saw disappear into a fissure at the foot of the crater Aristillus, were able to transport themselves into the vicinity of the crater Hansteen—which is to say, about sixty degrees, or more than four hundred and fifty leagues of four kilometers each?"

"That's true," murmured Mathieu-Rollère. "I didn't think of that."

"Well, if they've been able to travel such a distance in the conditions that exist on the surface of the Moon, according to the astronomical evidence, it's difficult to believe that they succeeded in doing so by means of their own resources—it's evident that they were helped. By whom? How? It's impossible for us to know. All that we can conclude, and we already know it from the discovery of the ball that determined their departure, is that the Moon really is inhabited and that our friends have been able to enter into communication with the beings, whatever they are, who live there."

"But how is it, then, that with the powerful telescope we have at our disposal, which permits us to distinguish objects nine feet long, we've never perceived anything that denotes the presence of living and intelligent beings?"

"That's certainly something inexplicable—or, rather, un-explained, for everything comes with time. For the moment, what is certain is that our friends have arrived on the Moon, have survived there, have crossed a considerable distance and made signals whose existence we can have no doubt. If you think that isn't a magnificent result, you're very hard to please. Let's not begrudge them time, and wait patiently."

The assured tone in which the American astronomer had spoken had a salutary and comforting effect on the somewhat troubled soul of the aged scientist. So it was with an entirely youthful ardor that he occupied himself, in company with the engineer Georges Dumesnil, in preparing the large signaling installation designed to ensure future communications. They hastened to return to France.

It had been agreed that during their absence and every time the moment was favorable, Sir William Burnett would renew, at regular intervals, the signal already sent and as yet unanswered. The three voyagers would thus understand that their message had been received and that further communications on their part were awaited. If anything new showed on the surface of the satellite, the director of the Long's Peak Observatory would immediately inform Mathieu-Rollère.

With everything thus arranged, the old astronomer set forth resolutely on campaign.

It was a matter, it will be recalled, of obtaining permis-sion from the French government to arrange in a plain in southern Algeria the electric apparatus necessary to the pro-duction of signals, and also to persuade the Observatoire de

Paris to dispose funds in favor of the enterprise that would be allocated under the rubric of "scientific research."

The authorization was obtained, but not without difficulty. While the scientist had been in America the Ministry had been overthrown yet again. The powerful friends on whom he had been counting had been turned to the peace of private life. Under the pretext of purification, the entire senior administrative staff had been renewed, and the astronomer no longer knew anyone. In consequence, things did not go as quickly as he had expected. At the first step be bumped into the customary routines of bureaucracy.

To begin with, no one understood what he was asking. When they understood, it was necessary to decide to which ministry the authorization ought to be granted. It seemed that it was within the purview of Public Education, but as it was a matter of an installation on the territory of a French département, that might well be the concern of the Interior. On the other hand, the plain chosen was in the zone submissive to military authority, so it was difficult to by-pass the consent of the Ministry of War. The documents that required to be piled up, the requests to be redrafted, the journeys to be made and the steps to be taken would be incomprehensible to those who have not had the ill luck to have to deal with those infatuated autocrats, as peevish as they are unapproachable, who, because they behave self-importantly, believe that they have some importance.

The unfortunate scientist ran breathlessly from one ministry to another for several weeks, and was able to verify for himself the exactitude of the saying of a man who was very familiar with the administration that Europe is wrong to envy us: "It takes longer for a dossier to cross the Seine than for a sailing ship to cross the Atlantic."

Finally, a day came when the fortunate authorization, decorated with all the seals, stamps, signatures, countersignatures and visas required by a formalism as puerile as it is inquisitorial found its way into Mathieu-Rollère's hands.

It was now necessary to occupy himself with the problem of money. That was something else entirely.

At the first overture that the astronomer made to the director of the Observatoire de Paris, the latter, while not disapproving of his project, declared that the attribution of funds was outside his prerogatives, and dependent on a committee without the decision of which nothing could be decided. He did, however, declare that he was willing to convene the committee.

The discussion was stormy. The objections to the project proposed by Mathieu-Rollère were numerous and passionate. What was this visionary doing, whose fantasies flew in the face of all official science? Had it not been agreed for a long time that the Moon, devoid of air and water, was uninhabited and uninhabitable? What was he saying about human beings having reached the moon, survived there and manifested their presence? If that were true, damn it, it would be known, and nobody knew anything about it. It was him, Mathieu-Rollère, who was on the Moon; it was necessary to leave him there and not occupy themselves with such follies.

In the midst of that unleashing of furious clamors, a few timid voices rose up. Why condemn thus, without wanting to examine it, a proposition that might be serious? If they did not want to trust the word of the American observer, they could nevertheless grant some credence to the more reserved affirmations of the director of the Observatoire de Nice. He was certainly no hoaxer; he had certainly seen something. Was that not a precious indication? Was it worthy of an assembly of French scientists to pass by disdainfully without wanting to attempt anything? What would become of the good renown of France, which had always been proud of marching at the head along the path of scientific discovery? What shame would not rebound on her if some other nation, shrewder and bolder, stole the glory of such an initiative from her?

But the president of the committee, an old scientific stick-in-the-mud who lived on his reputation far more than any real merit, and who disliked any discovery of which he was not the author, got to his feet and, dominating the tumult, shouted: "Enough discussion! We're the strict guardians of funds that the State has put at our disposal. We don't have the right to risk them in insensate enterprises and squander them for the satisfaction of stupid vanities. Let someone give us a precious and definite goal to attain, and we'll see what it's appropriate do, but one doesn't bring nonsense here, the cracked dreams of a sick brain. We'd be culpable if we lent our ears to it for a moment longer."

"Well, so be it!" exclaimed Mathieu-Rollère, exasperated. "I bring you definite results, scientifically established, checked by repeated experiments. There's none so blind as those who will not see. Oh, you can talk about squandering, of making a show of prudence and economy! Isn't French money poured out every day by the handful to content paltry ambitions or to furnish cumbersome mediocrities with the opportunity to make themselves known? And today, when it's a matter of the most important work that modern science has ever attempted, you talk about scruples and conscience! You're unworthy of the name of scientists—you're wretches!"

Anger blinded him; he had to be dragged away.

"Oh well," he said, while he was being removed, "I'll do without you. It won't be said that the stupid obstinacy of a few encrusted minds made me renounce my projects. I'll succeed without and in spite of you..."

In speaking thus the old scientist firmly believed in his success, but when it was necessary to bring about the realization of his project, he ran into difficulties that he had not foreseen. At first he thought about a public subscription, but to do that successfully would require advertising—a great deal of advertising—and that is something, in the present condition of journalism, that costs a great deal. The editors of the scientific journals considered him, in the main, to be an old fool, and did not want to compromise the name and dignity of their periodicals by associating themselves with such a utopia. As for other organs of publicity, they only accepted articles at exorbitant prices.

Mathieu-Rollère, who had begun by paying with an unalterable confidence, saw his personal resources diminishing rapidly. The subscription had been open for a month and had brought in exactly 1,967.50 francs.

The astronomer did not understand it at all.

How could people be insensible to the solution of such a problem? He was indignant to see people coming and going, hastening to their pleasures and business affairs, spending considerable sums on futilities, without giving any thought to furnishing science with the means to achieve the most magnificent conquest of which the human mind could dream: that of a world.

It did not take him long to fall into a state of profound depression. He had lost the exuberance of life and the almost juvenile activity that had thus far kept him youthful; he thought in a melancholy fashion about al his disappointments; the fears and the remorse that he had already confided to Sir William Burnett came back to his mind and tormented him.

His daughter, who had never quit him since Jacques' departure, had maintained a firmer determination. The love that filled her heart seemed to close it to any other sentiment than faith and hope. When she saw the old man thus discouraged, she simply said to him: "Why despair, Father? If it's a miserable question of money that's stopping you, take the fortune that my mother left me and make use of it as you please. I'll sacrifice it with joy and I'm certain that the man I love, when I see him again—because I will see him again, I'm sure of it—will approve of my decision. We'll live in poverty, if we must, glad to have accomplished a great task.

"Child," said Mathieu-Rollère, emotionally, hugging his daughter and kissing her forehead, "you have a noble heart; you're a worthy daughter of a scientist and you deserve the great love of an honest man. But my darling, what is the seventy or eighty thousand francs of which you can dispose? It's hundreds of thousands of francs, perhaps millions, that we'll need. That's what the egotism and cupidity of a century devoted to the vilest interests is refusing us obstinately. Oh, I feel

227

profoundly afflicted, and fear that I'll die before having brought our great work to a successful conclusion."

"Don't talk like that!" Hélène cried. "Take the money that I scorn, and which now fills me with horror. Perhaps you can find a means of using it to shake the apathy of the indifferent."

The old man shook his head without making any reply.

He was consumed by his sad reflections, and his discouragement was increasing every day when he suddenly received a dispatch from Long's Peak announcing that the three luminous letters M, J and R had reappeared in the south of the Ocean of Storms, in the vicinity of the crater Hansteen.

That news rendered the old astronomer all his ardor and energy; he swore that he would succeed.

IV. The Return to the Observatory

Access to the observatory had been reopened.

The work had been long and difficult. First of all it had been necessary to find the fissure through which the mephitic gases were escaping, which, after having filled the elevator's chimney, had invaded the entire edifice and almost caused the death of Merovar and the three foreigners. To that effect, men dressed in the kinds of apparatus that permitted them to explore the lunar surface had carefully traveled the length of the chimney, examining its walls minutely.

Long days had gone by in that research, but they had ended up establishing that at a height of about six terrestrial leagues, the rocky wall had given way under the pressure of contained gases. A crack had been produced, and it was through an enormous gaping hole that the gas had rushed out and invaded the whole shaft. Fortunately, that initial outburst had not been followed by any other; otherwise, nothing would have resisted the pressure of the formidable torrent, and the upper part of the observatory would have exploded. However, the poisonous vapors had replaced the breathable air everywhere; they occupied the entire space and compelled the workers to take the most scrupulous precautions.

In order to block the large opening, it had been necessary to hoist up numerous stone blocks, embed them profoundly in the wall where the crack had developed, and seal them with a tenacious cement. That titanic labor had not been completed without hard and painful efforts. Thus was constituted a thick artificial wall forming a solid mass with the rock face.

When that was done, they had been obliged to think about clearing out the vitiated air that filled the chimney and the observatory.

In order to succeed in that, openings had been made in the upper windows of the hall occupied by the large telescopes and in the bays illuminating the inferior part of the monument.

Then powerful ventilators, disposed at the bottom of the chimney and functioning relentlessly, adding their action to the pumps in everyday use, had gradually replaced the mortal air filing the shaft with pure air. That had taken a long time, and while that work of purification was taking place the observatory had passed through the period of daylight into darkness again.

It was a strange spectacle to see that torrent of gas and vapors condensing instantly under the action of the cold of space and falling to the ground in snowy flakes.

The work had finally run its course, and the sage Rugel had hastened to go to Marcel, who, after his decisive conversation with Orealis, had returned without delay to the lunar capital, where he was waiting impatiently for the moment to arrive when he could renew his attempts.

Jacques and Lord Rodilan, who had not had the same reasons as Marcel to forget the goal they were pursuing, were in even more haste than he was to resume a more active life. All three of them received the news that Rugel brought them joyfully, and they returned to the observatory. Orealis' father, although he welcomed the three foreigners with equal affability appeared to testify a greater affection for Marcel, which had something paternal about it. In his frequent visits, he had not failed to notice the state of mind in which the young engineer had found himself, and as his daughter could have no secrets from him, he had been able to follow the passion through which Marcel had passed throughout its development.

Undoubtedly, he had never been anxious with regard to his daughter, only fearing that the sentiment of which she was the object might trouble the peace of her soul, but he had been unable to help feeling a secret sympathy for the mental suffering that the great intelligence understood; he had admired the strength with which Marcel had triumphed over it, and the energy with which that virile soul had pulled itself together. Now, in fact, Marcel seemed to have completely forgotten that moment of weakness.

The truth is that his heart was still bleeding, but he had sworn to Orealis to be worthy of her, and was determined to keep his oath.

Scarcely had they returned to the observatory than the three friends went to visit the apparatus that they had used to send their luminous signals. Everything was in good condition; there was nothing to prevent communications being resumed at the point at which they had been interrupted.

When the examination was over, Marcel and his companions had gone into the observation hall. The two worlds were in their first quarter, and the concordance of darkness was complete between the two points from which the signals were made. At that moment, however, the American continent was still illuminated, and it would be necessary to wait for several hours before night fell there and it would be possible to see the luminous point already glimpsed.

All three were prey to the keenest impatience.

"Believe it or not, my dear Marcel," said Lord Rodilan, "I'd give a thousand guineas to know what they're thinking about us on Earth. Do they regard us as madmen or do they take us for audacious scientists who have just revolutionized everything known or believed to be known about the Moon?"

"You do too much honor to our terrestrial compatriots," Marcel replied. "You can be certain that, except for our friends at Long's Peak, and doubtless also Jacques' uncle, no one, or almost no one in interested in us. I'm convinced that if the news of the appearance of our luminous letters has been communicated to the scientific world by the honorable Burnett, it will only have encountered the most stupid incredulity. Too many people would be distu6rbed in their habits and routines, and it's simpler to deny what one doesn't understand."

"Certainly," said Jacques. "Remember what happened before. Was the scientific world excited about the voyage, already so marvelous, of Barbicane, Michel Ardan and Nicholl when the experiment was attempted? The audacious explorers were carried in triumph, and there was a pretext for lavish banquets and long speeches, but that enthusiasm didn't last, and in order for the memory of it to be preserved, it was necessary for an illustrious French writer to become the historian of that incredible event, and describe its exciting incidents with his habitual talent. But for him, that whole fantastic history would have been forgotten and would be completely unknown today."

"Jacques is right," said Lord Rodilan, "but you're forgetting that no Englishman featured in that first voyage. Otherwise, England wouldn't have permitted such an exploit to remain unknown."

"Well," said Marcel, smiling, "this time we have a citizen of free England with us, and are assured of remaining immortal henceforth."

There had been a certain amount of irony in that reply, but as it contained a sufficiently direct eulogy, the noble lord did not think it appropriate to protest.

"In any case," he said, instead, "it won't be long now before we can be certain on that point, for you are, I assume, thinking about the return journey?"

Marcel's expression darkened. "I have, indeed, given it some thought. To tell the truth, if I only had my own inclinations to consider, I'd be glad to conclude my days in the midst of this human race, which holds such an elevated rank in the scale of living beings. To leave this near-perfect world, where everything is noble and great, to fall back to Earth, where everything is paltry, crude and small, doesn't tempt me very much. Many other motives could attach me to the lunar world, but I can't think only of myself. I'm fully aware of the reasons recalling the two of you, and when the moment comes, I'll go with you."

Jacques shook his hand.

"However," Marcel continued, "I believe it will be some time yet before we can think seriously about making preparations for our return. Above all, it's necessary to establish communication with the Earth. That's our task, and we must devote ourselves to it completely. In my opinion, it will take a long time. Judge for yourselves: since we were sent the signal to which we were unable to reply, our friends have had no news of us, but they obviously can't attempt anything without being sure that we're still alive. They'll shortly have the certainty, of course, that we haven't perished and have perceived them. Like me, you know them; we can't doubt that they'll immediately begin doing what's necessary for communications to become regular, continuous and useful. They'll look for the system that is both rapid and practical. What will that system be? We don't know yet."

"Indeed," said Jacques. "I'll add that it's improbable that they'll choose the region of the Rocky Mountains to send us continuous signals. They couldn't be easily established and function reliably in that tortuous country and at such an altitude."

"That's true," Marcel continued. "It's impossible for us to divine the region of the terrestrial globe from which the imminent appeals will reach us. What plain will they choose for that purpose? Only the future can inform us on that matter. In any case, we won't be able to attempt anything other than what we've already done before such questions are completely fixed.

While Marcel was speaking, night had gradually enveloped the Atlantic, and had already attained Long's Peak. The three observers took their place again at the oculars of the telescopes. Their emotion was great and the profoundest silence reigned in the hall.

An hour, and then two, passed with nothing appearing.

Suddenly, a luminous point lit up the midst of the darkness.

A triple cry of joy was heard.

This time, no doubt was possible; the signal was there, before their eyes, immobile and fixed. It was not an illusion, a dream of their overexcited imagination. It was a living reality.

And it seemed to them that those rays of light were bringing the voices of those who had launched them into space; they felt them quivering and vibrating; the souls of their friends were trembling therein. It was no longer just a luminous message; it was like a magnetic current making hearts beat in unison.

The problem was resolved; their signals, patiently awaited, had been perceived and understood. A reply had been sent, and without being discouraged by the long period of inaction that had followed, the response signal had been untiringly renewed.

What admirable constancy the observers at Long's Peak had shown! What sublime faith in the future of science! And how grateful the three voyagers were to them on recognizing today that that they had not allowed themselves to fall into despair.

The light was still shining; after an hour, it was extinguished.

"Quickly," said Marcel. "They've been waiting anxiously, for nearly four months, for us to show signs of life. Let's not leave out friends in suspense any longer."

So saying, he grasped the handle of the commutator, placed within arm's reach.

The profound darkness enveloping the lunar plain was suddenly illuminated. A gigantic blazing J was outlined on the ground.

"To you, friend," he said, turning to Jacques, "the honor of being the first to reveal our presence to those awaiting us. If your uncle and the one your heart has never forgotten are still in the Rocky Mountains, I want them to be reassured on your account without delay."

"Thank you," said Jacques, shaking his hand.

"You'll excuse me, my dear lord," Marcel added, smiling. "But neither of us is in love..."

"Oh, for myself," said Lord Rodilan, "it's a long time since my heart ceased to beat rapidly, if it ever did. But for you, my friend, it might be reckless to affirm that only the love of science has ever reigned in your soul." At that allusion, benevolent as it was, a cloud passed over Marcel's face. The Englishman pretended not to notice it and continued: "No one on Earth is waiting for me or missing me. I won't accord a few

234

indifferent individuals with whom I've rubbed shoulders the honor of reckoning them as friends. At least I owe to this voyage the good fortune of encountering two, and that's enough for me."

The amity that united the three men was now indissoluble. Born of chance, of the common idea of during something unprecedented, it had been fortified in the midst of redoubtable ordeals and the most various fortunes experienced together; now, the success obtained thanks to their indomitable energy had consecrated it forever. From the day when all three had embarked into the Columbiad's shell and had confided themselves to the hazards of the immensity, they had never been apart. It was while always supporting one another that they had confronted unknown perils, risked their lives a hundred times, and finally triumphed over nature, whose laws they seemed to have vanquished. Whatever happened henceforth, they were united by unbreakable bonds.

The magical letters succeeded one another at regular intervals, and every time their flamboyant brightness succeeded darkness, they saw the Long's Peak signal, immutable and fixed, gleaming in the distance.

"Our friends decidedly lack imagination," murmured Lord Rodilan. Their sentences aren't long. A full stop, that's all."

"You're joking, my dear Rodilan," said Marcel, "but even that confirms my expectations. It's certain, in my opinion, that if they intended to send us signals from America permitting useful correspondence, they'd already have found a means of ensuring communications. Obviously, they're making preparations. How long will they take to complete? Only they can know. But I'm convinced that at a given moment, perhaps soon, we'll see something new appear that will give us full satisfaction. I repeat that we have only to wait."

And it was agreed that, until further notice, they were keep to the signals thus far exchanged.

V. In Algeria

South-west of Biskra, about fifty kilometers from the Ziban capital, on the right bank of the Oued-Djeddi, a vast plain extends eastwards as far as Chott Melrhir and southwards as far as the Oued-Melah.

To the west, the horizon is limited by the hills of sand that separate the basins of those watercourses, dry more often than not. It was in that region, visited by the Romans, and then the conquering Arabs who expelled the autochthonous Berbers, that the engineer Georges Dumesnil had decided to establish the system of signals that would permit correspondence with the inhabitants of the Moon.

The old astronomer had sworn to succeed; he had kept his word, but not without difficulty. After the pitiful failure of the public subscription he had opened, there could be no thought of a further appeal to the masses. The egotistical crowd, enslaved to its material instincts, was incapable of getting excited about a great scientific idea still in the domain of theory, in which it saw no practical utility. Even those people whose studies or functions seemed to prepare them to welcome the great project favorably were incredulous and not disposed to loosen their purse-strings.

Mathieu-Rollère had even addressed himself to the generous donor who had already made so many sacrifices to the progress of astronomical science and had endowed the Observatoire de Paris with its most advanced instruments, but at that moment the rich banker who had made such noble usage of his fortunes had recently devoted considerable sums to the erection of the Observatoire de Nice, and in spite of the enthusiasm that Mathieu-Rollère's plan caused him, he was obliged to leave to others the glory of rendering the grandiose enterprise possible.

In spite of his confidence, the old scientist was feeling doubt invade his soul, when a note read by chanced in a newspaper retuned all his confidence. At that moment, the man sitting on the throne of Brazil was not just a sovereign but a sage. Emperor Dom Pedro II divided his life between the duties of his position and the study of the sciences, about which he was passionate.[24] Every year, when he had taken care of matters of State, he came to France, to that nucleus of enlightenment, which, in spite of the blows of ill-fortune, has never ceased to shine upon the world. A corresponding member of the Académie des Sciences, he was interested in all the works of that learned assembly. His broad mind, curious for knowledge, had never been able to lose interest in the important problems that astronomy poses incessantly to minds avid for speculative research. He had already met Mathieu-Rollère during a visit to the Observatoire de Paris in the course of a previous voyage. The latter's work on the satellites of Uranus had seemed very remarkable to him.

The prince, so different from the majority of those who wear the royal circlet, was poorly understood by the mass of his subjects, unaccustomed to seeing philosophers and scientists in government, so they were to rise up against him a few years later and expel him brutally from the throne.

One day, while casting a distracted glance over the current events section of Le Figaro, Mathieu-Rollère read these lines:

His Majesty Emperor Dom Pedro will arrive in Paris shortly. He intends to stay for some time, in order to put the

---

[24] Dom Pedro II (1825-1891), who had succeeded to the imperial throne at the age of five in 1831, was indeed passionate about science, and did his very best to promote research in physics, chemistry and astronomy, as well as fighting long and hard for the abolition of slavery. This part of the story must be set prior to 1887, when his health worsened dramatically, making way for a military coup in 1889. Within the story's chronology it is probably 1885, but the author's awareness of the coup must mean that the reference in question was added after that date.

final touches to an important work, about which he wanted to consult a few of his colleagues at the Institut.

The old scientist's face lit up. If he did not cry "Eureka!" like Archimedes, it was because he did not think of it, but he rubbed his hands together vigorously.

"Just what I need," he said. "That's the only man who can understand me and help me." Without delay, he went to see the august sovereign, who received him immediately with his customary bonhomie.

In that first meeting, Mathieu-Rollère told his imperial colleague everything that had happened: the voyage accomplished by Marcel and his companions; the appearance of the luminous letters on the lunar disk; the work already done at Long's Peak Observatory to sketch a commencement of communications. He showed him the telegrams exchanged with Sir William Burnett and the plans, already drawn up, to extract useful and desirable consequences from so many heroic efforts.

The emperor was enthused.

So, when Mathieu-Rollère told him about the failure of his attempt to raise the sum necessary for such work, his benevolent interlocutor was immediately disposed to come to his aid.

Several more meetings took place. In which the accounts that the engineer Dumesnil had carefully drawn up were examined. The total was rather high, more than three million.

Dom Pedro grimaced. "Damn!" he said. "I'm not a sovereign rich enough to pay for such a fantasy. The civil list my subjects grant me and my parliament balks at votes through every year couldn't support such an increase in expenditure. Oh, my dear friend, monarchs today are poor, and I sometimes think sadly about your great King Louis XIV, who drew from the purses of his subjects as he wished, not hesitating for a moment when it was a matter of making the marvels of Versailles and Marly spring from the ground."

"Everything degenerates," the old scientist murmured. "It's also to Louis XIV that we owe the Observatoire, and if it didn't exist, God knows whether our government would consent to pay its expenses today. I was however, counting on Your Majesty; that was my last hope, and if it fails, all is lost."

"Let's see," said the emperor. "Perhaps there's a means to reach an understanding. Can't you make a few modifications to the plan that's been drawn up, and reduce at least some of the expenses?"

A rescuing branch was being offered to the astronomer; he grasped it desperately. "Assuredly," he said. "Our collaborator has included a Decauville railway between Biskra and the chosen site, which is about fifty kilometers away. We can do without that temporarily, and carry out the necessary transportations with carts or other means that are available locally. That would be a big saving. The expenses for staff and accommodation could also be reduced, I think, but nothing can be spared with regard to the electrical network. I'll consult Dumesnil about it."

"Do that," said the Emperor. "I'll put a sum of 1.5 million francs at your disposal; that's the best I can do." He smiled and added; "And I'll be scathingly criticized for this new folly."

"That will be sufficient," said Mathieu-Rollère. "It will have to be sufficient. May Your Majesty be blessed!"

In the last days of January 188-, the banks of the Oued-Djeddi became the theater of an extraordinary activity. All the components necessary for the projected installation were brought by railway to Biskra, and every day, long processions of carts and camels, laden with heavy boxes or various bizarre forms that frightened the local natives, departed from the city. Life became unusually active in that usually bleak and desolate region. The grinding of gears, the whinnies of the horses and the oaths of the drivers troubled the silence of the wilderness.

Assisted by twenty carefully-selected electricians from Paris, Mathieu-Rollère and Dumesnil were seen everywhere, with their cork helmets and white garments, hastening the convoys and supervising the unloading of materials, Soon,

239

they were able to begin the construction of hangars and the wooden huts to accommodate the staff of the enterprise. In fact, they only had to assemble the sections prepared in advance and carefully numbered.

The work advanced rapidly, and by 8 February they were able to start preparing the ground where the electrical network was to be established. Over an extent of about two hectares of carefully leveled ground, they first disposed a massive framework of beams a meter long and connecting at right-angles. The edge of the framework constituted a rectangle 125 meters long and 80 wide, divided into ten thousand one-meter squares. To each of the intersections of the beams a powerful electric arc-lamp was solidly fixed, furnished with a silvered parabolic reflector fifty meters in radius. Each reflector was linked to its neighbors by means of grips and pressure-screws, which ensured cohesion of the ensemble.

For a month, the twenty electricians, stimulated by Dumesnil, who was devoured by a feverish impatience, worked relentlessly. To the great astonishment of the indigenes, whom curiosity drew continually to the work-site, the ten thousand lamps were laid out on the ground. Already, when the sun, so ardent in that hot climate, darted its rays at the polished surfaces, it made them shine with an unsustainable glare. More than once they were obliged to remove importunates whose persistence threatened to disturb the work, and Mathieu-Rollère ended up enclosing the site and its buildings with a solid fence whose boundary was patrolled by a number of sentinels.

On the network thus disposed, all the letters of the alphabet could be easily depicted in luminous lines. A system of carefully-insulated electric wires linked each lamp, on the one hand, to powerful dynamos that produced current, and on the other, to 25 commutators disposed like a keyboard, each of which bore a letter of the alphabet.

As a considerable number of lamps could enter into the composition of several different letters, they were careful to link them by different wires to the commutators designed to light up each of the letters in which it was to participate. Thus, some of the lamps serving to form the letter D also served to form the letters B, E, R, L and so on. Each of them was thus attached by wires to each of the switches that had to be activated to form those various letters. It was sufficient, to obtain the desired symbol, to depress an ivory handle. When it was raised again, everything was extinguished, and, by means of another maneuver, under the action of different currents, the lamps designed to form the next letter were illuminated.

That was the simple and practical application of the signaling system conceived by Georges Dumesnil. On a relatively restricted surface, always the same, all the characters necessary to express thought with the utmost precision could succeed one another at brief intervals. It was impossible to imagine a more complete and more reliable realization of the theory of the optical telegraph.

One of the huts had been fitted out to accommodate the series of commutators, situated some distance away from the electrical network, in order that the manipulation of the levers should not be hindered by the unsustainable glare of the luminous lamps.

To protect the rectangle thus established against the rains that fell every year in winter, large tarpaulins had been set up which, when unfurled, covered the entire surface.

All of that work, so delicate and scrupulous, had taken a great deal of time. A month had sufficed to fix the ten thousand lamps solidly on their framework, but to establish the multiple network of wires that ran side by side without confusion took five long weeks. In the meantime, mechanics set up the steam engines and the dynamos.

Everything was ready to function by 14 April. By that time, the new moon was approaching.

"Let's take advantage of the moment," said Mathieu-Rollère, to make sure that everything is working properly. We can now test our apparatus by night without fear of being seen by our friends, who surely aren't on the lookout. We ought not to be running any risk of giving them false hope by commencing signals that we'll be forced to interrupt. We ought not to act until we're certain."

The precaution was wise. Before arriving at perfect functioning there were several hitches. Wires were broken; others, in spite of the precautions taken, were entangled and the insulating material had been destroyed by friction. In consequence, there were perturbations in the current and repairs that needed several days to carry out.

Finally, everything was ready and they could attempt the final trial.

On a dark night, when thick cloud covered the sky, the ten thousand lamps were switched on, and that flood of light, springing abruptly from the ground, struck the clouds and made them resplendent with an unaccustomed glitter.

To complete the experiment and take an exact account of the fashion in which the apparatus was functioning, they caused all the letters of the alphabet to appear in succession, and the strange spectacle was seen of the gigantic characters lighting up against the somber vault of the sky. One might have thought that a mysterious hand were tracing those lines of fire, as once, at the feast of a barbarian king, the threatening letters announcing the collapse of an empire had shone upon the polished marble walls. The neighboring populations, struck by terror at the sight of that new kind of meteor, prostrated themselves in the dust, wondering what spells the accursed foreigners had brought to the locale, and murmuring the name of Allah.

All the Europeans living in Biskra and a good number of tourists, attracted by curiosity, gathered around the enclosure and saluted the events with their cheers and cries.

It was beginning to cause a stir in the scientific community. The Brazilian emperor's act of generosity had not taken long to become known, and the sacrifice of such a huge sum had impressed those who had so far been the most incredulous. It was said that for such a clear-thinking monarch to have made such a decision without hesitation, Mathieu-Rollère must have furnished him with precise information and conclusive evidence. And it was as if the tide of public opinion began to turn.

People returned to the question of possible communication with Earth's satellite, and the problem no longer seeming insoluble. The theories alleging that certain parts of the Moon might be habitable returned to favor; the appearances of luminous points that certain observers claimed to have seen on the lunar dusk at various times were remembered, and it was said that, after all, experience had frequently belied seemingly well-founded assertions in the realm of astronomy, and brought science unexpected revelations.

That agitation of minds crossed the narrow bounds of the Institut and scientific societies. Specialist periodicals took possession of the problem and examined it from every angle. In their wake, the great organs of publicity thought it their duty to inform their readers, and with the fever of reportage and need for rapid information characteristic of our epoch, they followed that path swiftly and for a long distance.

First of all, they wanted to be sure of the departure of the three voyagers that Mathieu-Rollère alleged to have reached the satellite's surface. Intelligent reporters went to Florida to see the Columbiad with their own eyes, interrogate the local people, magistrates or simple residents, and made it known to the entire world that a second departure of the shell founded by the Gun Club really had taken place on 15 December 188-.

Proofs confirming that extraordinary event arrived from all directions. In Baltimore, the official record was found of the sale at which Lord Rodilan had acquired the Columbiad and all its accessories. At Long's Peak Observatory, Sir William Burnett was interviewed many times over, telling the story of Marcel's life in the region, the discovery of the mysterious ball and confirming the reality of the appearance on the lunar disk of letters indicating the arrival of the three voyagers.

Before that abundance of information, spread everywhere in thousands of copies, doubt was scarcely possible, and the names of Marcel de Rouzé, Jacques Deligny and Lord Rodilan soon became famous.

It was in England, most of all, that the excitement assumed the sharpest character. As soon as it became known that a member of the English aristocracy was included among the audacious explorers, the snobbery of the inhabitants of the United Kingdom gladdened their hearts, and the columns of the *Times*, which always reflected the sentiments of its numerous readers so exactly, caused the name of the noble lord to resound. The role that he had played in the colossal endeavor was now known, and it was repeated endlessly that without him, nothing would have been possible, which proved once again that England was always and everywhere the foremost nation in the world. It would not have taken much for all the honor of the grandiose conception to be attributed to him, Jacques and Marcel being relegated to the role of modest collaborators.

The apathy and indifference with which Mathieu-Rollère had collided was succeeded by an incredible infatuation. The scientists who had previously treated him as a madman now spoke about him with emotional admiration. Everyone wanted to have foreseen the grandeur of his projects and encouraged them. In the confines of the desert he continually received the most flattering letters, and, now that he had no need of them, the most brilliant offers arrived from all directions.

Entirely absorbed in his work, however, the old scientist disdained this return to renown. He estimated the more or less self-interested praise at its true worth; he had collided too rudely with the egotism and ignorance of his fellow men to be able to be touched by the gestures of belated sympathy of which he was the object. He waited patiently for the moment when the lunar night would concord with the terrestrial night, and promised himself, as soon as the luminous letters shone again, to launch the first message that would inaugurate interstellar communications.

The monetary sacrifice made by the emperor of Brazil had not, in spite of the prince's generosity, answered all of

Mathieu-Rollère's dreams. Ideally, he would have liked to install in proximity to the electrical network an instrument similar to the one permitting our satellite to be observed from the Rocky Mountains. Communications would then have been more rapid and uninterrupted. It had been necessary to give up on that, however, and as the Long's Peak telescope was the only one in the world capable of making out the signals sent to Earth exactly, the old astronomer had been obliged to rely on his communication with it. A telegraphic wire linked him to Biskra; from there, by the ordinary route, he could correspond directly with Sir William Burnett. It had been agreed that as soon as a new signal appeared on the Moon, Mathieu-Rollère would be informed immediately. As observers were working in shifts at the ocular of the telescope, nothing could escape them and no delay in the transmission was possible.

Everything being thus prepared, Mathieu-Rollère wanted to reserve for the man he considered as his benefactor the honor of sending the first message, and Dom Pedro had immediately accepted that flattering mark of distinction. He arrived on 20 April; the Moon was then entering its first quarter and shadow would envelop the region of the Ocean of Storms.

The sky was cloudless and, in that limpid atmosphere, thousands of stars sparkled, in the midst of which our satellite, illuminated by the Sun, shone with a vivid light.

The moment seemed solemn. Mathieu-Rollère, Dumesnil, the aged emperor and all the witnesses were gripped by a vivid emotion.

At a sign from the old scientist, the emperor, with a rapid gesture, lowered the handle that was to illuminate the ten thousand lamps. Abruptly, they were all ignited, and the beam of light, which no longer lit up a vault of cloud, as it had in the first trials, launched into the sky, tracing a resplendent furrow as far as the eye could follow it.

That monstrous searchlight shone for an hour.

"Our appeal," said Mathieu-Rollère, joyfully, "will certainly have been perceived by our friends, and we can, I believe, begin sending our telegram without fear."

And successively, during the five hours that the Moon remained shining over the horizon, each lasting for ten minutes, the letters forming the first message were sent from the Earth to its satellite. That message, a testimony of gratitude and admiration for these who had dared so much, was conceived in these terms:

HONOR TO THE AUDACIOUS VOYAGERS

VI. The Earth has Spoken

Four months had gone by since Marcel, Jacques and Lord Rodilan had perceived the beacon in the Rocky Mountains, and the signals establishing the certainty that correspondence would be established and the hope of its soon becoming complete has never ceased to shine in the darkness of night.

The Englishman mocked. "By God," they said, "it was hardly worth the trouble of making such a long voyage to arrive at such a meager result. Admit, my dear Marcel, that your conversation with our friends in America is incontestable and rather wearyingly monotonous."

"Patience, my dear friend," Marcel murmured.

The three voyagers took advantage of the time when communications were forcibly interrupted in consequence of the relative positions of the two worlds. They traveled through all the regions of the lunar world, carefully studying the fauna and flora, attentively observing mores, penetrating the scientific progress realized by those intelligences of such a high order.

They did not seek to hide the fact that, assured as it was that communications between the worlds would be established, they could never be sufficiently complete and rapid to embrace everything that either party would be interested to know. Thanks to the various books, albums and specimens with which they were equipped, they had already given the inhabitants of the Moon a fairly accurate idea of the history and civilization of their terrestrial siblings. In the same way, when they returned to Earth, they wanted to be able to make known the principle features of the hitherto-unknown humankind in which they had discovered so many brilliant qualities and virtues that had simultaneously charmed their hearts and dazzled their minds.

Marcel and his companions set out to accomplish the necessary work with a feverish activity; they accumulated documents, multiplied the investigations of their research, as if they already sensed that their time was limited and that the moment would soon arrive when, their task concluded, it would be necessary for them to make preparations for a return journey.

That uninterrupted work made waiting less painful.

Every time the respective positions of the two stars permitted signals to be exchanged, they went up to the observatory and, while comparing their notes and arranging their documents, they never ceased to observe Earth's disk, eager to grasp any new manifestation. Then, when the period of concordance of nights had concluded without bringing anything except the luminous dot still shining on the summit of Long's Peak, they returned to their studies, saying to one another, not without a sigh: "Next time, no doubt."

On 20 April the Moon was at the beginning of its first quarter. Faithful to their habit, the three friends arrived at the observatory. As usual, they went in haste to the telescopes aimed at the Earth, and cast a rapid glance over the part plunged in darkness.

"Nothing yet," said Marcel. "It's certainly taking a long time."

Lord Rodilan shrugged his shoulders. "You have a robust faith, Marcel; it's to acquit my conscience and in order to be agreeable to you I've accompanied you thus far, for I'm damned if I think that we'll any luckier today. For my part, I'm beginning to believe that our friends lack imagination. I'd like them to be a little more prolix."

In the meantime, Jacques had taken Marcel's place at the ocular he had just quit.

"Look! Look!" he said, suddenly. And he rubbed his eyes vigorously, as if to see better.

"What is it?" asked Marcel, excitedly.

"Look out there, above the equator. What is it?"

Marcel rushed forward, and Lord Rodilan took up his observation post too.

A luminous dot, of an intensity far superior to the beacon in the Rocky Mountains, was shining in the darkness. Its sustained brightness and fixity removed all possible doubt; it was not a geological phenomenon like the eruption of a volcano, or an accidental one like a vast conflagration; it was obviously the work of human intelligence. What confirmed that opinion was that the nucleus from which the powerful beam was escaping had a regular geometric form; it was a rectangle with neatly-designed sides and angles.

"It's them, isn't it?" said Jacques.

"I think so," said Marcel.

"In truth," said Lord Rodilan, laughing, "if that's what we've been waiting for all this time, it really wasn't worth the trouble. A square dot instead of a round one—you can see that they're not breaking the habit."

"Whoever lives will see," said Marcel. "We'll soon know what we've got."

The mysterious rectangle was still shining.

"But where are they?" Jacques asked.

"That's easy to determine," Marcel replied. "You can see that the eastern tip of Brazil hasn't yet entered into the shadow that reigns over the major part of the Atlantic and the whole of the old continent. We can calculate with the aid of a micrometer"—he was maneuvering the delicate apparatus with which each lunette as equipped as he spoke—"the longitude and latitude of the place where our friends are located. We know that the tip of Brazil near Pernambuco is about 37 degrees west of the Paris meridian. Now, I find about 37 degrees between that point and the point where the signal is lit. On the other hand, following the direction of the terrestrial equator to the extent that the distance permits, I think I can affirm that the latitude of the location is about 35 degrees."

While he was speaking, Lord Rodilan, poring over a terrestrial planisphere, followed these indications attentively, and in naval terminology, took the bearing.

"Very good," he exclaimed. "That puts us in the Algerian region, somewhat to the south, between Algiers and Constantine." In a lower voice, he added: "The fools! Why didn't they choose Malta or Cyprus? At least England would have had her hand on the key of the communications."

"You're truly insatiable, my dear Rodilan," Marcel retorted. "Isn't the part of your glorious nation large enough, since you're with us? You have a foot everywhere, in Europe, Asia, Africa, America and Oceania, and you want to Moon too? For myself, permit me to rejoice in the fact that our friends have chosen a French territory to realize a French idea." As the Englishman grimaced he added: "Perhaps, in any case, they couldn't do otherwise; we don't know what has happened."

Lord Rodilan was about to reply when Jacques, who had not ceased observing during that brief argument, uttered an exclamation. "Oh! The light has disappeared."

All three of them resumed their places at the oculars' of the telescopes.

They did not have to wait for long.

At the place where the luminous rectangle had shone and on the same field that the sheet of light had covered, a flamboyant letter suddenly stood out, which they distinguished immediately.

"An H!" they exclaimed, simultaneously.

"What's that supposed to mean?" murmured Lord Rodilan.

"It's obviously he beginning of a word," said Jacques.

Marcel had taken out his chronometer. "Oh, the worthy fellows," he said, radiantly. "They've improvised a whole alphabet."

After ten minutes a change took place; the letter O appeared where the letter H had shone before.

"That's admirable," said Marcel, who had understood completely, with the practicality of an experienced engineer. "We're going to see all the letters of the first message exchanged between the worlds succeed one another in the same place."

As soon as they had observed the presence of the luminous rectangle on the Earth's surface the news of the event had spread through the whole observatory, and Merovar, its director, had hastened to send a notification to the lunar Head of State, who, as everyone knew, had a keen interest in everything to do with interplanetary communications.

Discreetly, and without any fuss, all those whose rank in the scientific hierarchy permitted it had come into the observation hall, and since the appearance of the first letter had manifested an enthusiasm in their facial expression that only their habitual reserve prevented from being ardent.

The fiery letters succeeded one another every ten minutes without any dissolution of continuity. One might have thought that those who were projecting them across space, knowing that they only had a few hours of darkness at their disposal, were hurrying in order to be able to send their friends a complete thought. After fifty minutes an entire word had been transmitted: HONOR.

As soon as he had understood that it was a matter of a verbal message this time, Merovar had sent that further information to the Supreme Council, and scarcely had the first word launched between worlds arrived on Earth's satellite that the word in question, reproduced by electric apparatus, was before the eyes of the hastily-convened Supreme Council.

The emotion was intense, for the moment was solemn.

The problem so long pursued by so many generations, thus far at hazard, had finally received a dazzling and definitive solution. Aldeovaze saw the fulfillment of the hopes that the arrival of the inhabitants of Earth had caused him to conceive, and in which he had maintained complete confidence. Henceforth, the two worlds would no longer be strangers to one another in their eternal orbit. They would be united by a common thought, and efforts toward increasingly rapid and more complete development of the spirit of justice and love could be expected of that unanimity.

Meanwhile, on the northern coast of Africa, the magic rectangle was still sending new symbols, and during the five hours that the transmission continued without discontinuity, the entire sentence was seen to unfurl, which made the hearts of Marcel, Jacques and Lord Rodilan beat violently: *HONOR TO THE AUDACIOUS VOYAGERS.*

Thanks to the rapid means of communication in use in the lunar world, the entire population had been promptly advised of the important event that had just taken place. The emotion had been great, and everyone, from those who were close to the Supreme Council to the Diemides who occupied the lowest ranks in the social hierarchy, waited anxiously for the continuation of a communication of which they evidently only had the first part.

It was, in fact, almost certain that from now on, throughout the period when the part of the moon in which the observatory was located remained in shadow, the friends of the three voyagers would continue to send messages.

As soon as the sentence sent from Earth was complete, as the point from which it had departed was still in darkness, they resolved to light up simultaneously and cause the letters M, J and R to shine without pause. The terrestrial correspondents would thus understand that they had been perceived, and could continue their communications in complete security.

The Head of State, Aldeovaze, had decided to go to the observatory in person in order to collect further manifestations of the sympathy of the two humankinds as soon as they were produced. He also wanted to arrange with Marcel the prompt execution of the measures it would be appropriate to take in order to reply to the distant siblings with the same precision and rapidity.

The members of the Council whose functions did not retain them in the capital—who included Rugel—accompanied him.

The beautiful Orealis and Azali, who had saved the lives and the reason of the three voyagers, one by his science and the other by her devotion, also came in order to witness their triumph, and what was a universal festival of sorts throughout the lunar world was for them a kind of family feast.

It was not without emotion, in such solemn circumstances, that Marcel saw once again the image that he still had in the depths of his heart, but the young woman's face respired a joy so pure, and there was such honesty and confidence shining in Azali's gaze that he would have blushed to hesitate on vulgar thoughts unworthy of those generous natures.

The young scientist shook Marcel's hand effusively, and it was evident that, far from having conceived any sentiment of jealous mistrust toward the engineer, he held him in even higher esteem by virtue of having understood how worthy of being loved his beloved was.

"Friend," Orealis said to him, with a radiant smile, "I'm very happy today. You have done what I wished; you have conceived and realized great things, and have acquired the right to the eternal gratitude of two humankinds."

Marcel bowed without making any reply.

The host of eminent visitors filled the observatory with an unaccustomed animation. There was no longer the silent calm appropriate to serious study, but a kind of buzz, in which was revealed, among those serious men, the joy of the great event that had just taken place, and impatience to see it confirmed.

As soon as the rotation of the Earth had brought back into shadow the point on the surface at which the message had appeared the previous day, Aldeovaze wanted to follow the observations that were about to continue with his own eye. And during the four terrestrial nights that followed, the following sentences shone successively on the luminous rectangle, which caused the souls of all of the watchers to vibrate.

First, they read:

GREETINGS TO OUR LUNAR BROTHERS

Then:

THE ENTIRE WORLD IS THINKING ABOUT YOU

Then the urgent appeal:

AWAITING RESPONSE ANXIOUSLY

And finally, Jacques and Marcel were able to read with a profound emotion the two names that, for them, said so much:

MATHIEUROLLERE DUSMESNIL

"Oh, my worthy uncle!" Jacques exclaimed. "I knew that with his indomitable tenacity he'd end up getting in touch with us. But if he's there, Hélène must be there too."

And his heart beat forcefully as he pronounced the ever-adored name.

"And my faithful friend Dumesnil," said Marcel, triumphantly. "If Mathieu-Rollère's was the guiding will, his has been the arm that it directed. I can see clearly how it must have happened. It's evidently him who organized the beacon in the Rocky Mountains. It's him again, I'm sure of it, who devised that luminous rectangle on which all the letters of the alphabet can be displayed in turn: an apparatus as simple as it is practical, of which it was, however, necessary to think."

"Always the egg of Columbus," murmured Lord Rodilan. "Oh, the two of you are lucky. Down there, at the other end of the chain of light, you have friends whose heart is beating in unison with yours. I don't have anyone..."

"What about us?" said Jacques and Marcel, simultaneously, shaking is hand warmly.

"You're right," he said. "I'd be an ingrate if I forgot all the evidence of amity you've given me."

For a long time, Rugel and the various members of the Council with whom the three friends had found themselves in communication had known all the details of their lives. They knew who the astronomer Mathieu-Rollère was, and the engineer Dumesnil and the honorable W. Burnett were no longer unknown to them. They had brought the prudent Aldeovaze up to date with all the details of the anterior life of his guests, and they all congratulate Jacques and Marcel now on being reassured on the count of those who were dear to them. They seemed to recognize themselves, in the two names that had shone in space, those of old friends from whom they had long been separated, and whom they were pleased to encounter again.

If Aldeovaze was impatient finally to consecrate the communications now commenced in a definitive fashion, Marcel was no less so. With the promptitude of intellect that distinguished him, he had soon explained to the scientists around him—whose intelligence had, in any case, anticipated his demonstrations—what the engineer Dumesnil had done, and what he intended to do himself.

"This is a revelation," he said, "but we need to do even better."

Immediately, he explained his own plan.

The idea of a rectangle arranged in such a fashion that all the letters could appear there in turn, an instantly, was evidently practical, and he had immediately grasped the mechanism. But he wanted the sentences he would send to Earth, if they were belated, at least to be more complete and more rapid. So he resolved to dispose on the vast plain where he had established his first signals twelve rectangles analogous to the one he had seen functioning before his eyes, which would permit him to depict entire words at a stroke. The majority of those of which our language consists, in fact, are no longer than twelve.[25] Nothing prevented, in fact, when dealing with words of one or two syllables, sending more than one at a time.

That plan having been settled, the execution was prompt, and there was soon an extraordinary animation in the plain neighboring the observatory. An army of Diemides, chosen from among those whose habitual labor rendered them most apt for the gigantic task, were agitating and swarming in apparent confusion, in which the most perfect order nevertheless reigned.

Under the direction of the scientists who had taken Marcel's idea aboard and shared his ardor, clad in the suits already described, they were all deploying a zeal and an activity that

---

[25] The reader is left to presume that some of the lunar observatory's astronomers will undergo a crash course in the French language, in order to continue sending and receiving messages during the absence of their guests.

would ensure the imminent completion of the work undertaken. Some were leveling the ground, others sealing directly into the rock the stems of powerful electric lamps, and yet others disposing the multiple wires that were all connected to a table situated in the observatory's great telescope hall.

After a month, everything was complete, and on the very day when the two worlds reentered their first quarter, they were ready to reply.

VII. The Moon Replies

There was great agitation at Long's Peak Observatory. Sir William Burnett, who had been in telegraphic communication with Mathieu-Rollère, had been informed of the precise moment when the latter had sent his first message to our satellite. At that moment, the region of the Rocky Mountains was still in daylight, and he had been unable to ascertain immediately that the message had been received and understood. As soon as night had reached the region and observations could be resumed, however, he had observed the presence on the lunar disk of the accustomed signals.

This time, however, something new was happening: instead of showing themselves successively, as they had done thus far, the three letters M, J and R all appeared together; they were not shining in a uniform and continuous fashion for a determined time; they were seen to go out and reignite precipitately. There was nothing regular about those abrupt and disorderly appearances. One might have thought that the mysterious correspondence, eager to act but not yet having more complete means at their disposal, wanted to say to their distant friends: "We're here, we've seen you; have a little patience and we'll soon be able to reply to you."

So dispatches succeeded one another rapidly and urgently between Long's Peak and Biskra.

Knowing the impatience of his French colleague, the American astronomer said to him: "Have confidence; our friends have received your greeting. The almost feverish agitation with which they're multiplying their demonstrations proves that up there, ardent preparations are being made. We're evidently close to a definitive solution of the problem in hand."

Mathieu-Rollère was in a state of excitement that was shared by the engineer Dumesnil and the emperor Dom Pedro, and had ended up infecting all the Europeans that curiosity had gathered around him. Burnett's dispatches were read publicly, commented on, and communicated to all the newspapers. For the several nights during which the signals sent from the Moon remained visible, the observers at Long's Peak never ceased to observe the irregular but continual appearance of the symbolic letters and thus to maintain the hopes of Mathieu-Rollère and his companions.

A month had necessarily to pass before the point on the lunar surface at which telescopes were desperately aimed all over the world would become observable again. During that forced delay, all the scientific periodicals were filled with interminable discussions and indefinite theories, which had the result of keeping public curiosity alert.

Further visitors were arriving incessantly in the vicinity of Biskra, and the entire region, previously almost deserted, was now buzzing with intense life. At the same time, many scientists, desirous of seeing their hypotheses confirmed or opposing theories belied, and many idlers avid for new sensations or unknown spectacles flocked to the observatory at Long's Peak.

Already, considerable sums had been offered to the honorable Burnett to purchase the right to put an eye to the telescope and collect the next signals, for no one now doubted that some decisive manifestation would be witnessed during the next favorable phase of the moon.

The director of the observatory was inflexible. "I want to be the first to receive the three voyagers' messages," he had replied, "but as the signals appear, I'll transmit them to the telegraph post in Denver, from which the whole world will be able to take cognizance of them."

The curiosity-seekers had to be content with that response, and the majority of the great newspapers of the two continents had send reporters to Denver charged with gathering information without delay regarding the great event that he entire world was awaiting impatiently.

They day so ardently awaited finally arrived; it was 18 May that was to remain famous in the annals of science.

As all the newspaper reporters and curiosity-seekers were pressing around the telegraph office and the crowding threatened to produce disorders, the public authorities thought it appropriate to intervene. It was decided that all the journalists who could prove their entitlement would gather in a kind of congress and choose one of their number to man the receiving apparatus in order to receive the communications from Long's Peak and transmit it to all his colleagues.

The interested parties' selection fell to the representative of *Le Figaro*, the French newspaper with the largest circulation, which had already defended Mathieu-Rollère's cause ardently.

It was eleven twenty-three in the evening at the Long's Peak meridian when the bell of the apparatus suddenly rang. Everyone held his breath and all expressions were taut. Leaning over the ribbon on which the typographic characters were printed, the representative of *Le Figaro* read in a voice tremulous with emotion: "Long's Peak Observatory. I can distinctly read the following words on the lunar disk: 'Thank you.' Will continue transmission if other words appear."

Cries of enthusiasm rang out. People congratulated one another; that simple phrase was the response to the greeting send from Earth. The voyagers had received it and understood it. They had found a means, in so short a time, to put themselves in communication with the Earth in a more complete and rapid fashion than anyone had dared to hope, since they could transmit at a stroke no longer isolated letters but entire words. Surely they would not stop there.

Scarcely ten minutes had gone by when the bell was heard again, and on the telegraphic ribbon the words "M J R alive" appeared.

They had not been mistaken; it really was the three bold voyagers who were talking to their friends from the depths of space and wanted to reassure them as to their fate.

That same day, at an interval of several hours, a similar animation reigned in the vicinity of Biskra. There too a new manifestation as expected; the regular communications sent by

Burnett had maintained Mathieu-Rollère and his companions in an absolute confidence. So, when the first telegram sent from Long's Peak arrived in that lost corner of Africa, the astronomer and the engineer Dumesnil felt inundated by a profound joy.

In the presence of the magnificent result they had obtained, what did the ordeals they had undergone matter, the difficulties surmounted with so much difficulty, so many struggles and so many sacrifices? They had emerged victorious against envy and ignorance. Thanks to them, a fecund era was opening up for humankind; science was about to see hitherto-unknown horizons opening before it. And the imperial benefactor, whose intelligence had understood everything that was great in their idea, and had rendered its realization possible, shared their intoxication.

At the first words transmitted by Burnett, the old scientist's soul had blossomed. The three friends, he was now certain, were alive, and he saw confirmed, in spite of his funereal anticipations, the indomitable hope that had never ceased to live in his daughter's heart. Hélène was beside him, and their tears of happiness mingled.

But the communications that followed soon gave his thoughts a new direction.

On the somber screen on the lunar disk, the telescope in the Rocky Mountains had read distinctly words that plunged all the witnesses into a profound amazement, which seemed to overturn scientific theories that had previously seemed well established:

Lunar surface uninhabitable. Interior inhabited. Lunar humankind glad to enter into communication with Earth.

What new perspectives those unexpected revelations caused to unfurl before their eyes!

If the first part of the message confirmed what science had long observed with respect to the surface of the satellite, how could the presence of life in the bosom of such a compact mass be explained? What could that humankind be like, living in conditions that the most audacious imagination could scarcely conceive?

To judge by the scientific character of the means employed to communicate with the Earth, it might be thought that the humanity living there had achieved a high level of intellectual development. On the other hand, the signs perceived had been made on the surface. How could that be done if it was impossible to live there?

There were so many mysterious questions that remained unanswered, and in the old astronomer's head the ideas were crowding and spinning in an inexpressible confusion.

The news of that extraordinary event spread throughout the entire world. All the Institutes and all the scientific societies had been rapidly informed, and passionate discussions did not take long to cast trouble into minds. The crowd, always seduced by the marvelous, greeted the most fantastic stories served to them every day by the overexcited imagination of journalists with enthusiasm; the more incredible they were, the more fervently they welcomed them.

Public opinion, overheated, was already criticizing governments for inertia and indifference; monstrous cannons had to be founded in haste in order to give further voyagers the opportunity to repeat the experiment, and construction began of gigantic telescopes equal or superior in power to the one at Long's Peak. National pride was involved. Why leave the United States with the monopoly on correspondence with the Moon? Did not every nation have a duty to make every effort to arrive first in the race for the conquest of great scientific truths?

In France, the demands were imperious. Was not the endeavor, in sum, primarily French? Of the three voyagers, one was certainly English, but it was now known that Lord Rodilan was not a scientist; he was only a blasé individual in search of new emotions, and his role in the whole enterprise was the most minimal.

Then again, Mathieu-Rollère was also a Frenchman, and it was his indomitable tenacity that had, in spite of routine, accomplished such great things. Was it not just that, after having soaked up so much disdain and bitterness, he should remain responsible for completing the work he had begun? He had taken the trouble; he ought to have the honor.

VIII. In Search of a Crater

Eighteen months had gone by since Marcel and his companions had arrived on Earth's satellite, and when they thought about everything that they had experienced, learned and accomplished they were tempted to wonder whether they had not been living in a continuous dream.

An extraordinary voyage in conditions that seemed to defy all human previsions; a new world discovered, a world whose moral and intellectual superiority realized the most sublime conceptions of dreamers and utopians attempting to imagine a better humankind; a grandiose chimera, regular communications between the spheres orbiting in space, realized amid a thousand difficulties and perils: that was what their audacity and faith in science had achieved.

But now that goal had been attained and the work was complete, their hearts felt a profound emptiness. The zeal that had sustained them so long as they had something to do was now extinguishing for lack of an aliment. And they rediscovered with regret the Earth that they had left behind them, the friends whose thoughts reached them through space but whose hands they felt a need to shake and whose hearts they wanted to feel beating against their own.

Nothing can replace an absent fatherland, and in spite of the enchantments that had delighted them, the Earth was decidedly lacking. In the narrow and closed environment in which they had been living for long months, where the temperate and light were constant, the horizons always limited, colors mild but dull, where everything was calm and placid, devoid of the unexpected, devoid of the accidental, where nothing excited desire or inflamed the imagination, they were often seized by regret for the vast and various horizons of Earth, the warm bright light of the Sun, the depth of the blue sky, the swarming life on the surface of the land, the aerial spaces and the liquid abyss of the waves.

Many times, they had desired a storm or a tempest—in sum, something to break the eternal monotony of that unalterable serenity. The life these superior beings led was no longer sufficient for them. That whole existence, so sage, so sober and so well-regulated, appeared to them to have something artificial about it, and they wondered whether, deep down, life such as it was led on Earth, with its struggles and uncertainties, its perils and adventures, its alternation of good days and bad days, was not preferable, for beings endowed with sensibility and activity, to that ideal uniformity, similar to a lake with still waters, whose surface was never rippled by any breeze.

Marcel, who still retained a vague sentiment in the depths of his heart, dormant rather than extinct, could perhaps have resigned himself, even though he had bid adieu to all hope, to leading that placid existence, which cradled his love so gently. Jacques and Lord Rodilan, however, were beginning to show definite signs of having had enough; they were urging Marcel to think about the return journey. And he, yielding to their pleas and faithful to the promise that he had made to them, decided to talk to Rugel about it.

"Friend," he said, "the desires of the great Aldeovaze are now fulfilled. The link that will link the two sibling human-kinds together is now established, and they can, as the sage's mind had glimpsed, march in convoy along the road of progress. Our task is complete. The result we've obtained far surpasses what we had dared to dream when we launched ourselves into an unknown adventure. If our highest ambitions and aspirations have been satisfied, our hearts have found sweet recompenses here; we have encountered precious sympathies, solid amities, and we shall remember them eternally; but—forgive us, my friend—that's no longer sufficient for us. You'll surely understand, having given your entire life, all that you have of strength and intelligence to this world where you have born and where those you love reside. We too have a fatherland that we cherish; we were able to avoid suffering from being separated therefrom for as long as we were sus-

264

tained by the desire to work for its glory and its happiness, but today the love of our native soil has reawakened imperiously in our souls; all the force of our souls is aspiring toward it, and we're suffering from its deprivation."

While Marcel was speaking thus, Rugel's face had veiled with sadness.

"What you say, friend," he replied, "afflicts me but doesn't surprise me. I've been expecting it. I understood that that once the surprise caused to you by a world so different from your own had passed, when you no longer had before your eyes the noble goal to which you had devoted yourselves, you would lack something that our affection would be powerless to give you." With a melancholy smile he added: "You want to leave us; your departure will cause us to suffer, but we love you too much to think of delaying it. For my part, I shall attempt to hasten the moment for which you aspire with as much zeal and as much care as I have put into guiding you within our society and assisting you in your endeavors."

Jacques' face, and Lord Rodilan's, lit up at the thought that they were going, one to see the beloved fiancée with whom his heart was filed, the other finally to exchange the chemical nourishment to which he had never managed to adapt himself for large and succulent joints of roast beef at the Pall Mall Club.

"Well," said the Englishman, "since we're in agreement on that important point, it will perhaps be appropriate to enquire as to the ways and means to ensure our return."

"The question appears to me to be resolved in principle," Rugel replied. "We only have to preoccupy ourselves with the execution."

Marcel recognized, in fact, that the sole means to employ was the one that had permitted the three voyagers to reach the Moon. The specific weight of the satellite being six times less than that of the Earth, the force of attraction that it was necessary to overcome would be reduced in the same proportion. In addition, the neutral point at which the two attractions canceled one another out being much closer to the moon—eight

265

thousand leagues away, in fact—the distance to be covered was far less and would necessitate a considerably reduced initial velocity. It was therefore necessary to establish a cannon capable of a puerile effort, which, although less vast in its proportions than the Gun Club's Columbiad, would nevertheless be enormous.

"We are not novices in the matter of constructions of that sort," said Rugel. "We did not have recourse to other means in sending you the numerous projectiles designed to attract your attention. The machine that served to fire the cannonball that you so fortunately discovered was cast not far from here. I'll take you there soon and you can appreciate for yourselves the extent of our knowledge of ballistics."

Shortly afterwards, in fact, dressed in the special apparatus, accompanied by Merovar, a few of his colleagues and a number of Diemides, they left the observatory.

Guided by Rugel they went down the slope of the crater on the opposite side to the one they had descended when they established the signals, and soon came to the entrance to a steep-sided gorge between elevations of granitic rock, which seemed to trace a sinuous furrow through the chaotic accumulation.

To their great surprise, they perceived a sort of thick ribbon of iron, set on the ground, which followed the contours of the ravine,

Marcel hastened to hook his telephonic wire on to Rugel's sphere and say: "You've had a railway here, then?"

"We still have one," Rugel replied, smiling behind is mask at the astonishment of the three friends—for Jacques and Lord Rodilan were also manifesting a veritable amazement by means of their gestures.

"One never finishes," Jacques murmured, "being wonderstruck by this extraordinary world."

"That would open the eyes of the cockneys in the City," said Lord Rodilan, at the same time.

"Let's follow Merovar," said Rugel.

266

The director of the observatory was heading toward a jutting rock, behind which a number of wagons soon appeared, similar in form to those they had seen circulating inside the cavern, and similarly equipped with gyroscopic devices designed to maintain them in equilibrium on the single rail.

"This railway," Merovar explained, "was constructed a long time ago specifically to facilitate the establishment of the cannon we used to send you the projectiles. Since you arrived among us, there has been no more reason to use it, and we hoped that we would not be obliged to have recourse to it so soon."

The Diemides had soon finished the preparations for the departure.

The railway wagons, designed to operate in the void, different from those with which the voyagers were already familiar, being completely sealed and having solid frames in order to resist the pressure of the air that had to be accumulated within them. In one of them there was an apparatus for generating breathable air chemically, which rapidly furnished an atmosphere in which the voyagers could live as easily as inside the laboratory itself. Elegant tables and comfortable chairs were disposed in the other vehicles, the lateral walls of which were fitted with thick glass that permitted all the details of the region through which it was traveling to be seen.

Rugel and his companions went into one of them, closing the door firmly, and as soon as the barometer indicated a sufficient atmospheric pressure, they took off the somewhat inconvenient special costumes in which they had been forced to dress.

Meanwhile, the Diemides responsible for that task had activated the electric motors and soon, the gyroscopic apparatus having achieved the normal speed of rotation, the train moved off and slid rapidly along the rail.

Comfortably seated in the large wagon, which moved without shaking and soundlessly, into which the light flooded, the three inhabitants of Earth thought they were dreaming. Traveling by railway over the surface of the moon was enough to trouble less well-equilibrated brains, and Lord Rodilan was surprised to find himself pinching his arm, as if to assure himself that he was really awake.

But it was not a dream, and the marvelous spectacle that unfolded before their eyes was quite real.

After following the sinuosities of the gorge for some time, between two harsh rocky slopes, the train entered an open region in which the gaze embraced a vast horizon. To their right they perceived the crater at whose summit the observatory stood, its crystal vaults and gigantic telescopes resplendent in the ardent sunlight. Seen from that distance, from which one could no longer distinguish the asperities of the rocks, it was an imposing mass crowned by a magnificent flamboyance.

In the distance, to the left, they perceived mountain chains whose jagged crests stood out sharply and clearly against the raw blackness of the sky, and that trenchant opposition of colors, to which no vapor lent the slightest transition, seemed magical in its effect.

Suddenly, the ground seemed to collapse and the train appeared to be moving through the void.

"What's that?" said Marcel, instinctively throwing himself backwards.

"Oh, that's a bridge," said Rugel, smiling.

Jacques and Lord Rodilan had stood up; their faces were slightly pale. Beneath them, an abyss was hollowed out whose bottom was lost in dense obscurity. The impression they could not help feeling, suspended on a thread that they could not see, reminded them of what they had experienced at the moment when, enclosed in the shell and reaching the surface of the moon, they had plunged into the bowels of the satellite, from which they had thought that they would never be able to emerge.

But their souls were valiant; they pulled themselves together promptly. Already the crevasse had been crossed and the track, describing a tight curve, soon allowed them to look back and that surprising edifice, which was now displayed at an angle to the wagon. There was nothing bolder and more unexpected than that audacious construction: a simple ribbon of steel resting on an immense arc of the same metal, spanning at least four hundred meters, embedded at its two extremities directly in the rock—that was all.

Marcel's imagination would never have dared to conceive anything similar.

"Damn!" he said. "Rugel, my friend, your engineers are fine fellows. That leaves far behind anything that their colleagues on Earth could contrive."

"Oh," said Merovar, charmed by the young man's astonishment, "there's nothing very extraordinary about it; that bridge, bold as it might appear, is nevertheless perfectly solid."

The train continued its rapid progress, but less than an hour later it began to slow down.

"We're nearly there," said Rugel. "It's time to put on our costumes. The place to which we're going is close by."

The train stopped without any jolt and the passengers got out.

They found themselves next to a massive building of considerable dimensions, into which they penetrated via an airlock similar to the one that connected the observatory to the outside. It was illuminated by large bay windows, hermetically sealed, and inside, they saw apparatus for manufacturing artificial air as well as machines and tools of all kinds.

"This is where the people employed here lived throughout the time the work lasted," said Merovar.

The travelers continued walking, and after half an hour they reached the objective of their excursion. The orifice of the cannon opened in front of them.

A shaft 2.54 meters in diameter had been hollowed out vertically in the rock to a depth of seventy meters. Its walls were lined with a metal alloy, a kind of highly resistant bronze, some eighty centimeters thick, which left the cannon a barrel of 94 centimeters. That was the instrument with the aid of which the inhabitants of the Moon had, on numerous occasions, sent messages to the Earth, the last of which, by such a fortunate stroke of luck, had fallen into Marcel's hands.

Merovar explained to them that they had been obliged to choose a location for its installation some distanced away from the observatory—eighteen leagues in a straight line—to avoid the vibrations imparted to the ground by the explosions compromising the stability of the monument and the precision of the instruments of observation it contained.

"It's a great pity," said Lord Rodilan, "that this cannon is too small for us to use; otherwise we'd be able to fix the date of our departure now."

"You're very eager to leave us, friend," said Rugel—and something akin to a reproachful sadness was detectable in his voice.

The Englishman understood that he had caused needless offense to that generous individual, and added: "No, but since it's necessary to separate, I think that sooner would be better, because, for you as for us, waiting becomes more painful as it's prolonged. You know that we love you and will never forget you."

"I do know that, indeed—but we'll be forced to wait. We need to establish a new cannon, capable of launching a projectile similar to the one that brought you here. That will be a long and difficult operation. I don't doubt that the Head of State, the prudent Aldeovaze, in spite of his desire to keep you among us, will authorize the enterprise and do everything possible to facilitate its realization. Nevertheless, our task would be made much easier if we could find, in the region where we are at present, a crater of restricted dimensions hollowed out in the right direction, which could be adapted in such a fashion as to serve as a receptacle for our canon. Experience has demonstrated to us, in fact, that the material obstructing the chimneys of craters only forms a layer, of varying but never very considerable thickness, and that when one has traversed it one finds empty space beneath. We'd thus have a shaft already hollowed out, and it would be sufficient to even out its walls."

At that moment, one of the Diemides who was standing behind Rugel came forward. "Master," he said, "I believe that I know of a crater not far from here that combines all the features you desire. I was among those who were employed in sending the latest message addressed to the Earth, and I've had the opportunity to explore the whole region. If you care to follow me, I'll take you to it."

"Let's go," said Rugel.

They resumed marching, and in less than an hour they arrived at the foot of a kind of truncated cone that only rose to a modest height above the ground. They climbed its slope and found themselves on the edge of one of the smallest craters on the lunar surface. Merovar and Rugel examined the location attentively, measured the diameter of the interior orifice, and confirmed that it combined all the conditions desirable for the planned installation.

"Well," said Rugel, in conclusion, "It's decided, then. This is where you'll depart from when the moment comes for you to leave us. And you can be sure that, although I shall be sorry to arrive at the moment of our separation, far from doing anything to delay it, I'll do everything I can to make sure that the work proceeds as rapidly as possible."

They went back in all haste to the place where the train had stopped. They all took their places in the wagons again, and were soon back in the observatory.

IX. The Invisible Surface

On returning to the lunar world, Rugel, accompanied by his three friends, went directly to see the Head of State and gave him an account of what had just occurred. Although the news of the intention of Marcel, Jacques and Lord Rodilan to return to Earth affected him painfully, he had too much intelligence not to comprehend their desire to see their fatherland again, and too noble a soul to oppose it.

The labor necessary to ensure their return was, therefore, begun without delay. In spite of the diligence with which the task was undertaken, however, it would take some seven or eight months, and that long delay weighed upon the impatience of the three voyagers.

The communications established with the Earth continued in a regular fashion every month, during the relatively brief intervals during which observation was possible, but the rarity of those intervals inevitably rendered exchanges of idea between the two worlds very slow. Mathieu-Rollère, whose curiosity had been greatly excited by the indication furnished in the early days of the existence of a human race living inside the Moon, multiplied his questions, to which Merovar replied in an unalterably obliging fashion. Things did not go quickly, however, and even though precious information had already been transmitted, it was obvious that a long time would go by before the inhabitants of the Earth had any definitive notion of the nature and condition of their lunar siblings.

From the beginning, Marcel and his two companions had followed the exchange of communications with interest, but the occupation soon became impotent to satisfy them. They frequently went to the place where, under the guidance of experienced scientists, the Diemides were adapting the crater that was to serve as a mold for the liberating cannon. But there too, in spite of all the activity deployed, progress was slow; the difficulties to be overcome were considerable, and their fever, further aggravated every day by the waiting, rendered any delay unbearable.

It was then that Marcel thought about undertaking a voyage of exploration intended, in his mind, to complete his study of the new world that he was to reveal to the Earth. He had, of course, had before his eyes the maps drawn up by lunar scientists of the mysterious part of the satellite that was eternally hidden from the curiosity of terrestrial observers; he had been able to see that it was almost entirely similar to the visible part: just as arid, similarly bristling with mountains and strewn with numerable craters. He knew that only the imagination of a few dreamers had been able to suppose the presence there of immense seas, profound forests, rapid rivers and, in sum, an entire life: a hypothesis in absolute contradiction to the general law presiding over the evolution of worlds. He wanted to make sure of it himself, though, and bring to those he counted on rejoining soon the testimony of his own experience. He wanted to be able to say: "I've seen it."

Jacques and Lord Rodilan welcomed the proposal; it responded to their secret desires, by giving satisfaction to the purposeless agitation that prevented them from holding still.

They mentioned it to Rugel, who was entirely ready to assist them in the enterprise, and even offered to go with them.

"It's a bold plan," he said, "worthy of your courage; and since you're determined to carry it out, perhaps we can investigate an important question that has preoccupied me for a long time, and which I'd be very glad to be able to settle. If old traditions conserved in our histories can be trusted, there is, a long way to the east, a vast depression of considerable depth. Our scientists have often wondered whether a certain quantity of the atmosphere that once surrounded the planet might remain therein, and that it might have been able to support a residue of vegetable life. It's a matter I've often thought of clarifying, but I've never had an opportunity."

Those words provoked a great enthusiasm in Marcel. "Ah!" he exclaimed. "Some terrestrial astronomers have thought that they perceived light vapors and variations in hue

273

in the depths of certain craters, which they attributed to the presence of highly rarefied air, capable nevertheless of maintaining traces of vegetation. People refused to believe them. What a glory it would be for us to bring back evident proof that they weren't mistaken!"

Marcel's enthusiasm infected Jacques, and even Lord Rodilan, in spite of his lack of interest in purely scientific questions, seemed full of ardor.

Although they had become increasingly rare as life was concentrated in the bosom of the planet, the inhabitants of the Moon still carried out a few explorations of that nature, and the employment of all the machines necessary to their execution was familiar to them. Light and portable apparatus designed to manufacture air chemically, and powerful accumulators capable of storing electricity at high tension and furnishing sufficient lighting during the long lunar nights, were kept in a permanent state of readiness, at the disposal of those whose love of science prompted them to venture on to the uninhabitable surface.

The greatest difficulty with which explorers who undertook voyages of long duration would have to content was the considerable drop in temperature during periods of darkness. The ingenuity of the scientists had made provision for that. Before putting on their impermeable vestments, the voyagers covered their bodies with a kind of coat of mail formed by a light and flexible metallic mesh that allowed the limbs complete freedom of movement. Beneath the reservoir of air that they wore on their backs there was a small but powerful electrical accumulator, connected by wires to the metallic mesh, which caused a current to circulate therein of sufficient intensity to maintain the body and the surrounding air at a consistently tolerable temperature.

As for the necessity that the three inhabitants of Earth had to replenish their strength by nourishment, provision could easily be made for that. Inside the sphere that covered their head a small metallic receptacle was placed filled with the mysterious liquid that had constituted their principal aliment for some time, to the despair of Lord Rodilan. A tube departing from that receptacle was fixed to the sphere in such a way as to be within easy range of their lips. A slight movement permitted them to grasp it and suck in the chemical elements sufficient to nourish them.

As the observatory was thirty degrees—which is to say, more than nine hundred kilometers—from the region invisible from the Earth, Rugel had judged that the distance in question could be crossed during a single lunar night of fourteen terrestrial days, and that they could reach the other hemisphere at daybreak. It would be interesting for Marcel and his companions to be able to travel over the part of the satellite's surface with which they wanted to acquaint themselves in daylight.

In consequence, they left the observatory on 1 June, as darkness was beginning to envelop it. In addition to Marcel, Jacques, Lord Rodilan and Rugel, the little caravan included sixty Diemides. Ten scouts marched ahead, carrying powerful electric lamps, whose rays illuminated the whole area around them and permitted them to distinguish all the features of the landscape through which they were traveling for several kilometers around. The three voyagers and their guide advanced in the center, and the remainder of the Diemides brought up the rear, carrying, as well as numerous scientific instruments, the apparatus that manufactured and stored the air necessary for respiration. The alternations of marching and resting had been regulated in advance in such a way as to save the strength of the voyagers.

It is necessary not to forget, moreover, that the force of gravity on the surface of the Moon is much less than on Earth, so they hardly felt the weight of the vestments that they were wearing and the apparatus they were carrying. They were capable of crossing distance, without fatigue, that would have surpassed the limits of human strength on our world.

They felt light and carefree, full of ardor.

The first days of the journey were free of incident; they traversed the vast plain at the center of which Hansteen crater was located, heading eastwards with a slight inclination southwards.

Examination of the detailed maps with which they were equipped had informed them of the presence of deep fissures, one situated in the vicinity of the crater Grimaldi, the other a little further on, both of which were uncrossable.

As they approached the hills forming the eastern edge of the Ocean of Storms, the ground rose up noticeably, and they soon found themselves on the continent not far from the crater Sirsalis. There they were delayed somewhat by the necessity of climbing the buttresses of the crater, a mass of sheer rocks through which they could only advance with great precaution, in spite of the light projected by their electric lamps. Rugel had taken care to attach to each of his three friends two young Diemides with special responsibility for helping them in difficult passages. Proud of that task, which they considered a mark of honor, they did their very best to support those confided to them, and on more than one occasion, without their aid, a dangerous fall might have cut the journey shot for one of the bold explorers.

When that obstacle had been overcome, they found themselves on the plain again, and, still heading south-eastwards, passed at an equal distance between the craters Cruger and Asaph Hall.[26]

From that point on, the voyagers, still guided by Rugel, headed more directly eastwards, advancing without too much difficulty until they arrived in the foothills of the Cordilleras, a mountain chain whose mean elevation was nearly four thou-

---

[26] Hall crater, named after Asaph Hall, is in another part of the moon, and the direction in which the explorers would he heading to reach the invisible surface, given their starting-point, would be south-west rather than south-east, probably taking them between the craters Cruger and Eichstadt. Similarly, Troubelot is nowhere near the area they seem to be in, so the author's lunar geography seems have gone seriously awry in this passage.

sand meters. There was no possibility of tackling that formidable granite wall head on. Fortunately, the Diemides forming the advance guard knew the region well, having traveled it before. They knew that in the vicinity of the southern extremity of the crater Troubelot the chain was interrupted, and that there was a narrow but easily practicable pass through the mountainous masses. They set forth into it with confidence, therefore.

At the exit from the gorge, once they had circled around the crater, they found themselves close to the limit beyond which human gaze had never penetrated.

The long fourteen-day march, undertaken in darkness— in spite of the electric lamps, they had traversed many regions almost blind—had not diminished the ardor of Marcel and his companions at all. Every step they took brought them closer to the goal of the marvelous voyage, and as their impatience grew their strength seemed to increase.

When they crossed the meridian eternally limiting the visibly disk of the satellite, they felt a keen excitement. They knew full well that the spectacle awaiting them on the other hemisphere would be much the same as the one to which their gaze had long become accustomed, but they were doing something that no human being would ever have thought possible and that no one else would ever accomplish.

Already they were approaching the moment when day would abruptly succeed night.

In the absence of any atmosphere in which the luminous rays could be reflected, there is no dusk or dawn twilight on the lunar surface. Instead of the subtle and changing tints that render the tradition from night to day so poetic on Earth, the invasion of light is somewhat brutal; the sun suddenly emerged, illuminating everything with an equal glare.

Rugel, as jealous as an artist skillful in managing his effects, had decided to choose an observation post for his friends that would permit them to enjoy the curious phenomenon as completely as possible.

Some distance away from the point at which they had reached the invisible hemisphere, an isolated mountain loomed up, easy of access. They climbed its slope to await the appearance of the day star.

A few minutes before the moment when the light was due to burst forth, the electric lamps were switched off, and the whole country was plunged into a darkness whose profundity the eye sought in vain to fathom.

Suddenly, it was as if a curtain had been torn away.

A dazzling light inundated the space; the shadow, as if chased away by the golden arrow launched by the solar disk from the edge of the horizon, seemed to flee toward the Occident.

The panorama that extended before the gaze of the marveling voyagers was imposing and sublime. The mountain on which they were positioned was standing on the edge of an immense depression, a dried-up sea bed that extended to the left as far as the eye could see, in the background of which isolated craters could be made out—which, as Rugel explained to them, had once formed as many circular islands rising out of the mass of the waves.

Facing them, limiting the distant horizon, a chain of mountains appeared, much higher than the Cordilleras, whose jagged summits stood out clearly in spite of the distance. The entire region that extended to their base, even more profoundly tormented than all those they had already seen, offered an image of indescribable chaos. There was nothing but convulsed masses, bizarre in form, cut by broad crevasses, hollowed out by countless craters of all sizes. The irresistible power that animates the universe, employed in the formation and destruction of worlds, had never been manifest to them with a similar character of magnificence and horror.

To their right, the nearest of those craters drew an exclamation of admiration from them. In the center of an almost perfect circle of colossal dimension stood a needle of rock of enormous height, almost pyramidal in form, which the already-ardent sun caused to glitter with an unbearable brightness.

"How magnificent it all is!" said Jacques, putting himself in communication with Marcel and Lord Rodilan. "How imposing and terrible that eternal solitude and silence is!"

"That leaves the famous Cirque de Gavarnie far behind," said Lord Rodilan.[27] "if the peak we have before us were in the Pyrenees, a suspension railway to the summit would have been established long ago, and there'd be a hotel on top in which waiters with black jackets and white cravats would serve famished tourists with mutton chops decorated with the pompous name of izard."[28]

"I had a strong suspicion that neither of you would regret this voyage of exploration," Marcel said. And he was filled with joy at the thought that he had before his eyes a part of the unattainable region on which the imagination of scientists had so far been exercised at hazard. No vain theories for him: it was the reality that his gaze was embracing.

---

[27] The rounded valley in the Pyrenees known as the Cirque de Gavarnie is about 800 meters in diameter.

[28] An izard is a kind of chamois.

X. A Dead City

After sating themselves at their leisure on that grandiose spectacle, the voyagers went back down to the plain and resumed their march under Rugel's guidance.

They headed for the edge of the dry sea bed that they had contemplated from the height of the mountain and soon arrived on the crest of a steep cliff, whose vertical wall the waves had once battered. They followed it for some time, always having the vast arid basin to their right, over which their gaze slid to the limits of the visible horizon.

The march was monotonous and difficult over that rocky and pitted ground. They had to scale long slopes and descend steep ones, following all the sinuosities of the irregular coast, wondering where their guide was taking them. The painful trajectory, which it was necessary to interrupt with frequent halts and long rests, lasted for several days.

By Marcel's reckoning they had covered more than sixty kilometers in that fashion when, the cliff becoming abruptly lower, they found themselves before a large plain that sloped gently down into the ocean bed.

Toward the middle of that plain, and the place where the waves of the vanished sea must once have expired, the eye distinguished confused masses that could have been taken, at that distance, for the debris of rocks that had collapsed in a cataclysm, or a random accumulation of boulders.

It was toward that point that Rugel was leading them.

As they drew closer, what they had first taken for an irregular and fortuitous heap took on an appearance of regularity and symmetry. The distance diminished, the forms became more precise; one might have thought that there were the remains of mighty walls, vast quadrilateral formed like plazas, and the stumps of gigantic broken columns scattered here and there, around which heaps of rubble had accumulated.

"There," Rugel told them, extending his hand, "are the ruins of one of the cities in which, in the times when lunar humankind lived on the surface, its arts and civilization flourished. I've often talked to you about the life of our ancestors, when necessity had not yet constrained them to take refuge in the caverns we occupy today. You now have before your eyes one of the rare vestiges of their presence that has survived the frightful upheavals in the wake of which life disappeared from this region."

They were close enough now to be able to appreciate the considerable dimensions of the ancient city. All the private habitations had been reduced to dust, crumbled by the slow and ineluctable work of time. Nothing remained standing but a few remains of monuments constructed to resist the centuries, and that imposing debris gave some idea of the great strength and intelligence of the beings whose life had filled the region.

Rugel had folded his arms and seemed to be plunged in a profound meditation. All the Diemides forming the escort had stopped too, standing motionless, as if the sight of the ruins had struck them with a religious respect.

"I can't help feeling a profound sadness," Rugel said, "in thinking about that ancient existence, so different from the one to which we're now reduced. Once, life circulated in abundance around these locations. Water filled those vast basins plowed by numerous ships; dense forests crowned the mountains whose slopes were covered with verdant vegetation. In this city, now destroyed, a numerous active population enjoyed life, breathing in the intoxicating sea breezes and the penetrating odor of the great words. And it has all gone! What remains to those of us still alive today is enclosed within a narrow space, deprived of sunlight, and its days are numbered! Who knows whether some frightful cataclysm might not cut short its duration, and destroy the last vestiges of that wretched humankind?"

The grandeur of the scene could not leave Marcel and his two companions insensible. What they had before their eyes was the gripping image of the destruction of a world. This was the conclusion of the formidable interplay of the forces of nature, which, after having created a habitable globe and developed and maintained life there for long centuries, began to destroy their work with irresistible obstinacy. In the presence of that fatal evolution, what were the most magnificent discoveries of human genius, and the highest aspirations ever alert and ever unslaked, toward which its mortal nature tended?

With time, everything dissolved and vanished; and, extinguished in the turn, the worlds orbiting in space around a center of light and life were irrevocably destined to be nothing more than inert and sterile matter once again.

And the destruction would not stop there.

Those cadavers floating in the void would, in time, be disaggregated in their turn, returned to the state of cosmic dust in order to form other worlds, which would end in the same way, in an eternal recommencement.

A sign from Rugel extracted them from those grave thoughts. They went into the ruins of the dead city and wandered through them with a tender respect. They rediscovered the traces of edifices where the men responsible for giving laws to the city had sat, the squares where crowds had assembled, and all the places where they had lived—which is to say, loved and suffered. Nothing remained of all that but the shadow of a memory.

Rugel stopped them in front of a ruin whose form was reminiscent of a mausoleum, but of vast proportions.

"This," he said, "is the tomb destined to perpetuate the memory of a man whose virtues and great actions rendered him worthy of public gratitude. Time has not respected that refuge of death any more than the monuments in which life agitated."

The collapsed sepulcher allowed a kind of light dust to be perceived in the interior, perhaps all that remained of the person whose final abode it had been.

Marcel was astonished by its vast proportions.

"That's because the humans who lived on the surface of the Moon were taller than us. During the many centuries that lunar humankind has already been living in a more restricted environment, their stature has gradually diminished."

"So," said Jacques, "the generations that succeeded one another here, as on Earth, left mysterious memories to those who came after them, and those who lived in this place, if they had anticipated our coming, could have said with the poet: *Scilicet et tempus veniet cum finibus illis / Agricola... inviniet... Grandisque effossis mirabitur ossa sepulcris.*"[29]

It was necessary to set off again, but it was not without regret that the voyagers tore themselves away from that desolate spectacle, the sight of which had stirred up so many disparate emotions in their hearts.

They resumed their route, following the gradual slope of the terrain.

Rugel had intended for some time to take them to visit the bed of one of the ancient lunar seas. The opportunity was favorable; the voyagers had ten days of light in front of them, which could not be more usefully employed.

As the distance that separated them from the shore increased, the ground became progressively lower. The soil over which they were advancing offered a singular aspect: the dazzling whiteness that had been presented, under the sun's radiance, by the region they had just quit, was succeeded by a darker hue. Instead of the rough and harsh surface, uneven and difficult, over which they had been marching thus far, their feet were now treading on a kind of felted matter, supple and resistant at the same time, which seemed to yield underfoot. Strangely surprised, Marcel bent down to examine it at closer range. He even broke off a few pieces, not without effort, and was studying them attentively when Rugel intervened.

---

[29] The quotation, slightly misrendered in the original text, is from Virgil's *Georgics*. The passage translates, approximately, as; "The time will come when the plowman...will marvel at the giant bones he has exhumed."

"A little while ago," he said, "you saw what remains of human life. You now have before your eyes one of the last vestiges of the transformations of matter on the surface of the world, where everything is now dead."

Marcel continued to examine the debris he was holding, curiously. There were flexible silky fibers of great tenacity, offering a striking analogy with asbestos, which is encountered on Earth in places where the magnesium silicate commonly known as serpentine is accumulated.

Rugel explained to him that the waters that had originally covered a vast area of the Moon's surface had contained considerably quantities of a substance that terrestrial chemists call magnesia, or magnesium oxide, which is only encountered in nature in combination with other substances. As the seas had dried up, that magnesia had combined with the silica held in suspension in the water and had gradually formed enormous deposits, of which they were now looking at a curious specimen.

"That," said Marcel, "is the solution to a problem that has long preoccupied the scientists of Earth and suggested many hypotheses. People wondered how the dark and greenish tint observed in the vast lunar depressions could have been produced, which some stubbornly tried to explain by the presence of otherwise-inexplicable vegetation. It's evident that this mineral moss absorbs a considerable fraction of the light that strikes it; the light reflected by large expanses of it is therefore faint by comparison with that reflected by the continents and bare rocks."

"Well," said Lord Rodilan, who had been interested by that conversation, "our exploration will not have been futile if it enriches astronomical science with one discovery more."

They continued walking, still moving deeper and deeper into the bed of the ancient sea. Sometimes, they encountered a few craters of mediocre elevation, which had doubtless once formed submarine volcanoes, and, thinking about the multiplicity of those outlets that were to be found on the Moon's surface, even in the depths of the seas, they could not help

284

wondering what a powerful force the interior fire that filled the planet must have had, and what frightful revolutions those incessant expansions had produced in the solid crust that covered it without suppressing it.

They had reached the utmost depths of the sea they were crossing—a depth estimated by Marcel at four kilometers. There. the mineral "moss" carpeting the ground had accumulate in thicker layers, and when the necessity to rest obliged them to stop, the three inhabitants of Earth were able to lie down on something resembling thick grass. They might have imagined that they were in some valley in Switzerland or the Pyrenees if the silence and desolation around them had not recalled them to a sentiment of reality.

The appearance of that layer, with its uniform dark green tint, over which no tree extended its shade, where no flower grew and whose implacable immobility was never disturbed by any breeze, penetrated them with an insurmountable sadness. They hastened to escape its depressing influence.

When Rugel set off in a direction that would bring them back to the continent, therefore, they followed him eagerly, and it was with a sort of sentiment of liberation that they set foot once again on what, on the world they had quit, they would have been able to call firm ground.

They then found themselves, without transition, in a tormented region in which, the further they went forward, the more difficult marching became. Enormous blisters and abysms with sheer walls obliged them to change direction continually. Nevertheless, they were edging gradually northwards, where a crater appeared on the horizon that appeared to be the objective that Rugel wanted to reach. Having faith in their guide, they went forth bravely; the marvels that they had witnessed were a sure guarantee that they would be rewarded for their trouble.

Having arrived at the last of the crests forming the mountainous region, they saw a rather vast plain extended at their feet, in the middle of which stood, in majestic isolation, the crater whose summit they had already distinguished from afar.

The ground before their eyes presented a very particular appearance; from the summit of the mountain where the crater opened dazzling white streaks radiated in straight lines over its flanks and far into the plain, where, gradually diminishing in width, they ended up petering out. Between these luminous stripes, the rocky ground seemed dull and almost dark. Marcel, Jacques and Lord Rodilan were struck with surprise and admiration.

"Ah!" Marcel exclaimed. "A crater with a ray system!"

Rugel smiled. His friends' astonishment appeared to cause him considerable satisfaction.

"I would have liked to take you to see the gigantic circle to which your astronomers have given, as you have told me, the name of the scientist Tycho Brahe, but the time and the means were lacking. I wanted at least to set before your eyes a specimen of one of the most astonishing cosmic phenomena that our planet presents. A few more steps and you'll be able to examine it at close range."

They descended to the plain and advanced toward the nearest of the strange stripes. As they got closer they distinguished something akin to a layer of polished vitrified material evenly distributed on the ground, as smooth as a mirror, which reflected the sun's light in all its intensity.

"Our scientists," said Rugel, "explain this phenomenon as follows: at the time when the lunar surface began to solidify and the central fire as still fully active, enormous quantities of gas and vapor formed in the bosom of the igneous mass. At certain points, where the interior pressure was irresistible, either because the crust was thinner or because the volcano's chimney was insufficient to give passage to the gaseous materials, the crust around the crater was split in a star-shaped pattern. Gases escaped by that means, raised to a temperature of which we now have no idea, and, under the action of the extremely intense heat, the ground was vitrified, the sides of the fissure welded together, and these regular bright strips were formed, which must present a strange appearance to those who contemplate them from far away."

"That will put an end to all the controversies on the matter in question," said Marcel, "and give full credit to the theory formulated by Camille Flammarion, one of the most celebrated Earthly astronomers, the only one to glimpse the truth."[30]

The ascent of the crater was long and difficult. The uneven ground bristling with numerous asperities and scoriform blistered only permitted the voyagers to advance with extreme slowness. When they had reached the summit, however, the dazzling spectacle before their eyes soon made them forget their fatigue.

Beneath their feet, an infinite number of luminous strips departed, which formed as many radii of a gigantic star, which seemed to have fallen from the sky, and those polished and transparent surfaces, in decomposing the light, were resplendent with all the colors of the prism.

"How beautiful it is!" Marcel exclaimed. "On this arid and desolate world, nature has still found the means to produce grandiose effects, and our old Earth, varied as it is, offers nothing similar."

"Let us admire the Sovereign Being," said Rugel, "who imprint all his works, until death, with the marks of his supreme grandeur and inexhaustible magnificence."

Jacques and Lord Rodilan gazed in silence. The meditative soul of the one and the skeptical mind of the other were overwhelmed by the majesty of the sublime scene.

It was, however, necessary to tear themselves away from that contemplation.

"We've arrived at the extreme limits of the region that the inhabitants of the Moon have thus far explored," said

---

[30] Alas, Flammarion, working on the hypothesis that lunar craters are volcanic, had no chance of finding the true explanation, which is now generally thought—according to the hypothesis advanced by Eugene Shoemaker in the 1960s—to be that the "ray systems" associated with Tycho and some other craters are streaks of ejecta thrown out by the impact that was actually responsible for the crater.

Rugel. "When I talked to you about the possibility of taking our research further, you welcomed my proposal enthusiastically. Now, in the presence of the difficulties that await us and the perils we might have to overcome, I hesitate to pursue that enterprise. If it were to have a tragic outcome, I would never forgive myself for having involved you in it..."

Marcel interrupted swiftly. "Thank you for your solicitude, Rugel, my friend, but we're not men to recoil before obstacles of any sort. Those who have crossed the distance separating the Noon from the Earth won't allow themselves to be frightened by a few molehills to climb and ditches to traverse."

"Ditches and molehills!" Rugel replied, smiling. "But what do your companions think?"

"I'll go wherever you go," said Jacques. "I too revere science, and if this expedition will bring us a few new revelations, I want my part in the glory. Anyway, I'm certain that we'll come back safe and sound. I'm sure that I'll see the Earth again."

"As for me," said Lord Rodilan, with the phlegm that never abandoned him in the gravest circumstances, "I only ask to go forward. If there's danger, well, so much the better—that's one attraction more. I ought to have been dead a long time ago; anything that might happen now is of no importance."

"Well, so be it," said Rugel. "We'll launch ourselves into the unknown.

"After resting for a few terrestrial days and carrying out a minute inspection of all the apparatus they were carrying, which was in perfect condition, the voyagers set off resolutely in an eastward direction.

For a month, they continued their route in the same direction, and to their great surprise, the region through which they were traveling had an appearance quite different from those they had already traversed. The granitic ground on which they were walking no longer presented violent asperities and the abrupt outcrops of inferior strata that gave the other hemisphere of the Moon such a tormented character. Immense spaces extended before them whose almost flat surface only exhibited faint undulations. Nothing blocked their path or limited their gaze; the horizon continued to flee before them, and formed a perfect circle no matter where they were, of which they were always the center.

The 354-hour night took them by surprise, and then gave way to a day of equal length, and still they were advancing through those bleak solitudes in which no cry vibrated and in which no breeze lifted the dust beneath their feet, where everything was frozen and motionless. It was like an immense sea suddenly petrified wile calm. Had it not been for the somber hue of the rocks on which they were treading they might have believed that they were in the vast Sahara desert. Here, though, no oasis offered the shade of its palm trees and the murmur of its spring to their thirsty gaze. No caravan saluted them in passing.

They went on and on, guided by the stars alone.

The voyagers required well-tempered souls and intrepid hearts not to succumb to the burden of that frightful isolation.

Even in their saddest hours, Marcel and his two friends had never felt their resolution weaken, but in spite of their firmness, they were gradually penetrated by a mournful sentiment, and in those open spaces they were oppressed, as in the depths of a sepulcher.

Sometimes, Marcel tried to react against the sentiment, and words of encouragement came to his lips into which he strove to impart some cheerfulness, but his attempts were unechoed. Jacques' melancholy seemed to have increased, and Lord Rodilan could no longer find his joyful humor and mocking bonhomie. Rugel remained grave; his face had never lost its affability and softness; he seemed inaccessible to fatigue; discouragement had no purchase on that heart, full of the love of science.

The troop of Diemides marched with marvelous unison, in which no trace of weakness showed. Recruited from the youngest, most vigorous and most intelligent member of their class, they understood the importance of the mission that their leader had accepted, and as they had absolute confidence in him, they had no doubt about the final result of the enterprise.

The second period of night had just ended and the first rays of sunlight were already inundating the sky when an irregular black line appeared on the horizon, which the voyagers greeted with joy. They were finally coming to the end of the interminable plain! Compared with that desperate monotony, the most abrupt and difficult terrain that might be offered to them would at least offer them the image of life.

They soon arrived at the foot of a kind of wall formed of gigantic blocks of black basalt, which rose up sheerly, as if the igneous masses, under pressure of incredible force, had been ripped from the surface of the ground, hurled into space and then, suddenly seized by the low ambient temperature, had crystallized without being deformed.

That formidable upsurge was prolonged as far as the eye could see in both a northerly and a southerly direction; there was no possibility of going around it, and they resolved to get over it, still heading east. The undertaking was difficult, and would have made lesser men retreat.

Between the violently-projected blocks, which, more often than not, were tangled and overlapping at their base, there were only narrow and dangerous passages hardly large enough for them to penetrate one by one, whose floor, as smooth as glass, made walking uncertain and perilous. The feet slipped continually; the falls thus produced might have been fatal if the voyagers had not taken the precaution of attaching themselves together with long cords. When one of them was about to lose his footing and threatened to fall into some fissure in which he would unfailingly be crushed, he was caught by those preceding and following him. Then it was necessary, with great difficulty, by hauling on the rope, to bring him back up to the surface and continue the interrupted march.

Sometimes they found themselves facing some colossal block whose compact surface offered no way through. They were obliged then to attempt to climb over. A few Diemides, hoisted on to the shoulders of their companions, hollowed out holes in the rock with the aid of their pickaxes, plunged iron spikes into them, and then, climbing on to those improvised steps, dug further holes over their heads, all the way to the summit of the obstacle. Everyone followed them, and more than once, Lord Rodilan, suspended by his hands and feet from that parrot-ladder congratulated himself on having conserved a flexibility and vigor in his limbs that permitted him to execute acrobatic feats.

When the block was surpassed, they found themselves in the presence of new difficulties and perils, but the marvelous spectacles offered to their gaze by that strangely convulsed nature offered Rugel and his friends abundant compensation for their troubles.

Arranged in perfect symmetrical order, long series of enormous columns loomed up there with cylindrical bases and capitals that might have been carved by the hands of the most delicate artists.

Elsewhere, slender grooves jutting out from thick walls, came together in ogival arches, and they might have thought that they were in one of the Gothic cathedrals elevated by ardent and mystical faith by the Christians of the Middle Ages.

Often, densely-packed ridges arranged in stages of different heights and dimensions, depicted gigantic organs, and it was astonishing not to hear torrents of harmony springing from their flanks. In their capricious formation the rocks affected the most varied forms; Marcel pointed out to his companions an ancient burg similar to those overlooking the banks of the Rhine. Everything was there: the long ramparts with battlements, pierced with loopholes, flanked at intervals by pepper-pot towers and surmounted by a keep from which it seemed that the voice of a watchman announcing noble visitors might ring out at any moment.

Elsewhere again, there were imposing cathedrals, with their powerful buttresses, their bold arches, and their slender steeples raising their pointed tips toward the sky.

At one moment, Lord Rodilan gripped Jacques' arm, stopping him suddenly. "Oh!" he exclaimed. "Westminster Abbey!"

Before them, in fact, isolated in a large space, stood a marvelous Gothic construction with slim colonnettes, regular ogives and dentellate rose-windows, unmistakable reminiscent of the architectural gem that mirrors its lacy stonework in the waves of the Thames.

"That's utterly astonishing," said Jacques. "The caprices of nature are infinite! Never, it's necessary to admit, have the chisels of the most skillful artists produced anything more regular, more finished and more perfect."

Rugel and Marcel had been seized with admiration, and behind them, the troop of Diemides stood mute with surprise.

No human eye had ever contemplated those sublime spectacles, and they all felt a legitimate pride in having dared to penetrate into that inaccessible region in order to discover its astonishing secrets.

They went on, and the fantastic palaces were succeeded by enormous basilicas and vast arenas that seemed to be disposed to receive innumerable crowds of spectators. And over all those architectural treasures, whose astonishing variety even the richest imagination would not have been able to conceive, the sun poured its rays, the intensity of which was untempered by anything. Under the ardent light, those walls, pilasters, columns, steps, obelisks and pyramids were resplendent with a dazzling glare.

That accumulation of marvels left far behind everything that had been celebrated on Earth by enthusiastic voyagers or sung by poets, the famous colonnades of the coast of Antrim constituting the Giant's Causeway, which glorify Ireland, or even Fingal's Cave, where pale specters, the heroes of the legends of Ossian, gather by night to talk once again about battles and love.

In spite of the difficulties of every sort presented by walking through those disorderly masses, it was with a sentiment of regret that the voyagers drew away, and they often looked back to see once again, before they disappeared over the horizon, the bizarre silhouettes of those monstrous edifices, which seemed to have been built by the hands of genies.

The country into which they penetrated on emerging from the basaltic region offered a totally different aspect. There, by a strange fantasy of nature, the ancient commotions of the ground had projected to the surface an enormous layer of primitive rocks in which porphyry was dominant. The route became much easier, for the cooling seemed to have gripped the molten mass at a moment of calm. Save for a few blocks strewn at hazard, no serious obstacle impeded their progress.

Underfoot, however, everything was blood red; the rocks they were now skirting sometimes presented bloody streaks to their astonished gazes and sometimes the pink and violet tints of freshly cut flesh.

The inhabitants of the Moon, strangers to any idea of carnage and murder, felt no other impression than that of excited curiosity before this new spectacle, but Marcel and his two friends, who had often witnessed human fury on Earth, and had seen blood flow and mutilated bodies writhe on battlefields, were gripped by a sentiment of horror. Their imagination evoked the memory of those cruel scenes; they felt oppressed, and uttered a sigh of relief when they finally quit that region, which seemed to them to be accursed.

XI. The Eruption

The little caravan continued its eastward march intrepidly. Night made the sky resplendent again with a thousand fires, and the transparency of the ether was such that the eye could distinguish stars of the tenth magnitude without any difficulty.

The Milky Way, which striped the celestial vault above their heads, no longer appeared to them as a splash of diffuse light, but as an accumulation of countless suns, which distance caused to appear very close to one another, and each of which shone with its own light.

They were now traversing a continent quite similar to those which are encountered in large numbers on the visible surface of the Moon; there were the same tightly-packed craters, perforating the rocky crust everywhere, unequal in size, which they had continually to go around, while conserving the determined direction. They had stopped to rest. All of them, weary from a long march, had abandoned themselves to sleep, when one of the Diemides suddenly got up, showing all the signs of great astonishment.

He went to Rugel.

"Master," he said, "If I'm not mistaken, my ear has just perceived something like a dull rumbling deep underground. One might have thought that it was carts rolling over an iron bridge...."

Without letting him finish, Rugel bent down, commanded silence with a gesture, applied his ear to the bare rock and listened attentively.

A distant noise was audible, transmitted by the vibrations of the solid crust.

Hastily, he woke Marcel and his two companions.

"I believe some formidable cataclysm is in preparation," he told them, "and that we're going to witness one of the convulsions of nature that were once so frequent on our globe, and which made the surface so strange and tormented."

The subterranean noise had become more distinct; it was perceptible without putting an ear to the ground. All the Diemides were on their feet, and their attitude betrayed their apprehension.

"I thought that the lunar surface had been completely re-frozen for many centuries," said Marcel, "and that the central fire had been relegated to such depths hat it was impossible for it to have any external effect."

"But is that theory well-established?" Jacques observed. "Haven't certain astronomers, even in our day, observed appreciable changes on the visible surface several times, such as the appearance of new craters and modifications in the form of those that are already known?"

"All that's very vague," Marcel replied, "and doesn't qualify as scientifically demonstrated truth."

Rugel interrupted them.

"Since lunar humankind has been obliged to renounce living outside and to enclose itself in the caverns that now shelter its existence, no profound commotion has modified the part of the spheroid that extends over our heads, but the central fire that maintains our life still occupies a considerable space in the core and its action is always to be feared. The accident that occurred in the chimney of our elevator, to which you fell victim, proves that the gases that form in the interior and are subject to formidable pressure there can sometimes find fissures through which they escape and spread outside. It's quite possible that a phenomenon of the same kind is occurring where we are now, and that we might witness some redoubtable eruption. So it's best not to remain any longer in this country strewn with rocks, and to return to broadly open ground where we'll be less exposed."

The voyagers retraced their steps, and stopped in a vast plain that they had traversed after emerging from the porphyry region. The subterranean rumbles could still be heard, and the ground beneath their feet was already beginning to move. But it was not like our globe, where the profound shocks we call earthquakes are manifest, with undulations of varying amplitude. The density and thickness of the crust covering the interior fires could not lend itself to those movements, which resembled ocean waves; it was a sort of continuous trepidation, an agitation on the spot, in the midst of which muffled cracking sounds could be discerned.

Those symptoms seemed to Rugel to be menacing. He advised moving even further away from the point that seemed to be the center of the geological phenomenon.

They did not have time.

A dull sound, transmitted by the solid layers, suddenly burst forth, similar to the distant discharge of a hundred artillery pieces firing simultaneously. At the same time, the space lit up with a bloody glare. One of the craters whose summits they could see had just opened up.

The expansive force of the gases had projected into the air, to an incalculable height, the obstacle of solidified lava that had sealed the chimney for centuries, and an enormous column of molten matter was hurled from into space from the gaping opening. That column rose up vertically; in the center it looked like liquid gold; on the edges it was dark red, while green and violet flames burned at its periphery.

That torrent of fire, which launched outside the crater, dragged with it enormous incandescent blocks, which, abruptly seized by the cold of space, burst into sheaves of sparks.

In that airless milieu no sound wave could reach the ears of the witnesses to those detonations, which would have been formidable in the terrestrial atmosphere. The gigantic vomit of flame, spreading out silently into the profound night, seemed to have something supernatural about it, which chilled the soul with a religious terror. At the same time, dense fumes emerged from the volcano, charged with a frightful quantity of ash and scoria, which, rising up in a sinister dome, soon formed a kind of somber vault that hid the entire sky.

The stars had disappeared; the electric lamps, in that environment saturated with solid molecules, no longer gave out any but a wan light.

That spectacle of sublime horror struck all hearts with an indescribable terror.

In spite of the solid temper of their souls, Rugel and his three companions felt overwhelmed by the terrifying grandeur of that convulsion of lunar nature, of which nothing that occurs on Earth can give any idea. The frightened Diemides gathered tremulously around their leader. It seems, in fact, that in great cataclysms, beings of inferior intelligence instinctively draw nearer to those in whom they have observed a mental superiority.

After a moment of trouble and hesitation, the four valiant hearts had rallied.

The ground was trembling underfoot and was threatening to open up at any moment; somber and impenetrable clouds were spreading above their heads; they remained impassive and immobile, their arms folded, opposing to the unchained elements that were threatening their frail existence the tranquil calm, of an indomitable energy. Resigned, having made the sacrifice of their lives, they were entirely devoted to the contemplation of the imposing scene.

Meanwhile, the matter projected to prodigious heights by the volcano was beginning to fall back on to the shifting ground. There was a rain of ash, with which were mingled blocks of burning rock that were rebounding around them.

"We need to disperse," said Rugel, "and get as far away as possible from this deadly place."

At a sign from him, the Diemides scattered; they thus offered less purchase to the stones whose fall was becoming increasingly abundant. And they all launched themselves precipitately in a westward direction.

Like leaders anxious for the survival of those they command, who insist on remained in peril longest, Rugel and the three inhabitants of Earth brought up the rear, to make sure that no one was left behind. But their movement of retreat had hardly begun when two of the Diemides fell to the ground, struck by the incessant rain of stones.

The other Diemides, who were fleeing, had not noticed them. Rugel and his companions ran forward, but the vital air had already escaped from the breached suits, and asphyxia was complete.

Obedient to a generous sentiment, Marcel and Jacques bent down to pick up the cadavers and carry them away, but Rugel stopped them with a gesture.

"The poor fellows are dead," he said. "No human effort can bring them back to life; let's not hinder ourselves with such a burden. We have no other chance of salvation than to get away as quickly as possible from the circle in which the ash and scoria are falling. Later, if we're still alive, we'll come back to search for their bodies and address a final farewell to them."

They resumed their course.

The Diemides preceding them had not taken long to perceive their absence. Anxious, and neglectful of concern for their own salvation, they came back. Rugel ordered them to keep going and renewed the order to scatter, in order that if some further misfortune occurred, the number of victims would be minimized.

After a few hours of that hectic flight, the situation became less perilous; the fall of rocky debris had ceased, nothing was falling any longer but fine ash, already cooled, forming a thick layer that slowed their progress down, but they were out of danger.

They all gathered around Rugel.

"Friends," he said to them, "the frightful cataclysm that we've just escaped has claimed two victims among us. It will be impossible for us to return their mortal remains to those they have left behind; they will not repose amid their relatives and friends, but their memory will not perish and their names will remain forever engraved in marble in the Temple where we piously maintain reverence for those who have sacrificed their lives in the interest of all. As soon as we can approach the place where they fell, we shall go to render them the final duties, and we shall resume our route toward the goal we have assigned ourselves with a new courage."

The eruption continued for several days. At the distance that the voyagers now were, they could still make out the yellow glow of the column of fire vomited by the crater on the horizon. Gradually, however, its intensity diminished. It passed from bright yellow to somber red, and ended up being extinguished completely.

The ground was still subject to faint tremors, however, and it would not have been prudent to advance over terrain agitated by the final commotions of the interior fire. They were obliged, therefore, to wait until nature, recovering from the shock, had recovered its previous calm and immobility.

Then they went back, and reached the place where the two unfortunates surprised by death were lying. It was difficult to locate them; the ash escaped from the volcano had extended a sinister shroud over them, and it was necessary to dig down through the thick layer for some time in order to reach them. A hole was hollowed out in the rock; the two cadavers were laid within it side by side.

Standing up in the middle of all the others, who were kneeling down, Rugel extended his hands and said: "Rest in peace, you who died in the flower of your youth, one this road to which love of science and the sentiment of duty has drawn you in our wake. May the Sovereign Spirit receive your souls in tranquil peace, and reserve a new existence for you in some superior world!"

Large boulders were heaped up over them, and a funereal monument erected for them such as no mortal eye had ever seen.

After a few days of rest, the march was resumed, but everyone felt sad. The length of the journey and the shared fatigue had drawn the members of the unprecedented expedition closer together in bonds of fraternal sympathy; they formed a sort of family, and the death of those who had been killed had given birth to an impression in every heart that, without diminishing their ardor, left a profound trace in their minds.

They could not resume the route they had been following before directly. The agitation in the solid crust was still tangible, and the thickness of the layer of ash rendered the route both difficult and perilous. It was, therefore, necessary to go around that region by heading north, in order to resume an easterly direction after having circled it.

That part of the journey, accomplished in profound darkness, was particularly difficult. It was necessary to walk with great precaution, for at every moment they saw crevasses opening up underfoot, and sometimes wide precipices, where a fall would have been irremediable, so great was their depth and so many sharp and trenchant asperities protruded from their walls.

The action of the volcano had made itself felt well beyond the radius in which the matter projected by the eruption had fallen. Everything was disturbed. It seemed that the blocks that rested on the surface, shaken by the commotion, had not yet recovered their equilibrium and were incessantly threatening to crush the reckless individuals who dared to violate the mystery of those solitudes.

They marched on for a long time, and the lunar day succeeded the night yet again. As far as the eye could see, however, nothing could be seen but an immense plain whose uniformity was unbroken. It was like another Sahara in which immobility, silence and death reigned. The circle of the horizon was rounded out in an inflexible curve, like that of the ocean when the sea is calm, and it retreated incessantly as they walked toward it.

Where were they going? When would they see an end to that interminable voyage?

They kept advancing, but it was no longer with the almost joyous ardor of the early days. Gradually, they were all overtaken by the infinite sadness that emanated from those bleak spaces.

They were marching heavily and pensively now; they only exchanged rare comments; discouragement seemed to be overtaking them.

Jacques' soul, perhaps more impressionable than those of his friends, was invaded by a poignant anguish. Thus far, the incidents of the route had interested him and sustained his courage, but now he felt oppressed; one might have thought that all the weight of that dead nature was falling back upon him as if to crush him. He was now only walking with a hesitant stride, sometimes falling behind, and seemed to be following his companions regretfully.

Marcel noticed that. "Friend," he said to him, "I fear that your strength isn't a match for your energy. The task we've undertaken is more difficult to fulfill than I thought at first, and perhaps I've dragged you too far. But no matter how strong my desire is to fathom the unknown of this world that we'll soon be quitting, I'm ready, if you wish, to retrace my steps."

"Thank you, my dear Marcel; I never doubted your heart, and I know that you'd sacrifice your dearest hopes for me without regret. I confess that I feel prey to a depression that astonishes me. It's doubtless the desperate monotony of this endless desert in which we seem to be lost that's affecting my mind. I sometimes wonder whether the goal we're pursuing might not be a chimera, and whether we might be destined to see it fleeing incessantly before our eyes, like those shadows one pursues without ever overtaking."

"How can we believe, though, that the traditions on the strength of which we've engaged in this adventure can have been transmitted, without any variation, from generation to generation, if they don't contain a foundation of truth? Do you think that Rugel, so wise and profound, would have consented to serve as our guide if they were nothing but deceptive dreams?"

"What serious foundation can one attribute to vague indications that seem to be belied by everything that we already know about the lunar world? Have we ever encountered anything whatsoever that resembles traces of life—even vegetable life? No, everything really is dead on the surface of this old world, and it's folly to believe that there might be anything alive here except imprudent adventurers."

"Oh, if that's what you think, we need to go back!" And Marcel's voice was pierced with a note of regret.

"Who's talking about going back?" said Lord Rodilan. "Have we come this far to retreat shamefully? Are we children, then, who become irritated and discouraged because they can't grasp the object of their desire at the first attempt?"

"Oh, I know, Milord, that nothing could stop you. There's also nothing calling you back. We've almost reached the middle of the invisible surface of our satellite, more than a thousand leagues from our point of departure, and we haven't yet discovered what we came to find. There's no reason for that to change. Have you resolved, then, to go all around the Moon?"

"The prospect doesn't displease me," said Lord Rodilan. "You can't deny that the expedition has been sufficiently eventful thus far, and we're traveling in conditions that, given the world we're in, aren't uncomfortable. With the apparatus we have, we're protected from the cold. I'm beginning to resign myself only to being nourished scientifically, and thanks to the benefits of specific weight, we can undertake journeys easily before which the most intrepid globetrotters would recoil. We climb mountains with the agility of acrobats; falls that would be fatal on Earth are absolutely inoffensive here, and save for the unfortunate accident that befell the two poor devils we buried back there, we've accomplished a voyage whose story would make all the Livingstones, Stanleys, Camerons and—meaning no offense, my dear Jacques—Bingers past present and future pale with jealousy."[31]

---

[31] Verney Cameron was, like Livingstone and Stanley, a pioneering explorer of central Africa, the first to cross the continent from shore to shore in 1875. Louis Binger conducted his explorations at a later date, publishing an account of his 1889

Rugel had come closer, and had been listening to the three friends' conversation for a few moments.

"I understand the lassitude that has gripped you," he said to Jacques. "We all feel the influence that's oppressing you. But I think I can reassure you, and affirm that we're getting close to the objective we proposed. The traditions piously conserved among us do, in fact, mention a vast desert that it's necessary to cross for several days to arrive at the region whose mysterious depths retain the last vestiges of the life of old. We've been walking for a long time already; we must be close."

"Well, let's go on," said Jacques, rallied by what Rugel had said. "My courage won't be inferior to yours, and I can't let you miss out of the fruit of so much effort."

They resumed the route with a new ardor.

Rugel's assurance had dissipated all doubts. Even Jacques no longer seemed to be feeling the lassitude and depression that had triumphed momentarily over his energy.

Meanwhile, the ground began to rise in a gradual slope, although nothing was revealed as yet to anxious eyes and the line of the horizon still offered the same implacable rectitude.

A few Diemides, forming a kind of advance guard, were walking quite a long was in front of the bulk of the caravan, and their silhouettes stood out against the background of the sky. Suddenly, they were seen to stop and make broad gestures of astonishment. One of them soon separated from the little group and ran back to Rugel and his companions.

"I think we've reached the end of our journey, Master," he said, as he came close.

---

expedition in 1891; Rodilan could have known of Binger's earlier activities in 1885, when other evidence within the text suggests that this passage ought to be set, but it is unlikely. It is possible that the novel had been set aside for some time during the writing.

They had picked up the pace, and after a few moments the spectacle they had before their eyes drew exclamations of amazement.

The desert they had just traversed formed an immense plateau, which extended as far as the eye could see to the right and the left, but whose circular form could be distinguished in the distance.

In front of them there was an immense hole, on the edge of which they had paused, the other side of which was barely visible in the distance, the slopes of which descended steeply.

In the depths of the yawning hole—O prodigy!—far below the ridge on which they were huddled they could see vapors forming clouds, on which the sun's rays fell; one might have imagined them to be the fleecy waves of an immobile sea.

"Clouds! Genuine clouds!" exclaimed Marcel, Jacques and Lord Rodilan, simultaneously.

"Our traditions haven't lied," said Rugel. "Life isn't completely extinct on the surface of our world. We're going to explore its last vestiges."

XII. The Mysterious Valley

The descent was effected without too much difficulty. The certainty of having attained the goal of their enterprise, the strangeness of the phenomenon they had before their eyes, of which nothing thus far had given them any inkling, and the hope of enriching science with new discoveries had reanimated all hearts.

At several points there were perilous passages to tackle; they encountered a few sheer slopes down which it was necessary to let themselves slide, while roped together; there were numerous falls, but without any deadly result. What was all that to men who had accomplished such an audacious odyssey?

As they got closer to the vaporous layers that had appeared from above to be clouds, the presence of an atmosphere, very rarefied as yet but nevertheless certain began to be detectable. Their sight, which had extended over prodigious distances on the lunar surface, became more limited; the variations in the terrain did not stand out as clearly; the contours were softened, the colors less vivid.

They finally reached the moving sea that they had contemplated from high above.

Suddenly, the voyagers found themselves enveloped by a kind of thick milky white fog, sufficiently opaque for them not to be able to see more than two paces ahead. They felt isolated from one another, as if lost in a limitless and bottomless ocean. They hardly dared take a step, not knowing which way to go or where to place their feet, fearing at every moment to be separated from their companions and unable to find them again.

It was necessary to take new and minute precautions.

On Rugel's orders, the electric lamps were switched on again, but their light, rendered ruddy by the thickness of the fog, could only be perceived within a small radius, and only projected a dubious light on the ground.

Again it was necessary to rope themselves together.

Two of the most vigorous of the Diemides were placed in the lead; armed with pickaxes, they were to sound out the route, only advancing when they were sure that the ground on which they were about to set foot could support them.

In such conditions they could only descend very slowly, and the thickness of the cloud layer that they had to traverse was considerable. Rugel explained to his friends that its very thickness gave them the certainty that they would find vegetable life beneath it.

"These accumulated vapors," he said, "which must reign permanently over the inferior region, form a kind of thick curtain, which tempers the torrid heat of the sun while it's above the horizon, and prevents the heat stored then from radiating into space during the night. Thus, a kind of temperature equilibrium is established, without which life would be impossible."

As they plunged more deeply into that wan daylight, into the atmosphere whose density increased incessantly, it seemed to them that their movements became less facile and less free; it was not as easy to walk.

On perceiving that, Marcel attributed the phenomenon to the pressure of the ambient air operating on the surface of the suits in which they were clad. He told himself that the pressure would inevitably increase as they penetrated further forward, and that a moment would doubtless arrive when the air would become respirable for humans. That prospect, which he hastened to communicate to his friends, filled him with joy. Whatever services the ingenious, complicated and delicate apparatus rendered them, they would not be sorry to take the suits off for a while and live a more human existence.

Finally, they came through the cloud layer. The voyagers emerged from the vapors that enveloped them, like the Homeric gods suddenly revealing themselves to mortal eyes—but there was no one there to witness their sudden appearance.

They found themselves on the side of a mountain covered by a few meager vestiges of vegetation. Unknown plants, which offered considerable analogies to Earthly mosses and lichens, extended underfoot, covering the bare rock with a thin layer of yellow-tinted vegetation, in leprous patches. Below them, they could make out stunted bushes with gnarled, rampant branches and discolored foliage: a languid and etiolated flora to which it seemed that the atmosphere from which it sought life was only furnishing an insufficient nourishment.

In the bottom of the large valley there was an immense lake, whose dull waters were not rippled by any breeze. On its banks, bordered by aquatic plants of a slightly more vivid green, there were a few clumps of trees, whose mossy trunks were denuded, and whose crowns only bore a few twisted branches.

Over that impoverished nature reigned a veiled daylight, uniformly gray in color, through which no rays of sunlight filtered, not dissimilar to the dull winter days that precede long polar nights on Earth.

That residue of life so strangely conserved on the dead surface of the Moon was exceedingly sad and melancholy. In the eyes of Rugel and the Diemides who accompanied him, however, it seemed delightful and charming. It offered a striking contrast with the arid regions they had traversed, which gripped their imagination. Since leaving the observatory, they had been living in an environment in which everything was hostile and inhospitable. It seemed to them now that they had rediscovered a corner of their native planet, such as it was in ancient days, before the revolutions of the satellite had obliged its inhabitants to take refuge in its core.

Marcel and his two companions experienced quite different sensations. What was dominant in them was the joy of having, at the price of countless fatigues, resolved a problem that no one had even thought accessible. They had before them, on the ever-invisible part of the Moon, one of the depressions at the bottom of which they eyes of a few obstinate astronomers thought that they had recognized traces of vapor and vegetation.

Marcel's mind, however, reached beyond that. What was unfurled before his gaze was one of the last phases of the life of a world. In this remote corner where, by virtue of exceptional circumstances, the evolution of the planet had been delayed, he was, in a sense, witnessing the death-throes of the world.

Before reaching the state of complete dereliction that reigned over the whole surface, Earth's satellite had passed through successive transformations, and, at a given moment, it had all been similar to the miserable valley where the last glimmers of life seemed on the brink of extinction. With the diminution of the central heat, the slow disappearance of water and the atmosphere, the conditions necessary for life had gradually weakened; the cold had invaded everything, and everything still alive had ended up disappearing. And it was like a miracle to see this fragment of the world belatedly alive, as if forgotten at the moment of universal destruction.

And his thoughts returned to the Earth.

This, he said to himself, *is the fate that awaits our planet. In a few thousand centuries, it too will see the evolution whose beginnings we are witnessing today come to an end. While the central fire diminishes, the sun that lights and heats its surface will become weaker. The polar ice-caps will extend and confine the human race to a progressively more restricted area. In time, life will be concentrated in a narrow strip around the equator, and the debris of humankind, not having, like the inhabitants of the Moon, the recourse of taking refuge in the bowels of the globe, will perish miserably, cursing the Earth that has become impotent to nourish them, and cursing the miserly heavens that are refusing them light and heat.*

Meanwhile, the travelers had completed the descent of the mountainside and reached the valley floor.

They were all in a hurry to take off the apparatus in which they had been imprisoned for so long and to breathe open air, but it was necessary not to leave anything to chance.

Thanks to Rugel's foresight, measuring instruments had been brought in the luggage carried by the Diemides. They were consulted.

The metallic barometer indicated a pressure of 528 millimeters, still inferior to that of the city of Quito on Earth. The centigrade thermometer marked three degrees. That was undoubtedly a little low, but supportable. It was nevertheless evident that it would drop considerably during the 354-hour night, and paralyze the momentum of life.

The results were satisfactory, and on their leader's order, the Diemides took off their costumes.

Marcel, Jacques and Lord Rodilan had not waited, so great was their haste to recover the ease of movement and the free use of speech.

"Ah!" said Lord Rodilan, stretching delightedly and breathing in long draughts of air, which seemed so sweet to him. "How good it is to breathe easily! I was beginning to weary of that artificial atmosphere with which we've been obliged to content ourselves since our departure. Chemical air and chemical nourishment are all very well, but I've lost the taste for them, and if I ever get back to Earth, I shall swear a mortal hatred against chemistry, all its practitioners and all its inventions."

"Don't speak so ill of chemistry, my dear lord," replied Marcel, laughing. "Without it, neither of us would be here, and I'm sure you'd regret not having followed to the end a voyage so fecund in astonishing discoveries."

The troop of Diemides had spread out along the edge of the lake, the opposite shore of which could barely be distinguished in the distance. It did not appear to have any great depth; the surrounding region was flat and smooth. The forces of nature had been active; the rain and running water, incessantly drawing the friable particles toward the bottom of the valley, had gradually filled it up, and only a thin liquid layer remained, which evaporation was incessantly decreasing, and would not take long to disappear.

Silence reigned everywhere; there was no birdsong to be heard, nor the rustle of alarmed beasts. Apart from the languishing plants slowly perishing in this corner bound for death, nothing seemed to be alive.

Some distance away, a fairly extensive wood was visible, toward which they headed. The ground on which they were walking was covered with short coarse grass, growing as if regretfully on the thin layer of humus that was still resisting all the causes of destruction.

They went into the wood. They light was duller and more somber there that outside, and the sight of the strange, melancholy and lugubrious forest inspired a profound feeling of sadness. There was none of the bushy undergrowth that forms in Earthly forests, populated by so many various species, forming a backcloth so easy on the eye. The blackish trunks stood up rigid and bare. They were conifers of some sort, similar to those that grow on Earthly mountain-sides. Only toward the top were a few etiolated branches covered with sparse foliage.

A damp and penetrating cold reigned beneath that dome of verdure; they went through it in a hurry. When they emerged on the other side the voyagers found themselves on the bank of a stream running over a bed of mud, without producing the joyous murmur that is so conducive to reverie when one pauses to breathe the perfumed evening breeze after a warm summer's day in the country.

The stream descended through a narrow valley seemingly hollowed out in a pleat in the ground. While Rugel and his three friends lay down in the grass to take a little rest, a party of Diemides set off to explore.

"We've now reached the goal that we set ourselves," Marcel said. "We've verified the accuracy of your old legends, and we can report to your scientists who are interested in the problem the certainty that, if residues of life still subsist in remote areas of the lunar surface, they're on the point of disappearance, and that death will soon have extended its somber empire everywhere. What are your plans now, friend? Do you intend to stay here for long?"

"We'll doubtless require a long enough interval to explore the region in its full extent, study its layout and collect a few specimens of this dying flora."

"How large do you think the dimensions of this strange valley can be?" asked Lord Rodilan.

"It's difficult to measure exactly," said Rugel, "But as far as it's possible to judge by the curve of the kind of cliff that encloses it, the valley, if oblong in form, doesn't seem to be more than fifteen or twenty of your terrestrial leagues in its longest diameter."

"One of our French départements would have difficulty fitting into it," said Jacques, "And it's not probable that the exploration we'll undertake has any great surprises in store for us. There are no very significant changes in the terrain: no hills, no major watercourses, and no large forests. We haven't found any trace of animal life thus far, and it doubtless won't take long to complete our research. But in order to return to our departure point we still have long fatigues to endure, and in spite of the strength of resistance of which we've given evidence thus far, I think it would be appropriate to stay here for some while, in order to recover our strength and enable us to confront the ordeals that wait us."

"Wisely spoken," said Lord Rodilan. "The place pleases me, and if I could only hunt hare and snipe, I'd gladly get used to it."

"Incorrigible gourmand," said Marcel. "You always remain subservient to the material, and can't rise above those vulgar needs and gross enjoyments that weigh the soul down and turn it away from the contemplation of the ideal."

"You say that very casually, Marcel, and are easily disgusted, but I'd like to see you in the presence of one of those plates of venison that smell so good and have such a flavorsome taste. It makes my mouth water just thinking about it. The ideal is doubtless very jolly, but plunging into it with an empty stomach doesn't seem at all cheerful to me. After a good meal, when my stomach is satisfied and a few glasses of a generous wine have warmed by blood, when I see everything in a rosy light, I'm disposed, as you are, to let my mind wanted in the blue yonder, but when I'm hungry, my ideal is limited to having that good meal."

Marcel and Jacques could not help laughing at that sally. Rugel looked at the Englishman, not without surprise.

"So," said Jacques, "you've never envied the condition of our friend Rugel and those like him, who are freed from the ever-troublesome care of replenishing bodily strength by means of nourishment? You haven't admired the way that their minds, liberated from those preoccupations, could become subtler and finer? They've attained the degree of perfection glimpsed by our ancient philosophers of having no needs, of not having to labor to satisfy them and not having to suffer when they're unfulfilled."

"Oh, no," replied Lord Rodilan. "Doesn't all the charm of life consist of being able to increase the sum of one's enjoyments, and isn't the man who is most needy also the one whom, in satisfying all his needs, procures the greatest sum of pleasures? You make fun of me in condemning mine, but what are you doing when you're impassioned about science, when you expend your efforts to enrich it with some new conquest or unexpected discovery? You've created artificial needs and you're striving to satisfy them. One of your sages said that people ought to live in conformity with their nature. Now, my nature wants me to eat and drink; it doesn't urge me to find out what's happening on Jupiter or Saturn; so I'm closer than you are to veritable wisdom."

Jacques laughed frankly.

"That," said Marcel, "is an entirely unexpected application of the maxim of the Stoics, and old Zeno would certainly be surprised to find himself rallying to the banner of Epicurus. Materialist as you are, though, haven't you ever thought of distinguishing the noble needs of the spirits from the base appetites of the body"

"Bah!" said Lord Rodilan. "I don't know any philosophical maxim that's worth as much, when one's hungry, as a slice of roast beef and a pint of claret."

Rugel had listened to that discussion attentively. "I have no entitlement," he said, "to intervene in this debate, since, in his sovereign wisdom, the Author of all things has simplified the conditions of material life for us. If appears to me, however, that the joys whose lack our friend feels so strongly—which I cannot appreciate, never having known them—don't merit so much regret. To judge by what I know of your mode of existence and the organization of your terrestrial societies, the satisfaction of these needs is not achieved, for the greater number of the inhabitants of your planet, without effort and suffering of every kind, and what you call the struggle for existence appears to me to comprise more sadness and bitterness than veritable joys. It seems to me that it costs very dear to buy a few pleasures of short duration, and if one compares them with the pure joys of the mind, the choice can scarcely be in doubt."

They were chatting in this fashion when they saw some of the Diemides who had gone upstream coming back. Their expressions were strangely troubled.

"Master," said one of them, "We're not alone in this valley; we've just seen a human creature here."

XIII. The Last Family

With a single movement they all got up and surrounded the Diemide.

He told his story: "We'd been following the course of the stream for some time, and we'd just gone around the small hillock you can see from here, when we saw something unexpected. Some distance from the bank, on the hillside, we made out a mass of stones that we mistook at first for a landslide. When we got closer, though, we realized that it was the remains of a construction, evidently built by human hands, with regular walls and symmetrically-pierced openings. It was half-destroyed; the roof had collapsed and its debris was strewn on the ground. A few wild plants were growing in the midst of the ruins, which had been abandoned for a long time.

"That discovery excited us profoundly. There was no doubt about it; human beings had lived in this place, which we thought uninhabitable, for a long time, and we wondered how long it had been since the last representatives of that forgotten race had died. We went on, and the traces of an anterior life became more frequent: more ruined walls and devastated habitations appeared, and our feet even encountered a few recognizable fragments of instruments that had served the functions of life. Our emotion increased; we were only advancing hesitantly, somewhat troubled, through those remains of a past that still seemed recent, when we suddenly stopped, struck by amazement.

"Some distance away, a human being appeared. With his back to a fragment of a wall, he was standing still, seemingly insensible to his surroundings. He was wearing a thick, dark-colored garment, and his silhouette stood out clear against the whiteness of the stone.

"No sound had betrayed our approach; he had neither seen us not heard us. Gripped by astonishment, we were contemplating him, not daring to take another step, when the stranger straightened up and, without looking in our direction, suddenly disappeared from view. All that happened so rapidly that we hardly dared believe our eyes. Some of my companions wanted to run after him, but I stopped them, wanting to tell you about the discovery first and letting you decide what we ought to do next."

That story plunged Rugel and his three friends into amazement. Reflections full of anxiety and hope presented themselves to their minds in confusion.

The debris of a human race still survived! They had been able to discover the descendants of ancient ages, conserved on the surfaces of the world, where everything seemed to have perished! What could these vestiges of lunar humanity be, reduced to living in such wretched conditions? Had they retained anything of the intellectual culture of the civilization of old? Had they, on the contrary, reverted to primitive barbarity, fully occupied in defending themselves against the nature that was oppressing them?

The explorers were agitated by a poignant emotion; an entirely new interest had just appeared to them.

While they had believed the place to which their spirit of adventure had led them to be deserted, they had been unable to defend themselves against the impression of sadness it communicated. Now, everything was animated. Beings like them were living here. It was necessary to see them, to hear the story of the mysterious past through which their existence had been prolonged from their own mouths—and perhaps to rescue them from the death that threatened them.

"It's necessary to find that man at all costs," exclaimed Marcel. "Doubtless he's not alone, and if there are some of our fellows here, our duty is to save them."

"Yes," said Rugel, "and if this voyage, which we've undertaken in order to satisfy scientific curiosity, is to conclude with an act of humanity, if we can save some of our siblings from misery and death, we will have the finest of rewards for our efforts and fatigues." He turned to Jacques and Lord Rodilan. "Don't you agree?"

315

Jacques' only response was to shake Rugel's hand,

"As for me," said Lord Rodilan, "it hasn't often been given to me in life to do much good, but since the opportunity is presenting itself to accomplish something virtuous, I'll seize it gladly. It will make a change."

"You're ever ready to slander yourself," said Marcel, "but you're worth as much as the best of us, you know. Let's go, without further delay."

They selected the most alert and most vigorous of the Diemides, because they did not know how long the search would take and over how large an area it would have to be extended. The rest of the troop was to set up camp on the bank of the stream and guard the baggage.

Under the guidance of the Diemide whose story had excited them so much, Rugel and his three companions set forth.

They soon arrived at the place where the inhabitant of the rugged country had appeared. The voyagers went through the ruins that had once been human habitations but were no longer anything but scattered vestiges. In any other circumstances they would have paused to search for relics of times past, but they were animated by a more powerful interest. They were in haste to know what these human creatures were who were surviving, against all expectation, the death-throes of a world.

Impatient as they were, however, they thought it necessary to advance with the utmost precaution. They did not know what sort of beings they were going to find; it was as well to guard against surprises, and they were also afraid of frightening the unknown creatures. It was necessary to try to approach them without alarming them, and without having anything to fear from them.

They had passed through the destroyed village and were advancing along the floor of a narrow valley, at the end of which the plain seemed to broaden out, when they suddenly saw a man emerge from a small clump of trees to their right, weighed down by a heavy load of wood.

They all stopped.

"That's him," said the Diemide.

The stranger had seen them. Dropping his burden, he stood there motionless, as if frozen by amazement.

Rugel made a sign to his companions to stay where they were, and he advanced on his own, slowly, toward the unknown man.

The latter had not moved. His eyes, wide with alarm, were staring; his face expressed a superstitious dread. He was doubtless wondering whether these beings, who had appeared so suddenly, were celestial creatures come to hasten the last hour of the slow destruction. His limbs were agitated by a convulsive tremor.

Rugel advanced until he was close enough to touch him.

He appeared to be between thirty and thirty-five years of age. His face, pale and emaciated, bore the traces of long suffering; his intelligent eyes were veiled by a habitual sadness; his taut lips seemed never to have broadened in a smile. Beneath his garments, made of a coarse fabric, his limbs could be divined, thin but nevertheless robust.

"My brother," Rugel said to him, "the Sovereign Spirit has permitted us to reach you, in order to save you from the fate that is threatening you. Rejoice: your troubles are at an end."

The unknown man did not appear to understand. Overwhelmed by emotion, he was distraught, and murmuring something like a vague prayer.

In the words that he pronounced Rugel recognized, to his great surprise, an ancient language that the inhabitants of the Moon had spoken when they lived on the surface of the planet, which had fallen into disuse a long time ago, and was now only studied by scientists as a dead language.

Rugel was familiar with that ancient language. He made use of it to reassure the man who was so frightened by the sight of him.

"Have no fear," he said. "We are not beings descended from the sky to harm you. Like you, we are human beings. We have come, through a thousand perils, from the distant regions where the remnants of the human race who once lived on this world, now condemned to death, still survive in security and the abundance of all good things. We are your friends, your brothers; speak to us without fear. Are you the only representative of the forgotten race in this lost valley? Do you have companions—a family? It is salvation that we bring you."

While he was speaking the face of the unknown man had cleared, and it was now illuminated by a profound joy. He had immediately been reassured to hear the newcomer speaking in a language he understood, and his heart was opening to hope.

"Stranger," he said, "I don't yet know how or why you and your companions have come into the place whose approaches are all defended by death, but the sound of your voice and the expression of your features inspires confidence. You have before you a member of the last family that still populates these solitudes. My father, my brother and a younger sister are, with me, all that remains of a once-numerous and prosperous humankind. Bound for an imminent death, we were awaiting with resignation the moment to join those we have loved and who preceded us to the grave. Your arrival gives birth in my heart to hopes to which I dare not abandon myself."

All that was said in a soft and melancholy voice, and Rugel was astonished to find in that disinherited being such a nobility of sentiment and so firm an acceptance of the fate to which he was condemned.

"Count on us," he said. "We shall do everything possible to save you."

At a sign from him, Marcel, Jacques and Lord Rodilan came closer.

"These are my companions," said Rugel. "Like me, they are committed to removing you and your relatives from your sad condition. Take us to those who are dear to you."

The unknown man gazed at him with eyes veiled by tears. "Oh," he murmured, "will it be permissible for me to believe in better days for those I love? May mercy be granted to you, who have made that gleam of hope shine in our darkness."

None of the others knew the language that the unknown man was speaking, but Rugel served as his interpreter, and in response to the testaments of sympathy that they lavished upon him, his face brightened with a joy that he had not known for a long time.

"Before introducing you to our dwelling," he said, "Let me warn my family. My father is crippled by age, my sister frail and delicate, like a plant that flowers sadly in this desolate earth. Too sharp an emotion, too sudden a joy, might be fatal to them. Follow me, but pause a short distance from where we live. I'll go in alone, and tell you when I've prepared for your reception."

In the meantime, on Rugel's orders, the Diemides stopped to, wait for them, and they set forth, emerging into an extensive plain. The unknown pointed at a small hill on the horizon. "It's behind that hill," he said, "that the dwelling stands which shelters what remains of our sad race."

While they were walking toward it he told them how, for many generations, life had been diminishing in this prison of sorts, from which it had been condemned never to emerge.

"Once," he said, "our ancestors lived here peacefully, isolated from the rest of the world. Having no needs, they led a tranquil existence, unaware of what was happening around them. Gradually, however, as a result of long and gradual changes, the conditions of life became harsher. The air seemed to lose some of its vital properties, the water in the valleys diminished, the temperature dropped, and during the long nights, the cold became absolutely intolerable. Those whose constitution was less robust died first; villages were depopulated; the number of families decreased, and it as soon impossible to avoid the realization that we were condemned to imminent extinction.

"Not knowing what the cause was of the disasters and ruination, our father thought about leaving the place where they had lived and emigrating to more hospitable regions, but it

319

was impossible to escape. When anyone climbed the mountains surrounding us, the air became inadequate after a few hours to sustain exhausted lungs. To go any higher would have been certain and rapid death. It was necessary to come back down and resign ourselves to a slow and inevitable extinction.

"When my father was young, there were still two or three families struggling painfully against destruction, but my father saw them disappear successively, and we're the sole survivors. I saw my mother die, a victim of the pitiless climate, in despair at the thought that those she loved would die as miserably as her."

As he spoke, Rugel translated what the stranger was saying for his companions. They were all saddened by the story of that long suffering; their hearts overflowed with tenderness, and they congratulated themselves for having arrived in time to snatch away the deplorable victims on whom death seemed to have set a fatal seal.

They had crossed the plain and reached the foot of the hill. The unknown man asked those accompanying him to wait for a few moments.

Jacques had difficulty containing the emotion that was causing him a poignant distress. Even Lord Rodilan was gripped by it. "Oh, the poor devils!" he said. "But how, friend Rugel, were your ancestors able to forget these people when they took refuge in the caverns that you inhabit today? That was surely culpable negligence."

"Friend," said Rugel, "lunar humankind did not quit the surface of our globe all at once and at the same time. Our subterranean emigration was accomplished slowly, little by little. Many generations went by before it was complete, and doubtless those who were most obstinate in remaining in the light of day, and only gave in regretfully to an imperious necessity, were unaware of the existence of those they left behind. Nothing in the traditions that have been handed down to us makes any mention of these forgotten families. Be certain that had it been otherwise, we would already have made every attempt to save them."

The unknown came back hastily. "Come," he said to them. "My family is waiting for you, as liberators."

As they went round the hill a heavy and massive construction came into view, whose good state of conservation contrasted with the ruined buildings that surrounded it. It was enclosed by thick walls designed to protect the inhabitants against the rigors of cold. The door was small, the windows narrow; it was like a lair in which discouraged beings who had nothing good to expect from life were sheltering from the threats of a hostile nature.

By the flickering light of a fire that was completing the consumption of a few logs, they perceived an old man with a bald head and a long white beard lying on a crude bed, who appeared scarcely able to move his wasted limbs. Standing beside him and holding his hands were a young man with energetic features, who seemed to be about twenty-five years old, and a young woman with blonde hair and symmetrical features, whose unhealthily pale face took on a faint blush as the newcomers approached. She seemed scarcely out of adolescence. Both of them fixed Rugel and his friends with avid gazes; hope, a long time lost, had reentered their hearts.

"Bless you, whoever you are," said the old man, in a tremulous voice, raising himself up with an effort, "who are bringing a ray of light into our darkness. I shall die happy if I can have the consolation of thinking, as I expire, that the children I love will escape the fate that menaces them."

The two young people extended supplicant hands toward Rugel.

"You shall not die, Father," said Rugel. "We will take you away from this accursed place, and you will live for long years, to witness the happiness of your children."

"My days are numbered," said the old man. "Even if I could, I would not want to quit this land in which my ancestors are buried; I want to sleep my final slumber beside the companion of my life. Let the young folk depart with you, if you have the means to take them away. Their life is in flower, the future belongs to them."

On hearing these words the faces of the two young men had darkened, and the young woman's eyes had filled with tears.

The condition of the old man, weakened by long suffering, scarcely permitted Rugel to think of taking him away. He was in no condition to support the fatigues of such a journey; to impose them on him would have been a needless cruelty. Furthermore, life was gradually abandoning him; no one could be under any illusion as to his condition; he would soon reach the end of his sad existence.

A few days went by.

The most intelligent and active of the Diemides were given the task of exploring the whole region and compiling an exact account of it. Rugel and his three friends did not want to leave the unfortunates that they had discovered so miraculously, and took up residence in the dwelling where they would have ended their lives if deliverance had not come.

In their long conversations by the bedside of the moribund old man, they told their new friends how lunar humankind, expelled from the surface of the globe, had found a refuge in the immense caverns of the interior. They gave an account of the new, somewhat artificial world in which they lived, describing their arts, their sciences, and painting a cheerful picture of the happy and tranquil existence that awaited them, assuring them of a future exempt from worries, offering them the hope of friends and families.

The old man, who felt life slipping away slowly, smiled at the enchanting images, and his heart was filled with joy in thinking that his children would be able to enjoy long days of happiness and live again in their descendants.

XIV. The End of the Voyage

In spite of the vigor of their constitution, however, the newcomers were beginning to feel the deleterious influences of the impoverished environment in which they had been living for some time. Their respiration became less facile, their strength diminished. They had to quit the ill-fated place soon.

Only Lord Rodilan seemed unaffected by the commencement of illness whose effects his companions were feeling. An unexpected change had taken place in him. He was been keenly touched by the charm emanated by the frail child that hazard had put in his presence. Her face, with its symmetrical and pure features, her large blue eyes, whose expression, ordinarily sad and melancholy, sometimes gave way to a sudden radiance, like a soul protesting against a cruel and unjust fate, her long ash-blonde hair and her supple and harmonious body, etiolated by the inexorable climate, all had an impression on him which surprised him. He felt moved by an entirely novel pity for the young person who had already endured so much.

All that he had of repressed affection suddenly came to light; a loving faculty of which he had been unaware had awakened in his heart, and he had been attracted to the child by an entirely paternal tenderness. He surrounded her with the most attentive and devoted care, seemingly striving to anticipate her desires, and, by means of the few words of her language that he had learned, trying to make her glimpse a better future.

That sympathy had not escaped the young woman's notice; with the sure instinct of weak individuals who can recognize reliably when they are loved, she sought out the society of her new friend. It was him to whom she had recourse in all circumstances, on whose arm she leaned most willingly in the excursions that they made in order to obtain, before leaving, a more complete idea of that strange region.

The change that had overtaken their companion had not escaped Jacques and Marcel either, and they smiled to see the man they had known so cold and so entire in his willful insensitivity humanize himself thus for that feeble creature.

Only the desperate state of the old man delayed the departure of Rugel and his associates. They soon understood that the final hour was about to sound, and that he only had a few more moments to live. He knew that his end was nigh, and awaited the redoubtable visitor without weakness.

"You have given me a joy to which I would never have dared aspire," he said, addressed Rugel and his three friends. "Your courage and audacity have guided you through a thousand perils to this sad place to accomplish a work of salvation. I'm departing in tranquility; I know that, thanks to you, these children will be saved. I entrust them to you and I die blessing you. May the Sovereign Spirit watch over them and over you."

Everyone was emotional; the young woman and her brother sobbed.

The old man's death left an impression of sadness in all their hearts. All the Diemides who had remained behind were recalled, and it was in the midst of a cortège such as the ruins and solitudes had been long unaccustomed to seeing that he was taken to his final resting-place.

He was buried in the modest field of rest in which he had dug the tombs of his forebears. A crudely carved stone monument marked the place where the woman with whom he had shared the anguishes of his life was asleep. They laid him to rest alongside those venerated remains, and the stone of the sepulcher—the last that the abandoned ground would receive—sealed it forever.

The despair of the two young men and their sister was great, and although they understood that they could not delay their departure much longer without peril, it seemed to them that they could not tear themselves away from the place where they had suffered so much, and where the man they have loved so tenderly now rested.

It was, however, necessary to go.

It was already more than four months since the voyagers had quit the observatory. Marcel, Jacques and Lord Rodilan had not lost sight of their return to Earth and did not want to put it off.

For some time, in anticipation of the length of the journey they had to undertake, the last survivors of the destroyed world had been initiated into the usage of the apparatus of which they would have to take advantage. Rugel had taken the precaution of including spare suits among the baggage, in case of possible accidents.

It was customary among the inhabitants of the Moon, whenever they undertook any excursion to the airless surface to take with them with all the equipment necessary to guard against the unexpected, and their routine procedure was quite simple. As soon as any damage was manifest in any of the suits, the person wearing it was immediately enclosed in a kind of small tent, hermetically sealed and impermeable, which, inflated by the air furnished by the reservoirs carried by the Diemides, offered sufficient space for the threatened apparatus to be taken off and another put on.

The moment of departure arrived. In order to climb the side of the immense depression, they chose the place where the slope was most gradual. Rugel was concerned to conserve the strength of the frail child he was taking with them, and whom Lord Rodilan had loudly declared that he was taking under his protection.

Before reaching the layer of clouds—which is to say, when the air began to become unbreathable—they put on the traveling apparatus, and in spite of her grief, the young woman could not help smiling when she saw herself thus clad.

They emerged on the crest of the cliff, some distance to the north of the place where they had contrived the descent, and headed westwards. First they had to cross the vast desolate plain forming the superior plateau, the traversal of which had been so painful for the voyagers. Now they were returning to the habitable regions, however, they were happy at the thought of reentering the living world they had quit; they had succeeded in the boldest of enterprises, and saved from frightful death unfortunate individuals condemned to perish. In consequence, their stride was firm and triumphant.

All the past sufferings were forgotten; the certainty of the goal to be attained had reaffirmed all hearts.

The surprise that the strange journey caused their new friends was an occasion for interesting studies on the part of Rugel and his companions. Everything was so new and unexpected for them in that extinct world of whose existence they had had no suspicion. That singular fashion of traveling, in suits that permitted them to move and breathe easily in an environment in which all life appeared impossible, was a continuous source of wonder for them. Their naïve astonishment gave rise to endless questions, to which the three inhabitants of Earth, proud of their new knowledge, did their best to reply.

It was necessary, most of all, to see Lord Rodilan in the new role that he had taken on with regard to the young woman whose paternal guardian he had become. He watched over her with a jealous care, not leaving anyone else the right to approach her, supporting her when she weakened, even carrying her in his strong arms when her gait betrayed some fatigue, responding with unalterable patience to all her questions. An attentive mother could not have shown more tenderness and devotion.

When the desert was traversed, Rugel decided to avoid the basaltic region where they had had so much difficulty. He therefore directed the caravan northwards, so as to go around the redoubtable massif. The route would doubtless be longer, but they would make up the lost time because there would be fewer obstacles to overcome and move more rapidly.

The country into which they set forth only offered the usual accidents that were encountered in the less tormented regions of the lunar surface, and for men who had surmounted so many frightful difficulties, that as mere child's play.

It was during the night that they doubled the cape formed in the middle of the plain by the basalt massif. The three young people that the voyagers had brought with them had not yet recovered from the astonishment into which the march through the darkness had cast them.

The electric lamps whose brilliant light, cutting through the darkness, projected their blue-tinted light into the distance and lent fantastic appearances to all objects delighted them with surprise and admiration.

The route they followed was free of incident all the way to the visible surface of the Moon. They were all in haste to reach the meridian that marked its limit, in order to see the terrestrial world again, which illuminated the long lunar nights with such a bright and yet gentle light, and of which they had been deprived for such a long time.

They had been marching for some time over extremely hard rocky ground, which had no jutting asperities, when the Sun, suddenly rising behind them abruptly illuminated the most dazzling scene.

As far as the eye could see, before them and around them, extended a plateau of the most marvelous coloration, in which all the colors of the prism were juxtaposed and combined.

The green, yellow and blue marbles, the gray and pink granites, the blinding white limestones, the red and orange sandstones, the black diorites, trachytes and crystalline schists, skimming the surface, mingled their pastels shades, forming a kind of incredibly rich carpet.

To their left, a narrow fissure opened, of unfathomable depth, whose walls plunged perpendicularly into the somber abyss. It extended indefinitely in a north-westerly direction. The sunlight, striking it obliquely, illuminated those formidable walls and made them resplendent with the most varied and unexpected tints. One might have thought that masses of precious stones had escaped in disorder from some giant jewel-case, spread over the ground and caught on all the asperities of the enormous walls.

"I've seen something analogous to what you have before your eyes in America," said Marcel. "It was in Arizona. In the depths of narrow gorges known as canyons, whose meanders

327

the Colorado River follows with its foaming waves, the country it traverses also presents the most singular colorations, but nothing equals the grandiose splendor and infinite richness of the magical region through which we're traveling."

"Yes," said Lord Rodilan, "this lunar world is truly very curious, and I don't really know what will be able to surprise us or interest us when we return to Earth."

"But my dear friend," said Jacques, smiling, "nothing obliges you to leave it. You're free to stay here, and although we'd be sad to leave without you, we'd resign ourselves to it if you were to find happiness in this new fatherland." With a vague gesture he designated the young woman whose guardian the Englishman had appointed himself, and added: "And perhaps there are other reasons that might retain you here."

"Oh, my word no!" exclaimed Lord Rodilan. "When one has the honor of being English, one doesn't exchange one's fatherland for another." In response to Jacques final allusion, he added: "That child interests me. She has stirred in my heart an old residue of tenderness that I had thought extinct. But when I've put her in a safe place and she no longer has any need of me. I'll refrain from imposing any gratitude on her that might become onerous."

"You speak sagely, and as a worthy man," said Rugel, who had witnessed the conversation.

The march continued through that host of marvels. For a long time they admired the varied play of the light, the changes of hue that were modified at every step, in accordance with whether the sun's rays struck the variously colored surfaces directly or obliquely. But there is something in spectacles that impress the sight vividly that is akin to sentiments that agitate the heart. One cannot support excessively vivid sensations for long, and one develops a nostalgia for the simple and the ordinary. The voyagers ended up wearying of the sparkling colors and the eternal kaleidoscope that reflected its continual changes into their eyes.

It was with a sigh of relief, weary of admiration, that they entered a region less richly endowed by nature, whose duller and milder appearance was a veritable rest for them. They rediscovered with pleasure the gray rocks and the craters that had been long familiar to them, and they continued their westward course gladly.

The abrupt invasion of the lunar night surprised them just as they reached the visible surface of the satellite. They reached it in the vicinity of the sixth degree of south latitude.

It was necessary to switch on the electric lamps again and recommence walking in the dark.

They still had many difficulties to overcome before reaching the observatory and a great deal of fatigue to endure, but the important discoveries they had made, and the joy of triumph—for such a voyage seemed a conquest of the impossible—sustained their courage. Then again, they saw the moment approaching when, their task accomplished, they would be able to return to Earth, to see those they loved, deliver to the world the magnificent results of their endeavors, and reap the recompense of their efforts.

They found themselves at the foot of the D'Alembert mountain chain.[32] They skirted it, inclining northwards until they reached the vicinity of the crater Riccioli. Then, going around the vast cone, they walked for a long time though the profound valley that separates it from Grimaldi. To their right and left, colossal walls rose up, their bases illuminated by the powerful reflectors that the Diemides were carrying, where their eyes vaguely distinguished confused masses of enormous rocks, heaped up as if by the hands of Titans.

When they had come through that gorge, they came out into a broad plain, but it was not possible to follow the northern rim of the crater Grimaldi, because wide and profound fissures beginning from the foot of the con blocked their path. They were forced to turn northwards in the direction of the crater Lohrmann.

---

[32] The name of the D'Alembert Mountains has been dropped from modern lunar maps, where they are nowadays simple regarded as part of the Cordillera chain.

That part of their journey was perhaps the most laborious. In fact, the entire region between the two craters was one of the most chaotic; there was nothing but craters, small in dimension but very close together, between which it was necessary to slide, with difficulty, or sheer and deep crevasses, whose edges it was necessary to follow until some swelling of the ground, forming a kind of bridge, allowed them to be crossed.

The voyagers admired the profound knowledge of the country that Rugel possessed. In spite of the difficulties of the nocturnal march, no uncertainty was ever manifest in their guide's mind. They progressed slowly and awkwardly, but reliably.

When the obstacles had been overcome, they found themselves on the edge of the Ocean of Storms. From then on, the journey was mere child's play; a gradual slope led them into the immense plain formed by the bed of the dry sea. The traversal of the broken region had taken a long time, though, and daylight surprised the when they were about a hundred kilometers from the observatory.

The voyagers greeted the return of daylight gladly, and twenty-four hours later they were reunited with Merovar and the other scientists, who had perceived them some time before and who greeted them with joyful enthusiasm.

The sight of the three young people that the voyagers had brought back with them, after having saved them so miraculously, caused profound surprise throughout the laboratory.

"We saw you from a distance," Merovar said, "And could not understand how your number had increased."

Rugel gave a brief and rapid account of the events that had marked the course of their exploration. He recounted the unfortunate death of their two companions, explained how they had found the vestiges of a living world of which the old legends spoke, and saved the sad debris of a vanished human race from a horrible death.

Everyone flocked around the three young people, who, now rid of the apparatus they wore, were very surprised to breathe easily and move freely, and delighted by the warm welcome of which they were the object.

People looked at them with interest and interrogated them benevolently; emotionally, not knowing how to reply, they looked around anxiously. Everything in that environment, for which nothing had been able to prepare them, was new to them; they went back and forth as if in a dream.

Soon, however, their entry into the lunar world was to provide them with many other surprises.

XV. Humanitarian Dreams

The works undertaken to ensure the return of the three inhabitants of the Earth to their homeland had lasted eight months. Begun in June, they were finished at the end of January. In the meantime, a silent but sustained activity and reigned around the crater chosen by Rugel. Although everyone, Diemides and Meolicenes alike, was sad to see the moment approaching when they would be separated from the guests they had learned to love, everyone did his best to bring the work to a successful conclusion.

The walls of the crater had been smoothed to a depth of 150 meters. That length might have seemed excessive, given that the neutral point of attraction between the two planets was only eight thousand leagues distant from the Moon, but the scientists responsible for the work, in agreement with Marcel, had thought it best to exaggerate it, in order that the projectile could cross the zone of lunar attraction and steer reliably toward the objective to be attained without there being any danger of a deviation that might modify the initial direction.

A cylindrical mold; leaving an empty space between its surface and the rocky wall of 1.35 meters, had been raised from the bottom of the crater to its orifice. Into that interval the metal alloy had been poured that would form the gigantic cannon. Then, after the metal, completely cooled, had become an absolutely homogeneous mass, the interior mold had been broken up and removed, the barrel of the gun had been carefully bored; everything was ready to function.

Before quitting the world that they would never see again, Marcel and his companions wanted to spend the few days before the departure at Rugel's villa, where their reason had almost succumbed, and where the care of devoted friends had restored them to themselves. However impatient they were to see Earth again, they could not help feeling, as they were about to leave, a sentiment of melancholy and regret.

The conditions in which they had been living for more than two years were so different from everything they had known and seen until then that their souls had, in a manner of speaking, been transformed, as if purified, in a nobler and more perfect environment.

Since they had been in the lunar world, their gazes had become unaccustomed to all the ugliness and misery that terrestrial humankind presents. There, everything was worthy and elevated, everything tended to the pursuit of the beautiful and the good; everyone's efforts collaborated in the communal endeavor; without competition and strife, without jealousy and hatred, without cupidity and envy, an almost ideal society seemed to realize the type of perfection.

Thus had been removed from their eyes a corner of the veil that hides the divine work of creation. Already, the most elevated minds have glimpsed that superior law of the hierarchy of worlds, which, departing from the most infimal conditions of life, rises by insensible gradations along the path of a limitless advancement. They had had before their eyes one of the steps of that infinite progression, and they wondered to what degree of intellectual and moral superiority the inhabitants of even more favored spheres might rise.

They told themselves that, in returning to Earth, it would be as if they were awakening from a marvelous and magical dream. Everything of which they had had no knowledge for two years would assail them again; they would fall back into the midst of the struggle for existence; they would find themselves mingled with a crowd enslaved to gross needs and harsh appetites. It would be the end of the calm and tranquil life, the serenity of the spirit, the peace of the heart. They would have to reenter the battle, collide with the interests that never disarm, the ambitions that no scruple stops, which do not even recoil before crime in order to satisfy themselves. They would have before their eyes the depressing spectacle of triumphant force, honored injustice, sin crowned in the fact of persecuted virtue, verity shamed and unmerited misery.

If they had only listened to the voice of their reason, they would gladly have remained members of that society whose concord and harmony charmed them, but the memory of the people they had left behind and the love that nature puts into the heart of every man for his native soil, no matter how disinherited he might be, attracted him invincibly. In addition, their magnified souls had conceived noble projects, and even Lord Rodilan, to his great surprise felt gripped by a generous ardor that he had not known before. Already, many times, the three friends had promised themselves, when they returned to the old terrestrial world, to put all their efforts at the service of their wretched brethren, to soothe as much as was possible the evils from which they were suffering.

Those were the subjects they usually discussed with their hosts in the days preceding the separation.

In spite of his desire not to give the inhabitants of the Moon too poor an idea of terrestrial humankind, Marcel had been led to inform those that such questions interested the most about the sad conditions and shocking inequalities of the present existence of humans on Earth.

He had not been able to hide the fact that, even in the most advanced nations and beneath the external appearances of the most brilliant civilizations, profound abysms of vice and misery were concealed. He had told them about the unfortunates who struggled painfully to live in an environment of egotism and indifference, of the abandoned whom no one sustained or encouraged, and whose despair often led them to crime or suicide. He had shown them old people without a hearth, young women without protection, children without families or shelter, wandering in the vast cities, displaying their rags to the gaze of inattentive crowds, soliciting in vain a pity that might save them from dying of cold and hunger.

Thos who had received these sad confidences had been profoundly surprised, and they had been moved by the thought of these evils, and a moral degradation that they found difficult to imagine.

Orealis, in particular, had not been able to hear, without being moved in the utmost depths of her being, the description of such suffering. Her heart had filled with indignation against the injustice, and pity for the unfortunate. One day, when the three voyagers were talking to Rugel about their imminent departure, and plans they were thinking about putting into execution, Orealis appeared before them. Her expression, ordinarily so lively and frank, was veiled by sadness and her voice betrayed a slight embarrassment.

"Friends," she said to them, "Everything that you have told me about the world to which you're returning has interested me, and when you have left us, my thoughts will follow you to the places that I have learned from you to know. But my heart is particularly moved by the picture you have presented of the fate of the many unfortunates that terrestrial humanity still includes.

"I know what your plans are; I know that you want to devote yourselves to the relief of so many miseries, and I want to associate myself with your efforts. You will not refuse me, I hope, the joy of aiding you in that task; it will be a link that with connect us across space, which will subsist between us when you have gone. It will seem to me that we are not entirely separated when I think that I am making some contribution to the good that you are doing.

"You have told me that on Earth, someone who possesses certain rare and precious objects can secure more satisfactions and also do more good around him. I know that among the objects that are held in very high value are certain shiny stones that have no other utility for us than to decorate our monuments and increase their sparkle. I have gathered some together, and would like you to take them with you as a souvenir of those who have learned to esteem and love you, and who will never forget you."

At a sign from her, two Diemides appeared, carrying a coffer in precious metal, curiously shaped and sculpted, on which living figurines, interlaced foliage and delicate arabesques were depicted. The imagination of the dexterous artists of the lunar world had made a masterpiece of grace, richness and elegance.

Orealis opened it; there was a dazzling glitter. It was full to the brim with diamonds of marvelous clarity and unusual dimensions; there were also enormous sapphires, rubies, emeralds, opals and topazes, all of them beautiful. At first glance such a treasure evidently represented an enormous, inestimable fortune.

In spite of the detachment from terrestrial things to which they had grown accustomed in two years, Marcel, Jacques and Lord Rodilan felt a frisson, and the old instinct of possession that atavism had put into them reawakened. Their eyes shone with a more vivid gleam, and without their being aware of it, their hands moved toward that treasure, worthy of the *Thousand-and-One Nights*.

Rugel looked at them, smiling. They soon got a grip on themselves.

"You are the noblest and most generous of souls," Jacques set to Orealis. "We accept what you're offering us; we'll employ the riches that you're lavishing upon us to render confidence and hope to those disinherited by fate. We shall only be their distributors, and the unfortunates whose woes they relieve will learn from us to bless your name."

"Such an offering," said Rugel, "doesn't merit such thanks. These stones that you call treasures are almost valueless to us, and we would never have thought of utilizing them in this way if you hadn't told us about the purpose they might serve on Earth. If they can aid you in the accomplishment of your plans, if they can ameliorate a certain amount of suffering, we're glad to offer them to you, and regret that you can't take more of them with you."

While Rugel was saying that, Marcel had drawn nearer to Orealis. "My heart did not deceive me," he told her, "when it drew me toward you. I had understood that your heart enclosed great virtues, and I shall retain far from you the regret of not having been able to vanquish your indifference."

She made a gesture of protest. "You have never been indifferent to me, friend; you know that; but you dreamed the impossible, and I would have been culpable not to open your eyes. Far from me you'll forget, and I hope that a companion worthy of you will soon give you the happiness you deserve."

"Never," Marcel replied. "If I have been obliged to renounce the hope of uniting my life with yours, I have not renounced the sentiment that you have inspired in me. The love that is in my heart will never leave it; I shall retain it there with jealous care; it will be my strength and consolation in the ordeals that await me."

"Time will do its work, friend, believe me," Orealis replied. "It scars all wounds."

Marcel bowed without making any reply, but the expression on his face seemed to belie the hopes that the young woman's words had just expressed.

Azali, who had conceived a sincere affection for those who owed their lives to him, and in whom Marcel's character inspired more than esteem, had wanted to be near them during the final days that they were to spend in the lunar world. By virtue of a sentiment of reserve and delicacy, he had postponed his marriage to Rugel's daughter. The love that Marcel had felt for her had not put any cloud between them. Azali's mind was too elevated to be accessible to paltry mistrust or troubling jealousy; never had the slightest doubt crossed his mind with regard to the woman he loved. He knew very well, in any case, that if her heart had been touched by Marcel's affection, she would neither have wanted nor been able to conceal the change in her inclination—but nothing had ever troubled the serenity of her face or veiled the limpid charity of her gaze.

In any case, a profound transformation had been wrought in Marcel's sentiments: the noble virtue of Orealis, and the eventual conviction that his desires could not be realized, hand ended up triumphing over his initial ardor. Certainly, he still loved the young woman with all the force of his being, and he was sincere when he affirmed that no other woman would ever

337

take her place in his heart, but that sentiment was purified; disengaged from any vulgar aspiration, it was no more than an ideal worship to which he wanted to remain piously faithful, an exquisite flower whose perfume was to embalm his entire life.

A sympathy had developed between the two men, and the love they experienced only made it stronger. Azali took an interest in the projects that Marcel had often mentioned to his hosts. He questioned him frequently; he wanted to know about the state of mind of the disinherited masses curbed by the wind of misery, and what might be attempted on Earth to remedy such frightful iniquities. Marcel told him about everything that generous souls, animated by a profound love of humanity accomplished in favor of their unfortunate brethren, inspired by the divine word that had once resounded over the world: "Love one another."

Azali listened, and could not help feeling admiration when Marcel told him about the devoted men who, braving mortal contagions, risked cruel death in order to steal from nature some secret from which their fellows would profit, and the saintly women who sacrificed their youth and beauty, renouncing the pure joys of the family in order to devote themselves entirely to the service of the wretched, who lived in poisonous atmospheres, always in the presence of the most horrible wounds and the most frightful agonies, and often died as victims of their abnegation.

"That is great, and beautiful," he murmured. "You have the right to be proud of such courage and such magnificent virtue. And I bow down respectfully before the Sovereign Wisdom that has permitted such precious flowers to blossom, in a humanity less well endowed than ours. In truth, one cannot regret injustice and misery too much, if they are the condition of such sublime actions.

"Yes," said Marcel, "good and evil share our poor world, but there are somber hours in the existence of the people who live on Earth, when evil seems to have the upper hand. I won't hide it from you, friend, that the most advanced nations of our

338

humankind seem, at this moment, to be going through one of those fatal crises.

"A wind of hatred and anger that is blowing revolt into the hearts of the poor has risen among us. Men of bad faith, exploiting an ignorant and unfortunate crowd to the profit of their ambitions and their avarice are exciting the most detestable passions. They willingly close their eyes to all the good that people attempt to do; devotion appears suspect to them and charity an offense; they envelop in the same disapproval those who exploit the poor, enriching themselves on the fruit of their labor and those who make the most noble use of their fortune. They cause to shine in the eyes of those they deceive the mirage of some unrealizable city in which the leveling of a brutal equality will pass over all heads, in which, in a society from which all initiative and all love are excluded, silence and immobility will reign with the most implacable egotism. And to conquer that monstrous ideal, they dream of the destruction of the established order; they do not hesitate to arm fanatical hands, and it's through ruins, blood and tears that they claim to be founding the happiness of humankind.

"It is to be feared that, perhaps in the near future, the passions thus overexcited will be unleashed and that formidable struggles might hold back—God only knows for how long—all progress."

With a hint of melancholy, Marcel added: "I hope that with the treasures that the noble Orealis has just placed at our disposal, it will be possible for us to do some good. If we can neither prevent nor delay the fratricidal struggles that the wisest minds anticipate, we shall try, by diminishing the causes of misery for young generations and devoting ourselves to educating and moralizing them, to enlighten the ranks of that criminal army whose sacrilegious preaching launches them to assault society."

"The objective you propose, friend," Azali replied, "is worthy of you and your courage. If, as everything now permits the belief, regular communications continue between our world and yours, you can keep us informed of your attempts

339

and your success. We shall follow them with all the interest inspired by the affection we have for you, and will be happy to have been able to help you in some small degree."

Thus they conversed while awaiting the moment determined for the separation.

XVI. The Farewells

Everything was ready for the departure, which had been fixed for 25 February.

The shell in which the three voyagers had made their entrance into the lunar world had been placed in one of the rooms of the governmental palace and had been piously conserved as a monument of the most audacious enterprise that the genius of mortal creatures had ever attempted.

They had been obliged to construct another, equal in dimensions to the one that had made the first journey. They had chosen for its construction a violet metal as light as aluminum but even stronger—of which, it will be remembered, the metal plate had been made on which Marcel had read the invitation that had determined his departure from Earth. Only a few modifications had been made to it.

As seven-tenths of the surface of the Earth is covered by water there was a seventy per cent chance that the projectile would not fall on a continent. To those already considerable odds, the astronomers of the Moon had added the precision of their calculations.

Taking account of the givens of the problem—initial velocity, terrestrial and lunar gravity, the axial and orbital rotation of the Earth, and the orbital movement of the Moon—the shell ought to fall in a part of the Pacific Ocean in which its waters attained a depth between four and six thousand meters—more than sufficient to deaden the impact. The target area was on the equator, 130 degrees of longitude east of the Paris meridian—which is to say, in a region about fifty degrees distant from the American continent. The nearest land to that point is more than six hundred leagues away, which left a margin of error of twelve or thirteen hundred leagues, sufficient for a deviation, should any occur, not to offer any danger.

As the shell was to fall into the Pacific a long way from any land, it was necessary to provide it with sufficient navigability for it to be able to sail to any given point, if it were not picked up by a ship somewhere in the region. As it could float and was completely airtight, there was nothing to fear from the most furious tempests. In bad weather, it could only be tossed by the waves; it was only on a calm sea that it could be steered.

The scientists of the Moon, who did not want to leave anything to chance if they could provide for it be calculation and foresight, provided it with an ingenious mechanism. On the underside of the shell, in the vertical wall, a kind of chamber was fitted containing a helical propeller solidly secured between two strong metal plates. When the projectile came back to the surface after plunging into the ocean depths, it would be sufficient, by loosening the bolts holding it in position, to project it outside the exterior plate and using the thrust of the propeller, then able to rotate freely in the water, to move the novel kind of boat. In order that the vessel could be steered—which its cylindrical shape would render difficult—two cavities were placed a short distance above the chamber containing the propeller, in such a fashion that a movable rudder could be inserted therein, kept inside the shell until required and then passed through the upper porthole. The propeller would be powered by electrical accumulators capable of keeping it going at a sufficient speed for several weeks.

With such an apparatus they could not expect to make very rapid progress, nor to maintain a reliable direction, but as the imminent departure of the voyagers had been announced to their friends, with an approximate indication of the region in which they ought to fall, it was permissible to believe that vessels would be sent to search for them and that they would not be left at the mercy of the waves for long.

The system of breaking partitions destined to suppress the violence of the shock produced on the shell by the deflagration of the explosive that would project it into space, as well as the three sets of rockets intended to show its fall had been adopted by the constructors of the new projectile. All that had seemed to them to be ingeniously planned and sufficient.

As for the explosive itself, the lunar scientists, who possessed a very abundant collection, had been spoiled for choice. The one they had selected developed, in a very restricted volume, a formidable expansive force, and only occupied a height of eighteen meters in the barrel of the cannon—which, given that the total length of the gun was a hundred and fifty meters, left the projectile a hundred and thirty-two meters to travel before being launched into space.

According to the calculations, and in order that the shell would encounter the Earth at the target point, or at least in the region of which it formed the center, the departure on 25 February had to be effected at eight forty-five and twenty-seven seconds, calculated with reference to the Paris meridian. A month still separated the voyagers from that date. The weeks that followed were employed by them in visiting the world in which they had been living for two years one last time.

In that relatively limited population, in which everyone was interested in everything concerning public life, the news of the imminent departure of the strangers had produced a painful impression. In the long months that they had seen them living the common life, coming and going through the regions they had explored in every direction, everyone had got to know them, had become used to them and learned to love them.

Marcel's exuberant frankness, Jacques' slightly melancholy gravity and Lord Rodilan's familiar humor, with its unexpected sallies of wit, made a contrast, in the midst of that calm and thoughtful population, that rendered the sympathy of which they were the object even keener. For some time their hosts doubted it, because they could not get used to the idea of no longer seeing them, but when it became certain that their resolution was immutable, and it was known that the means for their departure were fully prepared and complete, there was a veritable sadness. Everywhere they went, crowds gathered; people wanted to see them one last time, to shake their hands and collect their final words.

By the marks of sympathy lavished upon them and the expressions of regret legible in all faces, the voyagers were able to judge the place that they had acquired in the life of that humankind, the importance in everyone's eyes of what they had accomplished, and the gap that they would leave behind.

They manifested their intention of bidding farewell to the Head of State.

"You've anticipated his own desire," Rugel told them. "The prudent Aldeovaze does not want to let you leave out planet without bidding you adieu. He's ready to see you."

Rugel and his guests returned to the capital, therefore, and went to the palace of government. They were introduced into the great hall, where Aldeovaze was surrounded by his Council.

As they contemplated, for the last time, that venerable assembly of men, whose wisdom and virtue elevated them so far above their own humankind, the three voyagers felt their hearts fill with respectful admiration.

In the two years that they had been living on the Moon, they had often been admitted to observe its solemn deliberations, and had always been struck by the calm and dignity that reigned in its grave debates. When they recalled the sessions of the legislative assemblies of the States that gloried in being the most civilized on Earth, they blushed for their compatriots. Here, there're was nothing similar to those gatherings of undisciplined schoolboys, turbulent and loquacious, which a quasi-pedagogical president had great difficulty in controlling, during which, in stormy sessions, abuse was exchanged, insults rained down, threats burst forth, and the sacred interests of the fatherland were bargained away in the clash of personal ambitions and paltry competition.

It seemed to them that they had before their eyes a rare cenacle that might have gathered together all the great figures that history had consecrated, and whom terrestrial humankind would always honor with a quasi-divine reverence: Socrates and Plato, Solon and Marcus Aurelius, John Chrysostom and Vincent de Paul, Michel de l'Hôpital and Descartes: all the geniuses, great in heart and intellect, that our inferior world honors, who seem to be the ransom of its vices and weaknesses.

The sages who formed the Council had, in their very nature, something more ideal and closer to absolute perfection than the purest terrestrial glories.

The envoy of the king of Epirus had thought, in the presence of the Roman sensate, that he was before and assembly of kings; the three friends could have believed that they were before an assembly of gods.

"Venerated leader of the lunar world," said Marcel, after having bowed profoundly, "we wanted, before returning to Earth, to express the sentiments of respect and gratitude with which our hearts are penetrated. Thanks to you, we have been able to attain the goal that we glimpsed, never daring to hope for such a complete realization. The communications between our two worlds are now an accomplished fact; the noble thought that you expressed when we arrived among you has been put into practice; the vast horizon of fraternal exchanges and progress accomplished in common now becomes accessible to two human races. Our work is done. Our duty, in accord with our affections, recalls us to our homeland. Others will continue what we have commenced, and we shall always retain in the depths of our hearts and eternal memory of your benevolence and generosity."

Aldeovaze had risen to his feet, and in spite of the austere gravity of his attitude, a contained emotion made his voice tremble slightly.

"Friends," he said to them, "we never expected that you would remain here forever, but we hoped that you would not think of leaving us so soon. We understand the sentiments animating you, however, and far from seeking to retain you, we have done everything possible to ensure that you could depart at the moment you have chosen. It will not be without sadness that we shall see those to whom so many bonds already attach us go away, but the memory of the great things you have done will not perish. Your courage has rendered possible what has only been until now a vain utopia, and for as long as the two worlds go side by side along the eternal route that divine wisdom has traced for them, your names will be repeated and blessed from one age to the next. Perhaps our globe, which has aged faster than yours in its sidereal evolution, is destined to end sooner, but so long as human life persists here, it will have the consolation of no longer being alone in space, and will know that it owes that inappreciable benefit to you. Return to our brothers on Earth, then; tell them that we love them and want to work in accord with them for the common happiness of our two humankinds."

The moment of departure arrived.

Aldeovaze wanted to give the voyagers, at the moment when they were about to undertake the hazardous journey so audaciously for a second time, a mark of his esteem and sympathy. With the members of the Supreme Council, he had gone to the observatory where the final adieux were to be exchanged.

All those who had lived in intimacy with Marcel, Jacques and Lord Rodilan were there: Rugel and his daughter, Merovar and Azali, and the two young men and the young woman brought from so far away, who would never forget those whose courage had contributed in such large measure to their salvation. They all felt gripped by a cruel sentiment of anguish.

No matter how exact the calculations of the scientists were that had fixed the moment of departure and marked the time of arrival, no one was unaware that the slightest error might suffice for the projectile, instead of plunging into the oceanic abyss, to crash on a continent. But those fears, which they all felt without daring to formulate them, had not troubled the intrepid souls of the three friends.

As the decisive moment approached, their valor seemed to increase. Now the resolution was firm, they were departing without casting a backward glance, and their gaze was rising into space toward the terrestrial world to which they were about to return.

Everyone had gathered on the terrace of the observatory, and the Earth, full at that moment, was brilliantly illuminated. They drank in the sight with all the ardor of their souls; they were impatient to be on their way.

They prepared to set off for the departure point.

Rugel, Merovar and Azali had offered to accompany them until the last moment. Emotion was at its peak.

The three friends shook the hands extended toward them one last time, and bowed respectfully to Aldeovaze. The young woman to whom Lord Rodilan had shown himself so paternal starred at him with wide moist eyes.

"Don't cry, my child," he said to her. "You've found a mother who will love you better than I would have been able to do"—Orealis had, in fact, taken in the sad orphan and was testifying a touching affection for her—"and you'll soon be consoled. If you retain the memory of the man who was your friend, you'll be able, in a few years' time, to give my name to your first-born son. You can call him Douglas."

Then, lifting the child up in his strong arms, he hugged her energetically to his heart. Putting her down again, he turned away in order furtively to wipe away a tear. That moment of emotion was brief, and almost immediately, he advanced with Jacques to say goodbye to the beautiful Orealis. She had been gentle and maternal to them; it was under her benevolent protection that their reason, temporarily obscured, had reawakened; they retained a profound gratitude for that, and the kisses thy deposited on her cheeks had something grave and meditative about them.

To Jacques, Orealis said: "Tell the one you are going to recover that she has a sister here who will always love her." Turning to Lord Rodilan, she added: "As for you, don't retain too bad a memory of the time you spent among us. Your heart, we know, is better than you want to let it seem, and we won't forget the good and generous man you really are."

Marcel was the last to come forward. In his turn he applied his lips to the face of the woman with whom he had dreamed of uniting his destiny, and put into that first and last kiss all of his disappointed hopes, and all the great love that nothing would ever efface from his heart.

They were both too emotional to say anything; their hands squeezed one another in a long and mute grip.

The three voyagers had gone.

All those who had stayed in the observatory were standing on the glazed terrace, their eyes fixed in the direction of the location from which the departure would take place. Suddenly, the horizon lit up with a vivid flash, which momentarily veiled the light that the Earth was pouring down on the surface of the Moon. Almost immediately, a dull rumble became audible.

Orealis fell to her knees in an attitude of prayer.

The grave voice of Aldeovaze was heard: "May the Sovereign Spirit that governs the worlds protect them, and bring them safe and sound to their journey's end."

XVII. In the Pacific Ocean

"Devil take your friends, my dear Marcel!" exclaimed Lord Rodilan, quitting the porthole through which he had been examining the surface of the ocean. "For three days we've been adrift in this region—they ought to have fished us out by now."

"Damn!" said Marcel, laughing "How our voyage to the Moon has changed you, my dear lord! You, once so phlegmatic, whose cold indifference nothing affected, are now as impatient as a little mistress."

"You're utterly content, then?" riposted the Englishman.

"No, of course not, but is it nothing to have above our heads, instead of a granite vault, that beautiful azure sky, those capriciously-formed clouds with shiny edges, to fill one's lungs with these saline breezes, to feel ourselves bathed by that bright and gentle sunlight, of which we've been deprived for so long? What do you say, Jacques?"

"Oh, as for me," said the young physician, "I'm as impatient as Lord Rodilan. I can't wait to get out of our floating prison and hug those who are waiting for us. Only then will I enjoy the happiness of having returned safe and sound to Earth."

"You're very lucky to be loved and awaited," Marcel murmured, dully, his forehead clouded. He soon pulled himself together, though. "My word, my friends, success has spoiled you. Everything has succeeded thus far, and you're still not satisfied. We've accomplished, the most hazardous journey in conditions for which we could hardly have hoped; we've fallen into the exact region of the Pacific for which we aimed; our projectile penetrated to the deepest larger of the ocean and came back to the surface without encountering any obstacle; now we're floating on a placid sea under a pure sky. What more do you want?

"Our friends, warned by the last dispatch we addressed to them, knowing the exact moment of our departure and arrival, are undoubtedly looking for us. As we discovered by taking a bearing that we fell at 136° 15′ west longitude and 9° 23′ south latitude—which is to say, outside any regular shipping route—there's nothing astonishing in the fact that the ships sent to find us haven't yet sighted us. We've done the wisest thing, setting a course for the nearest land, in the Marquesas archipelago, but our craft, excellent for interplanetary travel, would cut a sad figure in Yacht Club races, as you know, and in spite of the best efforts of our propeller, it'll take us a long time to come ashore."

"Well, so be it," said Lord Rodilan, with a comical resignation. "My voyage to the Moon won't have been a waste of time; I'll have learned to be patient."

Marcel was not mistaken. Numerous ships were in the region searching for the voyagers.

On 5 January the Long's Peak Observatory had transmitted a dispatch to Biskra saying: *Will depart 25 February 8:45:37. Will fall in Pacific near equator longitude 130 degrees. M. J. R.*

An immense joy had filled the hearts of Mathieu-Rollère and his daughter. Telegrams had immediately spread the astonishing news throughout the entire world. For a long time, no doubt had remained regarding the reality of the extraordinary voyage. The regularity of the communications exchanged, with the most incredulous had been able to verify with their own eyes, the precise information coming from the satellite, some of which had been confirmed by scientific observations already made, which others had furnished rational and satisfactory solutions to obscure problems, had reckoned with ill-will and routine.

At the announcement of the return of the bold explorers, all scientific societies had become excited. A great tide of curiosity and sympathy was manifest in all the civilized nations, and under the pressure of public opinion the great maritime powers of the world had sent ships to cruise the region where the projectile would fall. Mathieu-Rollère, his daughter and Georges Dumesnil had traveled in haste to Panama, and there had taken passage on the *Galathée*, a fast cruiser from the Pacific fleet placed at their disposal by the French government.

They had reached the region indicated by the lunar telegram without delay, where two other French ships from the same fleet and a number of English, American, Russian and even Japanese vessels were already sailing. The government in Tokyo, in fact, eager to keep up with all progress, had seized the opportunity to take part in all the scientific discussions.

A good number of pleasure yachts attracted by curiosity were also traveling in the region, ordinarily deserted, where an unusual activity had been noticeable for some days.

To facilitate the surveillance of the region of the Pacific in which the projectile would fall, and prevent the ships of different nations from wandering at random, and agreement had been made between the various governments. The officer of the longest-established rank was to take charge of the search and assign each vessel its observation post. To that effect, the region had been divided up into distinct zones, each of which had been allocated to a naval unit.

It was to Captain Francis Clayton of the United States Navy, an old sea-dog, commander of the first-class cruiser *Maryland*, that the command of the flotilla had devolved, which counted some forty ships of various tonnage. His instructions dictated that the first vessel to see the floating shell and pick up the voyagers would immediately head for the *Maryland*, situated in the middle of the region. At the same time, it would fire a cannon at regular intervals by day and launch powerful rockets by night intended to be seen at long distances. Those signals would be repeated by all the ships that perceived them, and when they were produced they would imply an order for a general rally.

When all that was settled, each ship had taken up its station, circling within the limits assigned to it.

Three days had gone by since the moment when the projectile departing from the Moon must have been swallowed by the ocean depths, and nothing had appeared on the surface of the tranquil sea.

While they were searching in every direction, Marcel and his companions, lost in the ocean, were making their way slowly toward the target they had selected. Their propeller was functioning efficiently, but the rounded form of their strange vessel rendered its maneuvering extremely difficult. In order to keep the shell moving in the chosen direction, it was necessary for one of the three companions to be permanently stationed at the tiller. They were, so to speak, sculling.

On the morning of the eighth day since the fall had taken place, Marcel, at the top of the ladder leading to the forward porthole, was searching the limited horizon that the slight elevation of the shell permitted him to see with his binoculars.

"There's land!" he suddenly shouted.

His two companions leapt to their feet, and each came in turn to observe the presence of the coast so ardently desired.

At the indecisive limit where the sea seemed to be confused with the sky, a blue-tinted line appeared, slightly indented—evidently the crest of a mountain chain of mediocre height.

"Finally," sighed Lord Rodilan, "we can get out of this damned prison, where I'm beginning to go moldy, and live on land again."

"Don't speak ill of our poor shell," said Marcel, smiling. "It's performed bravely. Do you know many skiffs that could have crossed such a distance at such a speed? It's not its fault if, constructed to fly through space, we've converted it into a pleasure-boat."

"Hélène! My uncle!" Jacques murmured. "I'm going to see them again."

They imposed maximum velocity on the propeller and resumed sculling madly, and the strange vessel, limping along as fast it could, approached the mountainous mass, whose contours stood out increasingly clearly.

Marcel had checked his map, and, having taken a new bearing, said: "That must be the island of Fatu Hiva, the most southerly of the Marquesas. We'll surely find a French post there where they'll hasten to welcome us."

"As long as they can offer us a nice slice of roast beef, or a steak," muttered the Englishman, his mouth watering at the thought of the lavish dinner he had promised himself.

As the distance diminished, the view of the coast became more precise. Dense forests, whose dark green cut through the blue of the sky, covered the mountains, which now closed the horizon. They sloped down toward a small beach limited to the right and left by rugged rocks; the sea breaking at their feet bordered them with a fringe of foam.

It was toward that inlet that the travelers steered.

It was about ten o'clock in the morning when the shell ran aground. Its considerable weight, augmented by the speed of the propeller, had sufficed to embed it profoundly, half a cable from the shore. As far as the eye could see, the place seemed deserted; there was no trace of human habitation.

Lord Rodilan was about to dive into the sea in order to swim to shore when Marcel stopped him.

"Steady on, my dear friend. It's as well, before descending on this coast, which we don't know, to take a few precautions. The Marquesas group undoubtedly belongs to France, but I'm not sure that we've landed in the vicinity of a post, and we might happen upon one of the savage tribes that still occupy the islands and, far from any surveillance, might do us harm. Admit that it would be unfortunate to come so far only to perish in some wretched ambush."

"By Jove!" said Lord Rodilan. "It wouldn't displease me to fire a shot or two. It would be a change from the monotonous life we've been leading for two years."

"Monotonous!" retorted Jacques. "You're hard to please! But Marcel's right—we mustn't neglect any precaution."

Having carefully wrapped their carbines, revolvers and some ammunition in an impermeable sack, the three men jumped boldly into the water, and reached the shore in a few strokes.

When they set foot on the soil of the Earth that they had quite such a long time ago, and had feared so many times that they might never see again, they let out a sigh of relief. They had triumphed over the impossible; their astonishing odyssey as now over, their ordeals had ended.

They had abandoned themselves to the joy of the return, and were shaking hands effusively, when a gunshot suddenly rang out, fired from a thicket bordering the strand, and Lord Rodilan's hat fell at his feet, traversed by a bullet.

"Ah!" said the Englishman. "Good! Now I'm sure that I'm on Earth. I've rediscovered the gentle and hospitable mores of my compatriots!"

Meanwhile, a dozen savages armed with long rifles emerged from the woods and advanced, firing, reassured by the small number of the strangers, with whom they thought they would reckon easily. Fortunately, their ill-directed shots had no result.

When the first moment of surprise had passed, Lord Rodilan and his companions, kneeling on the ground to steady their shots, directed the redoubtable fire of their repeating rifles at their assailants. Each one had a dozen savages in front of him. Already their long-range bullets had opened up gaps in the savages' ranks, and numerous cadavers were strewn on the ground.

Disconcerted by that resistance, which they had not expected, the indigenes were retreating when a larger troop of armed men emerged from the woods. Attracted by the sound of gunfire, the entire tribe had come running, brandishing rifles and uttering frightful howls.

"You wanted a battle, Milord," said Marcel, with fine self-composure. "I believe you've got your wish."

"We can't allow ourselves to be slaughtered by those brutes," said Jacques. "It would be too stupid."

"Let's fire into the mass," said Lord Rodilan, "while we fall back to the shell. Once there, we can stand them off without danger."

The barbarian host had spread out along the beach and was threatening to surround the three friends, who, retreating step by step, taking careful aim to save their ammunition, were dropping a man with every shot.[33]

Already, several of the savages, getting ahead of their companions, fearful of seeing the strangers escape, were racing between them and the shore, when there was a deafening racket, and twenty of the most fervent attackers bit the dust. While the ferocious horde fled in terror, Marcel and his companions, not knowing where that unexpected aid had come from, turned their heads. A troop of twenty sailors wearing French uniforms were calmly reloading their weapons.

A man dressed with supreme elegance in a costume that was half-naval and half civilian, who seemed to be in command, came toward the three companions, rendered immobile by surprise.

"Messieurs," he said to them, taking off his cap, "I bless the hazard that permitted me to arrive in time to rid you of that vermin. I have no need to ask you whom I have the honor of addressing; the shell that I can see run aground not far away tells me that I'm in the presence of the three illustrious voyagers for whom forty ships have been searching in vain for a week. I'm Comte Hector de Rochebrune; my yacht is anchored beyond that point, and I hope that you'll do me the honor of coming aboard in order to go with me to rejoin the people awaiting you with so much impatience."

The ease with which the newcomer expressed himself denoted a person of the highest society. His open expression and the frankness of his manners immediately gained Marcel's sympathy, and he shook the hand extended to him vigorously.

---

[33] This is the way that self-proclaimed humanitarians generally behave in fiction of the period; in reality, it was the diseases introduced by Westerners, rather than their bullets, that reduced the population of the Marquesas to considerably less than half its previous level within a few decades of the French asserting their control over the islands in the mid-19th century.

His name was, in any case, not unknown to him. Although still young—he was scarcely twenty-five years old—the Comte de Rochebrune was famous in the annals of voyages of circumnavigation. The master of an immense fortune, passionate about science, he had already traveled extensively in both hemispheres, and had brought back from each of his voyages precious zoological and ethnological collections, which had considerably enriched the natural history museum in Paris, to which he had presented them.

"Thank you, Monsieur le Comte," Marcel replied, warmly, "on behalf of myself and my companions, whom I have the honor of introducing to you: Lord Rodilan and Dr. Jacques Deligny."

The latter bowed gravely, but the Comte cried, cheerfully: "Enough ceremony, Messieurs. We are, with your permission, old acquaintances. For a long time, your names have been on all lips; I've been looking for you for a week, and I'm delighted to shake your hands." So saying, he headed toward the party of sailors, who had remained within range the range of their weapons, in an utterly military immobility.

"My friends," the Comte said to them, "Chance has served us marvelously. These are the three heroes for whom we've been searching, the men who have accomplished a voyage such as no sailor has ever attempted."

A formidable cheer was raised; all of them, including the Comte, gazed with respectful admiration at the three astonishing men surrounded by the prestige of such marvelous adventures. They seemed to be unable to sate their gaze. That testimony of ardent enthusiasm went straight to the three voyagers' hearts, but left them somewhat embarrassed, habituated as they had been for a long time to the calm and discreet manners of lunar humankind.

The Comte noticed that, and took out his watch. "It's noon, Messieurs, the time to go to table, and I hope that you'll do me the honor of accepting my modest hospitality."

At the idea of a meal, which, to judge by the distinction of the host, would be a fine one, Lord Rodilan's eyes lit up in satisfaction. His British pride would not allow anything to show, but Marcel and Jacques were not deceived, and looked at him, smiling.

An elegant launch was moored on the shore; the Comte and his new friends took their places therein, and the craft, propelled by twelve vigorous oarsmen, had soon doubled the rocky point behind which a superb 200-tonne steam yacht was anchored, slender and bold in form, its fine silhouette standing out against the sky.

The Comte climbed the ladder first and greeted his guests: "Welcome aboard the *Espérance*, Messieurs."

"We accept your hospitality gratefully," said Marcel, "And I've very glad, for my part, that the first hand I was given to shake on returning to Earth, was that of a compatriot."

The Comte took them into the sumptuous dining-room, where, on a dazzling white tablecloth, crystals and silverware were glittering.

At the sight of that luxury, of which they had been deprived for such a long time, Marcel, Jacques and Lord Rodilan most of all, could not help feeling a profound satisfaction. They regained true possession of terrestrial life and got ready to do honor to the delicate dishes and generous wines with which the table as covered.

Meanwhile, the *Espérance*, which had remained under pressure, raised anchor and set off at full steam to join Captain Francis Clayton. In conformity with the instructions received, the cannon was fired every quarter of an hour to advise any ships nearby that the search as over.

In the dining room, the four companions became joyful.

The Comte told his guests about the impression caused throughout the world by the announcement of their imminent return; he explained the measures taken to facilitate the search for the projectile as soon as it had fallen into the Pacific, and how, on the instructions of the *Maryland*'s commandant, each ship had received a share of the region to be explored.

"I was cruising," he said "at a hundred and thirty-five degrees west longitude and eight degrees south latitude when

357

the necessity of renewing my provisions of water obliged me to approach the coast. After having dropped anchor a few cables from the shore, I put a launch to sea and was about to land when I perceived your shell, run aground, I understood immediately that Providence had brought me to you, and was about to approach the projectile when the sound of a fusillade attracted my attention…and you know the rest."

"What we know," said Marcel, "is that you arrived just in time, for those savage brutes were beginning to become rather inconvenient."

"But what incompetents!" said Lord Rodilan. "There were a good two hundred, and not one of their shots hit the target."

"Except for the one that went through your hat," said Jacques. "An inch or two lower and we wouldn't be having the pleasure of savoring his exquisite French brandy with you."

It took the *Espérance*, whose progress was slowed down by the enormous weight she was towing, twelve days to reach the *Maryland*.

The time seemed short to the Comte de Rochebrune and his guests. Avid to know what had happened on the surface of the Earth since they had left it. Marcel, Jacques and Lord Rodilan multiplied their questions, and the Comte did his best to answer them—but he too, since he was the first to interview them, wanted to collect abundant details relating to the strange world that they had just quit.

Interrogations and responses succeeded one another relentlessly.

On the beautiful tropical nights, they lost track of time chatting on the deck, and scarcely remembered to get a few moments' sleep. There was so much to be said on both sides!

While the sun remained over the horizon the cannon never ceased to make its great voice heard, announcing to anyone within earshot that the mission had been completed successfully. During the night, rockets launched at regular intervals seemed to carry the good news into the heavens, and all the vessels that perceived the signals repeated them in their turn, so that by the time the voyagers reached the point fixed for the concentration, they were followed by twenty vessels forming a triumphal escort.

XVIII. Triumph and Good Works

When Jacques set foot on the deck of the *Maryland* he fell into Mathieu-Rollère's arms.

The aged scientist was quivering with a profound emotion; he was laughing and crying at the same time.

"Oh, my boy, my dear boy!" he stammered, squeezing the young man as if to stifle him.

"Uncle! My dear uncle!" murmured Jacques.

Soon, however, the old man, loosening his grip, turned to his daughter, whose was standing by his side, agitated by a nervous tremor.

"Embrace your husband," he said. "He's earned you!"

And Jacques deposited his betrothal kiss on his cousin's cheek.

Then it was the turn of Marcel and Lord Rodilan to receive the old astronomer's enthusiastic accolade.

"And me?" said Georges Dumesnil, advancing in his turn.

"Oh, my friend," said Marcel, embracing him, "What a joy it is to see you again!"

Jacques and Lord Rodilan also hugged that devoted friend whose collaboration had been so precious to them.

An indescribable enthusiasm reigned on the deck of the American cruiser. All the rules of discipline and hierarchy seemed to have been momentarily forgotten.

Captain Clayton and his officers, and all those whose rank or notoriety had permitted them to come aboard, all confused in the same surge, pressed around the voyagers. Everyone wanted to see them, to hear them and to touch them; shouts and cheers were uttered; there was a veritable delirium. Their hands were shaken, they were embraced frenziedly; everyone wanted to hug then, and in at crowd of excited admirers they were intoxicated, and had all the trouble in the world maintaining their composure.

"Oof!" said Lord Rodilan, finally freeing himself and mopping his brow. "What the Devil's got into them? Have they never seen people who've come back from the Moon before? What would our friends up there think if they saw such fanatics?"

The initial emotion had calmed down somewhat

In response to the boatswain's whistle, the crewmen had resumed their posts. Captain Clayton and his guests remained on the deck.

"Gentlemen," said the commander of the *Maryland*, "you're at home here. My mission is to take you wherever you wish."

After consulting one another, the three friends decided to head for Le Havre, and headed for the cabins that had been reserved for them on board.

The only people now remaining on the cruiser were Captain Clayton's guests. Among the visitors who had welcomed them were a considerable number of reporters, who had returned to their own ships, and we now heading for the nearest port at full steam, to telegraph the good and astonishing news to the waiting world.

The Comte de Rochebrune, who had had the honor of picking them up, did not want to leave his new friends, and left his second in command in charge of his yacht, which was to accompany the *Maryland* to Le Havre.

A French cruiser and an English cruiser, detached from their duties by their respective governments, were to form a kind of escort of honor for the American ship for the duration off its voyage. Before setting out en route, arrangements were made to bring the shell aboard the *Maryland*, because there could be now thought of towing it for such a long distance.

In spite of the large size of the cruiser—some 6,000 tons—the enormous weight of the shell rendered its loading difficult. It was decided, for the sake of prudence, to lighten the ship, and two of its heaviest guns were transported to the vessels of the escort. With the aid of a powerful crane activated by on-board machined, the shell, surrounded by strong chains, was hoisted on to the deck. The hatch of the main hold had been widened to let it through, and it was solidly stowed slightly below the water-line so that its weight, considerable as it was, could not compromise the stability of the ship.

Everything inside the projectile had been left in its original state. Marcel had decided some time ago to donate the specimens it contained to the Museum de Paris. There were numerous photographs, precious drawings and objects of all kinds fabricated by the inhabitants of the Moon, which could give an idea of their civilization as complete as possible.

Nevertheless, he was careful to set aside the chest enclosing the precious stones, Orealis' supreme gift, which, in accordance with the wishes of its generous donor, would be devoted to the relief of human misery.

Six weeks later, on 29 April, the four ships, sailing in convoy, were within sight of Le Havre. They were awaited.

The telegraph that spread the news of their arrival everywhere, and for days, trains packed with passengers and overladen ferry-boats had been pouring crowds of people into the city who had come from all over the world to see the three heroes, whose names were henceforth unforgettable.

The Minister of Public Education had come to meet them as they disembarked on French territory. The director of the Observatoire de Paris, the president of the Bureau des Longitudes and those of the astronomical and geographical societies had come, along with a large number of scientists, eager to collect from their own mouths the impressions they had brought back of the worlds so marvelously opened to science.

The President of the Republic had also wanted to be represented at the ceremony, which had taken on a patriotic character.

All the old oppositions previously raised by the spirit of routine and bureaucratic traditions were now forgotten. Before the reality of the accomplished fact, all resistance was disarmed, and an irresistible current of admiration and enthusiasm was carrying all hearts away. Those who, until recently, had been the most distrustful and rebellious were now the most prompt to proclaim the grandeur of a conquest unprecedented in the annals of science. How true is the saying that success overcomes all resistance, and that genius is only recognized when its light has blinded the most incredulous!

Députés, senators, representatives of all the constituent bodies, all the scientific societies in France, and the Parisian, provincial and foreign press, had joined the cortege. The city of Le Havre had never seen within its walls such a collection of everything France holds of the most illustrious and the most authorized, and it was in the midst of an indescribable intoxication that the voyagers set for on the quay where the flag-decked American cruiser docked.

After the inevitable speeches demanded by the circumstances, to which Lord Rodilan, for his part, only submitted with impatience, the three friends were obliged o resign themselves for a week to no longer belonging to themselves. Receptions, fêtes, banquets, illuminations and regattas succeeded one another without interruption, and more than once they came to regret the mental tranquility of the inhabitants of the Moon, of thoughtful and so reserved, in the midst of which they had lived for so long.

Everything comes to an end, however, and Lord Rodilan took advantage of the calm that ordinarily follows the most exuberant manifestations to head for Portsmouth aboard the Maryland, where further ovations awaited him. His compatriots, impatient at not yet possessing him, were determined to give him a brilliant welcome themselves, to claim their share of the final success of the glorious enterprise.

The train that took Marcel and Jacques to Paris also transported, on a wagon specially fitted out for that purpose, the shell in which they had accomplished their interplanetary journey.

That authentic monument to the industry of the inhabitants of the Moon, along with the scientific treasures it contained, which furnished such a precise documentation of our satellite, were to remain on show in a special museum, an im-

363

perishable souvenir of an immortal voyage and a fecund aliment offered to the investigations of science.

In Paris there was a further series of official receptions and popular fêtes.

The Head of State, surrounded by his ministers, his military household, the staff of the Chambres and scientific bodies made it a point of honor to receive them in a solemn audience.

Already, in response to the proposal of the President of the Council, the Senate and the Chambre des Députés had authorized the government to confer on Jacques and Marcel, by way of national recompense, the dignity of Grand-Officier de la Légion d'Honneur. For Lord Rodilan, a law was not necessary, for foreigners can be appointed immediately to the grade that their services have merited. Thus, the decrees bearing the nomination of the three explorers had appeared on the same date in the *Journal Officiel*.

The population of Paris, with its ardent spirit, quick to ignite, formed a cortege for them, and welcomed them with enthusiastic cheers. If ever they had dreamed of glory as a recompense for their efforts, they must have been fully satisfied; their names were on all lips, and the thousand voices of the press bore the story of the fantastic and triumphant adventure to every corner of the world.

A few months later, Jacques, recently married to the woman he had so valiantly won, received Marcel and Lord Rodilan at his table.

The latter, returned from London, where he too had been the object of the warmest welcome and the most flattering distinctions, had brought back for his two companions the diploma of Commander of the Order of the Bath, which, on the initiative of the Prince of Wales, Her Gracious Majesty Queen Victoria had hastened to grant them. Other governments and scientific societies, imitating that example, had spontaneously awarded them the most honorable and the most envied recompense.

They chatted while drinking coffee and smoking excellent cigars.

"Now that all the noise of our escapade is beginning to die down," said Marcel, "We need to think about what we're going to do with the treasures that have been confided to us and of which we're merely the depositories. Have you thought about the best use we can make of them?"

"Excuse me, my friend," said Jacques, blushing slightly and looking at his wife tenderly, "but I've scarcely had time thus far to think about it. The cares of my new installation..."

"Good, good," said Marcel, "I understand. You owe yourself to your recent happiness before thinking about those disinherited by fate." As Jacques made a gesture he added: "That's not a reproach, friend—you've suffered enough to have the right to be happy. What about you, Milord—do you have some project to submit to us?"

"In truth," replied the Englishman, the occupation of philanthropist is too unfamiliar for me to give you any useful advice. Use me for the action; I'm completely at your disposal, as you know."

"Well," said Marcel, "I haven't had the same reasons as you to remain inactive; I've reflected at length on what we might do for the greater profit of those who are suffering, and if you like, I'll tell you about the plan I've conceived."

"I hope," said Hélène, "that you've kept a role for me on the good that you intend to accomplish. Jacques has told me a great deal about the charming Orealis; I love that noble young woman like a sister; I want to associate myself with her generous designs, and do what she would do herself if she were in our midst."

"I never doubted the nobility of your sentiments, Madame, and Jacques would not have forgiven me had I not reserved a part for you in the task with which we're charged."

And he explained to them the vast project that he had conceived, and of which his practical mind had already traced out the broad outlines.

The sum of the stones contained in the chest offered by Orealis represented, in the estimation of the competent experts consulted by Marcel, an approximate value between eight and nine million francs, but it was necessary not to expect to be able to realize such a sum rapidly; that enormous quantity of precious stones, abruptly thrown on to the market, would inevitably distort the market and lead to a considerable loss. It was necessary to release them slowly and gradually, in accordance with the needs of the enterprises for which they were to serve.

As for their employment, Marcel had judged that, given the impossibility of soothing all human miseries—a task for which all the treasures in the world would not suffice, and against which the great law of inequality that weighs upon humankind loomed up—it was necessary to restrict himself to bringing some alleviation the most cruel and the most immediate. In the opinion of all economists and philanthropists, it was on the working population of cities that the present organization of society placed the heaviest burden of poverty. It was, therefore, in that direction that his efforts ought to be directed.

Old men whom age or infirmity rendered incapable of any labor, women left widowed young women without guidance and support, children orphaned or abandoned by unworthy parents, and all those afflicted by malady or unemployment, and whom in spite of their good will, could not find the means to sustain their lives, appeared to him to have incontestable rights to the benefits of which they were about to be the dispensers.

It was therefore necessary that the endeavor they were undertaking to found would include retirement facilities for the elderly, refuges for young women devoid of a family, workshops for those left without resources by long unemployment, and establishments where the homeless children swarming in the streets of great cities, from which the armies of crime would later be recruited, would be taken in, raised and educated.

Already, no doubt, public and private charity had multiplied institutions of those kinds, but thus far it had all been on a small scale. The tentative isolated attempts that often, instead of helping one another, harmed one another, routine, the bureaucratic mentality, the personal ambitions that made charity a means of renown, exaggerated regulation and dilapidation all made the results obtained meager in proportion to the efforts deployed and the good will expended.

The three friends, with considerable resources at their disposal, free of any attachment, disengaged from any personal interest, eager to work uniquely for the welfare of their fellows, could operate with more co-ordination and unity, and could extract the full benefit from the sums they spent.

They would establish in some of the most populous cities of the old world—Paris, London, Vienna, St. Petersburg, etc.—centers of action and model establishments in which everything would have been foreseen, equipped to provide for the immediate needs of the poor.

Marcel, Jacques and Lord Rodilan, who would form the superior committee of the endeavor, would each have their individual role. Marcel would take responsibility for everything concerning building, technical work and various appropriations; Jacques would supervise everything concerning hygiene, alimentation and medical services; Lord Rodilan would take charge of regulation and education, and would supervise monitoring. As for Hélène, the part she would play was neither the least important nor the least valuable; she would take care of the small children, who needed to be surrounded with maternal affection, and also those unfortunates, girls, women or widows, whom misery and despair often lead to the worst resolutions.

They would gather around them an elite staff, animated like them with an ardent love for humanity, and similarly resolved to devote themselves to that sublime task. In spite of the corruption of the century and the bitter egotism that was devouring it, Marcel had no doubt that he recruit those disinterested auxiliaries; he held his fellows in high enough esteem to believe that there still remained a few souls among them fond of pure virtue.

The engineer finished explained the general plan of the endeavor as he conceived it. His friends welcomed it enthusiastically, each one proud of the place reserved for them and eager to enter into the campaign.

Hélène shook Marcel's hand emotionally, saying: "Thank you—you've understood my heart's desire."

As soon as the sale of a certain quantity of stones—carried out in the largest markets in the world—had permitted sufficiently considerable sums to be amassed, they set resolutely to work. In the capitals they had chosen, benevolent establishments were soon built, in which all the resources that modern science could provide were brought together, sagely administered, from which everything resembling bureaucratic rigidity was banished, along with the brutal formality that sometimes renders the alms falling from public charity so bitter to its recipients.

All those who came were welcomed benevolently and treated with generosity; they felt that they were loved and went away comforted and reconciled with life.

Then a movement occurred of which philanthropists had long dreamed, but for whose realization they had never dared to hope. On seeing the admirable results produced by that truly Christian and entirely human fashion of doing good, a great surge of generosity and fraternity—not the fraternity that displays itself ostentatiously on public monuments, but that which truly ought to animate all hearts—became manifest with an irresistible force.

Everywhere, public powers were moved to action.

It seemed that people suddenly understood, for the first time, that humans are siblings, that those who have the mission to govern them ought before anything else to love them, and that, in a civilized nation worthy of the name, no one ought to suffer, except by their own fault or the effect of the fatal laws to which nature submits humankind.

Autocrats, legislative assemblies were seen to decree, with an emotional fervor, a series of measures designed to put an end, everywhere, to the frightful iniquities under which so many human creatures were weighed down, and which divided modern societies into two camps, one of human beings favored with all the gifts of fortune and who do not think sufficiently about the miseries of others, and the other of the unfortunates whose sufferings often render them unjust and too willing to listen to counsels of envy and hatred.

And thanks to the initiative of a few generous and devoted souls, an era of justice, happiness and love appeared to be commencing on Earth.

Conclusion

After having witnessed his friends' triumph, Mathieu-Rollère had resumed his position at the Observatoire de Paris. Modestly, he enjoyed the luster that all these events had cast upon his name. Now, people listened to him deferentially, treating him as a great man, and it was not without an ironic smile, thinking about the past, that he now received so many marks of respect from the same people who had treated him so unworthily.

Soon, moreover, the death of the illustrious scientist who directed the foremost astronomical establishment in France left that post vacant, and the Minister of Public Education hastened to call upon the man whose robust faith had contributed in such large measure to the solution of the great problem of interplanetary communication. That was the worthy coronation of a life entirely devoted to the veneration of science.

The engineer Dumesnil, whose name had also become famous, was passionate about the endeavor of which he had been the organizer, and made haste to return to Algeria in order to resume the series of conversations with the lunar world. A year later, great progress had been made. The French government had had no difficulty obtaining from Parliament the funds necessary for the construction of a telescope equal in power to the one in the Rocky Mountains, which was now installed on one of the highest summits in the Atlas.

A special telegraph wire kept Dumesnil is constant communication with that post, and he could then transmit without delay to Marcel and his friends all the information he received from the Moon.

The exchange of signals was undoubtedly slow, because it could only be carried out for a certain period during each lunar month, but it was achieved in a regular and continuous fashion. Precious information and interesting details were collected by that means, and the two worlds learned more about one another every day.

Those who had shared the same life for two years had not forgotten one another. Those on Earth kept their friends up to date with all that they were doing to realize Orealis' wishes. Those on the Moon, in their turn, had let them know that the prudent Aldeovaze was dead, that Rugel had been appointed to replace him, and that Orealis had married Azali.

Neither time nor distance could weaken the links of amity that united those elite souls.[34]

The communications had been going on for six years, and it was hoped that with the ever-increasing progress of science, they would become more frequent and more rapid, when Marcel received a telegram one day from Dumesnil which said: *Large flame appeared in field of telescope. Communications interrupted.*

And from that moment on, the eyes of observers searched the satellite's disk in vain; no evidence of life appeared on its surface, which seemed to have fallen back into death.

What had happened? What formidable explosion of subterranean forces had annihilated the human race in the midst of which the three explorers had lived? Had inexorable nature, whose laws it seemed to have violated, rendered it to oblivion at a stroke?

No one ever knew.

The years passed. The generous institutions due to the initiative of Marcel and his friends gradually fell into neglect, and were then abandoned; the world fell back into its routine and its indifference.

---

[34] The original text might well have ended at this point, the subsequent paragraphs being added by a different hand, perhaps on the instruction of the publisher, anxious that his readers, in 1896, would be too well aware that the world-changing events explicitly attributed to the 1880s had not occurred.

The very memory of those marvelous adventures faded away, and was no more, in the souls of those who had been their heroes, than a dream whose contours became more blurred every day.

Eventually, when, curbed by old age, he evoked the memory of it, Marcel wondered sadly whether it might all have been a dream.

SF & FANTASY

Adolphe Alhaiza. *Cybele*

Alphonse Allais. *The Adventures of Captain Cap*

Henri Allorge. *The Great Cataclysm*

Guy d'Armen. *Doc Ardan: The City of Gold and Lepers*

G.-J. Arnaud. *The Ice Company*

Charles Asselineau. *The Double Life*

Henri Austruy. *The Eupantophone; The Olotelepan; The Petitpaon Era*

Cyprien Bérard. *The Vampire Lord Ruthwen*

S. Henry Berthoud. *Martyrs of Science*

Aloysius Bertrand. *Gaspard de la Nuit*

Richard Bessière. *The Gardens of the Apocalypse*

Albert Bleunard. *Ever Smaller*

Félix Bodin. *The Novel of the Future*

Louis Boussenard. *Monsieur Synthesis*

Alphonse Brown. *City of Glass; The Conquest of the Air*

Emile Calvet. *In a Thousand Years*

André Caroff. *The Terror of Madame Atomos; Miss Atomos; The Return of Madame Atomos; The Mistake of Madame Atomos; The Monsters of Madame Atomos; The Revenge of Madame Atomos; The Resurrection of Madame Atomos; The Mark of Madame Atomos; The Spheres of Madame Atomos*

Félicien Champsaur. *The Human Arrow; Ouha, King of the Apes; Pharaoh's Wife*

Didier de Chousy. *Ignis*

Jules Clarétie. *Obsession*

Michel Corday. *The Eternal Flame*

André Couvreur. *The Necessary Evil*; *Caresco, Superman; The Exploits of Professor Tornada* (3 vols.)

Captain Danrit. *Undersea Odyssey*

C. I. Defontenay. *Star (Psi Cassiopeia)*

Charles Derennes. *The People of the Pole*

Georges Dodds (anthologist). *The Missing Link*

Harry Dickson. *The Heir of Dracula*

Jules Dornay. *Lord Ruthven Begins*

Alfred Driou. *The Adventures of a Parisian Aeronaut*

Sâr Dubnotal *vs. Jack the Ripper*

Alexandre Dumas. *The Return of Lord Ruthven*

Renée Dunan. *Baal*

J.-C. Dunyach. *The Night Orchid; The Thieves of Silence*

Henri Duvernois. *The Man Who Found Himself*

Achille Eyraud. *Voyage to Venus*

Henri Falk. *The Age of Lead*

Paul Féval. *Anne of the Isles; Knightshade; Revenants; Vampire City; The Vampire Countess; The Wandering Jew's Daughter*

Paul Féval, *fils. Felifax, the Tiger-Man*

Charles de Fieux. *Lamékis*

Louis Forest. *Someone is Stealing Children in Paris*

Arnould Galopin. *Doctor Omega; Doctor Omega and the Shadowmen* (anthology)

Judith Gautier. *Isoline and the Serpent-Flower*

H. Gayar. *The Marvelous Adventures of Serge Myrandhal on Mars*

Léon Gozlan. *The Vampire of the Val-de-Grâce*

G.L. Gick. *Harry Dickson and the Werewolf of Rutherford Grange*

Edmond Haraucourt. *Illusions of Immortality*

Nathalie Henneberg. *The Green Gods*

V. Hugo, P. Foucher & P. Meurice. *The Hunchback of Notre-Dame*

Romain d'Huissier. *Hexagon: Dark Matter*

Jules Janin. *The Magnetized Corpse*

Michel Jeury. *Chronolysis*

Gustave Kahn. *The Tale of Gold and Silence*

Gérard Klein. *The Mote in Time's Eye*

Fernand Kolney. *Love in 5000 Years*

Paul Lacroix. *Danse Macabre*

Louis-Guillaume de La Follie. *The Unpretentious Philosopher*

Jean de La Hire. *Enter the Nyctalope; The Nyctalope on Mars; The Nyctalope vs. Lucifer; The Nyctalope Steps In; Night of the Nyctalope; Return of the Nyctalope; The Fiery Wheel*

Etienne-Léon de Lamothe-Langon. *The Virgin Vampire*

André Laurie. *Spiridon*

Gabriel de Lautrec. *The Vengeance of the Oval Portrait*

Alain le Drimeur. *The Future City*

Georges Le Faure & Henri de Graffigny. *The Extraordinary Adventures of a Russian Scientist Across the Solar System* (2 vols.)

Gustave Le Rouge. *The Mysterious Doctor Cornelius* (3 vols.); *The Vampires of Mars; The Dominion of the World* (w/Gustave Guitton) (4 vols.)

Jules Lermina. *Mysteryville; Panic in Paris; To-Ho and the Gold Destroyers; The Secret of Zippelius*

André Lichtenberger. *The Centaurs; The Children of the Crab*
Jean-Marc & Randy Lofficier. *Edgar Allan Poe on Mars; The Katrina Protocol; Pacifica; Robonocchio; Return of the Nyctalope;* (anthologists) *Tales of the Shadowmen 1-10*
Xavier Mauméjean. *The League of Heroes*
Joseph Méry. *The Tower of Destiny*
Hippolyte Mettais. *The Year 5865*
Louise Michel. *The Human Microbes; The New World*
Tony Moilin. *Paris in the Year 2000*
José Moselli. *Illa's End*
John-Antoine Nau. *Enemy Force*
Marie Nizet. *Captain Vampire*
C. Nodier, A. Beraud & Toussaint-Merle. *Frankenstein*
Henri de Parville. *An Inhabitant of the Planet Mars*
Gaston de Pawlowski. *Journey to the Land of the 4th Dimension*
Georges Pellerin. *The World in 2000 Years*
Ernest Pérochon. *The Frenetic People*
Pierre Pelot. *The Child Who Walked on the Sky*
J. Polidori, C. Nodier, E. Scribe. *Lord Ruthven the Vampire*
P.-A. Ponson du Terrail. *The Vampire and the Devil's Son; The Immortal Woman*
Edgar Quinet. *Ahasuerus*
Henri de Régnier. *A Surfeit of Mirrors*
Maurice Renard. *The Blue Peril; Doctor Lerne; The Doctored Man; A Man Among the Microbes; The Master of Light*
Jean Richepin. *The Wing; The Crazy Corner*
Albert Robida. *The Adventures of Saturnin Farandoul; The Clock of the Centuries; Chalet in the Sky; The Electric Life*
J.-H. Rosny Aîné. *Helgvor of the Blue River; The Givreuse Enigma; The Mysterious Force; The Navigators of Space; Vamireh; The World of the Variants; The Young Vampire*
Marcel Rouff. *Journey to the Inverted World*
Han Ryner. *The Superhumans*
Angelo de Sorr. *The Vampires of London*
Brian Stableford. *The New Faust at the Tragicomique;The Empire of the Necromancers (The Shadow of Frankenstein; Frankenstein and the Vampire Countess; Frankenstein in London); Sherlock Holmes & The Vampires of Eternity; The Stones of Camelot; The Wayward Muse.* (anthologist) *News from the Moon; The Germans on Venus; The Supreme Progress; The World Above the World; Nemoville; Investigations of the Future; The Conqueror of Death*

Jacques Spitz. *The Eye of Purgatory*
Kurt Steiner. *Ortog*
Eugène Thébault. *Radio-Terror*
C.-F. Tiphaigne de La Roche. *Amilec*
Louis Ulbach. *Prince Bonifacio*
Théo Varlet. *The Golden Rock. The Xenobiotic Invasion; The Casta-ways of Eros; Timeslip Troopers* (w/André Blandin); *The Martian Epic* (w/Octave Joncquel)
Paul Vibert. *The Mysterious Fluid*
Villiers de l'Isle-Adam. *The Scaffold; The Vampire Soul*
Philippe Ward. *Artahe*
Philippe Ward & Sylvie Miller. *The Song of Montségur*

MYSTERIES & THRILLERS

M. Allain & P. Souvestre. *The Daughter of Fantômas*
A. Anicet-Bourgeois, Lucien Dabril. *Rocambole*
A. Bernède. *Belphegor*; *Judex* (w/Louis Feuillade); *The Return of Judex* (w/Louis Feuillade); *The Shadow of Judex*
A. Bisson & G. Livet. *Nick Carter vs. Fantômas*
V. Darlay & H. de Gorsse. *Arsène Lupin vs. Sherlock Holmes: The Stage Play*
Séamas Duffy. *Sherlock Holmes in Paris*
Paul Féval. *Gentlemen of the Night; John Devil; The Black Coats ('Salem Street; The Invisible Weapon; The Parisian Jungle; The Companions of the Treasure; Heart of Steel; The Cadet Gang; The Sword-Swallower)*
Emile Gaboriau. *Monsieur Lecoq*
Goron & Emile Gautier. *Spawn of the Penitentiary*
Rick Lai. *Shadows of the Opera: Retribution in Blood; Sisters of the Shadows: The Curse of Cagliostro*
Steve Leadley. *Sherlock Holmes: The Circle of Blood*
Maurice Leblanc. *Arsène Lupin vs. Countess Cagliostro; Arsène Lupin vs. Sherlock Holmes (The Blonde Phantom; The Hollow Nee-dle); The Many Faces of Arsène Lupin*
Gaston Leroux. *Chéri-Bibi; The Phantom of the Opera; Rouletabille & the Mystery of the Yellow Room; Rouletabille at Krupp's*
Richard Marsh. *The Complete Adventures of Judith Lee*
William Patrick Maynard. *The Terror of Fu Manchu; The Destiny of Fu Manchu*

Frank J. Morlock. *Sherlock Holmes: The Grand Horizontals; Sherlock Holmes vs Jack the Ripper*
Jean Petithuguenin. *The Adventures of Ethel King*
Antonin Reschal. *The Adventures of Miss Boston*
P. de Wattyne & Y. Walter. *Sherlock Holmes vs. Fantômas*
David White. *Fantômas in America*
Pierre Yrondy. *The Adventures of Thérèse Arnaud*

SCREENPLAYS

Mike Baron. *The Iron Triangle*
Emma Bull & Will Shetterly. *Nightspeeder; War for the Oaks*
Gerry Conway & Roy Thomas. *Doc Dynamo*
Steve Englehart. *Majorca*
James Hudnall. *The Devastator*
Jean-Marc & Randy Lofficier. *Royal Flush*
J.-M. & R. Lofficier & Marc Agapit. *Despair*
J.-M. & R. Lofficier & Joël Houssin. *City*
Andrew Paquette. *Peripheral Vision*
Robert L. Robinson, Jr. *Judex*
R. Thomas, J. Hendler & L. Sprague de Camp. *Rivers of Time*

NON-FICTION

Stephen R. Bissette. *Blur 1-5. Green Mountain Cinema 1; Teen Angels*
Win Scott Eckert. *Crossovers* (2 vols.)
Jean-Marc & Randy Lofficier. *Shadowmen* (2 vols.)
Randy Lofficier. *Over Here*

ART BOOKS

Jean-Pierre Normand. *Science Fiction Illustrations*
Raven Okeefe. *Raven's L'il Critters; Rave's Faves*
Randy Lofficier & Raven Okeefe. *If Your Possum Go Daylight...*
Daniele Serra. *Illusions*

HEXAGON COMICS

Franco Frescura & Luciano Bernasconi. *Wampus*

Franco Frescura & Giorgio Trevisan. *CLASH*
L. Bernasconi, J.-M. Lofficier & Juan Roncagliolo. *Phenix*
Claude Legrand, J.-M. Lofficier & L. Bernasconi. *Kabur*
Franco Oneta. *Zembla*
L. Buffolente, Lofficier & J.-J. Dzialowski. *Strangers: Homicron*
Danilo Grossi. *Strangers: Jaydee*
Claude Legrand & Luciano Bernasconi. *Strangers: Starlock*
Thierry Mornet & Juan Roncagliolo. *Guardian of the Republic*
J.-M. Lofficier, M. Garcia, F. Blanco & J. Pima. *Strangers in a Strange Land*